D0298323

KA 0033152 X

Life
Goes On

BY THE SAME AUTHOR

Fiction

Saturday Night and Sunday Morning
The Loneliness of the Long Distance Runner
The General
Key to the Door
The Ragman's Daughter
The Death of William Posters
A Tree on Fire
Guzman, Go Home
A Start in Life
Travels in Nihilon
Raw Material
Men, Women and Children
The Flame of Life
The Widower's Son
The Storyteller
The Second Chance and Other Stories
Her Victory
The Lost Flying Boat
Down From the Hill

Travel

The Saxon Shore Way
(with Fay Godwin)

Poetry

The Rats and Other Poems
A Falling Out of Love and Other Poems
Love in the Environs of Voronezh
Storm and Other Poems
Snow on the North Side of Lucifer
Sun Before Departure

Plays

All Citizens are Soldiers (with Ruth Fainlight)
Three Plays

Essays

Mountains and Caverns

For Children

The City Adventures of Marmalade Jim
Big John and the Stars
The Incredible Fencing Fleas
Marmalade Jim on the Farm
Marmalade Jim and the Fox

Alan Sillitoe

Life Goes On

GRANADA
London Toronto Sydney New York

Granada Publishing Limited
8 Grafton Street, London W1X 3LA

Published by Granada Publishing 1985

British Library Cataloguing in Publication Data

Sillitoe, Alan
Life goes on.
I. Title
823′.914 [F] PR6037.I55

ISBN 0-246-12709-0

Set in Baskerville by Columns of Reading
Printed in Great Britain by
Billing & Sons Ltd., Worcester

Life Goes On

Preamble

I, Michael Cullen, King Bastard the First, dodged the traffic like a London pigeon in its prime. Some got caught, but only the old ones, or the sick. Old ones shouldn't try to dodge the motors. Sick ones should stay at home.

Moggerhanger threatened to kill me. I believed he would like to. No matter how much of a bastard I was, there were always bigger bastards in the world. Moggerhanger was a rich bastard (he still is), which made him more effective than a poor bastard like me. He was also an older bastard, and we know what that means.

Come and get me. What else could I say? Bravado cost nothing, and he'd have to catch me. Maybe he'd have a fatal accident, though no doubt it was a condition of his will that the beneficiaries would have to deal with me before laying their maulers on the cash. He had many paid helpers, which was why I dodged the traffic like a pigeon. I ran across the light-on-green at Oxford Street. That was very close indeed. I didn't know his henchmen were driving buses.

Volume One of my memoirs was scribbled in a disused railway station in the Fen country. Where I am penning this account of even more extraordinary adventures will be explained at the end. If this tale is pasted on the billboards, Moggerhanger's a ruined man, though only in reputation. He is far too clever, and has too much influence in places that matter, to worry about going to prison, where he belongs. In any case, he is Lord Moggerhanger of Moggerhanger (Bedfordshire), whereas I am Michael Cullen, of no importance to anyone except myself, and with no distinguishing marks – at the moment.

I used to be a 22-carat no-good bastard, in the opinion of friends as well as enemies, but since my father married my mother twenty or so years after the event, I have only been a bastard to myself, which isn't saying much, because I am too fond of my own skin to be more of a bastard than is absolutely necessary. Once upon a time I was only enough of a bastard to keep myself sufficiently alert regarding what the rest of the world would do to me if I let it. I learned early on in life that the best form of defence is self-preservation. I'm more than halfway back to being a 22-carat no-good bastard because my mother and father don't live together anymore, thank God. I'd rather be a bastard than a nonentity.

However, as this story will reveal, I'm far more gullible than I thought.

Part One

One

Old lives for new, and new wives for old: it began when I came out of prison and fell into the arms of Bridgitte Appledore, the one-time Dutch *au pair* girl who became my everloving wife. Our married life in the disused Cambridgeshire railway station of Upper Mayhem lasted through a decade of idleness. We lived on the money of her first psychologist husband, Dr Anderson, bringing up Smog who was the son of the said dead husband and his first wife. Then followed three children of our own, and life at our station dwelling place had been so ordinary that the heavenly years passed too quickly to be appreciated, until that smouldering blond beauty with big breasts and a mouth too small for her heart, who acted but never talked about what went on inside, took the children out one day for a ride in the car while I was still in bed.

Harwich was two hours away, and none came back, a fact explained by a phone call from Holland next morning. She had, she said between sobs and god-fer-dommering curses, left me, and didn't know whether she would ever be back. To cover my shock and chagrin I told her she was full of gin, adding that as far as I was concerned she could stay away forever, and that I had always expected her sooner or later to go back to *them old* ways.

Grammar is always the first victim of a broken marriage. I knew my accusations to be a lie, which proved I was already halfway back to *my* old ways of lying, if I still had the backbone for it, which I had doubted till that moment.

I put in, for good measure, in case she misunderstood, that she was no better than a whore, which was a scandalous assertion because as far as I knew she had been as loyal as a turnip during our marriage. She shouted back, before this accusation was hardly through to the other side of my brain, and not yet fed into the wire, that I wouldn't have said that to her if Jankie (or some such name. Maybe it was Ankie) had been there, at which I screamed out: 'Who's Jankie, you double, treble, quadruple whore' – to which she retorted: 'I'm not a horse, you idle sponging no-good coward.'

'I never sponged,' I bawled. Every word, good or bad (and they were all bad), was a mistake. The only policy was a cool smile and lips well buttoned, but murder smouldered behind my eyes, waiting for the moment when I could pay her out. Silence wasn't my virtue, and it was too late to learn. 'You were living in *my* house!'

'You bought it on money you stole, you gold smuggler, you jailbird. I lived with you ten years in misery, hating every minute, with you hating me, and hating the children, and hating yourself, because prison turned you the bitterest man in the world.'

I buckled like a straw in the fire, because no man had spent a more contented time, with all the love from Bridgitte I needed, always thinking that no more was possible for her or anyone. I could have sworn to God she had been happy, yet here she was ranting her treacherous version: 'You thought you had it good, all the looking after, and me happy, but I was hating you, and you with your pervert tricks you made me do and thought I liked.'

Was my phone tapped? Was some lickspittle from MI5 tuned in to her perorations? And what about at the other end? Could those nice Dutch folks understand her English? I wanted to put the phone down.

'Wait till the children grow up,' she said, 'and I get them to know what ape and monkey tricks you've been up to, which I'll tell them if they ask for you and you try to get at me.'

'That's racism,' I broke in. 'Anymore of that and I'll get onto the Primates Liberation Organization.'

Nothing would stop her. 'I didn't want to live with you, because all the time it was rotten rotten rotten.' She was weeping again. Her parents were by her side, listening with pious faces, putting calicoed arms over her shoulders, waiting to snatch up the phone and threaten me with instant death by being thrown from the Butter Mountain or drowned in the Great Milk Lake. Better still, they would send her eight upright brothers (and three sisters) to reason with me. 'You were always looking around,' she went on, 'for every chance to get away from me. But you kept me like a dog chained to a post, just like your big, pig-headed father.'

She was half right, because during my early years at Upper Mayhem, after eighteen months in prison, the same thought nagged at me, so that I wondered, even before going for a drink at the village pub, why I hadn't slipped my prized transistor radio over my shoulder, or my treasured Japanese zoom lens binoculars. I would almost turn back to get them, but the idea seemed stupid, though it persisted for more than a year, and was finally cured by wise young Bridgitte suggesting that on my strolls I did indeed take my radio, binoculars, bank book, and even her, as well as the children, so that if I didn't come back it wouldn't matter, because everything I valued would be crowding unmercifully in on me – so that I couldn't help but come back, even if only to unload my burdens, by which time I would be too exhausted to care.

I was rueful yet full of wrath as I put down the phone. She had certainly picked up my language during our time together, so wasn't completely right when she said I had given her nothing. All I could do after receiving a call for help from my old pal Bill Straw in London was lock up the house for the day and set off to find out why he wanted to see me, and maybe get a sniff of what the future might hold, before Bridgitte recovered from her fit and came back to carry on as before. If it was the end between us, there was nothing I could do, though such finality was hard to believe because in my experience the only final thing was death, and I'd never be ready for that.

Comparisons were painful, so I mulled over my break with Bridgitte, which was a supportable agony because it was familiar. It seemed as if she had left only yesterday, but the unexpected savagery of her departure with the kids had bitten two weeks out of my life, leaving a wound so raw it would never heal. I could hardly account for the subsequent days except to say they were a nightmare, hours of misery from brooding at my loss, and a relentless ache at wondering how the kids were faring.

Bits of food and empty whisky bottles littered stairs and tables, but by closing the door that morning on the piggery of ten years, an iron test had been passed. The marks of the experience had bitten so deep that it seemed the disaster had had no effect on me.

Life goes on, I thought, settling myself into a first class seat on a second class cheap day shopper's ticket, which was tucked into a pocket of my Norfolk-style jacket. On the other hand, life had gone on since I was born, with little help from me, so there was no reason to suppose it would not continue until the day of my inevitable blackout. Even when my existence seemed too painful to last, or too good to go on forever, I stared side-on at the antics it played. After my stint in prison, ten years before, I preferred walking parallel to life rather than through the middle like a grenadier. But I was never less than up to my neck in it.

I reached for *The Times* left by somebody who got out at Cambridge. There was the usual front-page photo of a terrorist with a scarf around his head, trying to smile like royalty, and inside was the snapshot of an eight-year-old kid with a Kalashnikov which I supposed the photographer had given him a quid to hold so that he could get a good picture.

At thirty-five the grey hair had begun, which surprised me because I thought I never worried. Life had been calm, and nothing justified that hint of fag ash on the lower fringes of my sideboards. Worrying that I didn't worry would only make it worse. Bridgitte pointed to the grey bits as if they were the marks of a beast that had always lurked there, and ruffled them to see whether or not they were real.

I hoped the tormented expression on my face in the British Rail looking-glass was only temporary, because it spoiled my almost good looks, at which the only response was a crackling breakfast belch before sitting down.

What I dreaded most was going bald, like that tall, gaunt, randy old prick-head Gilbert Blaskin I had been lumbered with as a father. As for my mother, she hadn't been heard of for months, not since the old man began his new novel. While he was working he no longer tormented her, which meant that she was unable to get at him. Every so often they fled in opposite directions so as not to murder each other, and with Blaskin being a writer it worked out well. I imagined going to the flat and finding them dead on the mat by the door, a cleaver in her hand and an axe in his. They had struck each other's heart at the same second and with instant effect, though I thought it more likely that while one would be dead, the other would be so wounded that he or she would be pushed around in a bottle-type wheelchair for as long as he or she lived. Mother or father – I didn't care which – would gurgle reproachfully at me as the reason for their downfall. After a terrific struggle I'd get the bottle to the top of the Post Office Tower and let it go, hoping a gust of wind would swing it through a window of the Middlesex Hospital where they could accept it as an unsolicited gift from me.

My Irish mother of fifty-odd had a mop of Cullen-thick

hair which was duly passed on. She'd thinned her own and sprayed it with silver and pink so that she wouldn't look a day under thirty-five. Whether she was Irish or not I'd never really known, and neither had she, but she'd been unable to stand the thought of being taken for English, especially since Blaskin was a fairly pure specimen of the breed – at least, as she often said, in his talent for deceit and the versatility of his vices. I wanted to take after neither but, being my vain and pleasure-loving self, hoped I was closer to my mother's side as far as keeping my hair till I was a hundred and ten was concerned, though I found it painful at times that a bloke of thirty-five should be lumbered with parents at all.

Clouds floated over the flat fields, a fine picture of altocumulus castellanus – as I had learned from Smog's school books when I tested him for A levels, thus gaining qualifications which I hadn't been able to earn at the proper time. Such cloud varied in its direction with the sine, cosine and tangent of the moving train. April smelled ripe and dead, bits of sun filing through to the blackening earth.

The reason for my journey to London was because a letter from my old pal Bill Straw begged me to come *poste haste without restante* to help him out of a jam. When Bill, a man with a long past, wrote about a jam it was no mere logjam in a river of crocodiles near a thousand foot waterfall with natives shooting poisoned arrows from either bank. It was serious, though I didn't suppose he realized how much worse I might make his predicament.

A man wearing expensive clothes looked into my compartment as if to consider parking there. I had spreadeagled my coat, briefcase, cap and self in such a way that it looked filled, so he closed the door, gently for one so nervous, and walked down the corridor. I turned to *The Times* crossword, and tried to make sense out of nine down, a clue whose complexity made me feel like the kingpin idiot himself.

I noted in the car sales columns that the Thunderflash Estate had come onto the market, and was sorry I didn't have the wherewithal to buy one. The tall pin-headed man dragged the door open and settled himself opposite. He stank of scent, and looked out of the window while filing his nails. I tried to guess his profession, or the source of his money, hazarding soldier, barrister, remittance man, stockbroker's clerk, unfrocked priest, or of independent means, but none would fit. I observed a person of about forty who looked as if he had all his vices under firm control. With short, mousey, Caesar-style hair, he had more than a few, though I couldn't decide what they were, but he certainly knew all about them because he had the sour expression of someone who trusted himself absolutely. Whoever he worked for had fallen for his air of reliability.

His preoccupied gaze took me back to when I had been put in prison by the machinations of Claud Moggerhanger, an experience which reinforced my impression that the man opposite was untrustworthy to the core, though he might not look so to others. There were many such types in England. A man of similar phizzog in some countries would be immediately under suspicion but, living in a land where the borderline between loyalty and treachery had never been properly surveyed, and where he blended well with the surrounding populace, he would be considered a safe enough bet.

He was so taken up with himself that he didn't think I had noticed him, but a one-second flash over my newspaper told me more than any stare. I had been brought up in a place where, if you looked above two seconds at anyone, you were inviting him (or even her – sometimes especially her) to a fight. In prison, only one second was necessary, often less than that, so I had developed the knack of seeing all at a glance. Whoever the man worked for had put him through the aptitude tests and psychological probings of a foolproof selection board, but I knew they had boobed in the most basic way because they had never been in jail as a prisoner.

I was disturbed from watching the smoke of my morning cigar drift through the fitful sunshine by the ticket collector standing at the door. The passenger opposite gave his ticket to be punched.

'Thank you, sir.'

He then went back to his vacant gaze out of the window, continuing his manic manicure. I noticed how startled he was on hearing the collector say to me: 'You can't travel on a second class ticket in here, mate.'

I had set out that morning determined not to cheat, lie or commit any action while in London which would offend those principles which Bridgitte had tried to instil in me. She had taught me how much better it was not to lie or cheat, even if it meant, she said, losing all idea of your own identity. I realised how much she had gleaned from her former psychologist husband and – too late – that she wasn't as dreamy as she looked.

'Is this a first class compartment?' I asked, as if it was no better than a pigsty that had been used by humans for far too long. He was a middle-aged man, and fair ringlety hair fell to his shoulders from beneath a Wehrmacht-style hat. He pointed to the window. 'It says first class, don't it?'

I wanted to pull his earring. 'I suppose it would have to before somebody like me would notice.'

He leaned against the door, and yawned. 'That's the way it is, mate.'

Under the circumstances he couldn't be anything but honest, and do his job. The nail-filing man opposite, for all his preoccupation with the landscape flying by outside, took in every shade of the situation. And I, if nothing else, had my pride, which was all that ten years of peace had left me with. I took a twenty-pound note from my wallet.

'How much extra?'

He looked at the few foreign coins, plastic tokens, luncheon vouchers and Monopoly notes from his pockets. 'Can't change that.'

I reached for my executive-style briefcase. 'I'll write you a cheque.'

'It'd be more than my job's worth to take a cheque.'

'You'd better see what you can do about changing this legal tender, then.' I crumpled the note into my waistcoat pocket and went back to reading a report in the newspaper about a woman of eighty-six who had murdered her ninety-eight-year-old husband with a knife. 'He got on at me once too often,' she said in court, hoping the beak would be lenient. Then she spoiled it: 'Anyway, I'd always wanted to kill the swine.'

The judge sentenced her to fourteen years in jail. 'A worse case of premeditated murder I've never come across.'

'I'll get you when I come out,' she screamed as they dragged her down to the cells.

The ticket collector, reluctant to move, took a packet of chewing gum from his trouser pocket and put two capsules into his mouth. He lounged as if he had no work to go to, changing weight from foot to foot, happy enough to look at himself in the mirror above the seats. He swayed with the train, as if he'd not been long on the job and didn't care whether he had it much longer. I took a whisky flask from my briefcase and held it towards him. 'Why don't you sit down?'

'No thanks. Not that as well. It'd blow my mind. A train trip's enough for me.'

I wondered if he wasn't one of those scoundrels who, after buying a cap and clipper in Woollie's, hopped the train near a station, collected excess fares, then jumped off in time for the up-train. He did it every day for six months, and spent the rest of the year in Barbados. The millionaires there wondered where he got his money. He told them he was a plumber, but some of the snooty British thought he was only a window cleaner.

Yet he looked too genuine to be an impostor. His eyes, blue in white, spun like catherine wheels. With an effort he stood upright. 'I'll see what I can do about your change.'

We heard him dance his way along the corridor. 'Stoned out of his damned mind,' Nail-filer said. 'I've never seen anything like it. Even public servants. At least they're still changing the guard at Buckingham Palace.'

'For the moment,' I said, not wanting to be unsociable. He didn't turn his gaze from the window, and I noticed in the reflection that he held a map inside his newspaper on which he made pencil marks when a bridge, a cutting, a level crossing and, on one occasion, a pub swung close to the line. 'Are you planning another Great Train Robbery?'

Even in the glass I saw him turn white. The porcelain flash spread to the back of his neck, and to the knuckles of both hands. It was his business, not mine. Probably no one else would have cottoned on. He smiled as if I must be loony to say such a thing, but he wasn't reading that map for nothing, and that was a fact. Maybe he was doing a correspondence course from the Train Robbery Polytechnic, several of which must have opened in the last few years.

I don't know why I had been so awkward with the ticket collector. I had the right change, and could only put it down to the fact that I hadn't been to bed with another woman since before I married Bridgitte. I had banged a few on rugs and carpets, and behind summer hedges (and even on one occasion an aunt of Bridgitte's had had me in Holland), but never actually in bed. No other explanation seemed possible or desirable, except that such unnecessarily bloody-minded conduct helped to pass a few minutes on an otherwise boring journey. Or maybe it was those little flashes of grey hair which made me act the way

I did. Cheating made me feel young.

He put a folded map sheet away, and took another from his large sheer-leather hundred-quid briefcase, which was a far cry from the black plastic executive mock-up with a tin lock that I carried. I marvelled at his concentration. Sweat stood on his forehead. He wiped his cheeks, mopping the flood rather than the source. Anyone capable of such assiduous observation would certainly command a job whose salary allowed the purchase of such a briefcase.

The sun gleamed on factories as the train clawed its way closer to London. Well-kept houses reminded me that England was still wealthy, in spite of what the newspapers and the government wailed on about. Evidence of rich people made me feel better, though whenever I was on my way out of London the same fact depressed me.

The pin-headed, short-haired, well-shaven man sitting opposite put away his newspaper. 'Of course, it's entirely up to you, and I don't want to interfere, but what's the point of having a ticket which doesn't entitle you to the proper seat? You must know it's impossible to avoid paying.'

Just as I had whiled away a few minutes during my teasing of the ticket collector, so this nail-scraping fop was trying to pass the last half hour of our journey by a bout of moral finger-wagging, especially now that he had solved his calculations on the map. Having guessed his game, I could be courteous in reply. 'You might think so, old man, but I haven't coughed up yet.'

He laughed, as if he couldn't wait to see me do so. The fact that I failed to place him irritated me so much that I wanted to smash his mug to pulp. Then I twigged that beneath the old veneer he was ineradicably working class. He couldn't fool me, who was neither ashamed nor proud of having come from the mob, though my father was said to be descended from a long line of impoverished landowning wankers.

A lid of dark cloud stretched across the sky, a luminous mixture of blue up top and white below, which could only mean that it would rain the whole day over London. Such a prospect made the present conversation unimportant, but I played up to his need for chit-chat. 'I've no intention of not paying the extra, though it's true that by the time the ticket collector returns, if he ever does get back from the sort of trip he's gone on, we could be at Liverpool Street.'

I stubbed my cigar out too violently on the window, and had to brush ash and sparks from my newly cleaned suit. I looked at the half-hunter gold watch in my waistcoat pocket, as if anxious about a business appointment in town. He was interested in seeing how I would manoeuvre myself out of the predicament, and because I was in a good mood I decided to fall in with his expectations as a way of discovering something about him. Most of all, it was as if I was a candidate for a job and he was testing my suitability.

'I intended paying up from the beginning, yet I needn't if I don't want to. As soon as I see him coming with the change for twenty quid I can nip smartly back into second class, and nobody will be any the wiser. It pays to hold off till the last minute, because you never know what's going to turn up. It's because it's good exercise racking my brains for a way out, and probably as near to real life as I can get. In any case, suppose my briefcase above your head was full of explosives, and I thought somebody might be on the look-out for it. To divert suspicion, I'd cause a fuss about something insignificant, as a way of practising the theory of the indirect approach.'

He had turned pale, in the lurid light caused by the darkening sky. 'But what are you practising for?'

Raindrops splashed the window. 'Fun, as far as you are concerned. But you never know when the fun's going to turn nasty, do you? Or serious, for that matter. And therein lies the danger for anybody else who happens to be present. I just don't like a jumped-up, swivel-eyed prick like you trying to fuck me around, that's all.'

'Seems like we're going to become friends.' He brought out a silver cigar case of real Havanas. I smoked Jamaicans which were just as good. He passed one across. 'What sort of work do you do?'

'Work?' I dropped the crushed tube to the floor, and scuffed it under the seat with my heel. 'Work,' I said, 'is a habit which I gave up when I started living off my wife.'

He smiled, not knowing whether to believe me. The only blemish in his otherwise well-bred presentation was that his teeth were rotten, though not too much for a forty-year-old who hadn't yet got false ones, or too good for a perspicacious German not to recognise him for an Englishman. 'What sort of work do *you* do?'

'I don't think I could describe what I do as work,' he said. 'I'm a Royal Messenger, flitting not only between the Palace and the Foreign Office in my powder blue Mini-van, but occasionally using trains, and even planes, when engaged on overseas duties. I go from place to place as a courier.'

'I thought you were in something important. My name's Michael Cullen, by the way.'

He held out his manicured hand. 'I was christened Eric Samuel Raymond, and my surname is Alport. Call me Eric. At the moment I'm just back from Sandringham.'

I could only suppose that he had fallen arse backwards into that kind of an occupation, and yet I was convinced that he lied, and that if so he was more of an artist at it than I was – or used to be. He lied, right from the back of his throat, for he was no kind of Royal Messenger. I knew he had been in jail because the first thing people learn inside is how to lie. Learning how to become better criminals is only secondary. The lies they tell each other inside are picturesque. The lies they tell everyone they meet after they get out are calamitous and wild. It gives them something to do, and is a way of feeling their way back towards self-respect. But when they come out they betray themselves to people like me by the way they lie with such wonderful confidence. And lying is the first step that leads them back to jail where lying at least is safe.

He settled himself in his seat. 'It's a very nice occupation. The more responsible members of our family have done it for generations. It began when a great-uncle of mine worked at Tishbite Hall as a page boy. He was a bit of a dogsbody in those days. Whenever he made the slightest mistake in laying the table the butler kicked him up the arse and booted him out of the room. So my great-uncle soon learned to be good at the jobs he had to do. That kind of treatment went on even when he got to the age of twenty, but he had to put up with it because there was nowhere else for him to go. Then he fell in love with one of the kitchen maids, and decided he would marry her. That meant he had to give up his job, because at such houses only the butler was allowed to be married.

'So he wrote out his notice, and put on it that he was leaving because he wanted to emigrate to Canada. Now the butler already knew he was leaving to get married, and told Lord Tishbite. In those days that was a good job for my great-uncle to have. His father lived in a village ten miles away, and every so often he would get the word that he should go over to Tishbite Hall. So the father set off over the fields by footpaths, carrying a sackbag folded under his arm. When he got to Tishbite Hall he was given legs of lamb, pheasants and rabbits and all kinds of game, so much that he could just about carry it away. It was stuff that had been thrown out of the larders to be given to the pigs. So the father struggled home with it, and after taking out all that his family could possibly eat for the next few days he handed the rest to the poor of the village. There was certainly no need to starve if you had somebody in service at a place like Tishbite Hall.

'Anyway, when Lord Tishbite heard from the butler that my great-uncle had handed in his notice because he wanted to get married instead of emigrate he got him on the carpet. Lying was the worst thing you could do, in them days. It was almost as bad as murder. Well, my great-uncle, bless him, was trembling in his boots, because he thought this was the end. He wouldn't be able to get a reference, and it would be impossible to find another job. He might be able to get married, but he'd damn well starve. That was the days before the dole, remember.

'But Lord Tishbite, after rating him for a bit, told him he'd been such a good worker during his eight years in service that he wanted to do something for him. Maybe he'd taken a shine to him. I don't know. But he asked him if he would like to live in London, and the upshot was that he got him a post as a Queen's Messenger, in Whitehall. He was so outstanding at this that he eventually got his sons into the business, though he always put them in service first to make sure they had a good grounding in discipline and smartness. My early days, for instance, were spent working at a big house, mostly polishing boots. I could tell you a thing or two about shining boots! But I kept my eyes and ears open, and it certainly put the polish on me. Boning boots was the first step towards me becoming a gentleman's gentleman which was, after service in the army, from which I retired as a sergeant, to lead me to the post I have now. The old great-uncle insisted that none of us should get the job easily. After serving Queen Victoria he eventually became a messenger for Edward VII, and then King George V.'

'A very interesting tale,' I had to admit. 'If ever we meet again I must tell you mine. You've obviously rumbled the fact that I wasn't telling the truth when I said I had no job.'

He took a miniature make-up case from his top pocket

and extracted tiny tweezers, with which he began fishing about for a hair which he thought might be protruding from his nose, though I could see no such thing and knew that if he went on probing in so blind a fashion he would end up doing himself an injury. He took the telepathic hint, which somewhat increased my estimation of his abilities, and put the thing back into its box.

In prison you shared a cell with someone in a certain trade, and he talked so much about it that on getting out you could pretend to be in the same line of work. He couldn't fool me. I ran through the list of prisons and wondered which he had been discharged from that morning. I knew the names, populations, locations and reputations, but none seemed to fit. I'd been in one, but my information was so out of date that I decided to rummage at the next station bookstall through the current issue of the Good Nick Guide. There were more people inside in England, per head of population, than in any other country in Europe, so maybe somebody had published one. They would sell over forty thousand copies right away. It was a captive market.

'It's been very interesting talking to you.' He held out his carefully manicured hand as the train drew into Liverpool Street. I noticed a wad of yellow cotton wool in his left ear. 'I find it pleasant travelling by train these days. Can't think where that ticket collector's got to with your change, though.'

His hand felt like five baby cobras nestling in my palm, so I shook it free and jumped out of the carriage, zig-zagging through the crowd before he could catch me up to ask the loan of ten quid for a cup of tea. I won't see that lying swine again, I thought. How wrong I was.

Two

Making my way into the underground with a 10p ticket for a 40p journey I passed a gaudy and shocking poster of four hefty policemen using their truncheons on a man against a wall, with the caption underneath saying: 'Is it worth it for cheating on your fare?'

While waiting on the platform I noticed in the personal column of *The Times* a cryptic message meant only for me. 'You can't make hay out of straw when the cat is out. Bill.' This indicated that I had been tracked by persons known or unknown since leaving home that morning, and that the first to put tabs on me was that so-called Queen's Messenger. If Bill had got himself in trouble with Moggerhanger, or Lord Moggerhanger since the New Year's Honours List, then I would soon be in the shit as well. Tangle with Claud Moggerhanger, and the razors came out, and when they came out they went in – into your flesh. Or you landed in the nick on some framed-up charge, after buying a second-hand car from one of Moggerhanger's innumerable outlets, and driving off with a different number plate back and front so that the cyclops picked you up three corners away and had the laugh of their lives.

At Leicester Square I threw my ticket at the collector at the top of the crowded escalator and was through the barrier before he could pick it up. A fattish man in a shabby suit with wide trousers and a nicky hat rested his umbrella while browsing at a girlie-mag bookstall, and in passing I took the brolly and walked out into the open air, suitably equipped for my reappearance in the Metropolis. The London brolly was the equivalent of the Amsterdam bike, to be picked up without the stigma of stealing and dropped later on so that someone else could use it.

Rain splashed on dead beatniks, snow eaters and pavement artists. I felt sorry for a raving looney who stood by stills of big tits and fat arses outside a cinema shouting that they wouldn't get him, he'd beat them all, because he knew a thing or two, in fact he would get them first, yes he would, because they'd never get him, ha, ha, ha! Japanese holidaymakers took photographs of the AA offices. A split-skirted woman walked up and down with a magnificent Borzoi hound that pulled something unmentionable, even to me, out of a dustbin and walked off with it trailing like a Union Jack. Traffic wardens, in fear of their lives but wearing flak jackets underneath their overcoats, patrolled up and down in twos.

I made my way to The Platinum Hedgehog on Barber Street, and stood in line at the cafeteria. Upstairs was a sitdown restaurant, and downstairs a standup stripclub. Next door was a gambling den, and on the other side was the head office of the Flagellation Book Club in a cupboard, all owned by Moggerhanger, proving (if proof were needed) that buggers can't be choosers.

The man in front, who was certainly thin enough, took three apple pies, three custards and a cup of tea from the counter. Only Bill Straw could be so sweet-greedy, and I recognised him at once. 'The pies are full of sugared turnip,' I said, 'and the custards are made out of mustard and brothel-come, and as for the tea, piss would be positively safe by comparison.'

He turned. 'I knew you wouldn't let me down. But thank God you're here. Do you know, Michael, you are staring at the most stupid bleeder on God's earth?'

'When you sit down you can tell me why.'

He reached back for another custard and then lunged forward for a second cup of tea, so that his tray looked like a model of the centre of Calcutta. I was afraid to be seen with him. The last trouble had started after we had struck up an acquaintance on the Great North Road when Bill, straight out of prison, had begged a lift in my gradually collapsing car.

Instinct told me to put back the cellophane-packed sandwich from my coat pocket and run as far from the place as I could get in what time was left of my life. But I didn't, due to the sight of Bill's old-time face, plus a dose of curiosity, and a sense of boredom that hadn't left since Bridgitte had hopped off to Holland with the kids.

We sat at a table near the door. 'Just in case,' he said, looking round every few seconds as if he owned the place and was anxious to see how good or bad trade was.

'Keep your head still,' I said, 'because if anybody comes in looking for you they won't need an identikit picture to pick you out. They'll just look for the bottle of machine-oil on the table.'

He smiled like a dead man hoping to come back to life. The only time he was really unconscious was while slopping custard pies into his mouth. It was certainly a come-down for the smart man of the world and gold smuggler I had once known, the man in fact who had trained me at the trade. He was, however, well dressed in a smart suit, good shirt, tie, gold cufflinks and polished shoes, with a fleck of hanky at the top pocket, a briefcase of real leather by his feet, and a Burberry not made in Taiwan over the chair back. Only his manner had momentarily deteriorated. He still had a short back and sides, which was no longer the same with me.

'Your hair's a bit long, Michael. Get it cut,' he said. 'Doesn't look good. You're a middle-aged man now, or bloody close.'

I thanked him for the compliment.

He stared at a young man with hair down to his shoulders, who was demolishing a Sweeny Todd meat pie a few feet away. 'I can't stand all these hefty young lads with Veronica Lake hairstyles. They want a sergeant-major to sort 'em out. I sometimes walk behind one and don't know if it's a man or a woman. No good for blokes at my age.'

'If you have short hair these days you're a suspicious character.'

He didn't have that total confidence he once had. 'You think so?'

'You'd better stick to the business in hand.'

Having finished his breakfast he took out a cigarette case and lit up a fag, blowing smoke rings in the direction of two young women at the next table. 'They're lovely, aren't they? I wouldn't mind one for supper. Two, in fact. Do you know, Michael, I'm fifty-six, but I still like a feed now and then.' His lean features, suntanned and clean-shaven, wrinkled into anxiety when he saw my umbrella hooked onto the chair. 'Where did you get that gamp?'

'Oh, I just picked it up.'

The sight of it worried him. 'I don't like it.'

'You can lump it, then. It's mine, and I'm very fond of it. I'll love it till my dying day. Uncle Randolph used to go to Ascot with it before the War.'

'Nicked it, eh? Looks fishy to me. Anyway, do you want to hear my story or don't you? I know you do, and it's good of you to answer my call so quickly. Michael will always stand by a friend in need, I said. He's a good six-footer who not only looks after himself in a tight corner, but never lets an old pal down. I didn't have firmer friends in the Sherwood Foresters. I don't like the look of that umbrella, though. Where did you get it from?'

I told him.

'That's hardly calculated to set my mind at rest. It looks very suspicious.' He scraped the last stains of custard from all three dishes. 'Times have changed, Michael. You can't be too careful these days. Ten years ago things were comparatively civilised. If you strayed from the straight and narrow all you might end up with was a nasty scar on the lee side of your clock, but nowadays you might get chopped into bits and sprinkled over a Thames bridge from a plastic bag. You vanish without trace. The seagulls gulp every morsel. London pigeons are starting to eat flesh. A few months ago I happened to be the unwilling witness of a fight between the Green Toe Gang and Moggerhanger's Angels, and as a set-to it made the Battle of Bosworth Field look like a pub brawl at the Elephant and Castle. Things have altered, right enough.'

He plucked the small feather out of his hatband and put it into his mouth. 'You've been away, so you don't know how things are. How could you?' He spat the bedraggled feather onto a plastic pie plate. 'Well, it's not too bad, either, because otherwise I wouldn't have asked you to come down here and see me, would I?'

'Wouldn't you? Listen, I'll go right off my bonce if you don't tell me why you asked me to leave my cosily furnished railway station on such a foul day.'

Raindrops were running down the window. They broke out in separate places and made a dash for it, as I should have done, increasing in force and strength, born from stationary globules on the way down, like a crowd gathering on the way to a riot. Sometimes they travelled horizontally, lonely figures going a long way, till thwarted by the end of the glass.

'I'll tell you why I'm here, Michael, and why you're here. I want your advice and support. A few months ago I was at a loose end. My girlfriend had left me, my mother had died, and I was running out of cash. I'd earned fifty thousand pounds bringing back a consignment of don't-ask-what from Kashmir. I carried it in the false bottom of a butterfly collection, and got through the customs a treat. I had a beard (grey, unfortunately), little pebbledash glasses and a bush hat. I looked so theatrical they never thought I could be putting on an act. My false passport, fixed up by the Green Toe Gang, said I was a lepidopterist. I even had forged documents from the British Museum of Natural History. When those lads of the Green Toe Gang do something, they do it properly. No flies on them, Michael. No flies, no files, as they say. There aren't any marks where they've been, either, not like on the rest of us.

'It was the best job I ever pulled. Remember when we was smuggling gold ten years ago for Jack Leningrad Limited? Not a patch on that racket. At least this stuff doesn't weigh a ton. I brought in a hundredweight, all nicely hidden. In the East a column of porters carried it, and at London Airport they provide them nice squeaky trolleys for you to zig-zag your stuff through the Nothing to Declare gates. A word of advice, though: always get the squeakiest trolley. It's made for you these days. No rough stuff, or straining your muscles with three hundredweight of gold packed in your waistcoat pockets. No sweating with fear, either, as long as you act your part and keep a straight face, which we're always able to do, eh? Get me another cup o' tea and a custard, there's a good lad.'

'Fetch it yourself.'

'I was brought up in poverty,' he said, 'at Number Two Slaughterhouse Yard. If I don't stay at luxury hotels I feel deprived and underprivileged. You understand what I'm trying to say, don't you, Michael?'

'I think so.'

'Then get me another cup of tea, then, and two custard pies, the ones with the pastry a bit burnt.'

His face had a pallor, and his eyes a shine, that suggested he was about to die. 'What's up, for God's sake?'

He wiped a salt tear from his face. 'I'm in danger. I can't tell you – though I will. I'll come to it. I'm not afraid of dying, not me, not after going through the war with the Sherwood Foresters. That Normandy campaign was very rough. I nearly got killed once or twice.'

'I've heard that before.' I'd never seen him so frightened. 'Pull yourself together.'

He smiled. 'Another custard and a cup of tea will see me right.'

I came back with his supplies, and watched him devour them. 'Get on with your rigmarole.'

He wiped his lips. 'That little courier job brought me fifty thousand quid, but money doesn't stick to me, Michael. I like it too much to have it long. I give with my left hand, and grasp tight with my right, which means I get rid of it sooner than if I was just plain generous. I'm jittery with so much wadding in my pockets. I like to go round the clubs and have a good time. Shove fifty quid in a tart's hand and not even go to bed with her, then give another woman a good pasting because she won't let me have a feel. What's life for if you can't fix yourself up with an orgy now and again? Ever had three women in bed with you? You ain't lived.

'Anyway, I was broke, and then, providentially as I thought, I get this offer from the Green Toe Gang to be the driver of the third getaway car in a robbery. Now it ain't a bank or post office or a wages snatch, but the flat of a former member of the gang who had half-inched a hundred thousand of their money, and now they wanted it back, meaning to deal with him later. The Green Toe Gangers had been told he was on holiday in St Trop, and had left his loot in a suitcase under his bed. You still get people like that, though to do him justice he thought it was just as safe where it was than in a bank with people like him and the Green Toe Gang around.

'You can imagine how they trusted me absolutely? I'm a fool, Michael, always have been. You see, a few days before The Day one of Moggerhanger's men, Kenny Dukes, that bastard whose arms are so long he ought to be in a circus, and who used to be chief bouncer at one of

Lord Claud's lesbian clubs, said Moggerhanger would like to see me. Well, I thought, I've nothing to lose, and let myself be taken to his big house at Ealing, and over a whisky and soda he persuaded me to drive the getaway car straight up north to a bungalow in Lincolnshire called Smilin' Thru' on the outskirts of Back Enderby, and deliver the cash there. Instead of me getting five per cent, which was what the Green Toe Gang had promised, he would give me half. Well, I ask you! Fifty thousand instead of five is quite a whack, and by the fifth whisky I'd agreed. I must have been stoned, pissed, and just plain crackers. Claud was in his element. He knew what he was doing. He must have had someone placed right in the middle of the Green Toe Gang to know their plans in such detail.

'The actual robbery went smoothly. Nobody got knocked on the head. Not a gun was fired. Clockwork wasn't in it. The individual always collaborates, Michael. He gets a glint in his eyes because he wants to be part of the gamble as to whether it'll come off or not. It's the regimented law-abiding swine who causes trouble when you ask him to be part of a team. Anyway, the case of money was put into my car by the second getaway car, which the blokes in it then abandoned and walked into South Ken tube station. I set off, cool as if I had just come back from Brighton and was on my way home to lie to my wife as to where I had been. I was supposed to deliver the money to a house in Highgate for the Green Toe Gang. But Moggerhanger had given me instructions to take it to Smilin' Thru', and when I stopped to wait at the red traffic light (I'll never forgive that traffic light for being on red at that particular moment) I thought to myself: "A hundred thousand of real money is in the car, already checked and counted. It's too good to hand over to the Green Toe Gang, or to Moggerhanger. I'll keep it for myself."

'Ah, Michael, greed! That's the downfall of the human race, and especially of yours truly. What commandment of the Good Book is that? One of them, I'm sure, so don't tell me. Pure fucking greed, it was. I tell you I didn't know what greed was till then. The idea struck me so strongly that I thought I would faint, hit another car, get pulled in by the cops and be marched off to the nick with the loot being shared out in the police car behind. But I pulled myself together. A blinding white light flashing GREED, GREED, GREED in front of my eyes got me back on an even keel. That sensation is described very well in one of Gilbert Blaskin's novels, if I remember. It was on page one and I never got beyond it. But I was sweating, trembling, just how I was supposed to be. More than just a knee-trembler behind the dustbins in Soho would be mine for the asking with this amount of lolly. In a flash I wanted everything. You're getting my drift, Michael? I wanted a yacht, a high-speed boat with six berths and me as Captain Codspiece flaring across the Channel to have a triple bunk-up in Cherbourg. Ah, what dreams! The likes of you don't know one half.

'Well, some bastard behind me in a powder blue minivan with a coat of arms on the side was blaring the horn to tell me that red had changed to green, and from thinking I would get my dusters out and give him short back and sides by breaking all his windows except the windscreen so that he would at least be able to drive off and get them repaired, I shot away, jet propelled by nothing else but good old-fashioned greed. Greedy but unashamed, that's me.'

'The material world is so dull,' I said.

He winked. 'It might be. But it's got the best stories and the most money. I'll never forgive myself, I told myself as I left that traffic light behind. And neither, I knew, would the Green Toe Gang or Lord Moggerhanger. You just don't do that sort of thing. I've got two of the most vicious gangs in London (and that means the world) after my tripes to the last millimetre. They'll even kill the tapeworm as it tries to escape along the pavement, poor innocent thing. I honestly don't see how I can survive.'

'Neither do I,' I said.

'Fortunately, or unfortunately I now think, I had my passport with me when I shot from the traffic lights towards Sloane Square. That was because I make it a rule never to go out without it, not even to cross the street for the *Evening Standard* wearing my dressing gown. I'm too old a hand to be caught out on something like that.'

I wondered how I would survive after having been seen talking to such a soft-headed vainglorious lunatic. 'Stop boasting. Tell me what happened.'

He laughed, a tone of hysteria crossed by one of self-satisfaction. 'You must admit it was a brave thing to do, or would have been if it hadn't been so foolhardy. Daring and original, now I come to think of it. I just don't like being a dead man, that's all.'

'Neither would I.'

'But you won't abandon me, Michael?'

'First chance I get.'

'I drove straight to Dover. I was no fool. In Canterbury I gave a lift to a young woman called Phyllis with two kids named Huz and Buz, and before we had got to Dover I'd invited them to come on a continental holiday. She lived in Dover, and had to go home to get their passports. We looked as if we were going on holiday as we got on the boat. Police and customs waved us in with a smile. I never realised I could look such a family man. I even let the matelot wash my car when he asked me, though I locked the boot before going on deck for a breath of air. I can't tell you how good I felt. It was the high point of my life. Here was I, a man of fifty odd, with a car, a woman and two of the worst-behaved little bastards I've ever had the misfortune to lay my hands on, and a hundred thousand quid, on the way to lovely France. I felt like my old self again – rejuvenated, I think is the word.

'I spent a week at Le Touquet, then put my temporary family back on the boat at Ostend with a few hundred to keep them in ice creams and lollipops for a week or two. I then set off via Brussels and Aachen down the Rhine motorway, nonstop to Switzerland, that wonderful refuge of runaways and political exiles with money. Once there I headed for Geneva, where I put the money into an account I'd opened years ago, and still kept a few francs in to hold it open. A nest egg for a cuckoo, but the only thing is I won't live to enjoy it. That's the long and the short of it, Michael.'

I offered a cigarette to calm his nerves. 'But why did you come back? Why didn't you head for Brazil like Ronnie Biggs?'

'Have you got a cigar? Fags do my chest in.'

I gave him one. 'The same old scrounger.'

'I like generous friends. You'll never regret your friendship with me, Michael, even though it might cost you your life. Greater love hath no man . . .' He swung his head back, and hee-hawed like a donkey set free after twenty years going round and round the well. 'Why did I come back here? You haven't heard half the tale yet. I didn't return of my own free will. You think I'm daft as well as stupid?'

'Yes.'

'You're wrong. No, you may be right. The trouble is, Michael, there's no subtlety in my life, none whatsoever. I miss it sorely, and regret not having it. I feel what it is, and say that I must be subtle, and I spend hours deciding how I can be, but when the time comes, I act just like my old violent loud-mouthed greedy unlucky self. Anyway, to get back to Geneva, I was walking out of my hotel, on my constitutional to the lake. I like to keep up my walking. Five miles a day at least, one way or another. I even do a bit of running now and again. You never know when a sudden ten-mile sprint's going to come in handy. There's a gym I go to for boxing. I used to belong to a rifle club, just to maintain my marksmanship. I'm not that much of an idiot that I don't keep myself up to scratch, Green Toe Gang or no bleeding Green Toe Gang.'

'Get on with it.'

'It was a lovely day. I was on top of the world. My cigar tasted like the very best shit, a newspaper was under my arm, my hat was set on my head at the usual jaunty angle – and then it wasn't. Somebody knocked it off, and when I bent to pick it up, before lamming into them, I was lammed into by three of the biggest bastards you ever saw, and a shooter was stuck at my ribs. I didn't have a chance. They made sure I'd got my passport, and before I could say my name was Jack Straw or Bill Hay or Percy Chaff or whatever it was at the time (I honestly forget) I was on the plane to London and no messing.

'Everything looked normal as I walked to the check-in desk at Geneva, but there was one bugger behind me at four o'clock, and another chiking from eight, so that one false move and I'd have been bleeding all over the excess luggage labels. I went as quiet as a lamb. You see, they thought I'd left the money in England. Why? I'll never know, although I can speculate. The chief of the Green Toe Gang employs one of the best psychologists to help out with any problems, personal or otherwise, that come along. Every consultation probably costs a cool hundred. Mostly it pays off. So I assumed that in my case they put the problem before him, and wanted to know where in his opinion I'd gone and what I'd done with the money. So after much sweating at the temples the twit comes up with this scenario that even the big chief of the Green Toe Gang couldn't quibble about, since it had cost him so much. They traced me to Switzerland, which wasn't very clever of them. I could have done the same. This Dr Anderson chap must have told them that before leaving Blighty I'd stashed the cash in a hiding place I knew of, and that they would never find it until they got me back to the Sceptic Isle and made me talk.

'You see, Michael, the gangs aren't so cosmopolitan as they were in our day. They're too insular. They couldn't credit the fact that I would leave with the money and be happy to potter around continental resorts of pleasure for the rest of my life. They'd probably fed into this psychologist's computer-brain all the facts they knew about me, and he'd told them I had buried the cash under the floor boards of the house I was born in in Worksop – which had gone in slum clearance years ago. Well, when I said I'd left the money in Blighty they didn't even listen. They knew, poor sods.

'They got me back to London Airport right enough. Easy. There was a hire car waiting for us. All according to plan. When it comes to organisation, those boys are second to none.'

'They should run the country,' I said ironically.

'They do, Michael, they do, believe me. Anyway, we steamed onto the M4 and I pondered on the fate they had in store for me. My imagination wasn't up to it, though my expectations kept tormenting me. What those lads can do to you don't bear thinking about, but they try the sophisticated way first by locking you in for a couple of days with Dr Anderson. It usually works. Not a mark on you. But if it doesn't (and it wouldn't with me) out comes the tool kit. I was just about ready to be sick, but keeping a good face on it, when the car slows, to curses from the driver. A car in front had braked and we were too close to swerve out and overtake, so had to brake with it. Another car behind homed in. We were topped and tailed, the oldest manoeuvre in the book. My brain clicked into action. When I'm not using my brain I think it's turning into a cabbage and that I'm a walking case of senile decay.

I can't remember anything at times, or think through the simplest problem. But when it's a matter of being in peril, a time when action is needed, I'm as clear as tissue paper and as quick as a snake.

'The two cars were from Moggerhanger Limited, and I knew they wanted me safe in their manor because I was worth close to a hundred thousand when they got me. This was the hijack. The Green Toe Gang hadn't known that Moggerhanger had suborned me, so clearly they didn't expect it. Kenny Dukes got out of one car with three of his pals. One of them was Ron Cottapilly, the other was Paul Pindarry and the third I'd never seen before. Cottapilly had once been on footpad duty nicking wallets and jewellery after midnight in the West End. He held me up once with a knife – a terrible mistake for him, because I punched him so hard all round the clock and up and down the compass that he ended up pleading for his life. Him and Pindarry worked for Jack Leningrad, remember? Now they're going straight, being employed by Moggerhanger.

'Three blokes got out of the other car. One was Toffeebottle, one was Jericho Jim, and the other I didn't know. All of them had claw hammers, and Kenny had a shooter. While the others smashed the windows, Kenny shot the tyres. Two of the blokes came for me, but I hit one, kneed the other, and was up the bank with more bullets whizzing at my brain box than I'd heard since Normandy. I zig-zagged. Do you know, Michael, every chap should do military service. A stint with the Old Stubborns is absolutely vital, because there's bound to be some time in your life when you need the expertise, either to defend your country, or to defend yourself from it. It don't matter which. But the old infantry training's saved my life more times than I care to think about. Breaks my heart to see fat young chaps riding about on motorbikes or lounging on street corners. They should be learning unarmed combat, weapons handling, fieldcraft, marksmanship – basic training for life.'

My scornful look stopped him. 'I've had none of that, and I can take care of myself.'

'Ah, happen so, Michael, but you'd take care of yourself a lot better with it. Anyway, you're different. But to cut a long story short, one of 'em chased me up that bank, but at the top I turned and kicked him so smartly under the chin he went rolling right back onto the hard shoulder. I don't know what they feed people on these days, honest I don't, because the others down by the cars, instead of coming up after me, just watched me kick this bloke as if they was at the theatre and we was actors on the stage. Honest to God, I thought they were going to clap. I'd have waited if I hadn't seen Kenny Dukes reloading his shooter. Then I was off towards some houses in the distance.

'It was afternoon and would soon be dark, so I had to get my bearings and reach civilisation. I tell you, Michael, I felt like an escaped prisoner of war, because listen to the state I was in. After landing and getting through the customs, while we were in the car park, they took my wallet and passport and my shoes as well. Would you believe it? I'm surprised in a way they didn't give me the needle to keep me quiet till I got to a dungeon under Westminster Abbey or the London Mosque. They didn't think the expense was justified, I suppose. Even so, they were taking no chances, though an ambush wasn't expected.

'Another thing was that when I shinned up that bank I didn't realise I'd got no shoes on. Such was my impulse to get away I'd have run through hot coals and broken bottles. As for no money, a mere trifle. Identification papers had never bothered me. I'd never known who I was anyway, except that I was myself, and that's all that mattered. If you know who you are, other people can get at you, and we don't want that, do we? I can see those questions burning behind your eyes. Well, I'm in a right mess, I thought as I came to a lane. Luckily I'd done a bunk just beyond Junction Three, the London side, so the next exit for eastbound traffic wasn't till Gunnersbury, about six miles away. It would take them fifteen minutes at the soonest to turn round, come back to Junction Three and swing north to try and head me off. In that time I could do at least a mile and lose myself in the streets of Ealing. I'd driven so much around London I'd got an A to Z in my head – of the main roads and districts anyway.

'But money was the problem. It always is. It was what got me into the mess in the first place, and now it would have to get me out. I'd a few Swiss francs in coins in one pocket, and the equivalent of ten bob in the other – very useful for a bloke on the run, though not much cop for the likes of me. I had to think fast. I was walking so quick that in about twenty minutes – they hadn't taken my watch – I got to Southall station. The sodium lights glowed, and I skulked along as if wanted by every police force or outlaw gang in the world. This wasn't how I was feeling, Michael. It was tactical. I was really out of my mind with happiness at having got away. I knew that if they were looking for me they'd be expecting to spot an over-confident tall thinnish fellow walking along as if he owned the world – barefoot or not. So I pulled up the collar of my hundred guinea bespoke suit, fastened all three buttons, pulled my tie off and looped it round my waist, and sloped along in the shadows like a wino who'd just been given a talking-to by a do-gooder from Eel Pie Island. And as for that railway station, don't think I would go into it in my present physical state. Not on your big soft cock. If they swung off that Gunnersbury roundabout and looked at the map that's the first place their eyes would light on. They could be as tactical as I was when they'd been thwarted. I hope this tale's something you're learning a bit from, Michael. It's a bit cautionary, like, in more ways than one.'

I gave him a nod.

'Well, thank goodness the district was more like Bombay than Blighty, because I found an Indian Allsort store where I knew I could do a little trading, and went in out of the cold and dark. They had everything for sale, from cheap wristwatches and Russian junk radios to a second-hand clothes department behind a curtain. The chap who ran it was tall, very handsome and wore a turban. A couple of kids played on the floor, and his wife sat by the checkout.'

' "What can I do for you?" he asked me.

' "I'm in trouble," I told him. You have to come straight out with it at such times. I have an instinct, Michael. I can always spot a face that's going to help me. I knew he wouldn't panic, or turn me in after offering me a cup of strong tea with all the sugar I want, like your average Englishman – or anyone else, come to that. I laid my case straight in front of him. "I've been robbed, and this is how they left me. I'd just got off the plane after two years in the States, and these white thugs stuck me up at gunpoint, bundled me into a car, took everything I'd got and threw me on the motorway. Can you help me?"

' "Piss off," he said. "Get away from my shop, you National Front pig, or I'll call the police, and even if they beat me up, burn my shop, club my kids and loot any stock that's left they'll still pin something on you for pulling them away from their tea." These Good Samaritans always begin like that, but after half an hour's chat and several cups of liquid boot polish I sold him my hundred-guinea suit for two, bought a suit and a pair of shoes for a quid that he'd got from a jumble sale for two bob, gave him a quid for the loan of a razor and permission to use it in his lavatory, then gave my foreign coins to his kids in exchange for an old cap, and parted the best of friends. I'll never forget him. He saved my life and, what's more, Michael – forgive me if at this point I get sentimental – he knew it, too. The robbing bastard was the salt of the earth. Ah, Michael, I love people! They never let you down – most of 'em.'

'If you shove all your platitudes up your arse,' I said, 'you'll grow into an oak tree. Get on with your lies.'

He scratched his nose. 'After that, it was easy. I didn't get a train to Wales, or the Cotswolds – if trains run in them places anymore. Nor did I hitch as far out of London as I could get. Not your cunning old Bill he didn't, as that fiendish psychologist would tell them I had when they woke him up next morning. I got into London unspotted, and went to my flat to get money I'd stashed away for emergencies, and a case of things to tide me over. Then I rented a little fleapit room in Somers Town, thinking it better to be in the eye of the storm than on the periphery where an unexpected hurricane can blow up at any minute. That's bad for the nerves, and I don't like things playing on my nerves, especially when it's not necessary. We used to call it the indirect approach, Michael, remember? Nowadays it's known as lateral thinking. When I was a kid it was plain common sense. So then I wrote to you, and put an advert in *The Times* and here we are. And that's my story. Now you can see what a fiendish three-cornered fix I'm in.'

Three

I didn't believe a word of it. The only fact I got from such a rigmarole was that Dr Anderson the psychologist was in the pay of Moggerhanger and the Green Toe Gang. That rang true enough, because he was the brother of the ex-husband of my wife Bridgitte, the father of Smog, and both Andersons were as villainous and devious as they come. The present Anderson was obviously selling information from one gang to the other.

It didn't surprise me but, true or not, Bill seemed relieved that the story was off his chest and that he had found someone to listen to whom the information would be as deadly to know about as it was to himself. To me he was like the plague, and always had been, a carrier of downfall and death. Everything that had gone wrong in my life had been due to him, yet why had I answered his summons to London? He was brother, uncle and childhood pal rolled into one, and with me till the end of my life. It is only fair to record that a lot of the good things that happened had been due to him as well. 'I'm thinking,' I said, seeing the question on his lips.

'You'd better be.'

'I know you're in trouble. I believe it now, but don't you ever learn?'

'Learn?' He almost jumped off his chair. 'Learn?' he repeated, as if it was a new word he liked the sound of. 'Michael, I learn all the time. Every minute of my life, I learn. I go to sleep at night asking: "What have I learned today?" And I wake up in the morning wondering: "What can I learn?" But the sad fact is that I'd need six lives to learn enough to do myself any good. I could learn everything there is to learn and still get stabbed in the fifth rib down by that little fact I've left out.'

'But why someone like me, who can't help you in the least? The logic is absolutely beyond me.'

He drained his empty cup for the third time. 'You may not believe this, but the reason is, I've got nobody else. Nobody I can trust, I mean.'

I almost wept with pity. 'I've been out of circulation for ten years, living a domestic though far from peaceful life at my railway station, so I can't possibly be any help.'

He grasped my hands. 'You can, you can, Michael.'

'All I've done is wash up, play with kids, make do-it-yourself repairs on the waiting room, ticket office and station master's quarters now and again, and a bit of planting in the garden. I'm out of condition, as flabby as a baby seal.'

He put on his sulky look, knowing I was as fit as a flying pike. 'If there's one thing I remember about you it was your quick thinking and the startling versatility of your ideas. Makes my blood run cold, some of the things you got up to – which is better than it not running at all, or spilling over the pavement out of control. Come on, Michael, put that thinking cap on and let's have some good advice.'

'You know how to flatter me. But give me a minute.'

'Two, if you like.' He looked as if his worries were over, though I could have told him that, having brought me back into his life, they were about to begin. I was in no mood to impart comforting advice too soon after he had made it obvious that perilous times were on the cards for me as well. 'In view of the seriousness of your situation I believe the only game we can play is one of diplomacy. What I suggest is that you get into a taxi, drive straight to Lord Moggerhanger's residence and give yourself up. It's your only chance of survival.'

You'd have thought the National Anthem was about to

be played, the way he stood up. I'd never seen him paler. 'So that's what Moggerhanger told you to say? I can see it all now. As soon as I escaped from the hijack he got straight onto you, knowing I would contact you sooner or later. He offered you a good fat fee – half at the time and half on delivery – to meet me, listen to my woes, and then advise me to "drive straight to Lord Moggerhanger's residence and give yourself up". Michael, I would have thought better of you than to try and pull a thing like that. I suppose this place is surrounded, is it?' He looked out of the window, then sat down. 'Or maybe not. It ain't worth the expense, not when you can lead me there like a Mayfair poodle in a taxi. But it won't work. They'll never get me.' He tapped his pocket. 'I pack a little thing in here to help me.' He stared at me, and stood up again. He was acting, but it was too early to guess what his game was. 'I'm not such a fool as not to know that in the end I've only got myself to rely on.'

I did my best to look scornful, but I didn't move, which is perhaps what convinced him. 'Listen, if all you've told me is true, then you're trapped.' I was also a dab hand at acting. 'It's only a matter of time before you're caught, though nobody'll kill you, because they want the money back. That's what they all want. And they won't mind letting six months go by. They're patient. They'll only kill you after they've got their hands on the money. Now, if two gangs are out to get you (and they are, from what you tell me) then you've got to set them at each other's throats even more than they are at the moment. Of the two gangs, I think Moggerhanger's lot are the ones to deal with because both you and I know him from a long time ago. I don't see any other possibility.'

'You're a lunatic,' he said.

I put on a bright smile. 'Lunatics survive.'

'Michael, I don't think you're born.'

I disputed his flippant assertion. 'I was born so long ago

I'm dead. Bridgitte left me last week, and took the kids.'

'I'm sure it served you right. Even so, I don't see why you should want us both to commit suicide. The take-one-with-you attitude is all very well, but not among friends.'

'I'm not suggesting you crawl to the Villa Moggerhanger and blurt out pointblank why you've come,' I told him. 'Approach him on another pretext. Tell him you want to join up with his organisation. The Green Toe Gang got their hundred thousand back. It was in your suitcase. You didn't get your share, and you want your revenge. He'll understand that. Anyway, let's get out of here. I'm feeling like an alcoholic drink.'

'I don't think I need tell you, Michael, that I find our meeting particularly discouraging. I really do. Moggerhanger would just trade me in for half the money. He doesn't mess about. During the transfer he would take the lot. Come on, then. Let's go to The Hair of the Dog. They'll be opening about now.'

He put on his coat, and took my umbrella – being in such a low state that I couldn't tell the light-fingered bastard to put it back. We headed up Charing Cross Road, Bill in front, neither of us saying anything because of traffic noise and the difficulty of walking side by side among so many people. A middle-aged man with a dog on a lead intended passing us on our right but the dog, wanting to go along the wall for a sniff or two, got entangled in Bill's legs.

Even Dr Anderson the demon psychologist would be hard put to it to find a reason as to why some people are born with an animus against our canine friends. Perhaps whoever hates dogs had a particularly hard life in his (or her) younger days, which of course was true of Bill. Such types resent dogs because they regard them as lower than human beings and don't see why they should have a better and more carefree time than they did. Other people who dislike dogs may well be mentally unstable, or stricken with some physical ailment which makes them irascible and intolerant. In any case I don't suppose they can stand the whining fawning bloody pests shitting all over the streets.

Not that Bill reacted violently when the dog tangled with his legs and sent a few squirts of amber piss against his trousers. He had his own troubles, and wanted to be on his way with the least fuss. But he prodded it quite gently, it seemed to me, who had by this time caught up with him, with the end of my umbrella.

The result was extraordinary, to say the least. The black dog, of medium size and uncertain breed, and no doubt a gentle and fetching creature as far as dogs go, gave a squeak and rolled on its back, shivered along the belly, shook all paws and howled.

Bill stepped over it, and so did I. Neither of us realised the seriousness of what had happened. The man bent to look at what was ailing his pet, not for the moment relating its peculiar condition to the seemingly light prod dealt by Bill. He may not even have noticed. We speeded up, to the tune of the man wailing that his dog was having a fit. Perhaps it was dead. As quick as that. It maybe wasn't as bad as he thought, though something had certainly gone wrong as a result of the playful tap from the umbrella.

Running away from trouble seemed undignified, and I thought here was an opportunity to act on my idea of being more honest and responsible. 'Let's go back and see what's wrong.'

He grabbed my arm, the berserker tone in his voice taking on a quality that I hated but which my blood could not ignore: 'Run! For fuck's sake, run!'

We trotted up the road, glad so many people were about. They always came out when the rain stopped. 'Where did you get this umbrella, did you say?' he panted.

'I told you. I found it.'

'It must be poisoned.'

We darted across Cambridge Circus, then doubled back towards Long Acre. 'I didn't know. But don't throw it away. It might come in handy. And keep it away from me. My ankles ache already, it's so close.'

The Hair of the Dog, like auntie's parlour, was tarted up rather than down. The flock wallpaper was deep crimson and reeked of Jamaican rum. The corner of a condom packet showed from under the pseudo-Axminster carpet. I'd have known one anywhere. I looked around the walls at the plastic gold-leafed light-brackets for a sign of the condom itself. There was a framed picture of a child with big tears in its eyes, the sort that should have a microphone behind it. 'Why did we come here? Isn't it one of Moggerhanger's clubs?'

He looked as if the question was unnecessary. 'What I don't like about you,' he said, 'and I'm sorry to say there are some things I positively abhor, if you'll forgive my strong language, is that you are so simple, so, in other words, fucking crude. It's not even as if you're trying to hide something. There's virtue in concealment, when it's necessary, and even when it's not, providing you know what you're doing. But to show yourself as simple when you really are simple is inexcusable. The first sign of leaving it behind would be for you to know that you are simple and, being ashamed of it, learn how to keep your soupbox shut.' He leaned forward and held my hand. 'Do me a favour and make a beginning, there's a good lad. Then we might not only get somewhere, but reach wherever it is we're going in one piece. Are you getting my drift?'

I now knew beyond doubt that the story he had spun was as false and fantastic as he was. Behind his deviousness there was just a great blank sea – but one in which I might well sink without trace. He was working for someone, either Moggerhanger or the Green Toe Gang or both, and he had been asked to recruit me for some project that needed the skill, expertise (or perhaps just plain simplicity), that I was supposed to have. I didn't like it at all, if only because the pay wouldn't be good enough. Yet I had passed the test of loyalty and, in my determination to prove that I was nowhere as simple as I looked, I used the excuse of curiosity rather than loyalty to stay on and find out what it was all about. 'You're just a funny old windbag. Just tell me why you really got me out of my railway station.'

If I didn't like him it was only because he couldn't be straight with me, not through any moral fault or basic unfriendliness either on his part or on mine. On the other hand I did like him. I liked him very much. His thin jaws had flesh on them compared to a few years ago, but you could still see where the lines had been. The mark of hard times that had raddled his face for the first twenty-five years was sufficiently padded to give it a look of nonchalant ruthlessness, and that was what I didn't like.

'You're a bit of a chump, Michael.' Judging by his smile, if the room had been above ground, and had a window or two, the sun would have shone on his face. 'Untrustworthiness never got anybody anywhere.'

'Let's call it caution,' I said. Never trust anybody, was what I had believed all my life, though for reasons I could never understand it hadn't stopped me trusting more people than was good for me.

'That's different. If I thought you weren't cautious I wouldn't be talking to you, would I? Now me, I'm cautious. But I'm also careful. I think on two levels. All the time I've been talking to you I've been thinking. Do you know anybody else who can think and talk at the same time? About different things, I mean?'

'Only an old school pal called Alfie Bottesford, and he went mad.'

He looked as if he'd like to kill me. If we'd been on a

desert road fifty miles from anywhere, and he'd had a gun but I hadn't, he might have considered it. I told him.

'Too fucking right.' He patted my hand amiably. 'But seriously, Michael, let's make a plan of campaign.' After five minutes' silence he asked ruefully: 'Where shall I hide? That's all I want to know.'

I told him, quick as a flash of lightning at a garden party. My best thoughts always came without thought. 'We'll get a taxi to my father's flat in Knightsbridge. I can't think of a better place for you to hole up in for a while.'

'Not so loud. Even walls have ears.'

'Not this one. It's crawling with bugs.'

He snatched his hand away, as one bit the end of his finger. 'Bloody hell, so it is.'

'We'll hide you in Blaskin's flat, just behind Harrods. Very good for shopping. Their Chelsea buns are second to none. Not to mention the sausages. You can even buy a dressing gown if you want to go for a walk.'

He was impatient. 'Will your old man mind?'

'If he does though, you're made. He's an eminent novelist.'

'I know. I've met him, though I don't suppose he'll remember the occasion. It was in the railway station at Upper Mayhem the first time he came to see you there. He nearly went mad with pleasure when he climbed the iron ladder to get at the railway signal. He set it to derail the London express because he thought his publisher was on it, then burst into tears when you told him the line had been closed two years. I've never heard such language about poor old Beeching. It was all your fault though that he was so upset. I don't think I've known anybody as callous as you. The things you've done.'

'He wasn't upset. He's a novelist, don't forget. He was just dying with chagrin, but he wasn't by any means upset. If he got upset he wouldn't be able to describe the situation in a novel. He's far too canny to get so upset that he couldn't write about it.'

Bill looked worried. 'I hope he doesn't write about me if he catches me hiding in his flat.'

I squashed a bug on the table. Bill dropped one in his vodka and it died immediately. 'He may write about the situation in ten years. But he won't know you're there. He's got the top flat these days, and there's an attic he never goes to. With a bed and a pisspot, you can hide there for as long as you like.'

He gripped my elbow as though to break it. 'Michael, I know that some poor Jews had to hide like that in the war from the Germans, but I couldn't take it.' He pointed to his temple. 'I've seen that house in Amsterdam where Anne Frank lived. I'm not that strong. I'd go ga-ga after half an hour.'

'All right,' I said. 'Die. I suppose I'll be sorry if you do, but I'll have done my best, so you won't be on my conscience when I read about them fishing ossobuco from Battersea pond, Peking duck from Putney Reach, and searching vainly for the plain roast beef.' I stood up to go. 'I know Blaskin's loft isn't Claridge's, but at least it's central and you can almost stand up in it. Try it for a few days. What have you got to lose?'

I was bored with the situation and wanted to get back to Upper Mayhem to see if there was any sign of Bridgitte and the children. I was missing my pall of misery, because I thought, in my superstitious fashion, that being steeped in agony for lack of her might bring her back quicker than if I stayed to have a good time in Soho.

He squashed another bug, then pulled me back into my chair. 'All right. I'll do it. And I appreciate it. But I've got a request to make, and I hope you'll say yes.'

'The answer's no.'

'You haven't heard it yet.'

'You've got several score of the most ruthless mobsters

in London after you, and you're making conditions.'

'No,' he said, 'I'm finding you a job. I heard a couple of blokes say yesterday that Moggerhanger wanted another chauffeur. Why don't you apply for the post? He's good to his employees. You worked for him before, didn't you? No, don't take it like that. Sit down, old son.'

I did, before I fell. 'That was ten years ago, and I ended up in prison.'

'Didn't we all? You got mixed up with Jack Leningrad. And you shagged Moggerhanger's daughter. I don't know which was worse in his eyes. But Polly's married now, and Jack Leningrad's moved to Lichtenstein.'

My head spun, yet I was tempted to work again for Moggerhanger because I would get behind the wheel of a Rolls-Royce. Secondly, I would earn some money, and thirdly, I might have another go at Polly, married or not.

'What's in it for you?'

'The reason is,' he said, 'that if you're working for Moggerhanger – who as well as the Green Toe Gang is after my guts – you might pick up bits of information as to whether or not he's on my trail. I'll have a friend in the enemy camp, and feel safer with my own intelligence and security system.'

I was silent for a while. So was he. I didn't mind thinking myself at the turning-point of a long life, because I sometimes imagined it as much as twenty times a day, but what sent shivers up my backbone was to have Bill think it as well. I was horrified at having no say in whether things happened to me or not, so gave him my view on the matter as gently as I could. 'Drop dead. Get cut to bits. Count me out.'

'I can't fathom it,' he said after a minute or two. 'Here I am, telling you that if I'm alive six weeks from now I promise on the sacred memory of my dead mother to share with you – and to share equally – the hundred thousand pounds I've got stashed away. If that's not making it worth your while, nothing is. I know loyalty and friendship are precious commodities, Michael, but even they should have a price. I'm nothing if not realistic and generous.'

I was as greedy as the next man, and thought of all I could do with fifty thousand pounds. Corn in Egypt and the Promised Land rolled into one. I would turn the railway station into a fitted carpet palace. I'd repave the platforms, repair the footbridge, lay ornamental gardens on my stretch of line, as well as put in a new stove for Bridgitte and buy her a vacuum cleaner. I'd also give a flashing-light chess set to Smog, and if he failed to get into Oxford or Cambridge I'd buy him a degree from an American university, so that if he wanted a job he could become a secret member of the communist party and join the Foreign Office. Then, in our old age, after he'd become a colonel in the Red Army, we could spend our holidays in his nice cosy flat in Samarkand – or even Moscow, in the summer. Oh, the best laid plans of mice and men.

He grinned. 'Is it on?'

'You superannuated clapped-out Sherwood Forester,' I said, 'I suppose so.'

'You leave my old regiment alone. Sometimes I quite like your gift of the gab, but not when you insult the Sherwood Foresters. Best regiment in the British Army. We had four battalions wiped out on the Somme, and God knows how many in the last lot.'

I apologised. What else could I do? 'I don't stand a chance of getting a job with Moggerhanger.'

'Who knows? He's allus got a soft spot for a reformed rake. Nothing's guaranteed in this life, but you might just land it. You allus was game, I will say that for you. You don't get anything in this life unless you try.'

I was irritated by him. 'I'll just be able to stand you for as long as it takes to install you at my old man's flat. Let's get out of here.'

'Don't forget your umbrella,' he said when we were half-way up the stairs, and daylight struck my eyes like ball-bearings from a catapult. 'It might start raining.'

Four

The first new thing I saw while snooping around Gilbert's study – as he called it: he'd never studied anything in his life, except women – was a large coloured chart on the wall above his typewriter, showing the ages at which every well-known home, foreign and colonial novelist had died. His own name had a question mark by the side in brackets, at which I didn't know whether to laugh, or dab my eyes with his clean white blotting paper. He might be nudging sixty, but I didn't realise he was afraid to die.

The sheet in the typewriter seemed to be page one of a novel called *The Hijacked Vampire*. Below the line saying Chapter Three he had written:

> The privilege of learning from experience is only given to those who survive it. Many do survive, yet it is both pitiful and amazing to discover the numbers who do not, especially when one tries to imagine those people as individuals. Each life starts innocently enough, grows side by side with its dreams, and ends with its limbs broken amid pints of blood.

I crossed out 'pints' and wrote 'litres'.

> If we could profit from the experience of death, would we go more readily to die?

Such drivel went on for a few more lines, ending in a paragraph of exes. Maybe he was halfway human after all.

Bill lay on the settee in the living-room, smoking one of Blaskin's cigars and tippling a glass of Glenfiddich whisky. 'Can you get me something to eat, Michael?'

There was no reason to lose my temper at this late

stage, but maybe the Age Chart on the study wall had depressed even me. 'If he comes in and finds you in that condition, with delirium tremens and lung cancer, he'll slit your throat and tip you out of the window just as efficiently as a member of the Green Toe Gang or Moggerhanger's Angels. So let me show you to your six-week hideaway, then I can clear out. He won't be happy at finding me here, either.'

An old-fashioned antique gramophone with an enormous tin horn stood on one of the tables. In a cabinet behind was a lavish (locked) display of netsuke, such art and handiwork as I had only seen in museums. Some lovely old oil paintings of sailing ships and rustic scenes decorated the walls – as well as a portrait of Blaskin as a five-year-old, hardly recognisable except for the unmistakable signs of vice and wilfulness in that lovely face. I wondered how safe these treasures would be with a born marauder like Bill eating his heart out upstairs.

He swallowed the whisky and stood up, an athletic leap showing how fit he was. But there was panic in his eyes and voice. 'What am I going to do while I'm up there?'

'I'll schlep down to World's End and find you a harp.'

'I must have provisions, or I'll starve. You can last only so long trapping pigeons. And I'll tell you one thing, Michael, they don't taste very nice with all that petrol and grit inside 'em. I tried it once.'

I took a bottle of wine, a loaf, a German sausage and a jar of olives from the larder. He put them in his pockets. 'What a friend you are.' He was almost crying. 'I'll never forget you. A real friend.'

Maybe he hadn't invented the tale of his trip to Switzerland after all. He was too sentimental to be imaginative. Proper lies were beyond him. If they weren't, he'd be far too dangerous to himself. As it was, he was only a threat to others, me in particular. I had to help him for two good reasons: friendship and money, a combination impossible to deny, so I led him to the box-room at the end of the corridor. A bare light bulb illuminated water and wastepipes and old picture frames leaning against a pile of steamer trunks. A ladder with the first rung broken led up to a trapdoor – square in the middle of a map of water stains. He hung back. 'I'm not going up there.'

'Yes you are. Just imagine you're in prison and the lads have selected you as a volunteer to do a roof protest. Only don't start chucking slates on people going into Harrods. They might not like it.'

He relaxed. 'I'll never know why I let you twist me round your little finger. But before I go up, just nip back for a couple of candles or an oil lamp, will you? I draw the line at living in the dark.'

As I was opening kitchen drawers he shouted: 'And a blanket, while you're at it. And some more of them delicious Havanas. Oh, and a bottle of whisky and a few pats of best butter. And two pounds of sugar to put on my bread.'

Needless to say, I got him nothing except the candles and a blanket. We went up into the roof. 'You didn't happen to see a camp bed down there, by any chance?' he said.

The tank was part of the hot water system, so at least he wouldn't freeze to death. The roof arched above the whole flat, huge beams curving to an apex in a sort of cathedral for dwarfs. 'You can paint *The Last Supper* on the end walls.'

'I would if I could eat it,' he answered morosely, clasping my hands. 'You will come up and see me, won't you? And let me know how you get on with Lord Moggerhanger. I take a friendly interest in your career, Michael, you know that. I feel a bit like your elder brother.'

Only my head was visible above the floorboards. 'Stop

it, or you'll make me swear. I'll come and see you as often as I can.'

Or as often as I dare, I thought, treading carefully down the ladder and hoping he wouldn't make any noises that would lead to his discovery.

I sipped whisky and smoked a fag in the living room to think things over, wondering if I shouldn't phone the police, or Moggerhanger, or the Green Toe Gang, or all of them together, and tell them where Bill Straw was hiding and then get quickly back to Upper Mayhem before the cyclone struck. The police were just as interested in putting the fetters on Bill as was the underworld, though I supposed he was right to go more in fear of the latter, since legal capital punishment had ended years ago. If I did send out a general call to all interested parties even Blaskin might get winged in the crossfire for harbouring a man on the run, though it was futile trying to damage him because he'd only use the inconvenience as material for his writing, and end up richer than before.

I only mulled on the options of treachery so that I would never act on any of them. Then I wondered whether I should apply for the chauffeur's job with Moggerhanger. A spot of work would take my mind off Bridgitte which, after all, would be better than wallowing in misery at home. London always put me in a free and easy mood. With the naïvety of a newborn babe I thought that at this stage of my life I had nothing to lose, no matter what I did. The catch of the door sounded, and my father came in, singing a little ditty to himself:

> 'I knew a man who couldn't write
> He sat up brooding half the night
> Not because he couldn't write
> But because his shoe was tight, tight, tight!'

He stumbled in the hall as he took off his grey leather overcoat. 'Is that you, Michael? I can smell my cigars. Or is it the odious breath of yesteryear?'

How can a son describe his own father? Luckily I hadn't known about him till I was twenty-five, so that makes it easier. As for his description of me, I read it in one of his recent novels and it wasn't very good. It was slightly disguised, of course, as every fictional description must be but, slashing away the trimmings, he called me lazy, untruthful, mercenary and – words I hadn't heard till then – uxoriously sybaritic. Where he got such an idea I couldn't imagine. The description was so skewwhiff it's a wonder I recognised myself, and the fact that I did worried me for a while. And if it wasn't me, I was either trying to see myself as someone I wasn't, or I was someone I couldn't bear to see myself as. But such a description, bare as it was, certainly convinced me as nothing else that I was his son.

As for him, he was tall and bald, so bald that with the cleft in his head where a crazed husband had hit him with the blunt end of a cleaver, he looked like nothing less than a walking penis. I didn't for a moment suppose that this was the only reason many women found him attractive because he also, presumably, had a certain amount of what passed for charm. He had dead grey fish eyes, rubbery lips and a shapeless nose, but he was tall, energetic, talented (I supposed), and incredibly randy. As my mother, who knew him well, once said to me (though she hardly ever really knew him well for more than a few minutes at a time), 'Even a man has to stand with his back to the wall when that bastard comes into the room.'

'Well, Michael – it is Michael, isn't it? – what brings you here so early in the morning?'

I stood up, not wanting to act in any unusual way when I knew that Bill Straw was sobbing disconsolately in his upstairs prison. 'It's afternoon. I just thought I'd come and see you. Is it strange that I should want to visit my father now and again?'

He came back from the kitchen with two raw eggs in the bottom of a tall glass, poured in whisky to halfway, beat it to pulp with a fork, and slid it down. 'Breakfast. It isn't strange at all. It's positively perverse. How's Bridgitte?'

'She's left me. She's gone to Holland with the kids. I'm devastated. I'm lost without the kids around. I don't know which way to turn.' I encased my head in my hands, acting the hackneyed bereft husband in the hope of giving him some material for one of his novels.

'Good,' he said. 'I never liked the bitch for giving me what, with a proud simper, she called grandchildren. If there's one thing I can't stand it's the thought of grandchildren. Even if I die at a hundred-and-two I'll be too young to be a grandfather and I'm only fifty-eight. Or is it forty-six?' He poured another whisky. 'No matter. At least not after last night.'

He wasn't even good to me, so I didn't have fair reason to hate him, but I knew one way of making him jump. 'How's work, these days?'

He belched. 'Don't use that word. I've never worked in my life. A gentleman never works. I write, not work.' His eyes took on sufficient life for someone who wasn't in the know to imagine not only that he was alive, but that he was a normal human being. 'The worst thing I ever did was marry your mother so that I had no further right, in the technical sense, to call you a bastard. But you are a bastard, all the same. I never did like your insulting insinuations that I might be capable of the cardinal sin of work. All I do is write, and fuck. And never you forget it.'

'It's hardly possible,' I said, 'since you begat me.'

'So your mother said. But you're rotten enough, so it might well have been me.'

I poured another tot for myself. 'In my view the greatest disaster of modern times was when you first got blind drunk on the power of words.'

He threw his great cock-head back and laughed. 'You're

right, Michael. I've vomited over many a sofa in a dowager's salon. There aren't many decent homes I can visit anymore, but then, who wants to visit a decent home?'

We had something in common at least. 'All I wanted to know, in my clumsy fashion, is how the writing is getting on?'

'Why didn't you say so? If I have any love for you at all it's only because you're so ineradicably working-class – hell's prole, and second to none. Just like the lovely lads I had under me during the war. I'd acknowledge you much less if you came from within sniffing distance of the Thames Valley and had been to Eton – like me. The writing's getting on very well, since you ask. I've got so much to do I don't know which way to turn. I can't keep off it. Just a minute.' He went into his study, and I heard the clack of a single key on the typewriter. He came back, smiling. 'I wrote a comma. Now I can go out again, though not while you're here. You'll smoke the rest of my cigars. What did you really come for? I might be a writer, but I'm not a bally idiot.'

'I was on my way to Harrods to buy a waistcoat, and I nipped in on impulse.'

'A waistcoat? What colour?'

'A leather one.'

'Hmm! Not bad.'

'With horn buttons.'

'Better.' Then he went back to being nasty. 'And you thought you'd come here to disrupt me from my life's work? You'd like to stop me writing the novel to end novels, wouldn't you?'

'I expect it's been done,' I said, 'fifty years ago.'

'That's what you think.' He threw his empty glass on the sofa. 'I'd rather write a novel any day than a scholarly treatise on dumb insolence at the first Olympiad.' He laughed. 'But the thing is, Michael, my boy, I've got a commission to do something which is right up my street. A job wherein the research is going to take me to all the porn shops, strip clubs, lesbian hangouts, camp brothels, cat houses and underground cinemas in Soho. I can hardly believe it. I've just had a ten thousand pound advance to get started on it right away.'

'You fucking writers have all the luck.'

'I wish you wouldn't swear,' he said. 'There's nothing so charming as a working-class chap who doesn't swear. But as soon as he swears you know he's trying to pass himself off as middle-class. It sounds so uncouth. Mind you, I did swear when I was a young man, but it was only a happy-go-lucky fuck-this fuck-that sort of thing. I don't do it anymore. It restricts my vocabulary.'

'Don't tell me how to behave. But who's commissioned you to write that book?'

He chuckled. 'A peer of the realm. One of your self-made salt of the earth boys from the provinces who are periodically ennobled so that they won't cause more trouble to the body politic than they have to. He thinks he's God's gift to England because he has all the vice dens in the palm of his hand, and can be trusted not to let them get out of hand. He wants me to do his life story, a whitewash job if ever there was one. His wife read one of my novels, apparently, and didn't like it, so he thought I was just the writer to do it. But if he thinks I'm going to get much mileage out of making him into little Saint Claud Mogger-donger he's wrong. I'd much rather write the true story about him, except that I'll save the real material for one of my later novels, though I suppose I'd better go to his ancestral Moggerhanger village in Bedfordshire to write a nice lyrical opening chapter on his antecedents and their hanging ground. There's bound to be a gibbet or two I can go into raptures over, like Thomas Hardy. Why, Michael,' he shouted when I ran into the bathroom, 'have I said anything wrong? If I make you sick, you've made my day.'

The cold porcelain of the toilet struck my forehead. I tried to throw up, but not a grain of bile would rise. The hammer of a metronome was going back and forth, a decade one way, and a decade the other. It wasn't fear that turned my guts as much as that old familiar sensation of helplessness at being in the hands of fate. I tried to look on the bright side, but only a forty-watt light-bulb glowed. I couldn't imagine what side-swipe of chance had brought Blaskin and Moggerhanger together, especially when, unknown to the former, one of the latter's most wanted men was fretting in the attic above. I washed in cold water and, braving myself to meet whatever might come, went back to the living room.

'Did I say something wrong?' Blaskin said, with malicious perkiness. 'You look as pale as Little Dorrit, and you're trembling like the Aspern Papers. Do you have an appointment with fear?'

'I've got problems,' I admitted.

His eyes glowed. Sidney Blood wasn't in it. 'What are they?'

'If I knew I wouldn't have them, would I?'

After a two-minute silence he said: 'Michael, we've all got problems, but a writer, like a soldier, goes through life with his problems unresolved. I've been both.'

I was fed up with his penny packets of wisdom. 'You disgusting old bastard,' I spat back. 'I don't need you to tell me that everybody goes through life with their problems unresolved.'

He stared, maybe thinking there was something to the slum brat after all. He didn't like it. There was certainly no point in hoping for a bit of human kindness from a writer. He rubbed his head as if wanting it to come, then rubbed his eyes as if he wouldn't be able to stand the sight of what did. 'I had a bad night last night. I spent it with Margery Doldrum, and didn't get anywhere. So leave me alone. I've got work to do. The heart of darkness is within. It used to be outside in jungle or desert where we could handle it, but now it's back on home ground. It crept in to roost, with most of us unaware of its movement, but in reality it never left – not all of it, anyway.'

I hoped to cheer him up. 'You should write that down. It's not bad.'

'You think so?'

'I would, except that I'm not a writer, like you.'

He found a pencil and scribbled on the back of an envelope. There was an unopened pile of mail on the low-slung Swedish-type table. 'I'm going to give a talk on the modern English novel, so it'll come in handy. Sometimes even a son like you can be useful.'

'How is the novel going?' As his son, I thought I should at least show an interest in his work. But I only thrust him back into despair. You can't win.

'It isn't a novel, it's the Dead March from *Saul*, a chain-and-ball half-page a day, sometimes down to a comma a day, up a narrow valley with no blue horizon visible to cheer me on. I'm one of the poor bloody infantry lost in the moonscape south of Caen but soldiering on in the knowledge, but mostly the vain hope, that I'll get there soon and still have my feet left at least. But the joy of endeavour and solitude comes in now and again, Michael, sufficient to keep me going on this first draft route report. Fortunately, doing Moggerhanger's biography – or ghosting his autobiography, I'm not sure which yet – will bring in a few thousand, so I'll at least have enough hard cash to keep your extravagant mother at arm's length. I wish you'd stop turning pale when I mention Moggerhanger, by the way. It unnerves me. It's not that I don't love your mother, but I can't even write commas when she's around. So I'll deliver fifty pages of Moggerhanger's trash now and again to line my pockets. If there's one thing he knows nothing about, though he thinks he knows everything there is to know about everything else, it's writing. I can put one over on him there.'

'I don't suppose he knows what he's let himself in for.' I looked glumly at the netsuke to cheer myself up. 'It must be good being a writer, and able to make people so unhappy.'

'Wonderful,' he said, 'but do you think it's easy? If anybody comes to me and says they want to be a writer I tell them to get lost before I cut off their hands, blind them, and burst their eardrums. In any case, it's going to be impossible for a writer to flourish in the future. The manuscript of every book will have to go to the Arabian Censorship Office before it's published. So will all radio, and especially television scripts. The Foreign Office don't want us to offend anybody whose hands are on the oil taps. Every book and newspaper article will have to be passed by UNESCO after getting the go-ahead from the Third World nations to make sure you don't irritate them in their state of perpetual envy against better-off countries. No, it's not going to be so easy.' An unmistakable scratching sounded from the other side of the ceiling. His big head jutted up. 'What the hell's that? Are they up there already?'

I started to sweat. 'It's pigeons, I expect.'

'They must have broken in again. They don't breed. They multiply.'

I reached for my coat and briefcase. 'Must go. It's getting late, and I've got business to attend to.'

He came over to count the netsuke which he had seen me looking at.

'Shurrup!' I shouted, putting all the Nottingham ferocity into my voice, while hoping my eyes bulged and my cheeks quivered.

'What did you say?'

I laughed in his face. 'Shurrup!' I bawled again. 'Shurrup! I think I'm going mad.'

'Do you mind leaving, and coming back when it's a bit more advanced and so obvious I can't ignore it? Maybe you'll let me observe you then, and write about it. I've got work to do in the meantime.'

He followed me to the door to make sure I didn't whip a painting under my coat, and all but pushed me into the corridor, whose blank walls and escape route I was never so glad to see in my life.

Five

On the wall behind Moggerhanger's glass desk a notice said: 'While you are thinking about it, you can be doing it.'

I studied this cracker motto from The Little Blue Book of Chairman Mog, knowing that if wild horses pulled him apart, a thousand others would spill out. Even his big toe must have been packed with them. I remembered from ten years ago that if you tried to live by such rules you fell under his spell, so I knew I had to watch myself, especially when, on turning to the door I had come in by, I saw in a place where only the particularly anxious or the peculiarly double-jointed would look, a framed embroidered text saying: 'If you haven't tried everything you haven't tried anything.'

I wondered if there wasn't a microphone behind, but supposed the television scanner was in the fancy light-bulb above his desk. The furnishings had altered since I had last been there. A framed picture of the Queen stood on a shelf of the bookcase otherwise crammed with manuals on natural history and birdwatching. Behind the desk was a coloured map of England with a dozen pins stuck in different places, which I assumed were localities at which Moggerhanger had business properties, retreats of pleasure or hideaways. A single chair behind the desk suggested that everyone but Moggerhanger stood when in that room. Before he had become a Lord there were several chairs, but not anymore. He was even more English than Blaskin.

On the desk was a duraluminium model of his private twin-jet in flight which he kept at Scroatham aerodrome north of London. By the desk was a black-handled bottle of brandy six feet tall fixed in a brass frame on wheels. God knows how many gallons it contained. The cork was as big as a sewer lid, but the liquid shone like something out of heaven. I longed for a drink but didn't know how to tackle it. One false move and I would be missing, presumed drowned. I visualised Kenny Dukes pushing it through the Nothing to Declare door at London Airport, the contraption disguised as an old lady on her way back from a recuperative sojourn on the Riviera.

The bookcase swung open, then closed with the delicacy of a powder puff going back into its box. 'You seem to be fascinated by my exhortations.'

'I was admiring the needlework, Lord Moggerhanger.'

'As well you might. My daughter Polly did it. She went to the best Swiss finishing school.' She certainly had. I'd finished her off a fair number of times ten years ago.

He wore the best quality navy-blue pinstriped suit and waistcoat, a thin silver watch chain across his gut. He had lost weight, though not much. Nothing ever gets lost, he once said to me. It only goes missing. He had decided on his reduction at the time of his appearance in the New Year's Honours List, being unable to abide the idea of a fat lord. Vanity, I thought, will be his undoing.

'What brings you here, Michael?'

'I heard you wanted a chauffeur, Lord Moggerhanger.'

I noticed the dullness of contact lenses when he looked at me. 'Who from?'

'Kenny Dukes. I met him in The Hair of the Dog.'

'Kenny's in Italy, and not due back till tonight. He goes once a month to get the family shopping from Milan. So don't lie to me. Your wits are in cement. Do you want your feet to be? Why did you call, when you could have phoned first?'

'I didn't have your number.'

'It's in the book. You don't seem as sharp as you were

ten years ago, Michael. I'm surprised at you. You see, it's always been my contention that those whom the Gods wish to drive mad they first make ex-directory. All those pop stars and writers who scrub their names from the phone book as soon as they think they're too well-known are crazed with self-importance. Anybody wants to talk to me, all they have to do is look me up in the book and pick up the phone. I may be a Lord – and don't you forget it – but I'm still a democrat at heart.'

He was the only person I knew who you couldn't lie to, and get away with it. There was nothing to say. He looked at me for a while, with a gaze that seemed more pregnant than the *Encyclopaedia Britannica*. The last time I had worked for him I'd gone to prison because I was one of the expendables and now, facing him for the first time since, a thought flashed into my mind that promised danger and pleasure. The only emotion that can combine the two so neatly is revenge, yet how could someone like me dare to contemplate getting a Peer of the Realm put behind bars for a good long spell, even though he was the most crooked bastard in Great Britain – and that meant the Commonwealth, which probably meant the world? I let the suicidal, self-destroying notion go. 'It was a bit remiss of me. I'll know better next time.'

'I'm sure you will, if there is a next time. Are you sure you want to be my driver? I've had a few more applicants, as you can understand. One of them was Kenny Dukes's brother Paul, and I don't think I've ever seen a more wicked villain than that. On the other hand, he's the sort of driver who's been practising on stolen cars since he was twelve. Now he's twenty-five and in his prime.'

'I crashed my first car when I was five,' I said, which was true, 'and now I'm thirty-five.'

He took a box from under the desk that was big enough to put his feet on, and lifted out a cigar. To smoke it he needed one of those forked supports an arquebusier used to have. 'So you see, Michael, I've got a decision to make. However, I'm a born judge of men. I always was. I've got to be. I wouldn't last five minutes if I wasn't. I know that you and me had a little trouble ten years ago.'

I'd been waiting for that. 'It was my fault.'

'That's for me to say,' he snapped. 'But I suppose it inclines me more towards you than otherwise. You might say it taught us a lot about each other. Almost makes you part of the family. I like to learn from the past, and don't like starting with somebody from scratch unless I have to, or unless he's an exceptional case, as you were in those days, and as Kenny Dukes's brother isn't. They're ten a penny, that sort, in south and east London. They're well built, cocksure and clever, but if you stop looking over their shoulder for a second they get too clever. And even the cleverest of them can't think. Oh yes, they can move with cunning and alacrity in an emergency, but they can't think.'

'What do you expect?'

'I know, but there comes a time when you hope that a subordinate might be able to think to the advantage of the man who's paying him. I regard you as being in a different category. What's more, you're looking quite distinguished. Ten years in the wilderness seem to have made a man of you. In those days I didn't so much mind a young roustabout for my wheel man. Now I like a steadier chap, but one who still knows the tricks. I'll start you at five hundred a month, and you can have your old quarters back above the garage. You've got twenty-four hours to move in.'

The answer to everything was yes. His handshake was the grip of an earth remover, and my hands were neither small nor weak. He called me back from the door. 'How did you hear about this job?'

'I bumped into Bill Straw at Liverpool Street this morning.'

'Where was he going?'

'He wouldn't tell me.'

'What time was it?'

'Just before half past nine.'

He reached for the telephone. 'I wish you'd come earlier.'

'I didn't know it was important.'

'Piss off.' He didn't even look up. 'I want a call to Holland,' he was saying into the mouthpiece as I closed the door.

If poor old Bill had got on that Harwich boat train, as Moggerhanger wrongly surmised due to my quick thinking, he would have been met at the Hook, made to tell where the money was and put to a particularly grisly death before being dumped into the ooze. Luckily, he was safe in Blaskin's aerial foxhole, a fate which in no way would faze an old Sherwood Forester.

Not wanting to get back to Upper Mayhem too early, where I would only brood myself to death over Bridgitte's callous desertion, I decided to go into Town and get something to eat. A few hundred yards from the tube station a little dark girl who looked about ten but must have been thirty, judging from her big tits and almond eyes, was trying to carry a suitcase full of stones along the pavement. People passing were in too much of a hurry to help. Then she pulled the suitcase, till she had to stop. Then she pushed it. At that rate she'll get to the underground in the morning, I thought. It'll take another day to reach the platform, and she'll tumble into some railway station – the wrong one – in about three weeks. Luckily, it wasn't raining.

I passed her, but a soft heart forced me to turn and pick up the case. She thought I was a footpad after her worldly belongings and looked at me, raising a little bun fist, though realising that she couldn't win. I expected the weight to pull my arm off, but for my gold smuggling muscles it was no real burden, and I walked at a normal quick-march rate, with her half running by my side. 'I'll help you with it to the tube station. I'm not trying to steal it. It's on my way.'

She also had a satchel and a shoulder bag, so I slowed down. Her accent was foreign, and so was her lovely smile. 'Thank you very much.'

She was about four foot nothing, but full of promise. I asked her name, and she said it was Maria. 'You going on holiday?'

I thought she hadn't understood. 'Holiday?' I said. We got to the ticket office. 'Where to?'

'Victoria.'

I bought two fares, thinking to leave her after setting her luggage on the train. She'd clamped up since her first big smile and trotted by my side, while I was still wondering why Moggerhanger had given me the job so readily. It was as if he had been expecting me, though I couldn't dredge up a reason to prove it. 'Maria,' I said when we were on the platform, 'you going on holiday?'

A bearded wino in his twenties knocked her so hard as he pushed by that she almost fell onto the rails. I pulled her back, which was as well for him that I was so occupied, but then I elbowed him onto the bench. 'No holiday,' she said. 'I want to die.'

I laughed. 'You want to fly?'

'No, die.' She tried not to sob. Her accent was thick, but I could understand her. 'No more job.'

I was about to run away and leave her when the train came in. The last thing I wanted was a waif on my hands. I pushed her inside, and we faced each other over the luggage. The red woollen scarf that went round her neck and over her shoulder was only half as long as the braids of black hair that descended her back. She wore a white blouse under her coat, a black skirt, black ribbed stockings and black lace-up boots. Her face was oval and pale, a clean parting down the middle of her skull. Her brown eyes were almost liquid with tears, and the effort she made not to let them flow almost brought tears to my own – and stopped me getting out at Acton Town. I leaned forward: 'Where are you from?'

'Portugal.'

I held her warm hands, and tried to cheer her up. 'Nice place, Portugal.'

I wished I hadn't said that, because she looked up full of hope. 'You been there?'

'Yes. Good country. Lisbon is a wonderful city. You go there now?'

She didn't answer so I looked away, wondering where I'd go to eat before getting my train to Upper Mayhem. Something wet fell on my middle finger left hand, and I turned back to her. It was a tear. I don't know why I lifted my hand and licked it off. It was automatic, thoughtless, but with the hand that still held hers I felt a shiver go through her. I looked into her eyes, and thought I'd done the wrong thing in licking up that tear because as sure as hell – and the stare she gave hinted as much – such a gesture was, in the part of Portugal she came from, a kind of pre-nuptial ceremony that was binding forever.

My next chance of escape was at Hammersmith. I had enough on my plate at the moment. When she spoke, the shiver went through me and not her. 'I go nowhere. I lose my job working in English house. Missis Horlickstone throw me out. Mister Horlickstone hit me. Children hit me. Too much work. At six o'clock I get up, clean, do breakfast, serve tea, take children to school on bus, then go shopping, come back, clean, cook lunch, serve, clean up, make tea, get children from school on bus, feed children, bath children, cook dinner, serve, clean up. You know what money I get?'

I thought the cheapskates would have paid her about thirty pounds a week.

'Fifteen. I also babysit. No time off. For six months I work, live in box room, no air, no sky . . .'

I couldn't believe it. She was joking, but was breaking my heart. 'And they sacked you?' I said at South Kensington.

'I ran away. They're on holiday in Bermuda. They come back next week, so I leave.'

I wondered whether she'd got the family silver in her suitcase, but knew she couldn't be anything but honest. 'And now you want a better job?'

Another hot tear stung my wrist. I imagined a white acid spot when it dried. 'Yes. No. I don't know. I want to go home, but my family need money. They live on it. I have no money for train to . . .' She named some place in Portugal I'd never heard of.

So here was a lovely little down-trodden self-respecting intelligent thing like her with neither job, money nor place to sleep, in vast wicked London, sitting on the Underground facing a soft-hearted villain like me who also happened to be the son of Gilbert Blaskin. I supposed I could put her on the Circle Line and tell her to get off when it stopped. Where she would end up, I couldn't imagine. She looked blank, and dumb with suffering. I wanted to go to the house she had come from and burn it down, which would be futile because the owner wasn't in it, and would get the insurance anyway. 'Where will you stay tonight?'

She wiped her eyes with a white laundered handkerchief. 'I have money for room. Tomorrow I don't know.'

'Haven't you got any friends?'

'Missis don't let me out.'

'So what will you do?'

'Don't know. It takes time to get job.'

I drew my hands away and sat up smartly, as befitted a man who was about to become an employer. 'You've got one already, if you want it. Here's Piccadilly. We'll get out now, and go for something to eat. You hungry?'

'Oh, yes.'

'Good. While we're eating I'll tell you about your new job.'

We found a place which served flock steak, chalk chips, ragdoll salad, whale fat gâteaux and acorn coffee. She loved it, so I made out that I did as well. 'I'll tell you what's going to happen.' I lit my cigar. 'I have a country house in Cambridgeshire, as well as a wife and three children. Now, my wife and children are away at the moment, visiting our property in Holland, and won't be back for a few days, but I'm supposed to find a woman to help with the housework. I was going to put an advertisement in the *Evening Standard*, but don't need to now. What I suggest, Maria, is that you come with me to the house this evening and look the place over. I'll pay your fare. If you don't like it, you can stay the night, and a few more nights if you like, and then come back to London. My wife should be there, so you'll be quite safe.'

'You really got job?'

'That's what I said.' She tampered with my dessert, so I pushed it across. 'Come and see the house. At least you won't waste your money on a hotel.'

She looked even paler under the artificial light. It was dusk outside, and people were hurrying along the street. 'Why are you good to me, mister?'

The question tormented me more than it did her. I wasn't even sure I wanted to get her into bed. Maybe I couldn't stand living alone. She finished my dessert and I stood up. 'Let's go, then.'

Out on the street it started to rain, and I had left my umbrella at Blaskin's. I stopped, as if pricked with it, and snake venom was trickling down my leg. I saw the newsflash tickertaping across the Swiss Centre: NOVELIST ON MURDER CHARGE. Then I rubbed it away in the hope that it wouldn't come true.

'What's a matter?' she asked when I dropped the case. 'No job for me now?'

'No job for anybody,' I told her, hurrying on, 'if we don't get to Liverpool Street and hop on that train.'

Six

'Never,' I remember Blaskin saying, 'bother with a novel that takes more than five pages to cover one day.' Blaskin said many things. Blaskin is all wind and piss. Whatever he said, he meant the opposite. It was his silence you had to beware of. You were only safe when he had a pen in his hand. Even then, you had to be ready to duck in case, like James Cagney in *G-Men*, he mistook you for a fly on the door, and aimed it at you like a dart.

The day I got the job with Moggerhanger was one of the longest in my life, or so it seemed at the time, proved by the fact that when I got back to Upper Mayhem with Maria, my troubles were just beginning. There were more lights shining in our comfy little railway station than had ever been set glowing when main line expresses rattled through. You could see the light for miles over the flat Fen country, a glow in the sky as if a new hydroelectric dam had been opened in the Yorkshire Dales.

My first thought, walking with Maria and her suitcase from the bus stop, was that a band of squatters had occupied the place. I had often worked out what I would do if that happened. I'd phone Alfie Bottesford in Nottingham and tell him to get a posse of the lads together so that in one rough assault we'd have those squatters, including women, cats and kids, their pots and pans bundled into blankets, wending their lonely way in a refugee column across the Fens.

But I could hear no triumphant wassailing as I opened the gate and stepped silently down the platform. The radio was on, and I signalled to Maria to slow down and say nothing, which gesture alone should have indicated that all was not right with her prospects for the promised job. My adrenalin was whirlpooling too much to worry about her. I looked into the booking-office-cum-parlour. Three half-packed suitcases were on the floor, and Bridgitte sat at the table trying to hypnotise a cup of tea. I felt like a marauder, dagger in teeth, about to fade back into the countryside, as if I had come to the wrong house. But it was as much mine as hers, just as were the years we'd been together, whose miserable intensity came back the longer I stared.

She pushed the cup aside and reached for a sheet of paper and a pen, obviously intending to write the farewell letter she had been thinking about since the day we were married. Her expression of disgust caused a pain in my heart. I had never seen such a sad and saintly face. Though she may have been miserable for reasons known only unto God, both of us were locked in it together, and her despondency stirred up my muddy love for her, a love that was part of my marrow. Anything else might lack reality, but not what I felt for her. Whatever she said or did, wherever she went, whatever happened to me or to the kids, my association with her would never cease to have been the most vital of my life. I looked at her longingly and secretly.

She wrote a few lines, stopped, and stared in my direction without seeing me. With mouth open and head drawn back, she laughed, her fair tresses hanging down, so loud that I heard her though I was outside. It was a laugh of blind malice. Perhaps she thought I was funny, pathetic and useless. Scorn brought out the happiness in her. I'd never seen her so happy. She looked like a young and carefree girl I had never known.

I wondered what crime I had committed to have been lumbered with the catastrophe of meeting her. She had ruined my life with her humourless domesticity. I hated her. She was laughing now, but I'd never heard her laugh at anything funny while with me – if anything funny was ever worth laughing at. In our life together she had trudged unlovingly along, enduring rather than enjoying, and then, a couple of weeks ago, without warning, when Smog wasn't too far from taking his A Levels, had lit off to Holland.

As if picking up my thoughts, she saw the framed photograph on the sideboard. I'd never liked it. For reasons known only to herself, she had set it there, a blown-up snapshot taken at Cromer by Smog with his first camera eight years ago. Bridgitte had refused to be in the photo because she was pregnant. She reached for the frame and cracked it on the corner of the chair. Then she hit harder, till nothing was left. She bent down, broad and luscious hips beam on, picked the ragged photograph from the bits of glass and threw it on the fire.

In a wild rage, ready to batter her to death, I kicked the door open. Striding through the hall I trampled over fifteen pairs of wellingtons, a corrugated footpath of walking sticks and umbrellas, a jungle of anoraks, and kneed so hard against the parlour door that the latch burst. I stood with fists raised, a pain in my feet because they weren't yet kicking her.

She faced me four-square, and shrieked, 'Michael! You bastard!'

'You bitch!' I cried.

'Oh, my love,' she moaned, a glint in her eyes.

I reached out for her. 'Darling!'

We practically 'gonked on' in the middle of the suitcases, 'gonked on' being a phrase Smog used as a youngster when he brought two trucks together on his model railway. He once stumbled into the bedroom when Bridgitte and I were 'at it', and ever after would refer to the time we had been 'gonked on'.

We stood, embracing and kissing, mumbling dozens of tender words, apologies mostly, endearments among the tears, promises of undying loyalty and love. 'I'm so glad you came back,' she said. 'Oh, Michael, Michael, Michael, I'll never stop loving you.'

'I never did stop loving you. You're the one woman in my life.' The sound of something scraping along the floor like the enormous bandaged left foot of a mummy coming out of a pyramid broke into my consciousness. 'Rich, ripe, wonderful, beautiful! My only possible sweetheart.'

I kept it up as long as I could without turning back into a baby in the playpen until Bridgitte, looking over my shoulder, stiffened at what she saw in the mirror. I felt a stinging blow from my ever loving wife who then, stepping back a few paces, stumbled over a suitcase. She righted herself. 'Who's that?'

It had been obvious for some time who *that* was. First it was a suitcase, and then it was Maria, the waif I had rescued from a fate worse than death, pushing her luggage slowly across the threshold, panting as she did so.

'It's someone I hired in London to clean up the house and to look after you and the kids when you got back from Holland. Her name's Maria. Maria,' I called, 'this is Bridgitte my wife who I told you about. She'll show you what to do, though she may slap you around a bit in the process.'

Bridgitte stiffened, as if about to show Maria how right I was. But she held herself back. 'So that's what you do? As soon as I go to see my parents for two weeks you run off and get another woman. I should have known.'

It was no use trying to be angry. Yet if I wasn't she would believe me even less. I gave her an equally stinging crack across the chops. 'I was eating my heart out for you,' I said, 'and only went to London this morning. I met Maria tonight on the Underground. She'd just lost her skivvying job and had nowhere to go. So I thought we could use her here. I decided you worked too hard. You needed help.'

Bridgitte was crying.

'It's true.' Maria's tone was such that no one could disbelieve her, and I wanted to take her to bed from that moment on, but from that moment on knew I never would. 'He help me.' She pushed her case to the wall, took off her coat, picked a chair from the floor and set it against the table. 'Tomorrow, I leave,' she said. 'But it true what Michael say. English people in Ealing no good. Woman shout at me. Don't feed me. Children scream and kick. Mr Horlickstone put hand up my clothes, get drunk, laugh at me and say he want to stroke my tits. Englishmen, no good.'

I don't know why, but these sentiments took Bridgitte's fancy, especially the bit about Englishmen being no good. She swabbed her big blue eyes, and I was left sitting among the wreckage while she and Maria went talking into the kitchen to get something to eat. An owl sounded from outside, and an occasional car bumped over our level crossing. I sat, conscious that I had done the wrong thing ten times over, and that I wasn't wanted on voyage. I would have gone back to London except that it was too late. In Soho things might just be starting to jump, but in the Fen country, after eight o'clock at night the social amenities of civilisation are rolled up like a carpet and put away till next day. I had to tolerate their crazy laughter while I went to my room and packed a case to take to my quarters at the Moggerhanger domain. Bridgitte would laugh on the other side of her face when I told her I'd found a job.

Downstairs, there wasn't a sight of suitcases or broken glass. The table was set for a meal, *hors d'oeuvres* already laid out in dishes and platters, a bottle of Dutch gin and a packet of Dutch cigars and a box of Dutch chocolates and a red football of Dutch cheese. I almost expected to see a salt cellar windmill, a clog full of radishes and a wimple hat sprouting tulips. I'd known Bridgitte so long that lovely Holland was almost as much in my blood as hers.

The smell of roasting meat suggested she had ripped something from the deep freeze as soon as she got back. I was the luckiest man alive to have a Dutch woman for a wife, whether she hated me or not, but how long this lunatic confrontation could go on I had no way of knowing. Bedtime was on the cards and, after the meal, we made the most of it.

The Railway Inn, just across the road from the station, had the slowest service of any pub in the area. A quick drink was more of a possibility the further you got from that particular pot-house, and if you thought you could run into the Railway Inn for a pint and pork pie before catching your train you were bound to miss it – unless you left everything half finished on the bar.

The jovial bastard who ran that pub must have doubled his profits from unfinished drinks. No wonder he called you 'squire' and had his ninety-year-old mother serving behind the bar and washing the single glass they had for all their customers, while he looked out of the window at trains coming and going – mostly going – with a wide smile on his fat-chopped face. He had a sign saying 'Quick Lunches' tacked up outside, but even a paper plate of soapy cheese and sliced miracle bread took half an hour to cough up. No wonder he kept pigs at the end of his ten-acre garden. They were fed on the fat of the land, and produced pork that tasted of raw onions. He was notorious in the area for making people miss their trains due to slow service, yet the pub was often full. Perhaps it was a mark of the times that people didn't mind if they lost their appointment in London. In Switzerland they'd have chucked him off the Matterhorn.

Bridgitte drove me there so that I could catch the twelve-thirty. She was in a good mood after our night of unsolicited passion. Often this wasn't the case, orgasms making her itchy and nervous, like a hangover, but perhaps breaking the news of my job at breakfast, as she came in with a platter of sliced cheese, cushioned her morning mood. I suppose it did mine, as well, because after so many years together they often coincided.

'A job?' The shock was almost as great as the one I'd had when she went off to Holland. 'What can you do?'

'Chauffeur,' I said. 'And it's living in. I'll only get home at weekends. Unless I work weekends. Then I'll get home in the week. I'll get home as often as I can.'

She had become a person of order in the last few years. She liked to live to a pattern, to know what was happening and exactly when. Uncertainty depressed and irritated her, as it would anybody, so the fact that she might not know when I would turn up made her spill coffee on the cloth. I soothed her by saying I would never come home unless I telephoned from London first.

'And who are you working for?'

'An English lord.' I forked up a slice of ham. 'He'll pay two hundred and fifty pounds a month. It'll be very useful now that we're employing Maria.'

'She's not working for us.'

In the pub I ordered two pints, and we sat at a table by the window. 'Why not? She's a godsend.'

'I'll let her stay a few days. That's all.'

'She loves it at Upper Mayhem. She was as bright as a daffodil at breakfast. She likes you, anyway.'

'I like her, but we can't afford to pay her, not on your two hundred and fifty pounds a month.'

I could have kicked myself, but sipped at the jar of ale and looked at the clock. There were ten minutes to go before the train came, and I had to buy my ticket. 'I'll get enough money, don't worry. There'll be a bonus on top of my pay, every so often. Our financial worries are over.'

'Lord who?' she asked.

I hoped she wouldn't recollect. 'A chap called

Moggerhanger. But I've got to go, or I'll be late.'

I waited for her to rage at my foolishness. 'If you go to prison again, that's the end of us. You know that, don't you?'

'Come off it,' I laughed. 'Moggerhanger is an English lord. How can he do anything criminal? It's not like the sixties anymore. He's a reformed character. We all are.'

We had to get across to the station, so I picked up our glasses, the drink in them hardly touched, and followed Bridgitte to the door.

'Squire!' the publican roared. 'You can't take them glasses out there.'

I emptied the beer from both into a fever-grate, then took them back inside. 'Sorry, squire!' I hee-hawed aloud at his fury. 'Bit absent-minded these days.' Giving Bridgitte a quick kiss, I made a dash for the train.

A sixty-year-old grey-bearded chap in front of me emptied his leather purse on the counter and sorted his coins to decide whether any were false, in which case they were worth more than the real ones. I managed to get on board by jumping on the last carriage.

It would be untrue to say that nothing happened on the trip to London. Such a situation is unthinkable, certainly since Bridgitte had set the ball rolling by her strange behaviour in the last few weeks. But because events on the train had no bearing on subsequent occurrences, there's no point in retailing them, the plain fact being that I got back to Ealing just inside the twenty-four hours Moggerhanger had allowed me.

I'd thought of calling at Blaskin's to find out how Bill Straw was faring in his attic hideaway, but having got up so late after my night of homely passion with Bridgitte it hadn't been possible. Not that I worried about him. He would have to fend for himself, even if he did starve to death.

The flat over Moggerhanger's garage was furnished

little better than Bill's pigeon coop. There were plain wooden planks on the floor, and the walls were white-washed. If I wanted a face-swill there was a tap and sink in one corner. A single bed, a chair, a small table and a hotplate completed the amenities. For sleep there were two horse blankets, but no sheets. A forty-watt light-bulb hung on a wire from the ceiling, at which I assumed the electricity was included in my salary.

A red-white-and-blue biker's helmet with a hole in it was as far into a corner as it could get, as if it had been kicked there. I chose a paperback from a pile on the floor, and lay on the bed. Kenny Dukes's name was pencilled inside the cover. The story – *Orgy in the Sky* by Sidney Blood – seemed to be about a gang of five-year-old six-footers doing a warehouse robbery with a fight, a shoot-out and a fuck on every page. Towards the end, one or the other happened every second paragraph. Whenever it said something like 'He smashed his fist into his smirking face' Kenny had underlined it as if wanting to commit the immortal words to memory. Heavy scoring in the margin highlighted an occasional comment like: 'That's good!', so that with such marks the book was impossible to read without being brainwashed and ending up a replica of Kenny Dukes, the forty-year-old skinhead only half reformed. I honestly didn't know why Moggerhanger kept him on, because someone of his limited intelligence was bound to be more of a liability than an asset.

Maybe Kenny knew too much, and it would be embarrassing to do him in because he came from a very big family and was related to every thug in south London. Yet Moggerhanger had some affection for him, treasuring his qualities of loyalty and dumb violence. All I knew was that I didn't like Kenny Dukes and Kenny Dukes didn't like me, but as I considered myself to be at least six pegs above him in the social scale it was up to me to keep our relationship on a diplomatic if not friendly level.

Someone came up the stairs – and Kenny Dukes crashed the door open. 'Get off my fucking bed, or I'll smash your face to pulp.'

His portly and upright carriage was spoiled by the fact that he was slightly round-shouldered. Otherwise I don't suppose he was a very bad figure of a man, except that his arms were too long. In fact they were the longest arms I'd seen on a person who could still be called a human being. And he could – just. They were positively anglepoise, so that in a fight you had to close in as soon as possible to avoid their reach.

I leaned on my left elbow. 'Don't you ever use long words such as: "I'll obliterate your features so that your own mother wouldn't recognise you in Woolworth's on Saturday afternoon"?' Then I put on a pseudo-Yank accent straight out of Sidney Blood: 'Anyway, if you wanna know where the dough is, there's seventy-five thousand smackers under the bed, all cut out of newspaper. They passed us a dead duck, and we've got to get out and find 'em.'

He came in close, but recognised the style. 'That's my book.'

'Come closer, Sunshine.' The interior ratchet of my right arm drew back. I couldn't go on reading Sidney Blood's inspiring prose forever, without acting on it.

'Haven't I seen you somewhere before?' he said.

I wound up the springs in my feet as well. During ten years at Upper Mayhem I'd done plenty of labouring on the station and its surroundings. I'd helped local farmers at potato harvests. Every morning I did half an hour's jumping on the spot with dumbbells. Without being a fanatic, I believed in keeping the six feet and eleven stone of me supple and ready for action. Bill Straw wasn't the only one to develop his physical abilities. As for shooting, I could get two rabbits on the run with the twelve bore, in view of which I wasn't going to put up with any shit from

Kenny Dukes.

I shot off the bed like a rocket, and his fist went by my face and hit the pillow so hard that the frame shook. Being heavy he lost his balance, of which I took advantage by gripping him at the neck so that he couldn't move. He kicked around, but his boots couldn't reach me. I'd always known him to be the sort of courageous coward who wasn't afraid to come out from under his shell and turn into a bully.

'What's the excitement?' I said. But he wasn't the type who would plead for me to let him go, either. Whether this was due to obstinacy, or to a chronic lack of vocabulary I didn't know. 'We don't want bloodshed, do we? Not this early on in our relationship.'

He gasped as if his chest would burst. 'I've seen you before.'

I squeezed him harder into the half-nelson. 'I'm Michael Cullen. We met ten years ago, remember?' While his elastic-band computer was processing this bit of information I let him go and jumped clear, putting myself in such a state of defence that when he regained the vertical he made a rapid gut-decision not to carry on the feud, at least for the time being. 'I'm working for Moggerhanger as well,' I said, 'so if there's any argy-bargy he'll fire us both. You know that. Now lay off.'

His pig-eye cunning, which hid softening of the brain behind, stood him in good stead for once. 'You was reading my fucking book.'

'I needed intellectual stimulus.'

'And you was on my fucking bed.'

'I can't read standing up. And once I'd started, I couldn't stop.'

He sat down, mollified for the moment. 'Fucking good, ennit?'

'Best book I ever read.'

He smiled. 'Yeh.'

I sat on the bed. 'You read a lot.'

'Every minute, when I'm not fucking birds and 'ittin' people, and driving one of Lord Moggerhanger's flash Rollers with all the dazzle-lights on.'

I pulled on my whisky flask. 'Like a drop?'

He took a swig. I wouldn't trust him five minutes with a twenty-year-old banger. 'Can't drink much in case I'm called out,' he said. 'We're on tap all the time. Could be four in the morning. There's no night and day for Lord Claud.'

'What about time off?'

A laugh made him look human. 'When you're dead you get time off. But now he's got you, he might let me go home a few days.'

'You've been busy?'

His eyes narrowed, perhaps at the notion that I was pumping him. 'Just looking around for somebody to hit and kick.'

'Who for? You might as well tell me. I expect I'll have to find him sooner or later.'

'The boss tells, not me.'

'Fair enough.' I opened my case, and found *The Return of the Native* which I'd finished on the train. Bridgitte had read it three years ago when she'd done an Open University course. 'Try this. It ain't as good as Sidney Blood, but it's all right.'

He turned it over like a piece of cold toast. 'Don't like books about wogs.'

'Wogs?'

'Fucking blackies. Can't stand 'em.'

'It isn't about blacks.' I found it hard not to laugh. 'I'm a native myself.'

'You don't fucking look it. You're like me.'

I let that pass. 'We're all natives.'

'You're fucking pig-ignorant.'

'You're a native as well.'

He stood up, looked at himself in a piece of mirror by the door and straightened his tie. He wore an expensive grey suit and a silk shirt which was ready for the wash. Being of a similar build to his employer, I wondered if they weren't Moggerhanger's throwaways. 'I've drunk your drink,' he said, 'but you ought to be careful what you're saying.'

I don't know why I persisted. 'I'm a native of Nottingham because I was born there. Lord Moggerhanger is a native of Bedfordshire because he was born there. You're a native of Walworth.'

'Kennington.'

'Kennington, then, because you were born there. The blacks in London aren't natives, unless they were born here, and then they are. That's all it means. *The Return of the Native* is about a man who comes back to the place he was born at.'

His mind veered off my explanation. It was too long. 'I've got to be going. Got to go and see my mum. Knock her about a bit, otherwise she won't fink I love her.' He winked, as if he'd been taking the piss out of me. 'Don't break my wanker,' he said as he swaggered out of the door.

I lay full length on the bed, and decided I liked being at work, and went to sleep wondering how Maria was getting on with Bridgitte. Being so different, they seemed made for each other. Perhaps Bridgitte would send for the children from Holland. Maria thought Upper Mayhem a paradise and would work for nothing as long as she was allowed to stay, though she wouldn't go short of money – I'd see to that. She and Bridgitte would settle down and keep the place going for when I needed a refuge from the busy world. I laughed at the picture and, a final vision showing my homely settlement in flames, thought that at least I had done some positive good by finding Bill Straw a hiding place.

Kenny Dukes was right. At four in the morning the blower went. It was fixed to the wall by the door so I had to cross the room to answer it. 'Come to the house,' Moggerhanger said. 'And I don't mean in your pyjamas.'

I smartened up and, wide awake, crossed the yard to headquarters. The man by the door, no doubt with a gun under his coat, was Cottapilly, a big heavy swine who always went upstairs as quiet as a cloth-footed fly, so nimble on his feet that people expected to see a small man. He then put their surprise to maximum advantage. Afterwards, neat little turds of fag ash were seen on the stairs, as if someone had gone up on their hands and knees. He wore no collar or tie, but his boots were impeccably polished.

I was even more certain that some important scheme was being put into action when I saw Jericho Jim sitting in the corridor outside Moggerhanger's office. He was thin and of medium height, with thick grey hair and an incredibly lined face, though from a distance you would have taken him for thirty instead of fifty. Each icy blue eye shone like the point of a pen torch that a doctor shoves down your gullet to look at your tonsils. He'd been most of his life in prison, but had escaped so many times, even from Dartmoor, that they called him Jericho Jim, though his real name was Wilfred. He always ate the middle from a loaf first, on the assumption that he might die in the next five seconds or in case some well-wisher had put a file inside. It was a matter of old habits dying hard, and that by their feeding shall you know them. He stopped pulling the comb through his wavy hair to run his hands over my jacket and trousers.

'Do you think I'm barmy?' I said.

'Instructions,' he lisped. 'They're waiting for you.'

The room wasn't as empty as it had been the day before. Moggerhanger stood behind his desk wearing a flowered dressing-gown that came down to the floor, and smoking the kind of cigar that his doctor had said would put him in his bury-box. But I suppose it was a case of once a lord, always a lord. His manner hadn't altered from when I first saw him. There was an open map on the table, and as soon as Pindarry closed the door Moggerhanger pointed to it. 'Michael, can you read one of them?'

'Like a book.' I'd gone walking and cycling with Smog in the school holidays, and he was the one who had taught me to read maps.

'You're the only one who can, then,' he said, 'apart from myself. That's why I took you on.' The room was blindingly lit from a series of striplights flush with the ceiling. Two men I didn't know sat at a table by the wall, earphones on and their backs to me, and I heard the crackle of police voices from one and the bird noises of morse from the other. Moggerhanger looked over his shoulder and said to Pindarry: 'He'll be in time if he sets off now. The boat gets in at eight o'clock.' From behind his desk he asked: 'Do you know where Goole is?'

I was about to say I hadn't seen him in years, when I remembered it was a place. 'On the Lincolnshire coast?'

'It's a river port in Yorkshire,' said Pindarry.

I suppose I had to notice him. He didn't have a pot belly, but he was beefy at the midriff, and that's something you can't hide. I liked him less than Cottapilly. Even in the presence of the chief he always wore a little Austrian-type hat with a feather up the side. One of his teeth was missing, which you wouldn't notice unless he laughed – though he never laughed. He only smiled and then, so it was said, you were in trouble. But he had to eat, and Bill Straw told me he'd once shared a trough of rice and mutton with him on the pipeline road between Baghdad and Beirut in their smuggling days, adding that you no longer joined the Navy to see the world, but just signed on with Jack Leningrad Limited.

'I want you to collect some packages,' Moggerhanger said. 'Leave at five and you should be there by ten. We're sending you up in the Rolls-Royce, so take care of it. One scratch on the Roller means two on your face, only they'll be deeper. You'll be driving one of my prime motors, not a two-tone trapdoor estate with a battered right headlight and a crumpled wing, which has to be off the road before dark. If by any chance you should find yourself confronted by a police roadblock, don't try a Turpin and jump over it. Just say what your business is, and they'll let you through.'

He ran his organisation like the head of a country in wartime, and maybe not even he knew whether he made more money out of lawful business than rackets. He owned gambling houses, cafés and restaurants, hotels and roadhouses, caravan parks and amusement arcades, sex shops and strip clubs, escort agencies, garages and car hire firms, bucket shops for cheap travel called Pole-axe Tours, as well as loan and finance firms: 'Twelve thousand mortgages a day: just pay your money and you're safe for life.' Shadier operations involved smuggling and putting up money for criminal enterprises. If his connection with the Inland Revenue was frosty but correct, his association with some members of the police force was cordial, as I knew from the hand-in-glove manner in which he and Chief Inspector Lanthorn had got me put away for eighteen months. Lanthorn had to have someone to charge when the customs broke the smuggling gang, and Moggerhanger opted for me rather than Kenny Dukes – or himself. I had made plenty of money, so took the sentence as it was deserved and because I'd had no option. But I had grown less philosophical about it over the years, though I don't suppose I would have been bitten so hard by the cobra of revenge if Bill Straw hadn't dragged me back into the mainstream of a job with Moggerhanger.

'I can't guarantee a rotten little A40 won't drive into

me,' I said. 'The roads are full of anarchists these days.'

He put an arm around my shoulder. 'It's only a manner of speaking, Michael. I want you to stay in one piece: drive carefully, collect the goods, and take them to a place in Shropshire, where you'll wait till somebody collects them. Then come back here to me. If you want to know anything else, ask Mrs Whipplegate. She's my private secretary, and knows everything.'

She stood by a filing cabinet on the other side of the room, a tall thin woman who didn't have what I reckoned to be a good figure. But because she seemed inaccessible – with her grey svelte dress, a natty coloured flimsy scarf at the neck, and high-heeled shoes – I wanted to get to know her in the one way that mattered. Maybe because of her short darkish hair, slightly grey at the temples, and small black hornrimmed glasses, I assumed she was a widow (and if not hoped she soon would be) and reckoned she was in early middle age, though I learned later she was thirty-eight. The best part was her legs which, being shapely and plump, were out of character with her thin figure. I thought she might be one of Moggerhanger's girl-friends, but told myself she wasn't the sort he liked. She carried a handful of envelopes. 'If you'll come next door, Mr Cullen, I'll give you your instructions.'

'Before you go, Michael, I want to wish you luck,' Moggerhanger said. 'It's an important job, and if you do it well there'll be a bonus for you. I look after my lads, though I don't buy 'em. You won't see that sort of money. But I'll make it right with you.'

'Yes, sir.'

'It's loyalty all the way. No fucking around.'

'I haven't been to Oxford, so you can trust me.' But can I trust you, I wondered, you bombastic double-dealing bastard. He must have got my drift, so ambled over: 'Get going, then, before you get a knife in your back!'

A sense of humour was all very well, but not when it

was a camouflage for absolute villainy. He also used it as a trick to inspire confidence, and as a gambit to keep you energetic and alert.

I followed Mrs Whipplegate into her tiny office of desk, chair and filing cabinet, the advantage to me being that her unsubtle perfume filled the room and I was closer to her than when in the boss's big sanctum. She handed me the first large envelope. 'There's one map for the road to Goole, two to get you to Shropshire, and a large-scale one to find the cottage.'

'I love you.'

She blushed. 'Here's envelope number two, with your expenses of twenty five-pound notes.'

'I'll always love you.'

'Keep an account of what you spend, and let me have the list, as well as any monies still unspent when you get back. There are no written instructions except for the two addresses clipped to the maps. The cottage has a six-figure map reference because it's hard to find, and you're not under any circumstances to ask anyone the way to it.'

'I'd do anything for you.'

'After you get to each place, destroy the instructions. Lord Moggerhanger has many business rivals and doesn't like information to leak out. And please don't mark the maps. They can be used again.'

'When can we meet?'

'I don't see how we can.' She looked at me with grey eyes, and I saw there was no hope, until I also noticed that the little finger of her left hand was trembling. 'It's now half past four, and you're to start at five o'clock precisely. There's a dual carriageway almost to Doncaster, but after that you'll find the road somewhat twisted and cluttered . . .'

'Not as much as I am, until I've been to bed with you.' I regretted each stupid sally against her obvious impregnability, respectable demeanour, or plain distaste for the likes of me, but as usual in such situations I couldn't control myself. 'There's something inordinately attractive about you.'

'... as far as Goole. However, you should be in position by ten o'clock, and that will give you plenty of time.'

'I'm not being flippant,' I went on. 'There's something about you that I find profoundly interesting, and what I want is to get to know you a little better. I don't really mean much else. Or I might – if I did get to know you better. But until then all I'm asking is whether or not you'll have dinner with me when I get back.'

I was tired from my short night, but the effect was to sharpen the tongue and give me a hard-on for no particular reason. She passed a slip of paper, a form which I was expected to sign for receipt of the money. I picked up the envelopes, and brushed against her as I went to the door. 'Or even a cup of coffee.'

She twitched, then put on a thoughtful expression. 'I'm not sure whether Lord Moggerhanger likes fraternisation among his employees.'

Her naïvety frightened me, for she seemed to think he ran a lawful business and that this conspiratorial atmosphere was only a precaution against trade rivals. I wondered what the Green Toe Gang would think of that. A real clean-up, with a proper police force, would rope her in for ten years as well. I wanted to cry for her innocence, though mostly I craved to see her strip off that chic dress and clamber into bed with me. 'On the other hand,' I said, 'perhaps he would like it to be kept in the family. Lord Moggerhanger is a very paternal sort of employer.'

'You'd better leave. I didn't have much sleep either.'

I brushed by her again. 'Will you be on days next week?'

A smile was as far as she would go.

Back at the garage I collected my briefcase, which

contained underwear and a spare shirt, and a high-powered heavy duty two-two air pistol with a tin of slugs, as well as a carton of cigarettes and a small tranny for news and weather. With the envelopes stowed inside I felt as if I was on some kind of official business.

The garage-hand was a toothless, grizzle-haired, battered chap with a heavy Glasgow accent called George, who had been chief engineer on a coastal steamer. He showed me to the Rolls-Royce. The dashboard was like that of an old-fashioned airliner, and I called out for him to pull the chocks away. Moggerhanger was right: it was quite different to Black Bess, the old banger I pottered about in at home. I felt a thrill as I rolled forward, out of the wide gate.

Seven

I schoonered towards the North Circular, a forlorn man and woman waiting on an empty road for the Dawnliner bus to take them to work. The All Night Radio Station came up with a weather forecast: 'A warm and pleasant day everywhere. A real scorcher, in fact. Just a little mist on northern hills, perhaps, and some wind in the west bringing occasional drizzle, otherwise fine all over the country. A spot or two of rain in Central Wales and rather more prolonged downpours in the north, spreading south. Expect a little warmth, but a cold front developing in mid-Atlantic will reach the Midlands and north-east this afternoon to give snow and ice on high ground, with rain, fog, snow and hail just about everywhere. Further outlook dubious. Have a good day.'

Or something like that, causing me to wonder why I was in this floating palace and not in bed with Mrs Whipplegate, though at the first whiff of that lovely bleak romantic A406 my sense of adventure came back at the thought of going north again. The compass needle swung as I turned off into Hendon and passed a jam sandwich parked at the roundabout. One of the police lads inside waved in greeting, and I felt like the king of the road. Anyone driving around at five in the morning can't be up to any good, but I got a clear way through the traffic lights as if I had a control button on the dashboard. Maybe they photographed each car and flashed the numberplate to headquarters. Lights glowed from inside a filling station, an old man sleeping in a chair reflected in the glass. Dawn was seeping through as I turned right at the island. Trees were tinged with green, and dead grass bordered the roadside. I drifted in and out of a daydream, praying to see the first breakfast shack promising something to eat. Housefronts marched out of the melting darkness.

I slowed down for a hitchhiker, then remembered that Moggerhanger had said I wasn't to give lifts in his vehicles. In any case, I thought, he probably has fleas, muddy boots and concealed razor blades to slash the upholstery so slyly I won't notice the damage till he's got well away.

In the rear mirror I saw he was without luggage and wearing an overcoat. I got a clean snapshot of pink face and bald head, indignation and misery. Pylon towers stood grey against darker cloud. I speeded up, and saw him cursing me blind by the roadside. He waved his arms, and I knew that leaving him there was a bad business, not to say a sickly kind of omen, which kept me downhearted for the next two minutes. I wanted to go back and smack him in the teeth, but that idea made me feel even worse.

A bit of autoroute went by Stevenage (thank God) and not far beyond I saw a café that was open. I parked well to one side of a couple of decrepit lorries and a pantechnicon, and made my way between pools of water. The wind rattled two pieces of corrugated tin by the bucket-toilets. To the east there were clouds of dull red and gunmetal blue. I don't know where that weather forecast had come from. Thirty miles in that direction Bridgitte was curled up in bed and, so I supposed, was Maria. I wished them luck and long life, and went into the warmth.

I ordered a full-house of egg-bacon-sausage-beans-mushrooms-tomatoes-and-fried-bread. The lorry drivers looked at me as if I was a piece of shit that had crawled off the fire.

'Good morning,' I said, the worst thing you could come out with in such a place at that time of the day. You could say anything else, no matter how insulting, or even irrelevant – but not that. My tone was neutral, but my voice was clear, so I was taking my life in my hands. Fortunately they were too afflicted with lassitude to give more than non-committal grunts. I considered myself lucky and left it at that. Mike, the working-proprietor behind the counter, looked as if he was dying of starvation. He smoked a fag, and had half a mug of cold tea by his elbow. He poured a rope of charcoal into a mug for me and pushed it along. His wife Peggy was a solid-looking country woman with round steel glasses and a white apron. She actually smiled while buttering my sliced bread.

'How's business?' I had to say something, or lose the use of my vocal cords, but that, of course, was the second worst thing you could say – at any time of the day.

'Can't grumble,' she said.

'Why don't you tell him the truth?' her husband chipped in. 'It's fucking awful. We'll be bankrupt in a fortnight.'

'Sorry I asked.' I swigged the tea, which was strong and good.

'No, you're not,' he said. 'Don't fucking kid me. Of course you're not. You don't give a fuck, do you?'

'Well, not really,' I said. My third mistake was in being honest. 'Why should I?'

'I wish you wouldn't swear,' Peggy said. 'It don't do any good.'

Mike laughed, without mirth. 'Not to him it fucking don't. He's not a free enterprise businessman trying to keep his head above water. It don't matter to you, either, I expect,' he said to his wife. 'But it does to me, and that's all as matters, innit?'

'You're always fucking whining.' One of the lorry drivers had a slice of bacon half into his mouth. 'Every time I stop off here I hear you whining. If you didn't cook such good breakfasts, I wouldn't stop. You're a worse fucking whiner than the Aussies. I was four years down under, and I never heard so much whining in my life – except that they call it *wingeing*. But they do it in a loud voice, and only when they see no Pommies are around, so they don't think it's wingeing. But it's bad in this country as well. That's what's wrong with it. Everybody whines if they aren't making two hundred pounds a week just by lying in bed.'

'They think the world owes them a living,' said an older man, who had so many plates and cups on his table he looked as if he'd been lounging there all night. 'But they *are* the world.'

Mike threw my eggs and bacon into a pan of hot fat on the primus, while his wife boiled the beans. 'It's all right for you, Len, bringing illegal immigrants up from Romney Marsh to Bradford twice a month. One trip keeps you in luxury for weeks. I expect your lorry outside's full of Pakkies now, innit? Why don't you unlock the doors and bring the poor buggers in for some tea at least? Be good for my trade as well.'

Len began to choke. 'Keep your fucking trap shut.'

Everybody laughed.

'Well,' Mike said, 'stands to fucking reason, dunnit? Two loads of Pakkies every week and I might break even.'

'I do wish you'd stop swearing,' Peggy pleaded, devouring an elderberry-and-nettle pie. I went to an empty table, having had my fill of early morning conversation, though it seemed marvellous what arguments you could set off with an unrehearsed greeting. The breakfast was good when it came, and I could feel each mouthful waking me up. During my second mug of tea I heard a lorry hit the tin by the toilets as it slid through a puddle and drew up outside. The first person to come in was the man I had seen by the road thumbing a lift. He stood in the doorway and looked around with glittering eyes, which stopped swivelling when they saw me.

'I think I'll sit by the Good Samaritan,' he said to the

lorry driver who came in behind. I was ready to punch him in the face if he did, but I didn't. The hut was public property. He opened his overcoat, and showed a fairly good suit, with collar and tie. 'People don't get rid of me so easily.'

'Come outside and say that,' I said.

He gave me a particularly scornful look, then went to the counter to order breakfast.

'Where are you going to?' I asked when he came back.

'What's that to you? Anyone who'd leave his fellow man to die of exposure by the roadside at half past five in the morning hardly deserves to be greeted with cordiality when they meet later in altogether different circumstances.' When I said nothing in response, he added: 'I'm going to Rawcliffe, just before a place called Goole, which I suppose you've never heard of. You can drop me off at Doncaster, if it's on your way.'

He wasn't exactly reeking of aftershave, but he seemed decent enough. The trouble was, you could never tell. He looked amiable, with mild brown eyes, and smiled as he rubbed a hand over his bald head. 'You don't trust me,' he said, 'I can see that.' He held out the same hand that had stroked his head: 'Anyway, I'm Percy Blemish.'

'Michael Cullen,' I told him. 'I can't give you a lift because the person I'm working for has spies all along the road, and if he found that somebody else had been in the car, from that moment on I'd be seen to have a pronounced limp whenever the dole queue moved forward.'

'I understand,' he said. 'I'll just have to continue my journey with that uncouth lorry driver, in his draughty cab.'

The driver in question, who sat a few feet away, twitched his shoulders and turned. 'I heard that. You can walk. Too much fucking lip, that's your trouble. I was going to throw you out, anyway.'

'Oh dear,' Percy Blemish said, 'I talk too much.'

'We all do,' I said sadly.

'I do hate swearing,' Peggy said, though nobody heard but me.

Percy's hand was on the sauce bottle. Mine closed on the ketchup. It was a tie. 'Drop dead,' I told him, getting up to leave, and never wanting to see him again.

I took the map out of the envelope and saw that I still had a good way to go, but it was only half past six so I dawdled along. The sky was clear, except that red streaks in the east were turning yellowish. The wind was cold and damp, however, though after a mile or two the sun burned through the windscreen. I thought I saw a police car going up a slight rise in front, but it was a white car and a motorbiker just ahead wearing a blue helmet. The sight made me nervous, so I overtook them both.

While getting in the car after breakfast I'd noticed a container as big as a toolbox down by the back seat, and on opening it saw about three hundred Monte Cristos inside. I unscrewed a tube cap, and then drove effortlessly through green scenery on a full belly and with a delicious cigar between my teeth.

In the last few years at Upper Mayhem I had begun to wonder about the purpose of my life. Living modestly off Bridgitte and my savings no longer seemed the right existence for an active man. Prison should not have depressed me as much as it did, but what pushed me down even more was my natural born liking for idleness as long as life wasn't too uncomfortable. I'd never seen the point of stirring myself as long as I had a few quid in my pocket. Not that it could have gone on forever. My money was running out and Bridgitte realised that if she didn't withdraw her support she would never get rid of me. The call to London had come just in time.

Another factor was that the attitude towards idleness was changing. There were too many on the dole for it to be a virtue anymore. I lived on the edge of despair because I did not know why I was alive. It wasn't even a matter of reforming. Moral imperatives left me cold. But I had reached the stage where I had to do something to convince myself that I had been brought onto the earth for a purpose instead of rotting pleasantly at the disused railway station of Upper Mayhem. Almost accidentally and, so far, painlessly, I had got out of it, even though working for Moggerhanger was not the kind of job one could be proud of. But it was a start, and no matter what Bill Straw said, nor what I saw, or what I felt in my bones, I had no reason to suppose Moggerhanger's business affairs were anything other than legal. Even he, I hoped, had changed in the last ten years.

The thoughts that go through one's mind during a purloined luxurious smoke! A mouth doesn't show its true shape till a cigar's stuck in it, and when I took mine out between puffs I had an impulse to sing. I had set off from Upper Mayhem, forty-eight hours ago, determined to be honest in all my dealings. To put the cigar back where it came from was impossible. To throw what remained out of the window would be a criminal waste. I would finish my enjoyable smoke in peace, and steal nothing ever after. In the meantime, I would have a little music to soothe my faculties and make life perfect, so shoved a tape into the deck and waited for the overflowing balm of Victor Sylvester or Heavy Metal.

Luckily I was slowing down before the Norman Cross roundabout, otherwise I'd have swung off the road with shock. 'Remember,' said Moggerhanger, 'you are now driving for me, and don't you forget it. I don't want you eating, or sleeping in the car when you shouldn't be, or spitting, or dropping cigarette ends and sweet wrappers, or getting mud all over the carpets. Neither do I want you to help yourself at the cocktail cabinet, or interfere in any way with the emergency hamper. And keep your thieving hands off my cigars. I'm particularly insistent on that. For one thing, they're counted. And for another, if any are missing I'll cut you to pieces, though if you've already had one, consider yourself forgiven, but don't do it again. You have been warned. Just keep your eyes on the road and look after my car, which means never going above seventy. It's better for the engine, but most of all I don't want my employees fined for speeding. I don't think I need tell you that if that happens, you're out. And try not to let the fuel gauge show below the halfway mark. Now listen to the sweetest sound in the world. And have a good day.'

I looked around, as much as I dared, for the closed-circuit television, and wondered if there wasn't a built-in black box to register every stop. But his little joke seemed to be over and once more I was the captain of my ship, except that instead of music the tapedeck played a selection of church bells from parishes all over Bedfordshire, which racket I stood till I told myself that if another Quasimodo hung on my eardrums I'd belt the car into the nearest bridge support.

I was drifting north and without thought went more quickly, finding it hard not to stray above the stipulated seventy-mark especially as, now that traffic was building up, young blokes floated by in Ford Escorts at ninety-five, and their bosses flew in BMWs at a hundred and ten. I could have overtaken them all, but not with Moggerhanger breathing down my neck.

Some cars that overtook were plumbers' vans or salesmen's wagons, or old bangers with five men inside running a collective that got them to and from work (or the dole office) in the cheapest possible way. Others were smart and fast, and from a BMW window Percy Blemish waved his fist and pulled me a megrim as the car slid effortlessly by. It was my third view of him and I hoped it would be the last. His gloating and frantic face behind the Plexiglass reminded me of a baby deprived of its rights at the nipple, and I supposed he held every person he came across responsible for his misfortunes, unless he was given a lift. Even then, judging from the face that he turned on me, and which the benevolent driver of the moment could not see (luckily for him), I didn't reckon his chances of cheap and easy travel were very high, either.

I'd put back so much tea at breakfast that it was necessary to stop and wring out my bladder. I could get the petrol tank topped up at the same time. When I crunched slowly onto the petrol station forecourt, Percy Blemish was standing by the exit, waiting for another lift. I felt sure that the BMW man, goaded by one of his remarks, had dumped him there, and it was just my luck that I should be the next car along.

A Ford Cortina skidded in from the road and, by a fancy manoeuvre, the cunning bastard of a driver put himself before me at the pumps. It was a self-service establishment and in a few seconds he had the nozzle gangling into his tank. The manager came out and asked me, sir (seeing as I drove a Rolls-Royce), how much I wanted. He then motioned me backwards and wiggled another python into my tank to be sick. I was happy to let him do the work, while waiting to watch the Ford Cortina carry Percy Blemish away.

The driver was a young fair-haired chap in a polo-necked sweater who, having refuelled, went to the office to pay the clerk. I don't suppose he noticed me smirking. He drove slowly towards the exit where Percy Blemish, giving the sign for a lift, placed himself halfway across the drive so that the car would be forced to stop. When he bent to the window to say where he wanted to go, hand already at the door, a fist shot out and knocked him flying.

It was as blatant a refusal to give a poor chap a lift as I'd ever seen, totally unnecessary in its violence, though maybe the driver was wiser than he thought (and maybe not), for if he hadn't spoken with his fist he would have driven onto the Great North Road with Percy Blemish hanging onto his door. This did not make things look good for me. I went for a long piss to think things over, but was unable to decide on any viable course of action.

I strolled into the office to pay the reckoning. 'That's all right, sir,' the manager smiled. 'I'll put it on Lord Moggerhanger's account. He's very good at settling the bills.'

Percy Blemish had already gone. I wouldn't stop till I reached Goole, so there'd be no further trouble. A few spits of rain hit the window, but the road was still dry. I pushed in another tape, one of Tchaikovsky's jackboot symphonies which tried to do a rush job on decorating the inside of my head. He was pasting away with three walls finished and one more to go, with only the woodwork to scratch and the door to burn off, to a ball-and-chain finale, so that I couldn't stand it after five minutes, and flicked the button.

'I was enjoying that.' The disembodied voice came from behind, the second time I nearly had an accident that day. I was on the outer lane, overtaking a three-hundred-foot juggernaut which seemed to increase speed the faster I went, so that I was doing almost a ton by the time I came to a slight bend. But I got in front, left the lorry behind, and said to Percy Blemish who was grinning into my rear mirror: 'You'd better get out, or I'll stop at the next layby and do you in.'

'Why did you take the music off?'

If I stopped, I'd have to overtake the lorry again. 'Where did you say you were going?'

'You switched that music off,' he said. 'I like Tchaikovsky.'

'Why? He's only a block and tackle artist.' I decided to humour him until such time as I could get him outside and kick his teeth in. Then I saw the bruise caused by the young blood-pudding at the filling station, and decided it would be more humane to feel sorry for him. In any case, I had no option. 'It's better to talk than listen to that,' I said, 'and you certainly can't do both.'

'My wife liked it.' He shuffled around on the seat. 'At least she said she did, and I believed her.'

'You have to believe your wife, otherwise life isn't worth living.'

He sighed. 'I suppose so. You see, I'm the sort of person who thinks that everybody I see is older than me.'

'Interesting,' I replied.

He kept quiet for a while. Then the back of my neck tingled, for he piped up again. 'Do you know the best way to cause a fire?' There was a more sinister tone to his giggle. 'A friend of mine was in the fire service, and he told me.' I thought it best to let the bloody pest babble on, on the assumption that while he talked he was harmless. 'You put a couple of flashlight batteries in a shopping basket with a few packets of steel wool. Sooner or later they'll ignite – in the house or car of somebody you don't like.' His giggle turned into a laugh, and he rubbed his hands. 'If you put two tins of hair lacquer of the aerosol type in the bag as well, with a newspaper and a box of matches, with a few bits of shopping on top, an explosion will eventually ensue.'

'That's a lot of bollocks,' I shouted.

He pouted. 'It's not.'

'Have you ever tried it?'

After a few minutes he came back into the world with: 'No, but I might. You never know.'

'Just shurrup,' I said, thinking my Nottingham accent might have more effect.

'I won't shut up,' he retorted, in the poshest voice he could muster.

'Why don't you learn some poetry?' I suggested. 'Or learn to knit?'

'Don't want to,' he said sulkily. 'I was happily married,

I'll have you know, till I ran away from my wife. I'm fifty-eight years old, and I'm either running away from her or running back to her. At the moment I'm running back. We live near Goole, in a lovely little isolated house called Tinderbox Cottage. I can't understand why our marriage went wrong. I used to live in the south-east, and worked for Elfingham borough council as an engineer, but when I got ill they offered me early retirement and I took it, and came to live in the north with my wife. She can't stand me, and I can't stand her. We've tortured each other for thirty years. Out of what we thought was undying love has come unendurable suffering. Can you understand it?'

'Yes, and no,' I responded with perfect sincerity.

'I think it's economic,' he said.

'Economic?'

'You see, if the gross national product was sufficiently buoyant, the government could issue an edict saying that all those who are married are to live apart immediately. No argument. And those who can't afford to live apart get a pension in order to do so. Anyone caught staying married seven days from the date of this law will be shot. In twelve months, however, marriages can start again. You can get married to the same partner, if you feel so inclined.' His eyes glowed in the mirror. 'Good idea, don't you think? I spent years working that one out.'

'Good for some,' I said. 'But doesn't it bother you that you can't torment your wife when you're not with her? You must have fun as well, otherwise how can you be going back to torment her again?'

He hiccuped. 'I love her, so why shouldn't I?'

'It's all the same to me.'

'I'm going to kill her,' he said flatly. 'Or maybe she'll kill me. It wouldn't surprise me.'

I'd never met a loony who had a sense of humour, but then, if you were loony how could anything seem funny? It was too painful. I hoped he'd go to sleep, though because I was feeling sleepy myself I wanted him to keep talking. 'Do you spend all your time hitching lifts on the A1?'

'Yes. I've got a brother living in London, in Streatham, and I visit him every so often, and stay till he says I have to leave. There's enough money for the bus, but I prefer hitch-hiking because when I speak to someone on the bus the conductor puts me off for disturbing the passengers.' Grantham passed on the starboard and then Newark on the port bow. I lit one of my own cigars on crossing the Trent, always an obligatory and satisfying gesture at such a point. 'My brother burst into the room at four this morning and said I had to get out or he would strike me with an axe. That's why I'm on the road so early.'

'Life's difficult.'

'I'm really beginning to think it is.'

'You must be tired,' I said. 'Why don't you get your head down?'

He sighed, like a boiler about to burst. 'I can't. Sometimes I'm unable to sleep for days. I'm in such a phase now. That's why I'm going back to my wife.'

I felt like a cat having its fur rubbed backwards. Maybe I would murder him before he murdered his wife. 'Do you have any children?'

'Two daughters. Janet and Phyllis. Janet lives with another woman and Phyllis lives in Dover with two children but no husband. We don't see them, but they write now and again. They've got their own lives. Like all of us. Phyllis's two children are boys. She calls them Huz and Buz. When they last came to see us I told them a bedtime story, so she never brought them again.'

I was reminded of an incident from Bill Straw's adventures, but couldn't believe there was any connection.

'Phyllis left home at sixteen. We had a blazing row one day because she'd been hanging around the docks. I didn't receive a word from her for two years. Somebody told me she'd met an Irishman. Even the Salvation Army couldn't find her. Then she wrote to say she was married and having a baby, and asked for money. Her mother sent five pounds, and it came back by return of post, cut in two – longways. I don't know what we'd done to her. It's amazing what people can be like. Have you ever seen people who are happy?'

'I've seen them dead,' I said, 'so I suppose they were happy enough. But I've been happy from time to time.'

'There should be a happy medium, don't you think?'

'A happy tedium, more like it,' I said.

The smell of soot was in the air, the delectable breath of the north, which partly made up for the gloom descending on the car. It was impossible to throw him out. Nor did I want to. I was neither dead nor happy. There was a stage in between which he didn't know about, and that was his trouble. I thanked God first, and Moggerhanger second, and myself a close third, for including me in on it.

'If you had given me a lift right from the beginning,' he said, 'I wouldn't have had this black eye.'

'This is my employer's car,' I said wearily. 'I'm not supposed to give lifts. In my own car I always do. But not in this one. Do you understand?'

'And you switched off the music.'

'It was driving me crazy.'

A beautiful cream Mercedes passed us, and I glanced at it.

'You signalled to that car,' he said.

'You're off your head.' If he wasn't, I was – or would be soon.

'It must mean something – what you do.'

'It does if you want it to.'

'Everything means something.'

I'd never been so glad to see the Bawtry signpost, because it meant I would be back on the twisting arterial lanes and have to pay closer attention to driving. It also began to rain, big splashes coming at the windscreen, so I put on the wipers and hoped their rhythm would hypnotise him into sleep.

'It means something whether you want it to or not,' he said.

'Oh, bollocks.'

'Swearing reminds me of that horrible transport café.'

'I'll swear if I like.' I overtook a coal lorry, so that we missed dying by inches. That would have meant something, but he was in no condition to notice. I could see the faces of drivers who were coming to pass me on the other side of the road. Those with their mouths open hadn't yet learned to drink properly. The nipple still shaped them. One chap wearing a cap drove with a look of horror, as if death by fire could strike at any instant. Another man drove with so little of his face showing, he must have been three feet tall. Often the mouth was a circular hole in the middle of a plate of lard, just distinguishable between the dangling good luck charms and the India-rubber Alsatian behind. Most faces seemed angry, as if belonging to a body taking part in a bayonet charge, and set to kill every oncoming driver – unless it was the expression they put on at the sight of a Rolls-Royce. It was too common not to mean something, though I was inclined to think it their normal state. Those faces that didn't look rabid were gritted tight in concentration. A fair proportion of phizzogs sported a benign idiot smile, looking about ten years of age and as if delighted to be at the wheel of a lethal machine. I didn't know why, but most of the women's expressions seemed more or less normal. I wondered with a smile what my face looked like to those able to take it in – and immediately took the smile off it and assumed a mature sternness befitting the captain of a ship.

'What are you laughing at me for?' Percy Blemish said sharply.

There were pools of water in the fields, pylons crossing the road and colliery headstocks in the distance. I was too tired to give him a run-through of what I'd been thinking. 'There was something stuck in my teeth.'

'I'm sorry to have to insist, but you were laughing.'

If I ignored him I could expect a savage blow at the back of the head. If the car hit a pylon and exploded he would be laughing – for a split second. It was unjust that so many advantages should be on his side, and even more that he saw them as being only on mine. 'Would you like to tell me in what way you consider me to have been laughing?' If talk wouldn't calm him, nothing would.

'It wasn't so much your face, as the gesture of your body.'

I had met such people before, often worse than him, as well as a few marginally better (like myself), but in no case had I been imprisoned with one in a motorcar that wasn't my own and travelling along a road by whose side it was forbidden to stop, a road so narrow and winding that if you did stop a fully laden coal lorry would crush you within half a minute. I could drop him at the cop shop in Bawtry, double yellow lines in front of it or not, yet I was reluctant to because putting up with him till the end of the journey was a test of character I ought to be able to pass. If I had been old enough to fight in the War I don't suppose I would have survived with such sentiments. I decided that a little sharp talking-to was the only fitting response. 'You'd better be quiet, or I'll black your other eye. If I want to laugh I'll laugh, and if I want to cry I'll cry. It's fuck-all to do with you.'

He was offended by bad language, as I'd hoped he would be, so kept quiet till we were past Bawtry. On the other hand I was offended by the moral tone of *his* silence. He looked on me not as the personal agent of Lord Moggerhanger, but as a common chauffeur for someone whom he, with his superfine sensibility, was bound to scorn, in spite of the fact that he had hardly got two ha'pennies for a penny.

The country was flat, desolate, newborn, as if it had no right to be land at all. I thought that if I lived there I'd be suffering in no time from Backwater Fever. I got nervous if I didn't see rising ground, even if only a slagheap or a pimple with a tree on top in the distance. I had crossed some kind of frontier, and it didn't seem the right type of country for me.

Percy slept, or at least dozed, and I envied his ability to turn himself on and off like a well-oiled spigot, though even with closed eyes he didn't look peaceful. Tremors over the lids and flickers at the left corner of his downturning lips told of torments I would never have to put up with. But then I wasn't Percy Blemish, and I wasn't fifty-eight years old. I hoped I never would be, though when a souped-up black Mini with four young men inside, hooter going and headlights full on, came screaming around a bend, I took sufficient evasive action to suggest that my subconscious, such as it was, might have other ideas about that. Blemish stirred. 'You may set me down soon. I'll have only a short walk.'

I thought he was going to be with me forever. 'Is your wife expecting you?'

His laugh didn't seem quite real. 'She always is, though she hopes I'll never arrive. When I'm not there she sits by the telephone waiting for the police to call and say I've been killed. Or that I've been found by the roadside with a heart attack. It's understandable. I don't know what I'd do without her.'

'Why don't you get a divorce? Maybe it would make things more exciting.'

'We'd only marry again.'

'At least you'd have another date to remember. You can't have too many. The more you have, the longer your life will be. After all, you've only got one. You might as well make it as long as possible.'

The line of his lips straightened. A half-second glance in

the mirror gave me a fully developed snapshot image to add to my vast store of underground photographic material, many of them taken from as far back as I could remember. His eyes were glazed, and as he stroked his olive-drab cheek they became sadder. 'You make me sick.'

It was as if he had hit me. My foot accidentally slid off the clutch. I recovered, said nothing, and maintained my harmony with the bends of the road. Rain stopped, so I switched off the windscreen wipers.

'They were getting on my nerves,' he said. 'I suppose I'll sleep when I get home. Anyway, it was good of you to give me a lift. You see that house just ahead? Set me down there, if you would be so considerate.'

He could be charming when he liked, and I was sorry for him. I wondered which of the two cottages in the distance he would head for. 'I hope you go on all right.'

There was a bit of cinder-ground for me to park in, so I got out and opened the door as if he was Edward VII. He walked along an unpaved lane, while I sat in the car and looked at my map before driving the last few miles to Goole. This took almost as much time as doing fifty miles on the A1 because a car in front pottered along at twenty and it was impossible to overtake with so many lorries coming from the opposite direction. But as soon as we got to the outskirts of Goole, and past a thirty mile an hour speed limit, he increased his rate to fifty and left me behind, a phenomenon I'd often come across.

Caught in the usual scrag-end outskirts at a red light I watched a woman with grey hair and a blue overall-coat flicking a yellow duster at her door knob. She looked at me as if I ought to be at work instead of driving a Rolls-Royce. That's how they are around here, I thought. Then I got caught in a gaggle of Volvo lorries going over a wide bridge by the docks. Before I knew where I was I was across the river into Old Goole. Then I had to turn back, whereat a similar gaggle of Volvos swept me west again.

I turned right into the centre and pulled up not far from the town hall, where I oriented myself from the map and got to an unprepossessing thoroughfare on the outskirts called Muggleton Lane, on which I was to wait. It was nine thirty, so I set my alarm clock for five to ten, then put my head back and dozed. The sun shone on me, and I faded from the world, but after what seemed a few seconds the gentle pipping brought me back to life. Following instructions, I got out of the car, opened the boot and sat in the rear left seat reading a newspaper with the headline 'Terrorists state terms'.

Two minutes after ten o'clock (bad marks for being late) a powder blue Mini-van with a coat of arms on the side drew parallel. To my surprise Eric Brighteyes (otherwise Alport) who I had met a few days ago on the train into Liverpool Street, got out and opened the van door. He wore a blue boiler suit and a yachting cap, and gave no sign that he knew who I was, though I would have recognised him anywhere. 'Give me some assistance with these dog powders,' he said.

We took ten square packages, done up in brown paper and post office string, and laid them in a double row in the boot of the Roller. As I was signing the form on his clipboard he rubbed an open hand down over his face – once. 'Forget you've seen me. Right?'

I slammed the boot. 'No problem.'

We'd been together for two minutes, and he drove away in a cloud of blue smoke. All I had to do was exit from Goole the same way I had come, and though I anticipated getting lost in the maze of waterways and lorry routes, I was soon in the clear and on my way towards Doncaster.

Eight

Relieved at the completion of phase one, I lit a cigarette. The staff work had been exemplary, otherwise it might not have been such a skive. I was obviously working for a good firm. It was hard to believe that the British economy was in such a parlous situation with talent like that around. There was more of it in the country than was needed to compensate for the bone-idle, happy-go-lucky, feckless, come-what-may, jaunty, fuck-you-jack, how's-your-father, let's-have-a-lovely-strike sort of person which I had been up to a few days ago, and with which this country at any rate will always be overrun and no doubt affectionately remembered, at least according to the newspapers.

Fortunately the situation is generally saved by those with flair, improvisation, creative ability, hard work, love of money, flexibility, lack of panic in a tricky situation, luck (of course), a refusal to regard long hours as anathema and imaginative attention to detail when drawing up a plan or programme – which I hoped was the sort of person I was fast becoming.

Then of course there was the third type, which no country could afford but which England had somehow learned to tolerate, the one (he or she) who mixed up these qualities but was only held in check by a job that cradled them from start to pension and kept them out of harm's way. It certainly made it a cosy and exciting country to live in, I thought, wondering which category I fell into and not really caring as I set out on an intelligently planned route to south-central Shropshire where I was to offload Moggerhanger's batch of packages from abroad.

I saw someone standing close to where I had put down

Percy Blemish, and my spine turned to ice at the idea that it might be him again, this time heading south. I didn't want any more hitch-hikers in the car. Moggerhanger and I were now absolutely in one mind on the matter, though in my old Home Rule banger I gave plenty of lifts, which was no great sacrifice since I was never going very far. However, I decided to make an exception for an elderly woman of about sixty, because by the time I got close I hadn't the heart to shoot off and leave her, especially as a sudden squall of icy rain from Siberia clattered against the car. 'Where are you going?'

I hoped it would be to the next village.

'London.'

'I can take you as far as Doncaster.'

'It's very generous of you.'

'Get in the back.'

I glided on my way.

'It's a very uncertain kind of day to be out on the road,' I said.

She had lovely features, but her face was haggard and lined. I'd never seen anyone who looked less like a hitch-hiker. She wore a travelling cape and carried a good leather shoulder-bag. 'I suppose the bus services around here are lousy.' Silence between two people seemed more and more difficult to maintain. 'It doesn't seem a very convenient area to me.'

'It's not London, I agree,' she answered, 'but I've lived here for some years, and I don't think I have much reason to complain about the amenities. There's a certain starkness in the scenery, but it can be very beautiful at times.' It pained her to speak, as if she was made for better things than talking to someone from whom she had begged a lift.

'Do you have family in London?'

'Friends. At least I hope I have. I haven't seen them for a long while. Maybe they don't live there anymore. I also have a daughter, but she won't want to see me. Nor do I want to see her. The last time I heard, she was working in a vegetarian restaurant near Covent Garden.'

'You should be there by tea time.' It was hard to think of anything lively to say. 'I'll drop you on the M1, so you'll soon get a lift. I'm making for Shropshire.'

'I'll go there, then.' I detected a powder trail of uncertainty, almost hysteria, in her voice. 'I'll go anywhere, in fact, to get away.'

'Is it that bad?'

She leaned forward and said in my ear: 'You've no idea.'

The words chilled me. 'I probably haven't.'

'I can talk to you because you seem such a nice person. I can't say I've had a hard life, except insofar as I've been married to someone who is highly strung, if not actually poorly. I come of Irish stock.'

Such quick turnabouts got on my wick. 'So do I.'

'That's what most people say when I tell them. But I suppose it's what's given me the strength to support all I've been through. In our family there were five daughters which meant, going by popular belief, that my father was more of a man than most.'

Her expression of bitterness was not inborn, and I assumed it would go away with an alteration in her life. 'In the nineteen-thirties,' she said, 'he could afford to be, couldn't he? I rebelled, but against all the advantages, because I didn't know any better. He wanted me to go to University, like Amy Johnson, he said, but I got a job instead, and left home to do so. I went south and worked in the council offices, and there I met my husband, who was in the borough engineer's department. No one was happier than me when we got married, and no one, I thought, was more contented than him. Neither of us had to join up in the war. We stayed at work, and managed to save a bit of money. I had two daughters, and after the war we moved up here. You may well ask why.'

'Why?' I asked.

'I'll tell you. It's nice of you to give me a lift and let me talk to you as well. My husband had been very strange, right from just after we were married. I don't know why. His family was as right as rain. That was why they disowned him when he started going funny. One day he disappeared. It wasn't like him to do that. He'd always said when he was going out, even if only into the garden to water his onions. After a week he came back, filthy and in rags, his eyes glowing. "We're leaving," he said. "We're going to live near a place called Goole." "Where's that?" I asked. He got out the atlas and showed me. "Why Goole?" I wanted to know. He glared at me, and then he struck me. I struck him back – I was so shocked. Perhaps I shouldn't have returned the blow. He just wanted to do it once, and then life would have gone on normally. But life isn't like that. Well, we didn't go to Goole just then. He got stranger and stranger, until he lost his job. They called it voluntary redundancy, or premature retirement, but I knew what it was. They look after their own in this country, for better or worse.'

I was about to go off my head. First one, on the way up, and now the other, on the way down. If it hadn't been true I wouldn't have believed it. I was beginning to feel eaten, like the main course in the workhouse, as my grandmother used to say when I wouldn't stop talking as a kid. I decided to get rid of her as soon as possible, though while the rain belted down it was out of the question.

'Our married life has been decades of misery. He goes away for a day or two at a time, but the peace I get when he sets out is ruined by the thought that he could be back any minute. In fact I never know he is going till he's been gone twenty-four hours, and he could show up in the next twenty-four, though often, thank God, he stays away longer than that. But just as I begin to hope he's never going to come back, he kicks the door open and comes in like a whirlwind. This morning I could stand it no longer. After half an hour's raving he fell asleep on the couch, so I got out by the kitchen door, and decided that this time I would be the one to go.'

I couldn't believe it was the first time.

'It is,' she said. 'Up to now I've regarded sticking by him and making sure he doesn't go into an asylum as a test of character. That's what my father drummed into all us girls. "The harder life is," he said, "the more it tests your character, and the more you should be thankful it does because then you know it's doing you good." Growing up hearing things like that, and trying to believe in them, has ruined my life to such an extent that though I'll soon be sixty I don't feel older than thirty. I feel my life is yet to come, even though I may look worn out.'

She did, but only to a certain extent, because the more she talked the softer and more clear her features became, until she seemed nowhere near sixty. She folded her cloak and laid it on the seat beside her, and smoothed her grey hair which went in a ponytail down her back. 'Do you mind if I smoke a cigarette?'

I pulled two from my pocket and gave her one. 'Are you going to stay in London, or will you go back to Goole?'

'How can I tell? Maybe if he'd been in an institution years ago, as he deserved to be, he would have been out by now.'

'That would have been worse.'

She laughed, a pleasant surprise, showing good teeth. A pair of gold earrings shook. 'You seem to have had your troubles as well, the way you talk.'

'Who hasn't?'

'It's a pity wisdom only comes to those who suffer,' she said. 'I used to believe in progress, but I don't anymore.'

'That's a shame.'

'I suppose it is. Maybe I'll believe in it again as time

goes on. I'll get a job in London.'

I was almost beyond caring. 'What sort?'

'Who'll give someone like me a job?'

'You never know.'

'That's true.' She sounded more cheerful. 'I have a bit of money in my post office book, so I can look around. I'll get something, even if I go from door to door asking for work.'

'I'd never go back if I were you,' I said.

'I don't think I will.'

'Maybe he'll cure himself. Maybe he won't. But if you go back it'll be two lives ruined, instead of one. Troubles shared are troubles doubled.'

'You almost talk as if you know him.'

'I've just got a good imagination.' I didn't want to complicate matters. I was making headway towards Doncaster, and soon came within the suction area of the M1. It had stopped raining, and she seemed full of wonder as I scooted silently down the motorway. I couldn't resist going up to eighty.

'I can see why he likes getting lifts in fast cars,' she said. 'He often told me how it soothed him to be speeding along a wide straight road.'

'A pity life isn't like that all the time.' We had a good laugh over the fact that it wasn't. I quite took to her, and I think she liked me. I pointed out Hardwick Grange, a wonderful building up a hill to the left. 'A woman called Bess built it in the sixteenth century.'

'Hardwick *Hall*,' she retorted. 'I visited it with my father.'

Perfect signposting sometimes foxed me when I was tired and hungry, and coming off the motorway into a service area west of Nottingham I ended up behind the kitchens – though I soon got back to the proper place. In the cafeteria we sat with plates of steak and chips, sweet cakes and tea. She would be on her own from now on, because I was heading for Shropshire. 'You'll easily get a lift from the exit slip road,' I said. 'Anyone will stop for a respectable looking person like you.'

'I wish you'd let me stay with you.'

'It's more than my job's worth. But if things get desperate in London, here's how to find me.' I dribbled with the idea of sending her to Upper Mayhem, but couldn't guarantee Bridgitte's reception, so I gave her my address, care of Moggerhanger.

'I know you can't take me, and I didn't really mean to ask. Maybe I was testing your kindness again. I shall try not to contact you in London. I'm a very proud woman.'

We parted like old friends. I couldn't understand why I felt depressed after I left her by the slipway. Yet a mile down the road and she was out of my mind. I thought of nipping into Nottingham for an hour or two, to drive around the old haunts in my opulent maroon Roller. Maybe I'd see Alfie Bottesford cleaning school windows; or Claudine Forkes, now married with three more kids on top of the one I'd inadvertently given her before lighting off; or Miss Gwen Bolsover with her latest incompetent and tongue-tied lover. Or I might run into – or over, if I could – old Weekly of Pitch and Blenders the estate agents who gave me the push after I'd sold Clegg's house to the highest bidder and claimed an unofficial deposit of my own.

Business came first. I hadn't seen any of my Nottingham cronies for a dozen years. They could wait a bit longer for the pleasure, and so could I. Past midday I got onto the A52, and after the tangle of Derby was doing a header down the dual carriageway as far as Watling Street. Stirling Moss would have been proud of me. I was in my element at the wheel of such a car. Britain can make it. I sucked my way past two Minis and a lorry. A girl stood at an intersection thumbing a lift, black slacks and red hair, but even that didn't tempt me to stop. In any case she was no doubt a policewoman acting as a decoy to find clues as to who had murdered a girl hitch-hiker last month.

On Watling Street, the old Roman road, the A5, the London to Holyhead, that military ribbon laid out to keep the ancient Brits in order, I watched my compass needle swing back on the straight and narrow, heading towards more bucolic horizons. The day wore on through rain, shine and back to rain again, and beyond Shrewsbury into hilly pastures mottled with sheep.

I stopped to buy provisions in a village shop that was so small you could hardly move, but there was a pile of supermarket baskets for you to help yourself while the woman sat at the till waiting for you to stagger over and pay. She looked sulky, thinking I only wanted a bar of chocolate, but thawed on seeing me pick up milk and bread and cheese and bacon and eggs and sausages and oranges and tea and chocolates and sugar and fags and vegetables – all to go on the expense sheet – sufficient for forty-eight hours of incarceration at Peppercorn Cottage where I was to hole up till the ten parcels were collected.

By three o'clock I seemed to have been on the road forever, and wanted to sleep, but a downpour of hail and sleet, perfect spring weather, made me fearful of being slid off the hillside or sinking without trace in the mud if I went too far up the track to find a more hidden position where I could switch off for an hour. This was the time, I supposed, for a benzedrine or valium, or other such tablets that people swallow to keep them alert, but I had nothing like that with me and in any case had never taken drugs except an aspirin now and again. All through the sixties I thought people were crazy, the way they popped pills like Dolly Mixtures or Smarties. If I wanted to relax or blow the mind or have a great experience or find a new horizon I would either get it by my own head of steam or not at all.

I chewed a bar of chocolate and had a smoke, comfortingly protected in the car, watching a man in oilskins and wellingtons walk along the hillside with a collie dog towards a huddle of sheep by a distant gate – a biscuit-tin picture come to life. The freezing washdown was so intense he almost disappeared. I felt deprived, looking at a man and his dog battling their way to a cottage which became visible when the hail stopped. A luminous green gap between the clouds showed the outlines of the hills and the sheen on their flanks, and I felt more at home than in the Dutch flat lands around Upper Mayhem.

I stared at the network of lanes on the map till the approaches to my cottage-rendezvous were clear. The obvious way was to reach it from the east, but I preferred – since there weren't so many farms on that side – to come on it from the west, which meant doing a few extra miles. By seven the light was draining away. Rain washed dead gnats off the windscreen. I was at my worst because, in spite of the Royce's dazzlers, I was prone to see double or to see solids where there was only shadow. Pale sky above the turning drew me along a valley whose damp air I could sense but not feel, across a river, into a side valley, over a col and down again. Beyond Bishop's Castle and Clun I did a sharp sweep to the west and, when it was dark, drove through a tunnel of light with nothing but the black sides and the roof visible. I switched off the radio and counted junctions, forks and crossroads. There was a pub at one, a telephone call box at another, a farmhouse at a third. I passed Dog End Green, Heartburn Mill, Job's Corner, Liberty Hall, Lower Qualm and Topping Hill – or so I called them – and finally, after one wrong turning and a look at the map, I found the lane leading to Peppercorn Cottage.

I drove through a strip of wood and along a hillside. A rabbit panicked in my headlights, but saw sense and zig-zagged under a bush. The track was two bands of asphalt, grass in between brushing the underbelly of the car. A gate blocked my way and I disembarked to open it.

The lane rose gently for a further half-mile, then came out of another scattering of trees. At the top of the slope the stars were vivid, and I wanted to get out and walk, but dipped headlights and crawled along the narrowing track, worried that if the car broke down there would be no space to turn.

With the window down, flecks of rain hit my face and fresh air revived me. A bullock called from a field. A panel of tin clattered at some trough or hutch – from how far away I couldn't tell. Village lights glistened like orange tinsel on a hillside. The lane descended steeply. I was close to my reference point on the large-scale map, but no house was visible.

I got out, torch in one hand and the heavy airgun cocked in the other, hoping to catch a rabbit in a beam of light. A slug at close range, aimed in the right place, would blind or knock flat anyone posing danger. The noise of running water covered my approach. Behind, the Roller's shadow blocked out part of the sky. No human being was near for miles. I swore at getting my trousers splashed.

An owl hooted from the trees, and the stream rushed into a conduit under the muddy track which rose steeply beyond the dip. Then I saw a dark building to the left, a path leading to it through bushes and trees. There was space between the house and the stream to turn the car, but I was scared on each reversing manoeuvre that the back wheels would slip into the stream and get stuck, so that I needed ten minutes to get it facing outward bound.

I waded through a barrier of high nettles and, at the threshold, shone the torch on my watch. It was nine o'clock, and felt like two in the morning. I had been on the go for seventeen hours and was, to put it mildly, clapped out. Gun at the ready, I pushed the door open with my shoe, waited for a moment, and then jumped inside.

Nine

A large grey rat scuffled across the beam of my torch, and my senses immediately descended to a lower level of existence. The slug I fired knocked a crater in the plaster wall, ricochetted close to my head and went out leaving a hole in the window, spraying glass onto a truckle bed.

I lit a calor gas lamp hanging from a beam, and its hissing white light more or less illuminated the room. The damp air, one notch off being water, smelled of soil and foul rags, and I shivered with cold, sorry I hadn't had a blow-out at some place chosen from the *Good Food and Hotel Guide*, which Moggerhanger kept in the car in case he needed to look after himself while on the road. I could have charged it to expenses. 'You just don't think,' as Bridgitte used to say, 'do you?'

I set my radio going on the wonky table. An effort was necessary to create civilised comfort. At the end of the room was a huge fireplace made of boulders, by which lay a heap of newspapers and a pile of logs with a blunt chopper on top. I hacked out some sticks and got a fine blaze, though a fire would have to burn for weeks to cure the dank atmosphere. Under the window stood a calor gas burner and a blackened kettle which I filled at the stream. In a cupboard I found tea (mouldy), sugar (damp) and milk (sour), all of which I threw into the bushes, and got fresh provisions from the car. The room was filled with the smell of frying bacon and eggs, boiling tomatoes and toasting bread. Within an hour of arrival I was sitting by the fire, smoking a cigarette, drinking the best mug of tea since Mike's caff that morning and listening to a talk on the radio about a poet who killed himself while living in an isolated cottage in a remote and wooded part of the country.

To be cut off from the world, and from all normal life, was a not unpleasant sensation, though having been brought up in a street regarded as a slum, we'd at least had a tap and a gas stove, as well as a lavatory across the yard. At this place I dug a hole with a trowel at the side of the house, crouching with an umbrella in one hand, a flashlight in the other and a roll of white paper in my teeth. I supposed some shepherd had lived here with a wife and eight kids, as happy as the midwinter was long, but it certainly wasn't the sort of bijou gem a woman would walk into with her knickers in her hand.

It was quiet – I will say that – except for the scratching of a rat but he, or she (they, most likely), kept a fair distance after my hello of a bullet from the door. I threw another armful of logs on the fire, then stacked the ten packages from the car in the dresser-cupboard, hoping that with its doors shut tight the rats wouldn't get in and sample them. Above the dresser, just to give a homely touch to the place, was another pair of Moggerhanger's framed exhortations (though these had fly shit in the corners) saying: 'Eternal violence is the price of safety' and 'Morality knows no bounds'.

I went upstairs to see what condition the bedrooms were in. One to the left had heaps of rags under the window, and I didn't care to investigate for fear of finding a rotting tramp underneath. The rest of the room was stacked with red and white plastic bollards for organising contra-flow systems on the motorway, as well as red lights, yellow lights, road works indicators, men-at-work triangles and police 'Go-slow' signs. It was as if someone had broken into the Highway Code, because my torch also lit up the happy insignia of two children hand in hand on their way to school; a deer leaping merrily across the road; a nightmare avalanche of rocks hitting a car roof and the sign of a car halfway sunk in water after driving off the quay. Another showed a bus caught between the two jaws of a drawbridge, people spilling out with arms waving.

Fuck this, I said, let me go downstairs; but first I looked in the room opposite. On a low table between two iron beds stood a copse of bottles with candles stuck in their tops. The carpet was so covered with patches of grease that I resisted walking on it in case I slipped and broke my neck. A spider as big as an ashtray scooted across the room, but he seemed friendly compared to the rats twittering by the skirting boards, because he came slowly back to have a look at me.

I pulled the truckle bed in front of the fire, and lay down fully clothed. The blankets weighed like a bearskin that had been forty years in a damp pawnshop. The swollen brook was reinforced by rain which first beat against the windows above my head. The door was so badly fitted, or warped, that wind drove through and kept the room cold.

It was hard to sleep, due to the two mugs of strong tea and the fact that there were at least half a dozen rats scratching and squeaking behind the skirting boards as they held a council of war. I read the Riot Act in rat language and fired a slug towards a pair of beady eyes, which brought quiet for a few minutes, though the shot, having missed its target, tore down another square foot of plaster. The prevalence of so many rats led me to wonder whether the time wasn't far off when conventional weapons would no longer be appropriate, and I would have to go nuclear. Fortunately such an option was beyond my capability, and all I could do was reload the gun and lay it on the floor beside the bed. It would serve Moggerhanger right if the house was reduced to a ruin, for not providing a cosier relay post.

The road was in front of my eyes, pot-holes which I avoided, traffic lights suddenly on red when I was going at ninety. I came out of a café to find all four tyres flat (as well as the spare); then the Roller going backwards towards a cliff, with Moggerhanger, Cottapilly, Pindarry, Kenny Dukes, Toffeebottle and Jericho Jim ready to blast me with their shotguns if it went over. Or I was driving peacefully along a leafy road when a very peculiar kind of police siren, such as I'd not heard before, came in short loud squeaks.

Two rats scampered from the bed when I sat up. I felt my nose to see if it was still there. It was wet, though not from blood. I didn't know whether to laugh or whisper. I laughed. They were invisible in the dark. Their eyes glowed, but their arses didn't as they ran away. I shone the torch around the room and fired another slug at where their hole might be, just to show who was the boss as I wiped cold sweat from my face. I felt like an officer in the trenches in the Great War, except that I thought I might desert my post and make a bid for Blighty. There was a court martial in a room made entirely of mud. The rats sat at a table and condemned me to death. The joy of life induced me to fire off a dozen slugs. The noise of the stream outside affected my bladder, so I had a piss standing on the doorstep. Then I fell asleep. The human frame could stand only so much.

The light that woke me was like the reflection from a wall of cold porridge. I sat up, shot a rat, got out of bed, lit a fire, put a kettle on, laid sausages in the pan, then puffed at a cigar and awaited results.

The bullet had knocked the rat's brains out, which was not a pleasant sight before breakfast, but I swept the remains into a pan and threw them over the bushes. By the time my sausages were cooked they looked like turds swimming for dear life in a pool of fat. When I extracted the fat and threw it on the fire the room stank like Akbar's Snackbar. I was about to tuck in when I heard someone moving upstairs. Survival, a novelty at first, was becoming a problem.

During the day I'd intended sweeping away heaps of grit and plaster caused by my jittery gunplay. Then I would dust and wash where necessary, clean the windows to let in more light, and dry the blankets so as to make my second night a fraction cosier. But I was in no way inclined to share my abode, and if an old vagrant had shambled in during the night I was determined to get rid of him.

I went softly up, meaning to put a slug between his eyes if he showed any fight. The cargo enclosed in the dresser was too valuable to be at the mercy of a light-fingered tramp. If it was what I was beginning to think it was he would lick that white dust off with a beatific grin and at least die happy.

There was a noise of someone fighting his way from a cocoon of cardboard. A bottle fell on the floor and, welcoming the noise because it covered the creaking of the stairs, I leapt into the room and flattened myself at the door. Even full daylight wouldn't let me see across the room. I seemed the only one in it, which proved how far apart my senses and feelings were.

On the other side of the bed, by a fireplace from which a hundredweight of rusty soot had spilled like dust from a cold volcano, was a handsome brown owl, its eyes staring as if I had no right to come into its headquarters without a permit. First rats, and now an owl. Crosswise, it was almost as big as I was, and far too big even lengthwise to be out of a zoo. He was unmoving, as if my only hope was to sit down and talk matters over calmly and sensibly.

When I made a gesture with the pistol it flapped straight for me. I ducked. It clattered around the room, scored a channel through the bank of soot, knocked over two bottles and positioned itself by the door so that I couldn't get out. It had fed on the choicest rats – and now me. There was something human about its actions, so I couldn't shoot. One of the windows was open, and I edged forward in a dance, hoping it would have the sense to go out the way it had come in.

Maybe I shouldn't have frightened it, I thought, as it flew over the trees and I closed the window. Since it came every night and ate a dozen rats I should have kept it for a companion. It was just like me to scare away what would help me.

Consoling myself with a large breakfast, I thought what a good place this would be for Bill Straw to hide in, even though it belonged to Moggerhanger who was out for his guts – far better than being locked up in Blaskin's rafters where his skeleton would be discovered in fifty years' time when the block was knocked down for redevelopment.

It was blinding with rain, so I stayed inside. A band of trees along the course of the brook kept the place dim, and low clouds didn't help. I had the light on all day. A shelf nailed to the wall held a score of paperbacks, stained and full of grit, and as I shook each one separately I saw they were written by Sidney Blood. One of them, called *The Crimson Tub*, had underlinings and comments in the margins which proved that Kenny Dukes had been to Peppercorn Cottage.

The light lasted only a few hours in that hidden cleft of land. After a cowboy's lunch I lay on the bed and fell asleep for two hours, and was wakened by a rat running over my chest. I would suggest to Moggerhanger that the next courier to Peppercorn Cottage should bring a couple of tomcats from Stepney. I made tea and ate a packet of cakes, wondering how soon it would take me to go mad if I had to stay in this hotel forever.

Wearing wellingtons and oilskins I walked up the track, though now that I dressed for the rain, it stopped. Smoke came from the chimney of a farm about a mile away. I went into a field. A rabbit, young but fully grown, looked at me, and just as it thought to move, I pressed the trigger.

The isolation of Peppercorn Cottage had inspired me to

do a bit of living off the land. The rabbit ran a couple of yards, then stopped and began to spin, so I grabbed its back legs and delivered the chop that killed.

I sharpened a knife on the doorstep, drew out the guts and stomach, cut off the head, skinned and jointed it. For a stew I threw in potatoes, carrots and onions, and a few bay leaves from a bush by the door. I stoked up the fire, feeling like a cannibal, and swung the black pot over the flames.

The light from the beam didn't quite reach the four walls, so that the blazing fire turned the place into a cave. Perhaps the rats turned against me mostly because I wouldn't allow them to get too friendly. Some people say they are very intelligent creatures. I heard more squeals of resentment as I chewed at my broiled rabbit and threw the bones into the fire than I had while devouring salty and tasteless sausages. But I refused to share my delicious and plentiful food. They were big enough to go out and catch their own rabbits.

Shadows moved on the walls. I saw rats everywhere. I turned and fired the pistol and, because I shot out of malice instead of self-preservation, a ricochet struck my ankle. I swear to God the little bleeders laughed in chorus. When I took my sock off there was a dark bruise, and I hopped around the room till there was more ache in my foot from the cold than the bullet.

I was stuck till someone came for the packages. Maybe they wouldn't turn up for a month. I preferred not to think about it, as I pulled a stone from the fireplace and hurled it at a rat by the stairfoot door. I got it right on the arse, but a convenient hole swallowed it up. They were getting bolder.

The gap in the clouds when I stood at the open door showed brighter stars than I'd ever seen. One rat ran outside and another ran in. Then the one that ran out came in again. How long would they put up with me? I stood aside so as not to interfere with the traffic. All the same, I liked the isolation of the house. If it was mine I would set rat traps and lay poison, buy more lamps to hang up, bring stoves to heat the place, nail pictures on the wall, spread new carpets, install a battery television and record player, get a generator, and a pump to draw water from the stream, as well as fix a toilet in the shed by the side of the house and open a radio telephone line to the local exchange. I would clear the vegetation and lay out an ornamental garden, build a terrace and sun porch, and excavate a swimming pool. I would give parties and invite all the young girls from miles around.

I spat. Too expensive. Might as well buy a house in Clapham. When I slammed the door I almost trapped another rat on its way in. I decided to spend the night in the car which, seen from the window of this mud-smeared rat-infested hole in the hillside, seemed the height of civilisation. I wondered if being sent to this place wasn't Moggerhanger's notion of a test to see whether I wouldn't turn grey-haired or go mad. I filled a flask and made bacon sandwiches. Several trips were necessary to transfer provisions, blankets and the gun to the car. I was careful to lock the cottage door after me.

The stars beamed, trees swayed, water rippled a few feet beyond the fender. I was full and content, though not particularly drowsy. There was little rain. I was comfortable, yet felt more vulnerable in the car than I had in the house, in spite of my squeaking and scurrying friends. I listened to the radio, ate, drank tea, and got out now and again for a stroll, careful to open and close the door quickly. At ten o'clock there was nothing to do but sleep. Then I felt a rat run over my hand.

No, it was a corner of the blanket tickling me. But, I said to myself, blankets don't have little cold claws and damp noses, even at the corners. The tickling of a blanket is like that of a butterfly or moth, or even at the worst a bluebottle. In no possible way could even the edge of a blanket be compared to the snout of a fully fledged Shropshire rodent.

I jumped up, banged my head and the little bleeder ran squeaking under the steering column. To shoot in such a confined space would be foolhardy, and Moggerhanger wouldn't like slug scars all over his interior decoration. I dived across the seats to get at the rat with my bare hands, hoping it hadn't brought its mate as well, otherwise they would have at least two families by morning.

If I wasn't safe in a Rolls-Royce, where would I be safe? I had to put a stop to the invasion. A live rat in a car was no joke. I lit a fag and took a few minutes to think the matter out and to lull the rat into a state of over-confidence. I wasn't born yesterday.

I pulled on leather gloves from my overcoat pocket. The rat was near my boot, sniffing the leather. The light was on, and I could see it clearly – about eight inches long and quite pleased with itself. I actually saw its teeth, and felt them against the side of my boot.

That rat was never more surprised in its life – what was left of it. Neither was I. I gripped it like a vice around the soft belly then opened the window and threw it towards the stream. I listened for the splash, but to my chagrin it landed on the further bank, and then I heard the splash as it began swimming back. I battened all hatches and made as good a search as could be done with my torch, till I knew I was alone. I laughed like Boris Karloff after he'd strangled his seventh victim. I was safe from the rats, but even so, now and again through the night I heard one or two running over the roof of the car, and they sounded as if they had it in for me.

Ten

'I say, you there!'

I thought the rats had invented a miniature battering ram, and were tapping it at the window, but I soon realised that the collectors had arrived. I yawned and sat up. The day of my deliverance was at hand.

'Dammit, old man, why don't you shake a leg?'

He had, at least on the face of it, the sort of public school hee-haw that to me marked him as definitely untrustworthy. I may have been wrong, and no doubt I was, and he was no more untrustworthy than I was, which was why I recognised it so instinctively. I was never against clearly spoken English, though I'd heard people in London say that a northern accent was homely and cute. I dropped my Nottingham twang as soon as I began working at the estate agents when I was seventeen, otherwise people might not have understood me as quickly as I wanted them to, which would have been bad for a con-man's chances of success. When crossing frontiers as a gold smuggler, a neutral twang was the first requirement, which even Bill Straw used on his travels.

The man outside the car looked, with his blue eyes and blond locks, as if he had just left the changing-room by the sports field, but I knew immediately that he had come for the drug boxes inside the cottage. He smoked a slender pipe and had a scarf around his neck, though whether university colours or football emblem I didn't know. When he smiled there was something hard about the mouth. He was in his mid-twenties, but he could have been older. Whoever he was, he wasn't himself.

I opened the door and got out. There were two of them,

the other being dark-haired and wearing a scarf of a slightly different design. 'Sorry we pulled you out of the land of shut-eye,' the fair one said. 'I'm Peter.'

'I'm John,' the other called from the bank of the stream, where he was tying a red-white-and-blue canoe to a sapling. 'You may wonder what we're doing here.'

'So would I,' said Peter. 'We're paddling the whole length of the River Drivel, from its source to the sea, for charity – a sort of sponsored paddle. We were dropped about four miles north by landrover, but on most of the route so far we've had to carry the damned kayak.'

'It looks a shade better from here on,' said John. 'At least there aren't any roadblocks.'

'We need ballast, that's all.' Peter tapped his pipe a little too hard on the front fender of the Roller, and the bowl flew away from the stem. 'Oh bollocks!'

I detected a slight change in his accent.

'Fact is,' John said, 'we need five little counterweights to stow athwart the keel.'

'There are ten,' I informed him.

'We've been told to pick up five. I expect somebody else'll call for the others.' I noticed a scar down the left side of his face, and he hadn't got it from duelling with sabres. 'You get my drift, Mr Cullen?'

'It's in the dresser cupboard.' I nodded towards the door and gave him the key. Early morning wasn't my favourite part of the day, especially before breakfast, and I knew that with such people the fewer words the better, one trait which criminals have in common with the police. Talking never got you anywhere, unless you wanted it to.

He took the key grudgingly and opened the cottage door.

Peter saw the blankets in the car. 'I say, did you spend the night in there?'

'Sure.'

'Whatever for?'

'It's more comfortable, for one thing, and for another . . .'

There was a scuffle from the house and John, if that was his name, fell over the doorstep as he hurried out. 'Fucking rats,' he cried with a look of terror. 'The place is full of 'em.'

'I saw one or two.' I'd known there would be nothing more certain to establish his accent – which seemed to be mostly West Country. 'But they were quite tame. They won't harm you.'

He wanted to kill me, but realised that one or both of us would end up in the river if he tried. 'I'll make you some tea,' I said, 'if you've time. I haven't had mine yet.'

They sat on the stone bench while I got the stove going. The cups weren't of the cleanest and Peter wiped the rim with a folded white handkerchief. 'How long have you been here?'

'A couple of nights.'

John glanced towards the door. 'Better you than me.'

'I can take it or leave it.'

'Me,' he said, 'I'd leave it. I read a book once about the future. I forget what it was called. I always do. But some blokes put a cage over a chap's face with rats in it. I had nightmares for a week.' He stroked the scar on his cheek and downed the scalding tea at one swallow. He'd been in prison.

'We should be leaving.' Peter set his cup on the bench. 'Or we'll be late at the off-loading point. The tide waits for no man.'

I helped him out with five of the packages, and we wrapped each in a plastic container while John pulled the canoe onto the gravel. They slotted in neatly. 'I hope the stuff doesn't get wet.'

'No chance,' Peter said. 'If it does, we'll turn boy scouts and dry it out.'

We manhandled the boat across the lane, slid it over

half a field and down through some bushes to where the river came out of a gully. They hoisted a pennant saying SAVE ST DAMIAN'S and, laughing and shouting, wielded the paddles to avoid the banks in the swirling current. They certainly knew their job, I reflected as I went back to the cottage to wait for the next collection.

I ate breakfast in the feeble sunshine outside. The rats were already sensing victory, for I could hear them playing hide and seek. I lit my first fag, happy at the notion – mistaken as it turned out – that my job was half over. The weather was good, above the two walls of land. It was always the case that as soon as I got to thinking that life was improving, something bad happened to tell me that I should have had more sense. Optimism was never anything but a warning.

A car came down the lane, and I saw the blue flashing light through the bushes. Four of the biggest coppers I'd ever seen came running in, picked me up and flattened me against the wall. Thank God they hadn't used violence. I shouted all manner of threats about my lawyers and the Civil Liberties Association, but it had no effect. They threw me on the floor and the tracker dog sniffed me up and down. I think it was a mixture of Great Dane and Labrador, crossed by the Hound of the Baskervilles, though who was I to question its breed? It was certainly the biggest canine bastard I had ever seen.

'It ain't on him,' one policeman said.

I could have told them that, but they hadn't asked. In any case, it was hard to speak with my face in the mud.

'Where is it, then?' Number Two shouted, bending down to my ear. He yanked my face towards him.

'Where's what?' How could they have got at me so easily? I didn't know what hit me. They use blitzkrieg tactics these days: one at the back, one at the front and one down the chimney. Without standing up, he waddled over my body to get to the other ear. Number Three pressed a boot on my neck and the pain was so intense I thought he'd break it. 'You fucking well know where it is. Now where the fuck is it?'

I certainly did, and wasn't going to take any stick for Moggerhanger. 'In the house. In the dresser cupboard.'

I was pulled up like a rag doll, sat on the bench and given a cigarette. 'Why did you make things so difficult? Why didn't you say so?'

The inspector shouted to the bloke inside. 'How many?'

'Four, sir.'

'There should be five.'

The copper came out with the five boxes on his arm. 'It was too dark to count.'

'I'll deal with you later.'

The other went in, to fetch a biscuit for the dog. 'Got any water for our Dismal?'

I pointed to the stream.

'Don't be so sarky.'

My blood was racing with speculation. Would I get sent down for twenty years? Or forty? Next time, I'll do a murder and only get five. I wouldn't take the blame for Moggerhanger over this job, even if he had me cut to ribbons in jail. I was ready to cry at the balls-up that had been made, and wondered how it was possible that the coppers had got to know I was down here with such a cargo. I could hardly credit the fact that the Blemishes had been the most sophisticated kind of narks. Yet it was hard to disbelieve anything in this life. Before the arrival of the canoeists I could have assumed that the packages contained nothing but Epsom Salts or sachets of aspirins, as advertised on television, and that I was a decoy, but they couldn't have set up such an original and elaborate transport plan only for that.

'I don't know what you're after.' I stroked the dog, which seemed amiable after its biscuit and water. 'There's nothing illegal in those packets. In any case, I didn't see a search warrant, if you don't mind me saying so.'

I dodged a backhander, but it wasn't seriously meant, otherwise it would have got me. 'We don't need 'em these days,' the biggest bastard said. 'Don't you watch telly?'

'Do you mind if I go in for a biscuit?' I asked. 'I'm famished.' The inspector nodded. I came out with the packet, and Dismal pulled the first one from my hand. After a kick from the inspector it disentangled itself and went off for a piss.

In such circumstances my powers of observation go to pieces, but I saw that the inspector was, if nothing else, well built. He took his cap off to talk, and to scratch his bald head. I wouldn't have described him as white, but as pink – and I hope I don't go against the Race Relations Act in doing so. He had thickish lips, prominent blue eyes and a nose that seemed to have been broken more than once. He looked halfway civilised with his cap off, but the tone of voice was so reasonable it would have made anyone quail, except me. 'Listen, we're taking the stuff to our laboratories. It's not for you, or me, or my officers here to say what these packages contain until they have been properly examined by competent authorities. So shut your fucking mouth. I strongly advise you to stay at your present domicile – meaning here – until such time as you hear from us. There may be further questions, following which, charges may well be brought. Is that clearly understood – sir?'

'All right,' I said.

He put his hat on. 'Back in the car, lads!'

I waved them off with a smile, to show that I didn't believe I had anything to fear, or like a guilty man who thinks it's the best way to act innocent, but knowing that it's the surest way to be taken as guilty. But when the car was out of hearing I only hoped that an escarpment had formed at the top of the lane in the last half hour so that they would drop five hundred feet and never come back.

No such luck. It was the end. Half of Moggerhanger's precious loot was on its way to the cop shop, while I was condemned to stay in a rat infested hovel till such time, maybe two or three days, as they would come and take me away. I didn't even have the heart to go inside and make another cup of tea. My morale had gone, and that was a fact. I couldn't think for the noise of water from one direction, the triumphant scratching of rats in the other, and the rushing of wind through branches overhead.

But the one thing about your morale having gone bang is that you no longer need fear it will go. It's gone, and good riddance, and under the circumstances it had had fair reason to evaporate. Reflecting further, once your morale has well and truly gone, it can only come back. Nothing stays the same. That's the joy and excitement of life. I was more philosophical than in my early twenties.

The first indication of returning sanity was when Dismal the tracker dog came out of the bushes and licked my hand. It wanted another biscuit, and though my supplies were limited, I gave it one. The large brown head lay on my knees in gratitude. It was a big dog. If it stood on hind legs it would reach to the top button of my waistcoat, meaning that since he had become my guest we had exactly three hours supply of food left. How could those callous bastards, have forgotten such an amiable animal? By cheering me up it seemed anything but dismal.

The horrible truth came to me that they had left it behind to stop me getting away. What malicious ingenuity! I couldn't believe it. But what else could I believe? In my rage I kicked the brute. It made no difference. The bloody hound came back and lay at my feet. I gave it a slice of smoked bacon. By the time they returned the dog would be whimpering by my skeleton. Such a scene indeed was dismal. My sense of humour was coming back.

I smoked another cigarette. I was too depressed to

puff a cigar. The dog tried to pull it from me before I could light up, but desisted on being threatened by the flaming match. I walked to the edge of the stream. It was too wide to leap across. The dog pleaded for me not to drown myself. It had very expressive eyes for a police dog.

I went into the house, packed my things, including the remains of the food, and loaded them into the car. Then I locked the door, and settled myself in the driver's seat. Because I acted like an automaton I knew that what I was doing was right. Whether it was sensible, I wouldn't know for some time, but sense did not seem to offer much help in my predicament. It had always been my gut-feeling – and I can remember my Cullen grandfather saying so – that you never go to the cop shop on your own two feet. They have to drag you there kicking and screaming – after they find you.

It would not be tactically sound to depart from the place in daylight. I would pander to sense to that extent. I came in darkness, and I would go in darkness, like the thief in the night I was being made to feel. I would stay in the car and give Dismal more time to get used to me.

It rained, and he looked forlornly in. When he could no longer stand being wet he sheltered as much of his body as possible under the rotting porch by the door. Whenever I went into the house to make tea I was always careful to give him a dish, which he lapped dry. I spread the blankets in the back of the car, but would not let him get in till the time came. I was so bored waiting that I read halfway through the *Good Food and Hotel Guide*, trying to find out which establishment accepted overnight guests with dogs. There was a place called The Golden Fleece in an old fortress-and-market-town which had only survived from the Middle Ages because the Germans hadn't bombed it flat. It had plastic coffin baths in the bathrooms and four-poster plastic beds with flock mattresses that you disappeared into, which gave proof of its antiquity. There was, I felt sure, a King Arthur Bar and a Friar Tuck Dining Room, where a thug in Lincoln green stood by with a bow and arrow to pin you to the wall if they found out that your stolen credit card was counterfeit. The waitresses were called wenches and they all but served their own beautiful dumplings as they slopped frozen this and microwaved that onto your vast oval wooden platter, a look of horror on their faces at the fact that you actually wanted to eat it. The manager acted the grand swell and called you 'Squire' because he was charging forty pounds a night and getting away with it.

An Englishman would rather die than expose himself by complaining. 'These are jolly good turds. Aren't they wonderful turds, darling?'

'Eh? What? Turds? Oh, yes, excellent. Haven't had such good turds since I was in India. Quite delicious. We ought to compliment the cook. As I was saying about Rupert's school . . .'

'They're quite superior. You can't find good turds like this everywhere.'

'You could at one time, though. Now everything's plastic and ersatz. Convenience food, nothing else. What? Well, as I was saying about Rupert's report . . .'

When I'd played that one out, I perused a chapter of *The Crimson Tub* by Sidney Blood. Then I listened to my radio, fearful of using the one in the Roller because I had a horror of switching on the engine at zero hour and finding the battery dead. Acting senselessly did not mean that I could take chances like that.

Half an hour after lighting-up time I started the engine, and opened a door. Dismal climbed in as if used to such luxurious transport. The smooth movement over gravel and dead twigs onto the lane, all lights beaming, made me feel I was coming back to life. I only hoped I was right. My troubles at having lost half Moggerhanger's precious cargo may have been just beginning, but I was mobile, and nothing else mattered. If I had failed in my duty it was through no fault of my own. I switched off most of the car lights as Dismal and I travelled like two outlaws up the lane and back onto public roads.

Eleven

Whenever I put the radio on, Dismal slept. When I switched it off he sat up and looked over my shoulder at the road. Being almost human, he was fair company. When I got out for a piss, so did he. When I ate a biscuit, likewise. He even lapped up half a slab of chocolate and when I said it would ruin his teeth, he bit me. Life was perfect, except that the police and Moggerhanger were out for my guts.

The direct route to London was through Hereford and Cheltenham, but I set off for Shrewsbury and the A5, making easterly across the country to slide unobtrusively into London via the Great North Road, the highway I had come out on when heading for Goole – full of mindless optimism – a few days ago. I was so tense that life seemed real.

I drove carefully, meaning not too fast in the darkness, along winding roads. When headlights frizzled behind me I slowed down to indicate that the driver could overtake. Mostly they were youngsters in souped-up bangers going from one pub to another. Forty miles out of Peppercorn Cottage I began to relax. Because of my previous care with navigation I found my way onto the Shrewsbury road with ease. 'Dismal, I think we've got clean away.'

The car radio was an elaborate set, with extra wavelengths on which Moggerhanger could tune in to the police. I heard plenty of gabble about road accidents, abandoned cars, pub brawls and suspected break-ins, but nothing concerning a six-foot con-man and a kidnapped tracker-dog in a maroon Roller last seen heading towards the Severn.

Sooner or later I would get picked up, so I had to have sanctuary, and one place I reasonably expected to find it was at Moggerhanger's homebase. If I got caught, so would he. It wasn't my fault that the operation had gone wrong. If I got into London before anyone spotted me, Claud Moggerhanger, who was only human after all, would be obliged to keep me out of harm's way. Such an assumption cheered me up. I had always been an optimist, even if only in order to survive, believing that any action was better than no action, and any thought more comforting than none.

On the outskirts of Shrewsbury I spotted a fish and chip shop and parked halfway on the pavement with hazard lights going. The Chinese bloke gave me a funny look when I ordered fish, chips, roe, peas, sausages and pie twice, plus two bottles of lemonade. Hugging the parcels, I went back to the car and tucked in, to the noise of Dismal's disgraceful gobbling of his generous portions on the floor behind. I had brought a tin dish from the cottage, and poured out a bottle of lemonade so that he wouldn't get thirsty. He lapped that up, and belched into the back of my neck for the next ten miles. When we stopped at a traffic light I returned an even riper series of eructations, but he didn't take the hint.

After my stint at Peppercorn Cottage and my encounter with the police, I felt as if I had spent a fortnight going back and forth on an assault course at a very expensive health farm, and craved a wash and brush up. A public lavatory was still open, but there were no lights. Sinks were hanging from the walls, lavatory pans smashed, doors in matchwood, and the divisions in the urinal had, I assumed, been battered down with a sledgehammer. What they'd done with the attendant, I didn't dare think about. Maybe they were part of an adventure training school, which sent kids out suitably equipped, with score cards and umpires, to see how many toilets they could vandalise in one day without being caught. It looked as if this particular class had got inside with a fieldgun. I propped my torch on a ledge, turned on a tap, had a wash and put on a clean shirt. Back in the car I combed my hair and buffed up my boots with Dismal's tail. All spick and span, I could face the world again.

Huge raindrops thrashed at the windscreen. Dismal began to howl as if he'd never seen rain before. Or maybe the regularity of the wipers frightened him. I shouted for him to belt up. After passing Telford I was afraid of drifting into the never-never land from which you only wake up in death – or a very disagreeable fire. The clock glowed ten, and I fancied somewhere to bed down for a couple of hours. People would be coming out of the pubs and I'd need all my wits to avoid their antics, though I knew from experience that the worst time on country roads was before the pubs opened, when everyone was rushing to get their first drink. After closing time, when they were blind drunk, they at least tried to be careful.

Dismal was dozing, which didn't help matters. I drifted through space. The yearning to fall asleep came and went. I fought off the worst attacks by reliving the sojourn at Peppercorn Cottage, from which place my troubles stemmed. I should have known that the rats would bring no luck. The two jokers who had taken half my stock in their canoe must have been hired by Moggerhanger from a school of actors. I envied the skill with which they had made the collection. Clockwork wasn't in it. By now they had probably landed the stuff at some secluded bank of the Severn. The car that had picked it up was in London, and they were boozing with their girlfriends in some clip-joint roadhouse. Or they had transferred their cargo to a hired canal barge on the upper reaches of the Thames and were holidaying their slow way to Hammersmith – while I was driving east in Moggerhanger's car with a police tracker dog in the back.

Things could be worse. When I pulled up at an all-night café, I should have left Dismal locked inside, but he leapt over the seat, and though I tried with all my strength to pick him up and heave him back, he insisted on following me in case he missed something to eat. He had a collar, but no lead, and at the door he cleverly pulled the handle down with his teeth so that I could walk in.

Half a dozen black-leathered bikers were eating toasted sandwiches and drinking tea when the best trained dog in the police force rushed in. The laugh on a tall blond biker's face faded as Dismal sniffed forward and fastened his teeth onto the youth's trouser pocket, whining a signal that it was time for the back-up force to do its work and take the drugs off him.

The biker eased away from the juke box. 'I say, get this damned pooch out of here.' The other youths laughed. The only method of calling Dismal to heel would be to get a whistle out of my pocket and blow it.

'Jonas, you idiot, we told you not to bring that stuff back from school,' one of the bikers called.

'He's only a cuddly brown Labrador,' I said, taking a lump of sugar from the table and leading him to the corner of the room where I thought he would be safe. The bikers, donning their gear to leave, looked strangely at me, and made obscene comments about Dismal, to the effect that what did it feel like living off its immoral earnings? I wondered how I could get rid of him, because if the police who raided Peppercorn Cottage assumed I had taken him away I was a marked man. Riding in a Rolls-Royce down the Great North Road with such a conspicuous dog sitting in the back as if I was his lord and master would be too rash for safety.

'I don't allow dogs in here,' the proprietor called from behind his counter. 'Especially a big swine like that. He'll frighten my customers.'

'We only want some tea and cakes.' I put my fiver on

the counter and pulled Dismal's ear to make him be quiet. 'I'd like a bowl for him to drink his tea from, if you don't mind. He hasn't learned to use a mug yet.'

The man, too exhausted to care, slid the goods across. 'Dogs are a damned nuisance, urinating and breaking wind everywhere, and bothering my customers.'

'Dismal!' I shouted in my best police sergeant voice, 'let's go, otherwise we'll never get to Glasgow.'

'That's what I mean,' the proprietor said. 'Nobody's got a minute to spare. This is the worst kind of job to tell a story in. While I still had my factory and I told a story, people would listen. That was because it was in my time and not theirs. I was paying them to listen and they didn't mind at all. That was what ruined my business and brought me here, but having a café on a main road, nobody will listen because it's their time that's taken up. They run in, order their food, eat with a blank stare, then pay up and get out. It's no wonder the quality of life is deteriorating. They just want to get going on their journey, back to their homes, wives, children and' – a disapproving glance at Dismal, who took it well – 'to their dogs. Or back to their work, or businesses which in these times no amount of energy and good old British precision will save from going under the hammer.

'We live in times of change right enough. My factory manufactured doors, all kinds and sizes of door, but not so many doors were needed all of a sudden, or my doors were no longer competitive, or I hit a rough patch on the production line, or I didn't keep up with the times, or I didn't advertise, or the designs were no good. The order books were suddenly empty. The salesmen took too many days off. They came in late. They sat at home watching television when they should have been out on the road. When I spoke to one of them about it he said he was earning enough already thank you very much so why should he try to bump up his income when the tax man would take the extra money? He'd got a spare time job serving cream teas at the local stately home, and his wife did bed and breakfast in the summer, and they got paid in cash so that they didn't declare what they earned. So the order books were empty and I called the receiver in. My fault, if you think about it. Then my father died. He had a few shares in South African gold mines and when I sold 'em I bought this café.'

Though his story seemed banal, his complaints might have been justified. Dismal and I stayed by the counter. 'Well,' I said, 'I have to go.'

When he rolled up his sleeve I actually thought he was going to start work. But he lit a cigarette. 'Why can't you be like Charlie over there? He's never in a hurry.'

'That's because I'm on the dole.' Charlie was a fair-haired blue-eyed relaxed sort of chap in his middle thirties. 'Been on the dole seven years.'

I sympathised. 'It must be awful.'

He looked up from his tea. 'It's a lot better than getting up at six every morning and going out into the rain and cold five days a week, month in and month out. I pushed loaded cartons from one department of the warehouse to another, but then they got fork-lift trucks and six of us got the push. I thought the end of the world had come when I couldn't get another job, but I also saw that it was marvellous not having to go to work. I could do bits and bobs around the house, talk to my mates, go out on my bike, or sit in the public library reading dirty books. The dole's a lovely system. If we got a few more quid a week we'd be in heaven. I often help here in the café and earn a few quid, and I don't mind that because it don't seem like work. And I vote Tory now, instead of Labour.'

I was aghast. 'Tory?'

He laughed. 'Sure. Think what the Tories have done for the unemployed. Got millions of us on the dole. All you hear them Labour bleeders go on about is getting us back to work. Back to work! They want us building motorways, I expect, though I'm sure that lot wouldn't want to dirty their lily-white hands. If they ever did any work it was so long ago they don't remember what it was like.'

He amazed me so much, I bought him a cup of tea and six cakes. 'You're a bit of a philosopher.'

That pleased him. 'I never would have been if I hadn't got on the dole. I've had time to think. Labour don't want you to think. They think that if you do, you'll vote Tory, and how right they are. Thinking's always been the prerogative of the idle rich, but now it's within reach of everyone, and it's no thanks to Labour. The only time you'll catch me voting Labour is when they promise to double the dole money and stop talking about getting us back to work. I only wish the Tories would give us more money, but I expect they will as soon as they can afford it.'

The light in his blue eyes changed intensity, an increase in candlepower that almost turned them grey. 'I was thinking the other day what a nice place it would be if the whole world was on the dole. That's the sort of future we ought to aim for. Work is the cause of all evil, and it'll be heaven on earth when there's no such thing. Universal unemployment is what we want, and England will be the envy of the world when we've brought it about.'

Weary as I was, I did my best to point out his errors. Most people were driven mad by being out of work, I told him, apart from the fact that they had to live in poverty. They lost their self-respect, and the respect of their children. They lost the respect of their wives. They became prematurely old. They sat at home wrapped in self-hatred, a feeling of uselessness paralysing them body and soul. They deteriorated physically, and in a year became unrecognisable to what they had been. The houses they lived in fell to pieces around them. Their wives left them and their kids were taken into care by social workers who'd been hovering around rubbing their hands for just such a thing.

'That's as maybe,' he said, when I could say no more, 'but my mates don't think like that. As soon as they get the push they're like Robinson Crusoe who's just landed on that island after his shipwreck. They're a bit dazed, but they start picking up the pieces and learning to live with what they've got. In no time at all, they're happy, like me.'

A trio of white-faced young lorry drivers came in, and Dismal made a run for one in his capacity as a sniffer dog, but when threatened by a cowboy boot with glinting spurs, he ran after me to the door, changing his mind about whatever he knew to be in the man's pockets. He was learning fast, and I sincerely hoped I would break him of such habits before getting to London.

'Fucking dog,' one driver shouted. 'I'll have it on fucking toast if it shows its fucking snout in here again.' Such a crew must have cheered the place up no end, though I didn't suppose bone-idle Charlie buttonholed them with his nirvana of unemployment as they shared their joints with him.

I only felt safe in the car. We steamed along the great dual carriageways of the A5, under streams of orange or white sodiums, with occasional traffic lights to break the monotony. To the south lay the Black Country, a desolate sprawl of industrial ruination and high-rise hencoops. Traffic multiplied, mostly private cars, though a fair number of HGVs were pushing on in both directions. I sometimes thought that most of the lorries and pantechnicons were empty – Potemkin pantechnicons in fact, whose drivers were paid to steam up and down the main roads to persuade visiting Japanese industrialists that the country was in better nick than it was.

I was doing sixty on the inside lane when an armoured juggernaut overtook me at ninety, Mad Jack from Doncaster blasting ten horns as he did so. I watched him for miles weaving in and out of the traffic with a degree of manoeuvrability that could only be done by an artist at the game. He was laughing his head off, I supposed, open shirt showing a tea-stained vest, glorying in his fancy footwork as he told his younger mate to watch how it was done. 'All you've got to do is keep your eyes glued to the rear mirror for a jam sandwich.'

That, I explained to Dismal (in case he didn't know), is the name we road-busters give to a cop car with yellow and red streaks on its side. In the mirror I saw him yawn, bored out of his canine mind, but contented at the same time, while I got us mile by mile along the wonderful flarepath, also keeping a lookout for any jam sandwich drifting up on the starboard bow. If it never got light we would steam happily and forever along this lit-up dual carriageway through the enchanted Land of the Midlands at night.

No such luck. 'Down, Dismal!'

A blue flash worked overtime behind, as if to push me forward because I had strayed onto a runway at London Airport and a 747 was coming in to land. I looked at my speed, but the needle was pegged at sixty. Mad Jack had gone into the distance, so they weren't chasing him. The game was up. 'Get down, you melancholy bastard, or you'll give me away, and you'll be confined to barracks for fourteen days.'

He flopped off the seat, then began to howl at the flashing light, his perfect silhouette unmistakable even from a satellite wheeling in space. There was nothing I could do except stay calm, get ahead, whistle a tune, and wait for the four cops inside their Rover to overtake and slow down till I had to stop as well.

Dismal looked into their car. What other evidence did they need? They swung side-on, and I glimpsed their faces: fresh young lads out on patrol, the cream of the Staffordshire force, who seemed amused when Dismal flattened himself at the window as if pleading to be taken back to his air-conditioned kennel and ten pounds of gristle a day. I had looked after the ungrateful hound like my only begotten son, when I should have left him to live on raw rat and cold water at Peppercorn Cottage.

The jam sandwich slid ahead and was lost in other traffic. It seemed obvious, as Dismal lay on the seat and sobbed himself to sleep (or maybe it was indigestion after scoffing fish and chips, lemonade, chocky bars, several dishes of tea and three Eccles cakes), that they had got my number, if not my name and, radio communications being what they were, could afford to wait in a darker spot a few miles ahead, or pass me on to some of their more boisterous mates in Northamptonshire when I turned south for London.

But at this late stage I began to consider whether they really were after me. One of the coppers who had raided Peppercorn Cottage, on going in to search the dresser, had called out that there were only four boxes. At the time I thought maybe the rats had eaten one, but then the inspector answered that there should be five, and I was so numbed by their presence that it never occurred to me to wonder how he could have known what number there were. My brain, if it could be called one, spun like a millwheel. Questions came along on a conveyer belt like cars with one door missing. Who told them there were five boxes? There had been ten, until Peter and John – Peter and John, my arse! – paddled away with their half share in the canoe. The police had parked at the top of the slope and no doubt trained their binoculars to watch them paddling away, and only then came down to frighten the guts out of me and make off with the other five handipacks.

The only explanation was that the lads who had pinned me against the wall at Peppercorn Cottage hadn't been policemen at all. If they had, they would have left no roadblock unmanned to get their purloined dog back to base. To lie, perjure, resist arrest, even steal and murder, or hijack one of their cars and drive it the wrong way up and down the M1 shouting obscene defiance through their radio so that even the policewomen operators back at base shivered with rage and horror, was all part of the game, but to drive off with a superbly trained and well-nurtured poodle was asking for trouble. The fact was that the Peppercorn Cottage task force had been as much hoaxers as those two canoeists who had made off with their share of the loot half an hour before.

I turned left at the Cross-in-Hand roundabout for Lutterworth, and went over the M1 knowing that soon I would have to find a suitable parking place and bed down for a few hours, unless I wasn't to nod off at the wheel and wake up to find a policeman at my hospital traction-cot threatening to turn off my life-support machine if I didn't talk.

There was never anywhere to stop on the twisting arterial lane without fear of being hit from behind, so I drove on, always expecting to see something interesting around the next corner, such as trestle tables under colourful medieval awnings, laden with real food served by nubile wenches. Instead, I barged into a grim pub, and was stared at by drinkers who went silent at my advent. Even the one-armed bandit, a coin already in and the handle pulled, stopped working while the surly and ulcerous landlord asked what I wanted. I debated taking Dismal a tin of beer, but settled on lemonade, a bag of onion crisps and some peanuts. He certainly appreciated the attention I paid him, but it wasn't every day that I had a fully paid up member of the police force in my car.

Rain slowed me down, and the hypnotic rhythm of the wipers lulled me perilously. I rubbed my eyes so hard I almost mashed them back into my head and lost the sight of them altogether. When I switched off the engine and headlights beyond Corby, the sound of rain pounding on the roof was comforting. 'Dismal,' I said, 'we're on the loose. You've been abandoned by the world, but I'll look after you. As for me, if I survive explaining to Lord Moggerhanger how I let his precious packages slip through my fingers to the wrong people, I'll live forever, or for as long as makes no difference.'

A passing car lit up our habitation. Dismal yawned, and I let us both out, hoping dog piss wouldn't burn the rubber off the tyres. We farted, and got back inside. Dismal slept on the spare seat in front, while I stretched my legs in the back.

Twelve

Dismal's tongue felt like wet pumice on the back of my neck, and I came out of sleep as from a near fatal wound that needed a decent period of convalescence before I could consider myself halfway ready for the front line. I pushed him away. 'It's too early. Leave me alone.'

Crimson rags of cloud did not inspire me to be on the move, and for springtime it was as cold as winter. I lit a cigarette, glad I didn't have to share it with anyone, though Dismal looked as if expecting a puff. We weren't in the trenches yet, so I refused. To get him out of his sulk I threw a few scraps onto a sheet of newspaper and while he gobbled I looked at the map and listened to the weather forecast, which again was rattled off so quickly that I understood nothing, though perhaps I didn't want to, because today would be the day of reckoning, and the future state of the heavens seemed irrelevant. No matter how much I dawdled down the A1, I would be face to face with Moggerhanger by the end of it.

I was happy in a manic and probably dangerous kind of way, as I walked along the road breathing deeply. To the wonder of passing motorists I trotted back to the car and jumped up and down a hundred times to get my sluggish blood flowing. Rummaging in the boot, I found a length of rope. Did Moggerhanger keep it so as to hang himself when news of his financial collapse came over on Radio Two? Or was it to strangle somebody else who had displeased him by losing a valuable consignment of drugs? I looped it through Dismal's collar and took him for a walk, but it was too muddy underfoot to go far. He saw a rabbit, and almost pulled me face-down among the primroses and wood sorrel. A pigeon broke cover and climbed over the sheen of a bank of bluebells.

We floated down the ramp and joined the A1, and Dismal gave a half smile as I moved to the outer lane and overtook a macadam-breaking juggernaut. The sun polished my unshaven face through the windscreen, and instead of enjoying my run down the eighty-mile funnel to the Smoke I sweated at the prospect of getting there. Freedom ends where responsibility begins – or so I'd heard – but I would much rather have stayed in the muddy wood listening to the collared dove warbling mindlessly for its mate than come up against the Moggerhanger gang. In my feckless way I had fallen into the same mess that had forced Bill Straw to take refuge in the rafters of Blaskin's flat, and little did he know that I might be joining him.

Insanity was my companion and I stopped in the next layby to consider the feasibility of driving to Athens or Lisbon. Even if I didn't put the idea into operation, at least I would be delayed half an hour thinking about it. I stared at the map till its colours sent me boggle-eyed, then threw it flapping into the back, where Dismal, thinking it was some kind of toy, chewed it into tatters.

I tied him to the post of a litter bin while I walked up and down. All I lacked was Napoleon's hat and Caesar's sword. Lorries on the inner lane honked as they passed what seemed to be a man pushing a motorbike along the hard shoulder. To me it might have been a Japanese samurai on horseback – or on somebody else's back – till denser traffic cut the spectacle from view, and whatever it was had shinned up the bank to safety. The life of the road went on.

Not wanting to leave the layby, all I could do was reflect on the idleness which had afflicted me since birth. The few jobs I had taken since quitting school at fifteen had only been ways towards not having to work at all. Even in those days I considered it my duty not to deprive a fellow human being of regular and paid employment. To be without work was, to me, as natural as having work seemed to nearly everybody else, so I never wasted time making a decision on the matter. I had no conscience, because not to work was hereditary rather than acquired. I hadn't had the example of a father going out in overalls every day, which in any case would have convinced me as nothing else that I would never be so daft as to take on such drudgery myself. And seeing my mother go to work at the factory – though she had done it cheerfully enough – merely told me that no one ought to be subjected to it.

On the other hand, I sensed that it would not do for me to encourage anyone else to follow the same course into idleness. Somebody had to work and at the moment, thank God, a lot still preferred to. I had never wanted society to disintegrate into a state of chaos, because if I happened to be around I might get pulled in to help when the whole show needed rebuilding.

Before I could climb into the car I was transfixed by the apparition of a man in a blue forage cap with flowing hair and a dayglo orange cape pushing a laden pram along the hard shoulder towards the layby. A pennant said POMES A MILE EACH, and as he came into the space which seemed rightfully mine, with the tinny wail of music from a transistor, I saw that on one side of the pram had been aerosolled: POETRY COUNCIL ART-MOBILE and on the other RONALD DELPHICK'S ARTE-FACTORY. A huge black-and-white panda-doll in the pram looked as if it hadn't had its nappy changed for a week, and Dismal went into a frenzy of barking, pulling at the rope as if the panda's rotund guts were packed with the choicest hash.

'Call your tiger off,' he said. 'That panda is my living. And I'm very nasty when I'm roused.'

Dismal seemed to understand, and came away.

Delphick wiped the sweat off his face and parked his contraption behind the car. He sat on the ground, opened his cape, spat, shut his eyes, spread his arms and went into a rhythmic muttering, swaying back and forth. A deep grumble came from his stomach and he sounded like a gorilla trying to get at his loved one in the neighbouring cage. He had little bells on the ends of his fingers, but much of the sound was eliminated by passing traffic though Delphick, to his credit, didn't seem to mind.

The name was familiar, and so the face might have been, except that over ten years had passed since Blaskin and I had stumbled into one of his Poetry Pub readings. I'd heard of him from time to time, when his antics hit the papers, as when he threw a heap of bedding from the visitors' gallery in the House of Commons, which he said to reporters afterwards was intended to signify his blanket support for the IRA. No doubt he had moderated his opinions from those days, otherwise he wouldn't have got so many grants from the Poetry Council, unless they had made them only to keep him quiet.

He stood up, looked at the sky and yawned. 'That's enough of that. I've done me mantra.'

'How often do you do it?'

'Morning, noon and night, I give the Gods a fright. Night, noon and morning, I give them another warning.' He looked at me: 'Three times a day to you. Haven't I seen you sometime before? I never forget a face. You're Gilbert Blaskin's son. I saw you in that pub, when I was pumping a plump popsy's pubes – or trying to. I'm allus trying to.'

'That was ten years ago,' I said.

He closed an eye. 'It's ten days, with my memory. I'm cursed with total and immediate recall.'

'Lucky,' I said.

'Ain't it? Do you want to buy a poem?'

'What sort?'

His beard, and mane of black hair streaked with grey, swung around his face. He was about my age, but looked twenty years older because I was short haired and clean shaven. 'There's only one sort of poem,' he said. 'A poem-poem, a panda-poem, a polysyllabic pentameter poem. A Delphick ode, if you like.' He moved his panda pram a bit further from Dismal's frothing jaws.

'How much is it?'

Quick as a flash: 'What can you afford?'

'Fifty pee?'

'Drop dead. "Poems a mile each clean the mouth with bleach, though poems a killer-meter might sound a bit sweeter." That'll cost you a quid. I've got to have some toast with my tea. I ain't had breakfast yet, and I've been pushing me panda pram all night. You want me to whine? I'll whine if you like. Haven't you ever seen a poet whine, you well-fed, Rolls-Royce-driving millionaire swine? What's a quid to a well-fed underbled chap like you? That angry young man peroration will cost you two quid. I'd like a Danish pastry as well.'

I laughed. 'You won't get a penny out of me for a poem, but if you like to chuck your panda-contraption in the boot I'll give you a lift to the Burntfat Service Station and buy you breakfast, which I suppose will cost me more than a couple of quid.'

'I knew I could rely on you,' he said. 'If I remember rightly, we're working-class lads together, aren't we?'

'Listen,' I told him, 'any of that working-class crap and you and your pervert panda will spill straw all over the highway. Don't "working-class" me. I've never worked in my life, and neither have you.'

He looked at me through half closed eyes, while we lifted the pram off the oil-stained gravel into the boot. 'I'll talk to you after I've had my breakfast,' he said sullenly. 'The panda's hungry.'

I pressed the belly button, but it didn't squeak. 'What's

inside?'

'It's none of your business.'

Dismal insisted on sitting beside me in the front. 'I don't think he likes me,' Delphick remarked, when I wove through the mêlée of traffic.

I adjusted the mirror, flicked out of place by Dismal's tail. 'It takes him a long time to get to know people. Have you seen June lately?'

'Not since last year. It was a lousy wet month, if I remember.'

'I mean the girl you got pregnant in Leeds, and then left to fend for herself in London. She worked at a strip club to support herself and the kid. A little girl, wasn't it?'

I saw that half his teeth were bad when he laughed. 'There've been about five hundred others since then. You can't expect me to remember every one. I've got to do something in my spare time. You can't write poetry twenty-four hours a day. One of these weeks I hope to get married long enough to drive the wife into a loony bin. I'll never be a great poet till I've done that. Unless she's got a lot of money, then I'll have to watch my Ps and Qs.'

I wanted to set Dismal onto him, though I knew he wasn't as bad as he made himself out. 'I thought you had total recall?' But he didn't answer. 'What are you going south for?'

He took out a packet of cigarettes and didn't offer me one. I reached for my cigars and he put his cigarettes away. I didn't offer him a cigar, so he got a cigarette back from his pocket and lit up. 'I'm on tour,' he said. 'I've got a gig in Stevenage tonight. I'm on a POEMARCH to raise money for a new mag, so I stop at every place to give a reading. The mag's going to be run by the CIA – Community, Information, Arts. Some of it's going to be poems – my poems under different names. The first issue will have a hundred pages. There'll be a psychological analysis of the fiction of Sidney Blood and the difference between his influence on the working classes and the middle classes. Then some previously undiscovered poems from Bokhara by Ghengis Khan, each one a mountain of skulls made up of the word Delphick in tiny writing written by a German poet and translated by me. Chuck in a few Panda Poems, and there you have it. Maybe I'll get a slab of the latest book Gilbert Blaskin is working on. His stuff's real rubbish, but his name might sell a few copies.'

'He's writing somebody's life story at the moment.' For one dizzy second I saw a way of embarrassing this man who made my immorality look like the minor transgressions of a Sunday School teacher with TB.

'Whose?'

'Moggerhanger's.'

Dismal snapped at Delphick's hand, so that he dropped his cigarette. I punched Dismal and told him to behave in front of guests.

'Lord Moggerhanger's?'

'Why not? A chunk of that should look good beside the poems of Ghengis Khan.' Back on the inside lane, a couple of lorries walled by. 'What are you going to call your magazine?'

'Drop dead,' he said.

I didn't think I'd offended him. 'Fuck you,' I retorted.

'No,' he said too mildly for me to think we were arguing, '*Drop Dead* is what I'm going to call it.'

'A good title,' I said.

He pushed a form under my nose. 'Sign a subscription form. Ten copies for fifteen quid.'

I screwed it up and threw it out of the window. 'Come back next year.'

He didn't seem to mind. 'I'll have the best table of contents any mag ever had to start off with. Every item the epitome of spontaneous art.'

'How's the fund-raising going?' I passed Dismal a crisp from the glove box.

'Awful. But I've got a grant from the Poetry Council, and some money from the CIA. It ain't enough, because I need to decorate my house at Doggerel Bank in Yorkshire, and that'll cost a bob or two.'

'I thought it was all for the mag?'

'I'm starting a poetry museum in the parlour of Doggerel Bank, so some of it's got to go on that. I'll need central heating, for a start. There'll be an enormous plastic bowl for the public to slot money into as contributions for its upkeep, like in the Tate or the Royal Academy, and if they're cold it'll make 'em stingy. But with the old CH purring away they'll give everything they've got.'

I shut up, out of admiration.

'I'm only telling you all this because you aren't a poet yourself. Or a journalist. Tonight I'm giving a reading at the leisure centre, me and the panda. I might make a quid or two. I charge one pound fifty entrance fee, only I don't let anybody in. My poems, and Panda's, have to be spoken to the empty air. People's auras would spoil it. But they can hear us from outside, and they can applaud if they like. That's allowed. The door's locked though, and that keeps it a pure experience. Poetry is for space, the spice of emptiness. Emptiness eats it up, regurgitates it into the atmosphere so that it gets back into people in its purest form. They might not know it – how can they, the bourgeois pigs? – but it sweetens their soul. A single ear inside the hall when I'm speaking would desecrate it.'

'They should kick the door down,' I said.

'Then I would read my poems silently. You've got to let 'em know that poet power rules. Otherwise, what's life all about? Most of the time I'm at Doggerel Bank, but every so often I go on a Panda Tour to a different part of the country. It gets me out of myself. Doggerel Bank's very cut off. Do you want to come to my reading tonight? I need all the audience I can get, but don't bring the dog. They've had plenty of advance warning at the centre, so there'll be lots of fab women lined up to meet me. I sometimes end with two, and copulate to the rhythm of coryambics. "Them Greeks knew a thing or two, but you never reach the end of an ode/come in the middle of a line/like dying out of life/halfway through." '

He scribbled on a piece of paper, unable to speak for a few minutes. I was tempted to tip him onto the next layby, but unfortunately I'd promised him breakfast. When he looked up he was snuffling with emotion: 'Is it far to The Rabid Puker?'

'I don't know.' The sky in front was covered in broken jigsaw shapes, pieces of white and crimson cloud, with blue between. The light was orange and ominous. A car behind tried to tailgate me, but I pulled away with ease. Delphick snorted, a dead cigarette stuck to his lower lip.

I got the tank filled at the petrol station, then followed Delphick into the plastic dining palace. 'What do you want?'

'I'll start with a double whisky,' he said. 'I've been perished all night.'

'You'll have the basic meal, and pay for your own extras.'

He picked up the menu card. 'Bingo Breakfast, love.'

'What's that?'

'Full house.'

'Make it three.' Dismal had stayed in the car. Delphick grabbed the waitress's wrist. She was a lovely young blonde with a fine figure but a very sarky mouth. 'Do you want to buy a poem for fifty bob?' he said.

'You must be joking.'

He wouldn't let go. 'They make a lovely birthday pressie. Or a thoughtful wedding gift.'

'If you don't leave me alone I'll call the manager. I hate this job.' She looked at me. 'Tell the tramp to let me go.'

'Let her go.'

'Bollocks,' he said.

She glared, as if I was worse than him. 'I wish people like you hadn't got such soft hearts. You're allus picking deadbeats up and bringing 'em here for a feed. I can't understand what you get out of it. Makes you feel good, does it? Why don't you leave the dirty old bastard to die on the hard shoulder?'

Delphick's eyes softened with tenderness, but he had an iron grip.

'Look, crumb,' she said, 'stop it, or I'll call the manager.'

I was fed up. It was too early in the morning to tolerate unashamed con-men like him. 'If you don't let her go, I'll smash you in the teeth.'

He looked at me, as if to start a fight, then released her. She went to the counter with the little order pad swinging at her arse. 'The trouble with you,' he said, 'is that you don't understand the courtship ritual.'

'Neither does she,' I told him.

He took the top off the sauce bottle and swigged a mouthful, and a few driblets at his beard gave him the look of a vampire at dawn. 'I've been through the subtlety stage and, on balance, I get a few more successes by the direct approach. In war the indirect approach is best, but love is the opposite of war. Have you ever read the *I Ching*? Mao swore by it. He wouldn't have done the Long March if it hadn't been for the *I Ching*. But in matters of love, or lust, women get just as fed up with subtlety as men. A straight yes or no saves time. They're too busy these days, most of 'em going out to work and keeping men just to show they're more equal than we are. Lovely. So long as you say you love 'em you can just get straight in.'

I realised how much I'd been cut off in my ten years at Upper Mayhem. It was like listening to myself in the old days. I'd learned though, but Delphick hadn't, and I taxed him with it while waiting for our grub.

'I could learn if I liked,' he claimed. 'It's not beyond

me. But if I learned too much I might get no more inspiration – as a poet, per se, see? You've got to be careful, because poets don't get pensions. If they did, it might be different. Some of the eighty-year-old versifiers might well want to pack it in, but they can't.'

'I thought poets got good money, these days.'

He looked like a poxed-up old pirate. 'They earn a pittance now and again. There's all kinds of spin-offs, like grants, and talks, and performances, and editing, or anthologising when you use all your mates' poems and expect them to pay you back in kind for years to come. Then you might do an odd review and cut your enemies to bits; or you can waffle on on the BBC about a new working-class poet you've just discovered but who's blind, eighty, and lives alone on a wet hillside in Cumberland with his dog – but whose poems you've written yourself. It's not easy, but you can pick up a bob or two. For itinerants there used to be workhouses, now there's local arts groups if you want to go on tour. All you've got to do is write letters, and plan it well. I can write forty letters a day when I'm in full spate.'

'That sounds like work.'

'Well, it's better than filling in holes on the motorway. I never let work become a burden, though.'

The waitress put three plates of breakfast and three pots of coffee on our table. Delphick locked onto her wrist again, but she snapped it free and stood out of reach. 'If you do that once more, you mangy fucking tomcat, I'll pour a pot of boiling water over you. I will. I promise.'

'That's the stuff, miss.'

I took a plate of breakfast to Dismal. 'Wake up,' I said, opening the car door. His eyes widened, and a long purple tongue slid over an egg and drew it in. He paused, being a dog of good manners, and pressed his Button B nose against the back of my hand. I patted him a time or two, then left him finding his way around a piece of fried bread.

I got back inside to see Delphick three-quarters through the second plate of breakfast – mine. 'Hey, you bastard!' I pulled it away. 'Keep off my grub.'

He yanked it back without looking up. 'I thought you'd gone outside to eat yours. Anyway, you can afford to buy two.'

I prayed for boots big enough to make an impression. 'I don't own that Roll-Royce. I'm only the chauffeur.'

A lorry driver sat at the end of the room. 'Next time I see his contraption on the road I'm going to drive all twenty-four wheels over it. He's a right pest, he is.'

Delphick kept his head down and wiped up fat with a folded piece of bread. I went to order another breakfast while my coffee got cool. 'If that poet comes in here again,' the waitress told me, her dazzling green eyes looking directly into mine, so that I saw in even more sensual detail the delights of her undressed presence, 'I'm going to put rat poison in his grub, even though I swing for it. He don't respect anybody. And I like to be respected.'

'Why don't you put it in now?' My hand was at her waist, and she didn't push it away. 'You don't swing for murder anymore. The most you'll get is eighteen months, for aggravating circumstances. It's worth a try, don't you think?'

She smiled. 'I'll have to think about it, won't I?'

'What's your name?'

'Ettie.'

'I like that.'

'I'd have cut my throat if you didn't.'

'You are sarky, aren't you?'

'Sometimes. What's your name?'

'Michael. Do you want a drive in a Rolls-Royce to London?'

'Not if it isn't yours.'

'It'll be a lovely smooth ride.'

'I'll have to think about it.'

Maybe she thought a lot when she wasn't dishing up grub – which was most of the time. Her thoughts had to be short, though, which was the best kind to have, because they didn't take up much precious time. Neither did they keep her from action, I assumed. She was the sort of girl I liked, and couldn't have been more than twenty-three.

As a breakfast I could only compare it with the one from Bridgitte the morning I got out of prison. Perhaps because I had taken her part against Delphick, Ettie piled on bacon, two more eggs, beans, tomatoes, four slices of fried bread and half a tin of mushrooms. She either bribed the cook or she was having an affair with him. If she was, she wouldn't be for much longer if I had anything to do with it.

Delphick's eyes bulged with envy at the sight of my plate. 'Did you put grease on her nipples?'

I pulled him up by his coat and held my fist the requisite few inches from the bridge of his nose. It stayed there for ten full seconds. He didn't struggle or say anything, but turned whiter with each tick of the clock. I pushed him away, and he barely righted himself when the chair fell. 'Get that panda out of my car before I set the dog on it.'

He went, such pain and hurt pride on his face that only now did I think he was real. I didn't like him, because he was spoiling the day by making me feel sorry for him, and now making me feel guilty at an over-hasty reaction. But he'd insulted a woman, and I hated that, though I suppose I should have been cool and taken it like a man.

I sat down to eat, my appetite not entirely spoiled. In fact it returned, the more I put back. I hadn't realised how famished I was. I drained the coffee pot, then ordered another, and two Danish-style pastries. 'You're hungry,' Ettie said admiringly.

'I can't help it. It's you that's doing it. The more I look at you, the more I want to eat. And you know what that means?'

She blushed, the little trollop.

'I'm six foot two and weigh a hundred and sixty pounds, but if I lived with you, and you kept on feeding me like this, I'd weigh as much as Ten Ton Tommy. They'd have to lift me on and off with a block-and-tackle, but I don't think you'd be disappointed. I shouldn't talk like this, I know, but I'm only having a bit of a joke, though I was quite serious when I said you're the best-looking and most vivacious woman I've seen for a long time. You really are. I respect you enormously. I'm often up this way, so I'll stop more often on the road and say hello, if that's all right with you.'

'I don't mind,' she said. 'Only don't bring that fucking deadbeat ponce with the panda-wagon. I can't stand him. He came here once before and we couldn't get rid of him. The man who brought him suddenly took against him and wouldn't give him a lift away from the place. So he fell asleep on the floor. We didn't know what to do. He snored like a hacksaw. Then he woke up and started swearing. We couldn't throw him out because it was snowing. He said he'd phone up the television news if we did. I told him to crawl across the dual carriageway and fuck off to Scotland, but he wouldn't budge. In the end the manager gave a van driver five quid to dump him in Cambridge. But you're different. Do you want any more to eat?'

My early morning hard-on came back, and I thought I'd said enough already to indicate that I had nothing to lose by spouting a bit more in somewhat plainer fashion. 'Do you let rooms here, that's all I want to know. I'd give my right arm and more to be alone with you. As soon as I came in and saw you by the hot water urn I knew I loved you. I wasn't going to say so, though, because it didn't seem right. I respected you. And besides, there's a time and a place for everything, as it says in the Bible. My wife died five years ago, and I made a vow never to make love with anyone again, and as time went on it became easier to keep that holy vow' – I made my voice miss a beat, and held my head as if in pain – 'until I came in here and saw you.'

'I don't believe a word of it,' she smiled, 'but go on.'

'That's because you're a very sincere person. I wouldn't have told you this if I hadn't seen straightaway that you were a very sincere person. What I'm saying is the truth, and I couldn't have told it, except to a very sincere person. You're the first person I've told it to, and I respect you enormously for not believing me. If you'd believed me I would have got up and walked out. There aren't many sincere people left in the world, and now you've certainly made my day. You're busy, I know' – there was no one in now except us – 'but I'd like to talk to you properly, just the two of us, in a private room somewhere, any room where we can be alone.'

My face got closer, and my hands crept around her waist. She shook, and I thought she was going to come out with some filthy language and run, but she held my hand and looked back at me so that while she melted at the touch of my fingers I melted at the crutch and pressed close enough for her to feel what, for better or worse, was coming between us at the hour of our tribulation.

The windows and door of the flimsily built café rattled at the passage of some particularly weighty giant on wheels. I knew the time had come, that it was now or never, so pressed even closer to begin whispering sweet nothings into her pretty eggshell ear, my lips brushing against the plain wire earrings. 'I love you. I want to kiss your lips, suck your tits, and lick your sweet cunt till you come, then sink my prick into you, and grip your shapely arse and push your lovely guts around till my spunk shoots so far up you it comes out of your mouth and splashes against the opposite wall. Oh my sweet darling, I can't wait.'

'Oh, you dirty bastard,' she said. 'Come on, though.'

We leaned by the wall in a little cubby-hole of brooms and mops, and kissed ourselves into a frenzy. It was good to get back to somebody from the working classes (if I could find the right one, I'd always thought, and she was it) boiling for me because she didn't think I was a slum-brat from the working classes. She came with a long moan, assuming I was somebody different (and I suppose I was by now), and then I shot, knowing that she could have been the girl next door, fully grown up, who I used to play dirty games with in the air raid shelter. It worked marvels, and was all the better for being over in a few minutes. Some say there's nothing like a good fuck, and they could be right, but I say there's nothing better than a quick fuck that comes off for both participants.

I asked her again to travel with me to London, and don't know what I'd have done if she had said yes, but I only asked knowing she'd say no. 'Next time I might,' she said. Would I phone and write and call again, and then maybe we'd slowly get to know each other because she had never met anyone like me before. I was astounded and gratified that somebody could know me – or think they did, which was the same – in such a short time, when I'd been living in my own skin all my life, and was nowhere near knowing myself.

I thought, as I went out to the toilets, that you only had a chance of knowing yourself when you were acquainted with a lot of people who said they knew you and acted as if they did. But I also thought what a pity that somebody should fall in love with me, and me half in love with them, when I was on my way to London in a situation where, before many hours were out, I would get into an argument which might leave my face so cut up that Ettie wouldn't recognise me anymore.

I felt as light as air because whatever was supposed to happen could never be said to have happened until it had, and between one and the other was always a wider space and a longer time than you could imagine. I glanced at the wall and saw a piece of paper stuck there, which I thought was something about not hurling your fag butts into the piss channel, but on zipping up and going close I read:

> Ronald Delphick, poet lariot, roped into life with a naval cord, cabin-buoyed to the Wash and the Severn Seas. Yo ho ho on a fat woman's hornipipe. Poetry performance, panda-wise, at Stevenage Leisure Centre half past seven tonight. Admission one pound fifty. Programmes two pounds. Books for sail.

I'd hoped he had vanished, but when I got outside he was wiping gnats off the windscreen with a piece of wet cloth. 'Thanks for the breakfasts. I'm sorry for that bit of bovver in there.'

He seemed different, as if he'd been drunk in the café, or stoned, but was now fully recovered. While I'd been with Ettie he must have had a wash-and-comb-up in the toilet, because he looked cleaner and smarter. I couldn't tell him to walk to Stevenage, so opened the door for him to get in. Dismal dashed out and left a squalid mess by a dustbin. When I looked for his breakfast plate Delphick said he'd already taken it inside. 'I saw that waitress, and she was crying. What happened?'

'It's none of your business.' I passed him a cigar. 'Suck that.'

Dismal sat beside me, and I set off once more into the mainstream of motorised life. We were quiet for a while, Dismal like a statue in front, Delphick like a dummy behind and the panda sticking out of the boot like a waxwork. I didn't feel lively, either, but was otherwise happy. The clouds were white and dense, like those on engravings of Greenland in picture books. I almost expected to see a whaling ship come from behind one, then braked to avoid hitting a Cortina, and swung out to overtake after checking in the mirror that all was clear.

A dual carriageway took us between stunted trees, and in spite of a few attractive laybys I decided to drop Delphick at the slip road into Stevenage, so that he could push in with his panda-pram in appropriate style. The southern weather was better, open sky with few clouds, so neither he nor his cargo of literature would get wet. I told him my intention.

'That's good of you,' he said. 'If you're ever in Yorkshire, you'll be welcome to stay a day or two at Doggerel Bank. There's always a pan of stew on the Rayburn, and a demijohn of elderberry wine. Bring a sleeping bag, though, because I've only got one bed. And a bottle of whisky, if you can. It gets a bit damp at times, but you'll manage all right.'

He meant well. 'Thanks.'

'And a few tins of cat food might be useful.' He couldn't think of anything else, a bad silence because I dreaded the time when I would have to let him off. I wanted to go back and plead with Ettie to come with me, and even for Delphick to stay on, so that at least I would be among familiar faces when the big chop came.

If my depressions ever lasted more than a few moments maybe I would have learned something. But they didn't, and I never had the spiritual constitution to support mental pain long enough either to be destroyed by one, or educated and improved. I always sensed a feeling of regret when I began to come out of the gloom. 'Tell me a poem,' I said to Delphick, 'and I'll give you thirty bob.'

'Two quid.'

'Two quid, then.' I'd have given him five. 'There'll just be time before I put you off.'

He rustled a few papers. 'I'll tell you a love poem.'

'Is that the best you can do?'

'What's wrong with a love poem? Panda and me perform love poems perfectly.'

'Don't you have a funny poem?'

His laugh nearly cracked the mirror. 'There's no such thing. Laughter and poems don't go together. People only buy poems when they cry, or are moved. If I make 'em laugh they just feel good, and walk out by the overloaded table without buying one of my books.'

'Any poem will do,' I said.

He phlegmed out of the window. 'Listen to this, then. It's called "Dusk Queen" – by Ronald Delphick:

'A rhododendron for a rudder
as we steer the wild canals:
slither-lines of silver between black and green.
Geraniums on cottage windows
claw golden glass,
smokestacks pouring eye-shadow
in God's evening glare
grabbing the day and night to work in.
Headstocks of a coalmine draw
cages up at dusk as our barge
between the slag heaps steers its way,
and you on the burnished poop deck
sitting while you play
Gary Glitter on the wind-up gramophone.'

A Capri cut in a bit too close in front, playing his own little game. A Rolls-Royce is sport for everybody, and Delphick didn't notice my smart avoidance procedure. 'I know it's not that good, and that I'm still working on it, but you might fucking well say something.'

'If I had a lady in this car,' I said, 'I wouldn't have given you a lift in a million years.'

'Oh,' he said nastily, 'you're power mad, are you?'

'But I liked your poem. It was better than I thought it would be.'

'Oh, bloody good. Bloody *good.* Now I know why I sweat blood. Just to hear something complimentary like that. You've not only made my day, but you've made my life.'

'I enjoyed it.' Praise cost nothing. 'I was so engrossed you nearly made me have an accident.' The straight dual carriageway was fabulous for speed. I remembered the cluttered and winding ribbon of death on my first motorised trip to London nearly fifteen years ago. 'You really did.'

'A real accident?'

'Another split second and we'd have been a blazing funeral pyre on the central reservation: you, me, Dismal and Panda going skywards in a cloud of soot and flame – and maybe the four people in the offending car as well. A holocaust, in fact.'

'Marvellous.' He scribbled away. 'Go on.'

'There would be a multiple pile-up and a tailback for ten miles, and the sky would reflect ribbons of blue flashing lights, as police cars and ambulances tried to get to us. And if one car's petrol tank exploded, so would the one behind, and the one behind that, and you'd have the domino theory in action right back to York, like Dick Turpin's horse of flame called Red Bess jumping the turnpike gates.'

'Don't tell me,' he screamed, causing Dismal to bark. 'Don't tell me. Now I've got it: "Like the Fifth Horseman of the Apocalypse." That's it. Wonderful. What an image. Delphick does it again. "Dick Turpin rides a horse called Poker Lips through a multiple pile-up . . ." Now you can go on.'

His enthusiasm had dried me up.

'Well, go on, then!'

'Write your own poems.' I signalled to get off the motorway. 'Here's the parting of the ways.'

We lifted his panda-wagon out of the boot, and he didn't thank me for services willingly provided, but then, I was glad to see him go with pennant waving, making progress towards his triumphant reception in Stevenage.

I laid a hand on Dismal's head as we got back to the big wide track. He seemed pleased that we were on our own again and nudged me fondly. I was tired. Composing Delphick's poem had worn me out, making me realise how hard a poet's life must be. A graceful road bridge spanned the motorway and gave a perfect side-on view of a jam sandwich, at which Dismal merely twitched. There was something reassuring about the sight, and in the apparition of a London taxi which overtook me and was soon well in front. I stopped dragging my heels and went a bit faster, thinking it time to show everybody that the Rolls-Royce was still king of the road.

When I overtook the taxi at eighty he flashed me, and Dismal breathed down my neck with full approval at our speed. I floated effortlessly up to a ton and wondered who had been in that cop car crossing the overhead bridge near Stevenage. Moggerhanger had many contacts among the jam sandwich fraternity, and both organisations were interested in my whereabouts, so maybe the cop car had radioed my progress to the metropolis. I slowed down to ninety, not wanting a speeding charge to be the first of many stepping stones to twenty-five years. 'And it is recommended that he serve the whole of the sentence.'

There's some benefit to having a split personality, especially when you have constant access to the most cheerful, positive and optimistic side. That was one of the things Bridgitte couldn't stand, yet if I hadn't had such an easygoing side to my nature we would have been divorced years ago, which maybe was something else she held against me. I felt a vivid and passionate longing to see Sam and Rachel, as well as Smog, but crushed it down as being counter-productive to my scheme of survival. It was no use driving to Harwich and onto the boat to Holland with so much unfinished business in the air.

I slowed down further on the long slope before the island at the end of the motorway and slid into the path of a lorry to get around. The driver didn't like it, so told his mate to sit on the horn, the noise following me the whole way to Hatfield. It was bad driving, to bring such attention to myself. He tailgated me for a while, forty white halitosis headlights burning my neck and almost driving Dismal mad. Then he turned off, so I settled into a sedate trundle on the long grind to the North Circular.

From twenty miles away, on a rise of the road, I saw the sprawl of London. I could smell it, and the car seemed to speed up even though I didn't put my foot on the pedal. Half a hoarding was missing, where a lorry had smashed into it, and a large signpost a few miles further along was so covered in mud it could hardly be read. The pull was definitely on when I got to Barnet, orange sodiums fully lit even though the sun burned bright. I threaded the denser but quick-moving traffic through the matchless boxwood villas of Mill Hill, till I was turning west on the North Circular, passing places I had ticked off a few days ago but which now seemed from another life.

Every traffic light turned green at my advance, and I got into London too early for comfort. I had imagined a night approach, on the understanding that if there was a barney when I handed the car back there would be a chance to vanish like a cat in the blackout. I stopped at every pedestrian crossing to let anyone over who stood within fifty yards of the edge. If a traffic light did turn amber I was pathetically grateful for the favour of being held up.

'Are you going then, or aren't you?' I shouted to one old lady, who therefore felt she must hurry so fast to the crossing that I dreaded her having a heart attack. I should have gone to Delphick's gig in Stevenage, got him to take me on as his manager and press agent (or pander) so as to hold back from London for another few days.

Instead I decided to visit Blaskin's flat, and see how Bill Straw was starving along. I cut into Town on Watling

Street and Edgware Road and an hour later found a parking meter near Harrods.

PART TWO

Thirteen

This is me, Gilbert Blaskin, writing. Fasten your safety belts. Cullen's story has come into my hands, and there's a gap in his narrative which needs to be bridged. It's an unprecedented step for me to doctor an offspring's book, but art ever instills a striving for perfection – and that means in anybody else's work that comes to my always grateful hand. The reason Zhdanov Blaskin hates communism is that if ever it came to power, and I was made minister for culture, I wouldn't be able to trust myself. Knowing there are limits to human perfectibility, especially mine, saves me from committing a multitude of sins against my fellow men. I only wish I could say the same about women.

A few days after seeing Michael Cullen for the first time in months, if not years (how the hell should I know when I last saw my son?) he came in one afternoon and left a creature called Dismal with me. He was in a peculiar mood and I couldn't guess why, except that he was just back from a jaunt around the country on behalf of that bandit Moggerhanger. I hoped he hadn't done anything that would get him in trouble with the police. He kept lifting his eyes and looking at the ceiling, as if expecting God to come down from his Kingdom and help him. It worried me. Then it irritated me. When he wouldn't have a drink because he was driving I really began to worry. I had a ferocious headache after a long night on the town, so had the courtesy to drink his share with my own.

Nor did he stay long enough to change his mind. There's more of me in him, in the manner of obstinacy, than I sometimes like to imagine, and he's as firm in his ways as I am in mine. Though they don't touch at the moment, I expect they will more and more as time goes on. I wondered what he had done to deserve such a fate.

Nor have I any liking for dogs. The hound he left with me, by the name of Dismal, tore a packet of my cigarettes to bits as if he was the wrath of God sent forth by one of those lunatic anti-smoking types. It endeared me to it, nevertheless. I wished he'd knocked the whisky bottle over as well. I put the cigarettes that survived back on the table, thinking that life was too short to give up smoking and that in any case it was just my luck to get cancer if I did. Then I poured another glass of whisky, as a continuation of my afternoon breakfast, and when it had slithered into my stomach like an egg on fire I told myself that this style of life can't go on, something I always say when I begin to feel better, especially after a night out that ended in the police station and in court the morning after.

Down Sloane Street at midnight my car was halfway up a lamp post. 'I have reason to believe you've been drinking,' one of the young lads in blue said.

'Let's breathalyse the bleeder,' said the other.

I was about to deny all knowledge of drink when unfortunately I was sick, which seemed to confirm their suspicions.

'Unmistakable vomit,' said the policeman in court.

'Yes,' said the magistrate, 'you did rather stop a packet, didn't you?' He was a genial old cove, and I'd been up before him often.

'A pint, sir, not a packet,' said the constable.

'Well, a quart, if you like,' said the beak. 'I don't suppose Mr Blaskin has anything to say for himself. He never has.'

I'd been feeling queasy all night in the cell.

'Twenty-five pounds fine, and fifteen pounds costs,' grinned the beak. Then the bloody awful thing growled once more. The beak got panicky: 'Make it twenty-five pounds costs for the dry cleaning. And get him out of here. Quick! Quick!'

It was too late. He called for sawdust, and I could only commiserate. I was lucky to get off so lightly. Realising such behaviour would have to stop, I lit another cigarette and poured more whisky. Dismal walked out of the kitchen and jumped on my knee. I pushed him off, and looked through the mail to see if there was any money. I found a two hundred pound money order for the translation of one of my early novels into Serbo-Croat, which would just about pay for last night's foray. God looks after his own, and writers.

I went into the kitchen for something to eat. Every weekend I stocked up with goodies from Harrods, and though it was only Tuesday, there was nothing left. I gave Dismal a kick. He looked at me reproachfully, and ate a letter – fortunately not the one with the cheque in it. I patted him, sorry I had been unjust to such a clever dog who could get paté and sausages out of the refrigerator, or bread and tinned delicacies from the larder, or my best wine from the cupboard. I would have given a lot to see him working the corkscrew. I have a bad memory regarding the consumption of food, but I knew there should have been more than I saw.

At three o'clock my charwoman Mrs Drudge came in, and it was obvious that she hadn't put on extra weight in the last few days. I daren't say anything about the food shortage, because she was very sensitive about such things, perhaps because of her name. When she came into the living room and complained about the mess, as well she might, I said: 'Where the hell have you been, Mrs Drudge, to let the flat get so untidy? I can't put up with it. If things go on like this, I shall have to dismiss you.'

I suppose I must explain (being a writer) that her real name was Drudge-Perkins, and that she came from a highly respected family. She had a statuesque and severe aspect, and was forty years of age. For a brief period, in her early thirties, she had been my mistress. I say mistress advisedly, because that's what it was like whenever I got her into bed. I'd first met her when I gave a talk at Camp House (Contemporary Arts, Music and Poetry) on 'Art and the People', or was it 'The Novelist and the Moral Crisis of the Age'? She took me to task afterwards (her phrase) on my cynicism, which I called reality, but we climbed into bed before the argument got far, she because she wanted to hear my final views on the matter (I was very subtle and diplomatic in those days, not to say devious), and me because I needed to get to the fundamental parts of her matter. And so things went from bad to better and from better to ecstatic. She was one of the best women I ever had and she wasn't averse to indicating, by her concupiscent frigidity, that I was one of the worst men for her. She was a single woman with a private income, and I rode that one till she offered to give it to me, so that I could nobly refuse, which I did. She did my typing for a while, after the demise of poor Pearl Harby, until I got tired of correcting her myriad mistakes (and her trying to alter my style and take out what she considered the dirty bits but which were tepid pictures of what really flowed through the sewers), and took on somebody else, when she agreed, as she put it, to clean my pigsty now and again. Her flat was in the same block, on the third floor, so she didn't have far to come.

As for her appearance, what can I say, except that I still occasionally slavered over her, though of course, given our somewhat changed attitude towards one another, she was infinitely more difficult to get at. In order to emphasise the dignity of her position, and to show how far beneath herself she was stooping in cleaning up my slops, she never dressed below the standard of a Queen of Hearts out shopping. Her hair style was immaculate though severe, as befitted a personality which she had no intention of changing, even if she had been able to. She wore a conservative tight-fitting expensive dress whenever she appeared, sporting a string of pearls, a bracelet, a ring, and black shoes with a strap fastened demurely over the plump top of her foot with a shiny black button. She must have spent more time getting ready to come up and do my chores than on the work itself, but for the last five years she had never been less than frosty in her attitude to me who, though I have never done anything basically wrong, insulted her to the core by the fact that I had been born.

To say that I loved her would be strictly correct, and to say that she adored me, in her Greenlandish fashion, might also bear a taint of accuracy, but there was part of her which spoke in soft but irrevocable words to the effect that I was an animal to be avoided, and that since she couldn't stay out of my sight she must keep herself as tightly laced as the underwear designs of male chauvinist pigs would allow her to get. We had each other well assessed. My flat became a tiger cage as soon as she entered it, and we neither of us minded because we knew our places exactly with regard to each other. Whenever she found me, at three in the afternoon, in bed with the current girlfriend, or even with my wife, she was as frosty and correct as ever, but I knew she was seething underneath, and she knew that I knew, and sometimes I would ask her to get into bed with us, but she trumped my wicked card by declining in the most polite and civilised manner.

She was the only woman with whom I couldn't win, because we came from the same side of the tracks, but for that reason I could deliver her more painful blows than anyone else. And for the same reason, any blow she aimed at me could have no repercussions whatsoever. She was my perfect companion, and I was hers, but for that reason she would never marry me, and for the same reason I would never marry her. For the same reason again we had a nagging and eternal love for one another. Therefore she was only fit to be my charlady. From her point of view that was the only way she had of punishing me. We had an ideal relationship which it would be base to sully with wedlock. In any case, I was already married. It was not normal and happy, which would have pained her less, but unconventional and very light on my shoulders, which must have been torment to her. We were star-crossed lovers, both hearts walking in different parts of space yet indissolubly linked. I loved her as if she was a wayward brother I could never get to know, and if she loved me at all it was as a sister who had become a prostitute not to earn a living but because she liked it – a sister she could never get to know simply because she had no hope of bringing her back to the path of rectitude.

She went around emptying ashtrays into a plastic bag.

'And how's Mrs Drudge today?'

'Drudge-Perkins. And it's Miss, not Mrs. How's Mr Blaskin, the eminent public figure, this afternoon?'

'Awful. I threw my guts up in court this morning, all over the magistrate. Arthur Cobalt's his name. He's a director of my publishers, otherwise I suppose I'd have gone to gaol.'

'That might do you a lot of good,' she said, as I had known she would.

'Drudge by name, and Drudge by nature. Why don't you say something unexpected? If only there was a spark of originality in you.'

'Gilbert,' she said, 'I didn't come up here to be insulted.'

I lay on the settee. 'Then go back down.'

'No. There is something known as Women's Liberation.'

Being in a foul mood, I laughed even louder than usual. 'Women's Lib? You aren't into all that feminist stuff, are you? Or did you only hear it mentioned on Radio Four this morning? You know what feminism is?'

'I don't want to know.'

'I know you don't. I'll tell you. It's a lesbian trick to get black women into bed.'

She staggered, and gripped a heavy glass ashtray, and for one dizzying moment I thought she would have the guts to throw it. I often thought we'd end up murdering one another, supposing in the same breath that there were worse ways to go. But I had said too much. I could see it in her face. I touched her wrist but she snatched it away as if I was a walking hot poker. 'Sorry I said that, Drudgy. Feminism is the noblest movement of the century. I'm all for it.' All I wanted was to get down to writing Lord Moggerhanger's life story, or add a few paragraphs to my thirteenth novel, or crash off another couple of pages of the latest Sidney Blood exploit, which I was doing for an outright fee for Pulp Books.

'Mrs Drudge,' I said, in my Noel Coward writer-in-his-country-house-blithe-spirit-and-all's-right-with-the-world tone, 'would you be so good as to get me something to eat? I'm going into my study to work.' I stood up and, unfortunately, farted. 'I think I've got a novel coming on.'

Dismal watched us, like a nonentity at a tennis match.

'Mr Blaskin,' she said, 'this kind of behaviour isn't worthy of you.'

I smiled. 'All's fair in the sex war. I'm eternally grateful to Women's Lib for bringing it out in the open. Now I can really have a good time. It was so dull before.'

Stop, I said to myself. Write, don't speak. It was too late. She had decided to retaliate. 'You should get married to a nice young man and settle down.'

'I would, but women fit me better. Not that I haven't done a share of bum-fucking in my time, men and women, come to that. After all, I'm a proper Englishman, even though I don't spy for Russia. Especially when I was in the army, though we were only lads then, but I prefer to fuck women because they've got tits and, in general, nicer faces. Would you like to suck me off? I haven't had a gam for a long time. Not that it'll do me much good. I think I've got homeosexual tendencies more than the other sort.'

I had gone too far, which was just as far as I wanted to go. She huffed into the kitchen, and I went into my study. 'If you want to bring yourself off,' I shouted, 'don't use the coffee grinder. You broke it last time.'

Peace – but did I want it? I closed the door, then opened the rest of my mail. There was a letter inviting me to take part in a conference entitled 'Is the Book Doomed?' and calling for a quick answer. I didn't know whether the book was doomed, but I felt that I was. Domed, at any rate, but I couldn't tell them so without being impolite. I picked up the phone and sent the cheapest telegram I could devise. CAN'T COME BLIND DRUNK BLASKIN.

A letter from my publisher wanted to know what I would call my collected works he was foolish enough to think of bringing out. I scribbled a note to say he should call it The Dustbin Edition, to be printed by the Misprint Press, and sold at the Throwaway Bookshop. He didn't know that the only occupation a madman can follow is that of writer.

I'd had enough of letters for one day. All the income tax demands and bills were thrown into the paperbin for Dismal to play Post Office with, which left practically nothing, and that made it seem as if I had already done some work. To show willing, however, I looked at the electric typewriter, and noticed that the letter H had been popping up unbidden lately, in such a way as to suggest – which had probably been true – that I was drunk: 'It sheems as if I shtruck shomething shinister in the shcheme of thingsh.' I pulled the paper out and sent it flying after the bills and postcards, then picked up my favourite ballpoint and got to work on Moggerhanger's life, able to do so after a few days of nattering to various scarfaced Soho doorkeepers. The only way to begin was to reconnect the Trollopian tubes and sail in with no concessions to diplomacy precisely because the evil old windbag was paying me well:

> Serf Moggerhanger who followed his knightly master in the Crusades to Jerusalem unknowingly made a fire with part of the true cross. He was known as the master cross chopper, until the Infidels caught him one night doing the same to the crescent, so they sent back his head in a bucket. Sailor Moggerhanger went to the Spanish Main, returned with a sack of loot and two golden earrings. He also came back with a wooden leg – somebody else's. Soldier Moggerhanger went to Flanders in the wake of Uncle Toby, and swore more horribly than anyone else. Moggerhanger was a footpad, otherwise known as Muggerhanger, because he mugged and was hanged. Another Moggerhanger robbed on the highway, a handsome devil whom the ladies (and some of their dandies) loved. Ned Moggerhanger of Calverton broke machines, but he broke the wrong one, which was a device for dispensing small beer in greater quantities than had hitherto been thought possible, for which he was strung up on a greenwood tree by the weavers. Another Moggerhanger fell from the high tower of a church while stealing lead. His son enlisted and became a trooper in the Light Brigade. He rode into the Valley of Death, and came back with gold coins chinking in his pockets, and the teeth of a Russian gunner embedded in his fist. Sergeant Moggerhanger (a cousin of Crimean Moggerhanger) went to the Northwest Frontier of India, raping and looting, and made a tobacco pouch from a virgin's pap. Constable Moggerhanger of the London docks took bribes, and went blind in one eye from too much drink. The crew of the *Narcissus* threw Merchant Seaman

Moggerhanger overboard. When he swam back to the boat, they mutinied. He festered in brothels and learned how to smuggle. In the Great War, Lance-Corporal Moggerhanger got to within ten miles of the Western Front and, hearing the noise of massed artillery, deserted. He was one of the very few who got back to England and was never caught. In other words, he had turned as White as a Sheet, Wiped his face on a Cambric handkerchief, broke his Arrows, said his Amens, and walked halfway home from Passion Dale. He afterwards traded in Nigeria, came back destitute, and went on the Dole. That was Jack Moggerhanger, but Claud, who didn't know whether he was his father's nephew or his son, saw home territory as his prime concern. All in all, it must be said that a Moggerhanger loves his children, his mother, and his country, unless they stand in his way. As for his friends, count me out.

Mrs Drudge came in with a plate of steaming goulash, tinned peas, fried eggs, white toast and a pint of black coffee as weak as licorice water. 'Here comes old grumble-cunt,' I said to cheer her up.

She stiffened.

'Don't drop that tray, for God's sake.'

'You hate women, don't you?'

'Not more than most people. At least I'm not one of those Englishmen who holds his breath when he walks by a woman. I suppose that's the only sort you could really love.'

She drew a deep sigh. It was like water coming up from the deepest well in the desert. If there was one thing I admired it was breeding. I still do. 'I don't want to alarm you, Gilbert, but do you think there are rats in the building?'

'I don't see why there shouldn't be,' I said. 'There seems to be just about everything else. Anyway, you'd be looking at one if I weren't so bald.'

'Seriously, I heard a scratching above my head while I was in the kitchen. Maybe the pigeons have broken in again.'

I scooped up the food with relish, which may not have been good, but it was all I had. 'If I never wonder why you're so good to me it's only because I realise how rotten I am to you.' She flushed, whether with pleasure or pain I did not know. I was the only person in the world who could get either – or both – reactions out of her, and whatever it was, she felt more alive at such times, I swear, than when she was on her own or with other people. And when she had a reaction of any sort I felt waves of lechery rising in me, and having gobbled two-thirds of her execrable meal I put my arms around her fairly broad arse.

She made an effort to move away. 'Leave me alone, you beast.'

I set the plate down for Dismal to lick. 'You know I love you. The only true words I ever speak are those plain unadorned ones which describe my undying love for you.'

'You make it hard for me to believe.'

'Will you type out this bit of my Moggerhanger book? Jenny Potash won't be back from Benidorm till next week.'

'Perhaps I'll do it later – if you promise to mend your ways.'

I put my arms around her, her magnificent breasts against my waistcoat, my lips at her cheek as she turned her head away. 'You're not too old to be a mother,' I spooned. 'Don't you want a baby, before it's too late? Imagine having a son to support you in your declining years, a big handsome chinless wonder weeping salt tears over his O levels? Surely, my lovely one, you must have thought of it, and if so, I would feel honoured if you'd choose me for the supreme sacrifice.'

I eased the zip from the nape of her warm neck to the

valley of her ample bum. Two fingers unhooked her brassiere and my hands closed in front over her hot breasts. From early on I knew one had to be deft with hooks and eyes, and in my youth I had practised for days on a seamstress's dummy to make sure, drunk or sober, I had it off pat.

The muscles of her broad posterior relaxed as her perfume and make-up gassed me into further eloquence. 'Think of a little baby,' I muttered into her ear, pulling her dress forward and her brassiere off. 'All yours to bring up and turn into yourself with a man's face. You'd be the proudest mother by the sandpit, or pushing the perambulator through the park with the most cooing, laughing, puking, shitting little lovely kid you could ever have imagined. But if he picks up a pen, chop his head off.'

'Gilbert,' she exclaimed, 'it's not right to talk like that.'

'Just his hand, then.'

'You're too ghastly.'

'I know, but all the same, I mean it when I say it would be an honour for me to be the father of your child. I love you more than I've ever loved anyone, or shall ever love anyone, in my life. We're so much made for each other that it pains me to be near you. Unless I fuck you I'm burning in the fires of hell. Surely you must understand that, from your cave of ice?'

'I don't want you,' she cried. 'I don't want you.'

I put the three middle fingers of her left hand into my mouth, and laid her right hand against my erection, then put both hands down her bloomers, and found her burning like the inside of a compost heap.

Her protestations of 'Never! Never!' were belied by the state in which I found her. I knew her from of old. She had never wanted me. She always objected, right to the end. Even on this occasion she allowed herself – readily enough – to be piloted into the bedroom, as if I had just cut in on an excuse-me quickstep and we were going towards the refreshment table. I kicked the door in Dismal's face, who had followed us across the living room as if he wanted to be in on the nuptial roundabout.

'I shan't thank you for it.' She lay back, and lifted so that I could draw her bloomers off. 'I shan't thank you for it.' Though she didn't let go of that icy grip on her soul, she was let go of by a demon that was even more deeply in her, and up went her head and china-blue eyes and flickering lashes as she was taken out of herself sufficiently to stop her nagging that *she wouldn't enjoy it or thank me for it if she did.* Did she think I cared whether she enjoyed it or not, as long as I enjoyed it myself? She would certainly not enjoy it if I wanted her to enjoy it, so at least this way there was a chance that she would. I did want her to, though, I certainly did. The lid went off, and as I pumped in for the finals all I saw were her lovely breasts and her gorgeous swan neck, hearing her moans increasing in volume as if the breath was being pulled out of her, while near the end, when her legs would have floated across different continents if she had opened them any wider, the lid went off me as well with such a kettle of steam I thought it would never come back even if I sent a twelve month search party to look for it among my scattered entrails. And, after all, she did thank me for it. And I thanked her as well, which, under the circumstances, was the least I could do.

'I shall never forgive you.' She turned away to fasten her suspenders. 'Never.'

I wiped myself on her bloomers. 'You said that the first time, several hundred years ago. And you've said it every time since. What you mean is that you'll never forgive yourself. Didn't you enjoy it?'

She turned to me so that I could zip up her dress. Such little attentions were worth a thousand bitter quarrels – to her.

'I did not enjoy it.'

I pushed her away. 'You must have done. I heard it. I couldn't help but hear it. They must have heard it across at Harrods and thought another shoplifter had been caught. In fact every time you come it sounds like another execution in Red Square. I've never heard anything like it.'

Her lower lip trembled, but whether in rage or misery I couldn't say. I don't believe she could, either, and I almost felt sorry for her. 'I don't know why I love you,' she said.

'Could it just be that I make you come,' I said, fingers in the armholes of my waistcoat, 'in spite of yourself? Anybody else would take you seriously when you told him you were frigid, and be reduced to wanking himself off on your belly button while you looked on with your cold superior smile. You know, if there's anything I hate you for it's because you make me say what I really feel, and I can never forgive you for that. That's the only weapon you've got over me.' I kissed her again, very nicely I thought, anything to stop her weeping. 'I don't know whether I love you, but you have a fatal attraction for me, and I suppose that's more than I can say for practically anyone.'

She cried like a little girl for about ten seconds. I held up my watch and timed her. I had never understood her, and never would, and that fact more than her distress made me occasionally despise her. 'You should be smiling and happy,' I ranted, 'but you're too mean. You *should* thank me for it. You *should* be grateful. Every time it happens to me my backbone goes to pieces, but I'm still grateful.'

'You're vile,' she said.

'You say that because you only came once. You want to come forty times and fall dead into oblivion, then you'd think you had a good time and say thank you with your dying breath. I don't blame you. But this isn't Swan Lake. It's Southwest One, Knightsbridge-on-Harrods, the great

Middle East emporium. Nothing special anymore.'

She followed me into the living room. I put 'The Blue Danube' on the hi-fi and poured two drinks.

'You know I never touch that horrid stuff,' she said, so I knocked both of them back.

'You're like Messalina, the whore of the Roman world. You're getting above your Sunday schoolteacher self.' I felt an ugly mood coming on. 'And you haven't finished cleaning the place up yet. How much longer do you expect me to tolerate a slut like you?'

She stood straight, and put on her snow-maiden expression. 'I do wish you wouldn't drink so much.'

I went into a knot to prevent myself hitting her. 'Oh, do you? The reason I drink is that I'll soon be dead, and then I won't be able to do it anymore.' I heard noises, a heavy tread. 'Somebody's walking about upstairs.'

She put her hand on my arm, and listened. It stopped. 'There isn't anything. Are you all right, Mr Blaskin?'

'It was those two drinks. Maybe you're right, darling. I ought to go out and get some air. Oh my sweet. I don't want to die.'

She kissed me, as if convinced I was having a funny turn and might well be about to croak. 'Perhaps it would be best. You've done enough work for today, Gilbert. Shall I put you to bed with a hot drink?'

I know, and I've been told even more often than I've told myself that, being a writer, I should know exactly what I'm going to do before I do it, and that I should be aware of whatever I intend saying before I say it. Then I would be able to moderate my action and speech accordingly. Dear reader, believe me when I say that I am that dangerous beast who knows precisely what he will say before he says it, and exactly what he will do before he does it, but says it and does it all the same, to my everlasting shame but instant gratification.

I smacked her soundly across that lovely frosty face.

'Don't nanny me. I don't need you to tell me when I've done enough work.' I poured another drink before she could express her opinion of the wicked treatment I'd meted out. 'And stop gobbling all my food while I'm off the premises. I spent forty pounds on that last Harrods order, and there's practically nothing left. I've had hardly any of it, and Dismal doesn't know how to get in the fridge. No wonder you have such orgasms, eating so much rich food.'

I gripped her wrist as her fist came flying. She would put up with anything but that kind of accusation, and yet who else could be eating me out of home and gardens? It wasn't the cost that worried me as much as the mystery I couldn't solve. If Drudge hadn't eaten it I couldn't think who had.

I splashed around in the bath for a while with my plastic battleships, then scented myself up and changed into a clean suit, throwing the other onto the floor for Mrs Drudge to send to the cleaners. Dismal rummaged amongst it for something to eat – or was it smoke? Maybe I wouldn't send him to the dogs' home after all.

I took some money from my desk, and checked that all credit and club cards were in order. Drudge was having a rather satisfying weep, so I kissed her through the tears till she stopped, then went out, pleased at having given her something to live for, even if only me.

It was a chilly spring evening and I sloped along in boots, a long fawn overcoat, a hat and gloves, towards Piccadilly, afraid to cross busy roads after such a scene with Mrs Drudge in case I got run over. She was too highborn and civilised to send maledictions, but I took no chances on negotiating Hyde Park Corner.

After a single bullet of fire in The Hair of the Dog, I went along Shaftesbury Avenue and slipped into The Black Crikey, where the first person I spotted was Margery Doldrum, who I hadn't seen for a week. She was talking to Wayland Smith, a part-time sculptor who did something to the news at the BBC – one of those left wing intellectuals of the sixties who, unable to grow up, went into the media. Margery, who also worked at the BBC, had been my girlfriend up to a few months ago. She was thirty-eight, a willowy sort of woman, who only straightened up in a wind. At the wendigo sound of the gale she pursed her lips as if to give it some competition. She laid on make-up to improve the look of her skin, but only succeeded in showing an orange face to the world. Her disturbed eyes were probably the result of her experiences with me.

I met her when my last novel came out and she wanted to do something for it on the wireless. She flattered me, in a professional kind of way, so I did a bit of homework and peppered my talk with pallid witticisms trawled from old notebooks, and memorised them so that it wouldn't look too deliberate when I brought them out.

'The trouble with me,' I remember saying, 'is that I've got the sort of mind that considers clear thinking to be the death of intellectual speculation. Consequently I write the best parts of my novels when I don't know what I'm doing.' Other things, either stale or meaningless, were said in such a way as to make her think she had said them.

'How does a writer like you live as well as write?' she wanted to know.

'As you get older,' I said, 'your unconscious comes more to the surface. You're in the lexicographical fire service beating out words with a damp cloth. You realise that guilt is recognising your sins, and you haven't got much time left, so you write rather than live. A novelist has to forget about what the novel is or should be while he's writing one. It's none of his business. That's the only condition in which his art, if that's what it is, can move on.'

And a lot more such bilge. But she loved it – or so she

led me to believe by the serious cut of her lips and her stare at the little black tape recorder. Straight into the horse's mouth, they put it on the overseas programme as well. I invited her to lunch at my club and, two nights later, put on my topee and set out for dinner at her house on Grapevine Terrace in Richmond. The dugout canoe nearly sank crossing the Thames, so I was a bit late. I didn't even want to make love when I got there, but I did, as always, because I knew of no other way of getting to know women. But after making love I was never any nearer to knowing them than I had been before, except in a few cases where the uninhibited response of the woman not too long afterwards was one of absolute rancour. Then the relationship had the virtue of becoming lively. Margery Doldrum had made the first move, something which always disconcerts me, though it rarely happens. I had long made it a rule that if a woman makes the first move I don't follow up, because it means she has problems. But experience has shown that all women have problems, and so have all men, so the rule (as with every rule) seemed rather unnecessary and when Margery made the first move I was not slow in making the second.

From the bar stool in The Black Crikey she pinpointed me with that basilisk eye now so full of healthy hatred. 'Why are you looking at me so hatefully, Gilbert?' she asked with a smile. 'Are you going to drop us a few pearls of wisdom from your tired old snakepit?'

'I'm not playing that game tonight.'

Wayland Smith wore a beard, that National Service uniform of those in early middle age who had just missed the real thing – unless they were young and had a Jesus complex and wanted to be crucified by the Third World, which couldn't afford to do it anyway because wood was too expensive. They would just tie him on an anthill for reminding them of their poverty. If you liked Wayland you could say there was a benign twinkle in his blue eyes. If you didn't you could say he had a malevolent glitter. I was inclined to leave him alone, but since I was in the same pub I was obliged to buy him a drink. 'You have one too, my love,' I said to Margery.

'I'll have a double brandy. Wayland's driving.'

He put his pudgy hand on her thin thigh and opted for a pint of best bitter. Ugh!

If this is living, I thought, I would rather write. 'Have you concocted any good documentaries lately?'

His smile showed a tooth missing, presumably from when he'd asked one question too many. 'I'm doing something on the vulnerability of the British coastline, and I don't mean geological erosion.'

I downed my double whisky-and-dash. 'You mean drugs and gold, and illegal immigrants? I was talking to a waiter about that the other day. Or was it the man from the gas board who came to fix my boiler? My latest novel is about smuggling. I'm on the third draft, so maybe it'll be out before your documentary. And if your documentary's out first it'll help to sell my book. In any case,' I went on, 'how can an island like ours exist without smuggling? The English are a nation of sailors, as well as traders, and that's an unbeatable combination for making money. What luck that the radar coverage around our coast isn't as perfect as it's cracked up to be. Boats come in and out all the time, not to mention light aircraft flying under the radar screen and landing on one of those disused airfields in East Anglia. They don't even need to land. They just lob out a parachute with an attached radio bleeper when they see the beam of car headlights, then fly away back to Belgium. So if you want to interview me for your programme I'll tell you all I know – providing you buy me a drink. It's your round.'

I don't know why he didn't like me. Margery didn't know whether she liked me or not, which was much to her credit. I didn't know whether I liked myself or not, which was slightly less credit to me. When in the presence of some people destruction is the only form of creation. He swallowed another pint. 'I know something you don't know. There's someone at the middle of the smuggling ring who's in the House of . . .'

Margery stopped him. Maybe she was working on the documentary too. House of Lords, my arse. I tried to persuade everybody I met who was in press, radio or television that they should become a novelist. I told them how easy it was to write a novel, though not too easy, and then I flattered them by saying that they had talent, that they were wasting their time in press, radio or television. Many agreed with me, though none gave up their lucrative jobs to test out the truth of my idiotic assertion. I always hoped that one would, but the odds were so great against their having a go that perhaps I was not being malicious after all. I thought that if I tried to persuade Margery to do it, in front of Wayland Smith, who I patently wouldn't try to persuade, I may at least sow discord between them. I lifted my glass. 'You're far too talented to be working for the BBC.'

Wayland jutted his chin.

'No, Margery. I've heard her commentaries, and seen them printed in the *Listener*.'

She blushed under her Damart vest. 'I just knocked them off.'

'They read as if they've been very well polished. That piece about the old lady who was evicted during slum clearance in Richmond was damned good. I'm sure you could write a fine novel.'

'Stop it, Gilbert.'

'Or you could write your memoirs. Why don't you?' Wayland turned to studying the beer pumps. 'That kind of reportage would be just right for you. Your memoirs would be fascinating, the way you'd write them. You'd be certain to get them published by The Harridan Press, or

Crone Books. They publish anything these days, as long as it's written by a woman. Surely you can drum up something about a poor little Richmond girl from Eel Pie Island who inherits a fortune and gives nine-sixteenths of it to the Third World? I'm sure you could. In fact the Harridan Press is doing so well that the last time I saw my publisher he said, "Blaskin, old chap, you'll have to write your stuff under a woman's name. You do quite well, but you'd do far better, and so would I. We'll publish any drivel as long as you find a woman's name." '

I always spoiled it by going too far, but at least Margery was amused, and gave a wonderful and uninhibited laugh that you couldn't imagine her having when you looked at her face in repose. 'You're such a male chauvinist pig I almost think I love you, Gilbert. It's terrible, I know. Yet I don't think you really hate women. You're far too amusing for that.'

The only answer was silence, so I ordered more drinks and Wayland came out of his trance with a scowl. Everyone has to live, and he had a car and a cottage to keep up, and a flat in West Kensington to pay for. I understood that perfectly, but what I disliked was that he confused earning a living with doing a public service, which would have been unforgivable if it hadn't been so amusing. 'He's calling at my place to pick up some papers,' Margery said. 'Why don't you come as well, Gilbert, and have something to eat?'

I was feeling guilty, and a tiny bit disgusted with myself, so thought it a fit mood to go back and do some writing with a high moral tone. 'I'll eat at home – if I can find anything. My charlady's got half a dozen tapeworms, because no sooner do I fill the flat with food than she eats it all up. My whisky's been going, as well.'

Margery dropped me there on her way to Richmond. On unlocking my door, it seemed I'd made a mistake. Absent-minded, but by no means drunk, I'd gone to the wrong flat. There was the sound of music, for one thing, and my place was supposed to be empty. I could tell 'The Nutcracker Suite' anywhere, though I hadn't played it for twenty years. When I looked into the living room I saw this chap sitting at a low table with a feast spread before him of the sort I hadn't partaken of for a month. His jacket was on a chair, and he sat with shirt open and sleeves rolled up, a man with a brazen look and a thin face, hard grey eyes and short hair. Dismal sat nearby, and it was obvious that they were as thick as thieves. The man smiled at me, then threw the dog a goodly chunk of Hungarian sausage, followed by a piece of rye bread which he had shorn off with a carving knife.

'Who the hell are you?'

'I could ask the same about you, my old duck. Bring the bottle of milk in from outside the door, or they'll think the place hasn't been burgled yet and break the door down.'

'I'm asking *you*.'

He smiled. 'Shall I explain, or would you like me to run you through with this kukri-type bread-knife?'

I took off my hat and coat. 'If you're a burglar I'd rather you emptied your pockets and got out.'

He stood and, to my surprise, offered his hand to shake, after he'd wiped it up and down his trousers. 'You've got a lot of nice gew-gaws in here, but I wouldn't touch anything, because I think you must be Michael's father.'

'And you,' I said, 'have been helping yourself to my food. It's a good thing I caught you. I'd intended smearing it with poison.'

'You wouldn't do that to Dismal, would you? Listen, I owe you an explanation.' He poured a glass of Nuits St Georges and went on eating. 'Why don't you get a plate, a glass and some eating-irons and join me?'

It's no use saying I wasn't intrigued.

'My name's Bill Straw, late staff sergeant, Sherwood Foresters. I'm here because I'm a friend of your son's. I told him that the Green Toe Gang was out to cut my throat. So is Moggerhanger's outfit, and Michael hid me in your rafters. It's bloody cold up there, and a bit lonely at night, though your whisky was a help.'

'Why didn't you order half a ton of coal?'

He laughed, in such a way that I couldn't doubt his good nature. 'Next time I will. But seriously, my life's not worth a light at the moment.'

'And I thought I had bats in the belfry, hearing all that to-ing and fro-ing in the roof.' The food was very good as well. He had boiled potatoes, cooked cannelloni, opened ham, laid out sausage, hacked various breads, and made a delicious salad. I was enjoying it more than any food for a long time. 'You certainly know how to look after yourself.'

He rolled up a sheet of ham and threw it at Dismal. 'I'd have made a special effort if I'd known you were coming back.'

'And the wine's good.'

'Best I could find.' He winked. 'They didn't call us the Sherwood Foragers for nothing. I was only going to stay a few more days. I didn't want to impose on you.'

'I'm glad I was made to help.'

'As soon as I step outside I'm a goner. Though you never know: I might beat 'em yet. Life's full of unpleasant surprises. I wouldn't mind if only one gang was after me, but to have Moggerhanger's Angels on my back as well is a bit rough.'

I poured a second tumbler of wine, and at his resentful glance put another out for him. 'What do you know about Moggerhanger?'

He drained his glass. 'Everything.'

'Yes, but how much is everything?'

He crammed a potato into his mouth, but his speech was clear. 'Let me put it this way: I've been involved in all his enterprises for the last fifteen years. There's nothing I don't know about Claud. I'm familiar with all his girlfriends, for a start. I've met his wife and daughter, and his son called Parkhurst who's an even harder case than his father, except that he's bone idle. I know all his clubs – and I mean *all*. You'd be surprised where some of 'em are.' He leaned forward as if walls had ears: 'Moggerhanger has houses from Carlisle to Thanet, from Berwick-on-Tweed to Black Torrington. I expect he'll be training Michael to know where they are at the moment, making him a chauffeur-guide on how to get from one to another by minor roads so that anyone following would be lost within five miles – and there's no such thing as traffic jams. All the places tend to be hidden and somewhat humble from the outside, and often they actually are, though one or two have concealed fall-out shelters, because Moggerhanger has contingency plans in case of a nuclear war to establish a regional seat of gangsterdom.'

As he talked, my pencil went over the paper like a hovercraft back and forth across the Channel on Bank Holiday.

'These hide-outs are places he picked up for a few thousand in the sixties, before property shot up. At his London headquarters he's got a map on his office wall with pins indicating their locations. I have a copy of it. But if you don't mind, I've got to go now.'

He put on his jacket, and belched. 'Thanks for everything. I'm glad to know that Michael's got such a toff for a father, though we did meet briefly at Upper Mayhem, remember?'

'What's the hurry?' I said. 'You haven't had your coffee yet. Nor your brandy. Or Cointreau, if you like. And I have some delicious Jamaican cigars. I had a box of Havanas, but you seem to have finished them. I think we ought to have a long talk about Lord Moggerhanger. I'd like to know what else you have to say on the matter. You strike me as being an observant and self-reliant kind of chap. I'd hate you to get killed when you go out on the street. Moggerhanger's got stalkers everywhere. He'd be bound to know if you skedaddled from this well-stocked haven of refuge.'

I detected a waft of fear over his face as he caught my threat to betray him if he left. He was an unusual kind of chap. With a bit of polish he could pass himself off as a gentleman ranker. 'I see what you mean.' He reached for a box of handmade chocolates. 'Dessert!' he grinned. 'You forgot that. Well, go and sort out your tape recorder, or whatever you use, and I'll put the kettle on for coffee.'

I rubbed my hands. He would as good as write the Moggerhanger book for me, or a big slice of it.

Fourteen

I drove at dusk through the main gate of the Villa Moggerhanger, and didn't feel very good when I looked in the mirror and saw it firmly shut behind me by the garage hand. I had left Dismal at Blaskin's flat and Bill Straw wasn't happy at having a competitor at the trough but, being man's faithful friend, Dismal took obligingly to the parade-ground voice shouting for him to get down. I offered Bill the scraps of food left over from the journey, but he threw them into the trash can with a look of disgust, saying he was taking care of himself quite well, thank you very much, and in the meantime would I like another helping of Parma ham and melon?

On the way from Peppercorn Cottage I had mentally rehearsed leaping from the Rolls-Royce a score of times and fighting for my life, but once out of the car I knew I didn't have a chance of saving myself. I was convinced the yard was empty, but no sooner did I open the car door than Jericho Jim, Kenny Dukes, Cottapilly and Pindarry came towards me. Lights shone from the house, and a set of more callous and incompetent faces I had never seen. And yet, apprehensive as I was, at least I had come back to base and knew I would a million times rather be there than in rat-infested Peppercorn Cottage. 'I hope you've been good lads during my absence,' I said.

'The boss wants to see you,' Kenny Dukes hissed. 'I can't think what for. Maybe he wants to give you a pat on the back.'

If there was something I couldn't take it was the humour of those whose world view was narrower than my own. No retort would have been heavy enough to put him down, so I whistled a fancy tune while walking along the corridor to the door of Moggerhanger's sanctum. Jericho Jim went in to announce me. The boss was smoking a cigar and, dressed in a pinstriped suit and sporting a white flower in his buttonhole, he looked as if about to go out and celebrate his silver wedding with Lady Moggerhanger and the rest of his family at the Kaibosh Restaurant. Cottapilly and Pindarry stood to either side of the door, as if the fools thought I would make a run for it, or plunge a knife into the boss's fat gut. He came from behind the protection of his desk for a better look at me. 'I've got fifteen minutes to hear your account of the trip. Let's have it. But be brief. I want no lies and no trimmings.'

He went back to his desk and sat down. My legs were giving, but there was no option except to stay upright and tell everything – though without mentioning hitch-hikers. When my kitty was empty he opened his desk and held up a slip of paper. I wondered how I should react to such a signal. 'Are you frozen to the spot?' he said. 'Come and get the bloody thing.'

I turned cold. If I moved, would they put the knife in?

'You've done the best job anyone could have done,' he said when I went forward. 'Everything's safe under lock and key, exactly where it should be. I knew you had the steadiness not to panic and do something stupid. Now take this, and go and get some sleep. You look as if you need it. We've had the garage flat tarted up a bit since you left.'

I was staring at a cheque for five hundred pounds.

'Don't spend it all on lollipops and french letters,' he said, 'there's a good lad! You're one of us now, Michael.'

I was going to say I thought I'd kacked up the whole operation, but stopped myself in time. 'I didn't expect a bonus.'

'The best men don't, I've often noticed. But next time don't be so free on the rides to bums who want lifts, especially to that fool pushing a panda-pram up and down the A1. I've passed him many a time. He nearly caused an accident once when I threw a ham sandwich at him.'

Cottapilly and Pindarry sniggered. I wondered if they were holding hands.

'And where's Dismal?' Moggerhanger asked.

I gulped. 'Dismal?'

'That useless dog.'

'I left him at a friend's place.'

'Bring him back. He belongs to my daughter. He was a present from Chief Inspector Lanthorn. He was sweet on Polly at one time, poor old Jack!'

'Can I leave it till tomorrow?'

'You can keep him as far as I'm concerned. But clear out now. You're wasting my time. Wait a minute, though.' I turned from the door to see a smile on his clean-shaven chops. I could smell his aftershave. 'Did the rats bother you?'

'What rats?'

'At Peppercorn Cottage.' His joke wasn't taking effect.

'Not really. But they came a bit tough when I ate one raw. When I boiled a couple for breakfast they tasted a treat, though.'

He laughed, his whole face rosy. 'Not everybody's frightened to death of a few rats,' he said to Cottapilly and Pindarry. 'Those two wouldn't go near the place. Nor would that big soft turd Kenny Dukes. That's another reason I had to send you.'

It was my turn to laugh. 'I'll go any time you like.'

I went out to looks of dislike from those by the door, and unable to believe that the sky hadn't fallen in. My impulse was to run to the bank and get the cheque in before the ricochet hit me between the eyes, though in my heart I knew that Moggerhanger's cheques were as safe as the Bank of England.

I collected my briefcase from the car and climbed the outside stairway to the flat. There was a carpet on the floor, and the bed had been made, a flowered counterpane laid on top. An ashtray had been put down in place of the tin lid on the bedside table, and somebody had left a copy of the Gideon Bible as well as six tins of Baxter's Lager still in their cardboard handpack. On another table, under the window with chintz curtains drawn across, was a pot of plastic flowers. A sailing ship, framed on the wall, ploughed into snowy waves. In the corner was one of those big wireless sets from the fifties. I recognised the home-from-home style of Polly Moggerhanger. Or was it Mrs Whipplegate? Maybe Jericho Jim had been trying his hand at interior decorating, because there was something of a prison cell about the layout.

I wasn't in a state to appreciate it, not having slept properly for days – or weeks if I counted the argy-bargy with Bridgitte before she left for Holland. I opened a tin of beer (it was cold, as if it had recently come out of the freezer. Nice touch, that. Good to feel wanted) and smoked a fag. After being in the car for so long that it had become my skin, I hardly knew where I was. Blaskin would have said I was bemused, such was his talent with words, and I suppose he would have been right. Though it was only seven thirty I took off my clothes and got between clean sheets, sorry that Mrs Whipplegate hadn't been here to welcome me.

One afternoon at the end of April I was called to the house by Kenny Dukes. I'd had so much sleep in the week before that I thought it would take me a year to get back into one piece, yet as soon as I entered Moggerhanger's presence my wits slotted into place. It was a matter of them having to. 'He's sitting in there with Parkhurst,' Kenny said as we crossed the yard. 'So I expect he's organising another operation.'

'Didn't know he was a surgeon,' I said. 'Reminds me of that scene in Sidney Blood when he gets his worst enemy on the operating table.'

'Oh,' Kenny drooled, 'don't it, eh?'

'*The Running Gutter* I think it was called.'

'One of his best.'

'Who's this Parkhurst bloke?'

'His son,' Kenny said, 'by his first marriage. Born with a silver spoon in his mouth and sent to the best private schools – but you wouldn't know.'

Parkhurst sat on the floor with his back to the wall, looking so straight ahead that I thought he was blind. You could tell he was a man of few words because all the time the boss was talking he scraped match after match along the emery until flame crackled into life, and then he would lay each charred stick in the ashtray when the heat got close to his fingers. Maybe he spent more on matches than on clothes, because he wore a shabby grey suit and cheap suede shoes, and a tie that looked as if it hadn't been to the cleaners in months. He might have been good looking if he dressed better, in spite of his lank hair and thinnish face.

'You've been called in,' Moggerhanger told me, 'because we're going up to Spleen Manor, in Yorkshire.' He laughed. 'No rats, this time. There are servants' quarters, what's more, and a caretaker to keep the place warm, so we'll be well looked after. It's near Bluddenden. Work out a route. You'll be towing the horse box, but the Roller will handle it all right.' He looked at Parkhurst: 'This is my son, by the way, unless you thought he couldn't be. Parkhurst, wake up, for God's sake, and meet one of my best men. I wish you'd take a few leaves out of Mr Cullen's book, even if only chapter one – you bone idle bloody skiver.'

I expected a scowl from Parkhurst to indicate that he would like to kill me, but he wouldn't even rouse himself to that extent. Or maybe he'd heard such a spiel too often.

'All you do,' his father went on, 'is idle your time away

around the clubs. You don't even dress properly, though your wardrobe's full of good suits. Or get a haircut. Polly's worth fifty of you. When I was your age I'd been on my own feet for twenty years. I stopped you going to prison for as long as I could, and when they finally dragged you off all it did was give you a nickname.'

Parkhurst spoke in a low voice, as if he didn't want to exert himself. 'Bollocks!'

Moggerhanger winced, and smiled to cover his anger. 'One of these days you're going to get into such trouble that you'll shoot into real life and wonder what you were doing ever to be like this. But I'll tell you one thing: I'm going to stop paying your gambling debts.'

'They're your places I play in,' Parkhurst said in the same dead voice, 'and the tables are rigged.'

There was a pause. 'You can go elsewhere and see if it's any different. If you can't pay up then, you'll soon have no face left. See how you like that.' He changed his tone, or tactics. 'Oh, Malcolm, why don't you wake up? I've got no end of jobs for you. You could be a great help, if you'd decide to do as I tell you.'

The match he threw onto the carpet went out. 'Don't want to.'

'Is that all, Lord Moggerhanger?' I asked.

'Lord-fucking-Moggerhanger,' Parkhurst babbled, as if to himself. 'I ask you!'

'Be ready in half an hour, Michael. Get George to fix the horsebox on, and make sure the inside's spick and span.'

'I was going to bring Dismal back today.'

'He can wait. Polly won't mind. She's in Italy with her boyfriend – though she's supposed to be happily married. What children I've got!'

Parkhurst grunted. 'At least they don't have blood on their hands.'

I thought Moggerhanger would burst. 'But they have

money whenever they ask for it. You'll get no more cash from now on.'

Parkhurst smiled as if he'd heard that one before as well. I left them wrangling. George sat on a garden seat reading the *Standard*. 'Take a dekko inside, Mr Cullen. I've been working on it since five this morning. It's as neat as Montgomery's caravan.'

It may not have been as big, but along one side was a series of drawers and cupboards, their brass handles flush in beautiful mahogany. The top made a flat surface for a desk, or a sleeping place at a pinch, and there was a swivel chair (itself worth a fortune) as well as a small window with curtains, a night cupboard (with no doubt a golden pot inside), a discreet radio rack and a stove and picnic-set under the desk. A map on the wall showed Moggerhanger's properties, and on the table stood a photograph of the family when they were much younger. They also looked happier. Parkhurst, wearing the tie and blazer of some prep school, gripped his father's right hand and looked up at him with a frightening mixture of adoration and panic. Polly stood a foot or so away, smiling widely at something only she could see, but which she knew she would one day get, and it wasn't the camera.

George looked over my shoulder. 'Go on in.' He thought it would be a real treat. The length of carpet on the floor looked as if it had been cut from a precious Persian (to the best of my knowledge). On the wall opposite the table-desk hung a dressing gown on a hanger, wrapped in cellophane. 'Home from home,' I said.

'He could survive in the wilds for weeks. I can't open the drawers for you, because they're locked. He's got guns and fishing tackle, and food to last a while. Not that Lord Moggerhanger will ever need it, but it takes his fancy to think he might have to use it one day. I suppose he's got to spend his money on something. But when it's on tow, go easy on the corners. I'd have a nervous breakdown if anything happened to it.'

Cottapilly and Pindarry put Moggerhanger's luggage into the boot. Mrs Whipplegate, coat on, stood in the yard with a suitcase, and I almost fainted at the thought that she was on the trip as well. 'I have to go, because there'll be some secretarial work.'

I asked how long for.

'A couple of nights, but you can never tell with Lord Moggerhanger. He's thinking of buying some agricultural land adjoining Spleen Manor. Otherwise I'm as much in the dark as you are.'

The car had been vacuumed inside, and polished highly on the outside to double for a shaving mirror. The telephone had been plugged in and the cocktail cabinet unlocked, as if we were going on holiday. Moggerhanger came to the car with a cigar burning. Lady Moggerhanger was like a ghost from ten years ago. Her hair had been black. Now it was grey. She was a good-looking woman in her early fifties but had put on weight. I saw Polly's features embedded there as she held out her hand for me to shake in such a way that I thought she had been practising before a full length mirror since becoming Lady Moggerhanger. 'How are you, Mr Cullen? I heard you were back. You don't seem a day older.'

I said I was very well, and that neither did she.

'Drive carefully. And take care of Lord Moggerhanger.' They made their goodbyes and I got in behind the wheel, noting that the wing mirrors gave fair views to the rear. I was happy that Parkhurst had wriggled his way out of the trip.

By four o'clock we were locked into heavy traffic going towards the North Circular. 'It's the rush hour already,' Moggerhanger grumbled. 'You see 'em going to work at eleven in the morning, and they're on their way home by three. It's no wonder the country's sluicing down the drain. I'm sometimes at it twenty-four hours a day, except for a short nap. I'm lucky to get a round of golf in, these days.'

The horsebox wasn't much of a pull, but on cornering I had to go out a bit so as not to clip the kerb or knock a lamp post. I almost fetched a cyclist off his grid, and the obscenities he screamed through the window sent a reddish tinge over Mrs Whipplegate's liberated face, such an enjoyable sight that I blessed that grey-bearded irascible pushbiker.

'You have to watch 'em,' the chief said. 'I don't mind you cutting up some young blood in a BMW, but not a silly old bastard with soda in his eyes.'

'I'll do my best,' I said.

'Would you kindly pass me a brandy and splash, Mrs Whipplegate?'

He nursed the glass while I did my fancy footwork in order to put a few miles behind us. The sky was dull, but the road dry. You couldn't have everything. By five we'd gobbled a few miles on the same old route to the north. Not long ago I'd steamed down it with Ronald Delphick's Panda Roadshow, and I hoped he'd had a profitable gig in Stevenage, followed by a night-long bang with a bevy of nubile admirers. Some people have all the luck. When I first saw him he was plain Ron Delph, and read a Tube Map anticlockwise, which everybody thought was pure genius in action. But that was in the sixties.

A flick of the wheel and even the Rolls-Royce would concertina if I hit a bridge support at a hundred. But why would I want to do that? You may well ask, because I certainly asked myself. I had left Upper Mayhem intending to lead an honest life. Instead, I had landed a job with Moggerhanger in order to help a friend, and been enrolled to do work which I suspected was crooked to the core. Not that I thought it a valid reason to put an end to things. Life was wonderful, and would go on because I had a job, money, and respect (of a sort) from the man I was employed by. 'Do you think this is one of the best cars in the world, sir?'

'It's not *one* of the best, it's *the* best.' He was in his most bullish mood. 'There's nothing to touch it.'

'What about a Merc?'

He shifted in his seat and peered through the windscreen at a Mini in front. 'Get round him. The Merc's good, but I feel better in a Roller than I do in a Merc, so it must be that much better, eh?' He nudged me, but I stayed straight enough to thread the needle between a lorry and the central reservation. He threw a cigar-end out of the window, and I thought I saw the wheels of the Mini bump over it.

'I buy British, Michael. I'm not a founder member of the British Abasement Society, like so many people today, who go crawling around anybody from the Third World to try and make up for what the good old British Empire didn't do to them. Some people don't know they're born unless they grovel and run the country down in the process. I think we in the old country have to pull together.'

The thoughts of Chairman Mog didn't bear thinking about, but it wasn't my place to say so as we floated north towards Spleen Manor. Percy Blemish stood by the roadside with his thumb in the air, on his way back to Tinderbox Cottage, I supposed, after an unsuccessful foray to look for his wife in London. 'Run over his toes. I've seen him before. He's another nuisance.'

I kept a straight course. Twilight was coming on, that long slow drift into nothingness that marks the end of an English day. Mrs Whipplegate was the queen of her compartment, as long as Moggerhanger cared to be in the cockpit with me. Via the rear-looking mirror I glimpsed her face as often as I dared, that subtle and concentrated line of beauty shaped by a mind engrossed in a novel. I hoped there was some sex in it, and longed for the gaffer to get tired and move back for a snooze. Then Mrs Whipplegate would sit up front with me.

'There's still too much revolution in the air these days,' he said. Somebody seemed to have wound him up, and it wasn't me. 'It's doing nobody any good. Revolution is either for single people or childless couples, and then only as a parlour game. They'd be the first to go to the wall if it did come, as we all know, and as they ought to know but don't because they're too stupid.'

What seemed dead certain to me was that blokes like him would always come out on top. He asked Mrs Whipplegate to pass the food box, and helped himself to a smoked salmon sandwich.

'I know a nice café up the road.' I thought how pleasant it might be to tank up at the place next to Ettie's diner. She'd be pleased to see me back.

'I'm sure you do,' he said, 'but I like to eat my own stuff. Even when I'm going round my clubs I take my dear wife's sandwiches – especially then. London is the salmonella capital of the world. Never eat out in it.'

On drawing level to overtake some rep in his flash Ford he increased speed so as to keep up with me. Moggerhanger pressed the window button and bawled out: 'You fucking anarchist! Jam your shoeleather down, Michael, and then cut in.'

That was the most dangerous thing you could do, and as I was the captain of the ship I didn't do it. 'I'd rather not, sir.'

'I suppose you're right,' he grumbled. I pulled well out in front, then settled back into the inner lane at a steady sixty. 'The roads are crowded with maniacs,' he said. 'I'd go everywhere by train if I could have my own carriage. First class rail is no longer any protection. There's no way to travel on public transport anymore for a man like me. The riff-raff are everywhere.'

My headlights brought the road continually towards the

wheels. I suppose the driver of the Ford was familiar with the area and knew what he was doing. He overtook at speed, shot directly in front of us and went along at about thirty miles an hour. This was a difficult situation. He was determined to hold us up. Maybe he'd had a bad day and couldn't bear to have a Rolls-Royce – plus a horsebox, which hurt him even more – overtake him and stay close on the same road.

'Flash the swine with all beams,' Moggerhanger said, a youth again, who wanted a burn-up and a set-to. I shook my head, edged out and overtook as gently as I could. He tailgated me, two feet behind at fifty miles an hour, all lamps burning, so lighting us up that I felt we were in an operating theatre. 'And that's where he'll be soon,' Moggerhanger growled, 'if he doesn't pack it in.'

I increased speed to sixty, and when I thought he had given up and dropped behind, he roared by at eighty, cut in just in front, and tried to stop dead so that I would go smack into the back of him.

He misjudged the mobility of his car. I jammed on my brakes and swerved into the fortunately clear right lane, while he shot up the bank, turned over three times with bits coming away from all points of his car, and settled into a steaming wreck on the hard shoulder. I slid by and gathered speed. Let him get out of that one. He was insane. He'd tried to kill us.

'There's your riff-raff,' I said.

Moggerhanger went purple with laughter. 'Did you touch him?'

'No.' My guts were like jelly.

He banged both hands on his thighs. 'If only I'd had a movie camera. I'd play it over and over to my dying day.'

I felt guilty, though not at fault. 'It was too close for me.'

'You're a cool customer, Michael. By God, you were quick.'

I didn't like his tone of voice. If he thought I was getting too good he would send me on the job to end jobs. 'Lucky,' I said, 'not quick. We'd have been battered if I'd hit him. So would he. I don't know where they come from.'

I didn't feel easy that I'd made his day. 'You did right not to stop,' he said. 'Let somebody else pull him out. It's like being on the bloody battlefield. If he'd damaged my Roller I'd have blown his head off. I hope you got the number, Alice. Inspector Lanthorn can get me his particulars then.'

Hearing her first name made my fright with the maniac worthwhile, and I said it over and over to myself as we went through the night – with a wave at Ettie's diner to the right. She went back to her book, while Moggerhanger, after brushing the crumbs from his clothes, thumbed through a sheaf of estate agent's handouts.

The cloud had moved, and I saw star patterns high in front. Alice laid the book in her lap, and Moggerhanger put his papers away. He slotted in a tape, treating us for the next half hour to a concert by Jack Emrod and his Old Time Orchestra playing the honeysuckle favourites of yesteryear. By half past seven we were well on our way, with Retford to starboard and Worksop to port. Even Nottinghamshire was falling behind as we headed for the motorway by Doncaster.

He yawned, but didn't go to sleep. 'Yes, Michael, business is booming. At least my business is. My clubs can't do enough trade. I drive around Soho and look out on the world from behind smoked glass windows, and can't but reflect on how well I'm doing. When I see two specimens from the north wearing woolly hats and football scarves, I know they're going to spend a quid or two in one of my places before they go back to their train with bloodshot eyes and empty pockets. It used to be said that there was one born every minute, but nowadays, with the population explosion, there are two, if not three or four. I think it was an American president – and correct me if I'm wrong – who once said that in order to fool some of the people some of the time you've got to fool all of the people all of the time!

'I've got the top end of the market buttoned up as well. The fact is, there's a job to do in this country in the seventies and eighties – if not till the end of the century. It's a job of national importance, and I'll tell you why. There's a lot of oil money floating around, millions in cash accruing to those robed potentates of the Middle East, bless 'em, and it's my job to cream off as much as possible. By hook or by crook – it don't much matter which, as long as you don't make it too obvious – the sterling must stay in London. It's vital for our national survival. I've had word about it from on high, and I'm all set to do my bit. It's 1940 all over again, only money's involved this time, not blood, though in the long run it's just as important to a country like this. The sterling balance will ever have us by the short hairs, so we have to get the money out of them by women, the roulette wheel, select entertainment which they can't get anywhere else in the world (nudge-nudge, wink-wink); surgical operations that won't do them too much harm, but which won't do them much good either; flats and houses at exorbitant prices that are going to cost so much in maintenance that by calling on the services of an army of bodgers (a trade at which we British excel) it'll help the unemployment problem; and by palming off onto them all kinds of goods whether they need them or not, but goods that they think they'll die if they don't have. That's real business, Michael. And nobody can say it ain't honest. As for armaments, though, the built-in obsolescence factor is such that even I think it's a disgrace.'

There was a pause while he lit a cigar. 'The trouble is, I'm not the only one in the trade. If I was, everything would be all right, but some new organisations commit such daylight robbery it makes my blood run cold – and that's not an easy thing to do. Fly-by-night firms are popping up all over the place, as if the oil wells are going to run dry tomorrow. They can't get their hands in the till fast enough, and so far I've never seen any of them with bandages on their wrists. It makes the Great Train Robbery look like absconding with a blind man's penny-box. Investment banks go bust overnight. Ships full of goods disappear at sea. A man pays millions for a block of flats that belongs to somebody else. You name it, they get up to it. And it goes on even at the bottom end of the market. Some people are so unscrupulous that they add insult to injury by taking most of the money out of the country, to such places as Zürich and Lichtenstein. But me, though I make a lot, I plough it back. I buy houses and land, and invest on the stock exchange.' He held a finger across his throat. 'I'm up to here in National Savings. A pittance. But it looks good. I also employ people, such as yourselves. In other words, I keep as much money as I can in the country, and I spread it around, not only as security for my family, but as a patriotic duty. Yes, I've got a lot invested in good old England, Michael. If ever the ship goes down you won't see me in the lifeboat with a lot of rats.'

The thought of Moggerhanger in a lifeboat horrified me. How far would you get with such a shark on board? 'Well,' he went on, 'I shan't go on, except to say that there are more gangs than there used to be, and the worst is the Green Toe Gang. How they got that damned name, I'll never know. But what's in a name? Suffice it to say, they've given me more trouble these last two or three years than I think I deserve. They seem to know more about what goes on in my business than they should by any intelligent assumption, as if they've got somebody planted in my office. If I could find out who it was, well, I don't think I need tell you, Michael, what I'd do. A loyal man like you knows very well what I'd do. If there's anyone I can't stand it's a traitor. I've learned in my life, though, that a good man rarely sells himself for money. That's why I've taken you on. I sorely need someone like you within arm's reach because you know, and I know you know, that being a traitor's not for the likes of you or me, because we had similar upbringings, give or take a bob or two. I worship steel, not gold. Never turn your face on a friend, or your back on an enemy.'

'No, sir.' I spoke only to find out whether I still had a voice. The more he went on with such blarney the more I distrusted him. Bill Straw once said that Moggerhanger never told you anything without reason, and if he did it was always bad – for you.

'You can stop at the next layby,' he yawned. 'I want to change places with Alice and get my forty winks.'

The miles went quickly. I was near Tadcaster by the time I made the switchover and he bedded down under a thick patchwork blanket.

'Do you mind if I call you Alice?' I asked when I set off again.

'Why not?'

I caught a smile in the profile that peeped out of a flimsy headscarf.

'I still hope you'll do me the honour of having dinner with me after we get back to Town.'

She took the book from her bag. 'I'd like to read, if you don't mind.'

'Make free. What is it?'

'Something by Gilbert Blaskin called *The Warp and the Weft.*'

'Is it good?'

'I can't tell. I'm only halfway through.'

It was the one I had typed for him, and added a few bits in my own right, when I first met him in London. 'I know Blaskin.'

'You do?'

'He had an affair with my mother.'

She didn't believe somebody like me could possibly be acquainted with a novelist. Her laugh, however, encouraged me to hope I was more than halfway there. 'That was thirty-five years ago. He was a lieutenant in the army, stationed near Nottingham. Then he went overseas and left her pregnant. Out popped me.'

The book, at any rate, was back on her knee. 'What an imagination.'

'When we go to dinner, I'll tell you more. But I'm afraid I'll never be able to introduce you.'

'That's because you don't know him.'

'No. If I did, I'd lose you. He's the biggest lecher in the kingdom. And I'm passionately in love with you. It's as much as I can do to drive this car.' My hand was sliding up her thigh. 'Does being in a car make you feel randy?'

'Sometimes it does.'

'We'll have to contain ourselves. But I'd love to suck your delicious cunt till I made you come.'

'Stop it,' she said sharply.

'Did you see Gilbert Blaskin's last television interview?'

'I'm afraid not.'

'It was one of that series called "Writers and Their Habits" on Channel Five. He was interviewed by that lovely young person called Marylin Blandish. Do you know her?'

'I've seen her. She's pretty.'

'They were in his flat, and she started asking him pertinent intellectual questions about his work, and he gradually got his chair close enough to give her a kiss. It was so quick and light that she almost didn't know it had happened. Then he gave her one that she did know about. And then, Women's Lib being all the rage, she thought she'd equalise by kissing him.'

'I don't believe a word of what you're saying.'

'I'm not asking you to. The intellectual question and

answer game was kept up through long looks and subtly moving lips. Old Blaskin's patter was so good – or something was – and it was a full moon that evening, so she kissed him back, and the television crew, instead of closing the show as they should have done, were so mesmerised at what was happening, and at what seemed likely to transpire, that they just watched and carried on working.'

'I've never heard of such a thing.'

'Neither had I. But Blaskin – so he told me later – regretted not being able to control his actions, and he slipped his waistcoat off with the excuse that it was hot under the lights, and after a few more minutes he got her blouse off, both of them mumbling away about where a writer finds his ideas and discussing in an otherwise perfectly normal way how he lets politics in the twentieth century influence his work. The TV crews were fascinated by that – as Blaskin and Marylin slithered onto the medium piled carpet. Blaskin's hand went up her clothes and fumbled at her tights with a look of beatific malevolence as he told her about his horrible childhood at boarding school and the poems he wrote when he was seventeen on the Spanish Civil War.'

'You're joking.'

'I'm certainly not. It's as true as I'm sitting here. She unzipped his flies with salacious speed, while questioning him in deadly earnest about his first book called *Walking Wounded in Eritrea*. They kissed passionately, and went on about society and the writer, till his trousers came off at the mention of Suez. He said that for a writer reality is a prison and that you should live only in order to rub your nose in the delectable cunt of reality. He threw her tights in the air, saying he couldn't be a communist, but left that sort of thing to the Russians and those leftwingers who ought to know better. Her tights landed across a camera lens, and one of the quick-witted crew snatched them off and stuffed them in his mouth for a souvenir, so that they hung out of his mouth as if he'd swallowed an overdose of textile spaghetti.'

'It's disgusting,' Alice said.

'Maybe it is, but Marylin's legs opened as she mentioned the Two Cultures, and Blaskin said there was nothing like a bad novel to set you questioning the purpose of the novel, and then he got it in as he mentioned Flaubert's syphilis and hoped Marylin's husband Charles wasn't looking at the telly that night. "No," she said, "no, he's shooting grouse, and do you write with pen and ink or on the typewriter?" and he said, "Yes, of course, because all art is the product of an obsessively robust selfishness." Marylin unhooked her bra so that he could get at her delicious girlish tits, and told him that he should stick to the point and only answer questions that were put in good faith, at which some of the crew cheered while others nodded in agreement. With a hand under her arse and her hands around his, which were pitted with old shrapnel scars from an Italian fieldgun, she asked about the reviewers and at his devastating response she came, and moaned so that somebody put the mike closer as if she was about to phrase her final question. It was a useless gesture because Gilbert shouted that if God existed the novelist should be shot and, being as far into her as he could get, praised the Lord and passed the ammunition.

'The producer realised he had something priceless in the can, and cut at that point, having decided to tack the end credits over stormy waves beating on the seashore. It really made good television and letters from Birmingham pleading for more such programmes ran into thousands. The switchboards were blocked for days. It was submitted for the Italia prize and they even thought it'd get a Ramrod from Hollywood.'

She was breathing heavily. 'I didn't see it.'

'Neither did I, but with Blaskin, anything's possible. It

is with me, as well, and I only say so because I sincerely believe that everything's possible with you. But I'm sorry if I stopped you reading your book. I'm sure it's much better than my idle chatter.'

She pushed my hand from the top of her thigh, but still held two fingers. I didn't know whether that was because she thought I might continue my attempt to get them into her, or because she was prudishly affectionate. 'Perhaps it's safer if I get back to my book.'

'I wish you two lovebirds would stop billing and cooing,' Moggerhanger called out, 'so that I can get some sleep. We'll be there in an hour.'

Fifteen

Spleen Manor was a house, Moggerhanger said, in which you could fart without the windows rattling, or without somebody down the lane on his way to church turning away in horror at the unmistakable sound.

From a B road I went down a paved lane to a narrow bridge over a stream, and halfway up a hill turned left into the grounds. The first glimpse, through bushes and across the garden, was of a longish dwelling of two storeys, with lights glowing from the downstairs windows.

I carried in five suitcases for Moggerhanger's overnight needs, then mine and Alice's. Three of the chief's were so heavy they must have contained a thousand sovereigns apiece, or their equivalent in bullion, suggesting that he was to pay someone off for a very expensive job. The ceiling in the hallway looked low enough to bump your head on if you didn't duck because the beams, quite ordinary in their arrangement, had a motif of grey arrowheads painted in between, which gave the impression that the beams were closer to your skull than they otherwise were. Even Moggerhanger ducked, and he was used to the place.

The rooms were fairly well proportioned, as Blaskin might have said, and the house was quite large. Moggerhanger sniffed at the smell of cooking from the hall and said he was ready for his dinner. He wasn't the only one, but he told Matthew Coppice to show us to our rooms and said that we were to come down in half an hour.

A corridor along the second floor connected the five bedrooms. At one end, where the staircase came up from the ground floor, was Moggerhanger's quarters, because I saw Coppice taking his luggage in. He was well placed to hear anyone who might be tempted (me, for instance) into going down in the middle of the night to look through the house and see what I could learn. No matter how light the footfall, the floorboards creaked so that even someone in bed across the valley would stir in his sleep. Moggerhanger might even hear my lecherous thoughts meandering into Alice Whipplegate's room which, I was glad to see, was next to mine.

My own cell had no lock to the door, and I hoped it was the same with hers. I should have known better than to have nothing in my mind but sex, because the reason I'd locked myself into the cogs of Moggerhanger's big wheel was to find out as much as possible for Bill Straw so that he would be more able to protect himself when it was decided to round him up. An equally important reason was that such information might help me to get even with Moggerhanger for having put me behind bars ten years ago. My aim was a mixture of public duty and private revenge, which told me that I ought not to let lechery interfere with my actions. That kind of itch could well be left to Blaskin, who often only indulged in it to flesh out the characters in his books. Thinking rarely did me any good, especially the sort that put me off trying to go to bed with Alice Whipplegate, when to become intimate with her might be the only way of learning something about Moggerhanger which I couldn't come across in any other way.

Putting on a clean shirt and a different tie in the bathroom, I noticed another of Moggerhanger's framed quips on the wall saying: 'Look before you speak.' He must have had Polly working in a regular little sweatshop. I expect she posted one a week back from Switzerland when she was eighteen.

Matthew Coppice had laid a buffet-style meal on a round mahogany table in the middle of the dining room.

There was a dish of boiled potatoes, a flank of roast meat, a bowl of salad, a basket of sliced bread, a board of cheeses and a cluster of plastic-looking grapes. Four bottles of Italian red stood on sentry-go at various points. Moggerhanger's oval platter was already laden and he sat at a separate table with his own bottle of champagne, talking to someone who had not come up in the car with us.

Since reacquainting myself with Moggerhanger I decided that when I had enough evidence to get him sentenced to everything short of hanging I would go to the police station with my locked briefcase, to which only I had the combination, and spread the papers out on the large table in the interview room. 'Would you do me the favour of looking these over? It'll take a while, but I'll just sit down and have a smoke, if you don't mind.' Every few moments I would hear exclamations of shock and indignation from the honest constables and their officers. Eventually the inspector would say: 'We get the drift, Mr Cullen. Leave the stuff with us and think no more about it. There's enough here to send even an archbishop down. We've been waiting for stuff like this for years.'

You can imagine my chagrin, which included a twinge of despair, when I realised that the man talking to Moggerhanger at their separate table was none other than Chief Inspector Jack Lanthorn, one of the cops who was so bent he could get through the maze at Hampton Court in one minute flat. I knew now that the police raid on Peppercorn Cottage hadn't been carried out by a RADA acting class, but had been done by real coppers giving Moggerhanger a hand on instructions from Lanthorn. And the inspector had come up incognito to Spleen Manor to collect payment for services willingly given. I hoped he'd retire in a couple of years to Jersey, which might make it easier for me to sink the boots of retribution into Moggerhanger's backbone. His long thin face and pinpoint grey eyes beamed at me. 'Haven't I seen you somewhere before, lad?'

I did not like his disrespectful way of addressing me, and looked stonily back saying: 'You arrested me at London Airport for gold smuggling twelve years ago.'

He turned to Moggerhanger. 'I thought you had enough old lags on your staff, without having to take on a young one.'

'Here's somebody who doesn't intend to be an old one.' I resolved from then on to bring that bastard crashing down as well if I could. 'I don't live at Number One Kangaroo Court anymore, not in the Garden Flat, anyway.'

Moggerhanger laughed. 'Steady on, Michael. None of us do – or will.'

Lanthorn thought me too small to worry about. Perhaps I shouldn't have spoken. I was usually able to uphold my standard of being the quiet sort, except where women were concerned, but here I had slipped up, because I should have denied being who I was when Lanthorn recognised me. That was the expected response, so that he could have chuckled inwardly, both at having spotted me and made me lie. Maybe there were some lies I was getting too old to tell. He forked red meat into his cavernous gob, then slopped half a glass of red Polly after it. 'None of us knows what the future holds.'

'That's why we're here tonight,' Moggerhanger said. They were two crocodiles in the pool together.

'Among other things, Claud.'

I loaded my plate. The radiators along the walls gave off a faint warmth, but Moggerhanger called: 'I expected to see a fire in the grate, Matthew.'

Coppice stood by the door looking into space, a man in his late forties, with a pink face that would have seemed well fed if it hadn't had an expression of worry stamped indelibly on it. The lines must have been there from birth, or from when he first went to prep school at six. Wavy grey hair was spread thinly over his skull. He wore flannels and sports jacket and heavy, highly polished shoes. A cravat decorated the spread of his Viyella shirt instead of a tie. He stank of whisky, and shook himself out of his vacant stare, saying with no tone of apology: 'I thought the place was warm enough.'

'I know what you thought,' said Moggerhanger. 'I can usually tell a mile off what somebody like you is thinking. You didn't want to get your hands dirty, right?'

'Yes, sir.'

'Well, we all know that you can't make a fire without getting your hands dirty, but that shouldn't put you off when you know very well I like to see a bit of fire in the grate. It might not matter down south, but in Yorkshire it cheers me up. If you can't do better than that you'll find yourself back in Peppercorn Cottage. It's a good dinner, though, I will say that.'

Lanthorn walked to the window and pulled a corner of the curtain to look out. 'Throwing it down with rain. What a goddamn fucking hole Yorkshire is.'

'Steady on,' Moggerhanger said. 'It's no worse than any other, Jack.'

'I was born not twenty miles away. Thank God I got out of it at fourteen.'

'Stop worrying. He'll be here in the morning. Come and get some more of this lovely grub.'

Lanthorn took his advice and advanced on it, and plied with his knife and fork as if the meat was helping him with his enquiries.

'And I also noticed,' Moggerhanger said to Coppice, 'that my bed was made. Quite an advance on last time. Do you remember, when you served half-cooked pizza and a bucket of Algerian jollop?'

Several expressions passed over Matthew Coppice's phizzog which our self-opinionated boss didn't catch. If he had, he would have been careful from then on with his apparently humble servant. All the same, I felt sorry for Coppice and wondered why he didn't walk out. Instead, he took a cigarette from his case and lit up with trembling fingers, then came to the table and poured a glass of wine.

Moggerhanger pulled a bundle of papers from his pocket and passed them to Lanthorn. 'The only thing to do is do it, Jack.'

'I'm not so sure whether I dare,' Lanthorn said. 'Or care to, if it comes to that.'

'It's a matter of options.' Moggerhanger filled their glasses. 'And how many of those do we have, these days?'

Lanthorn said something I couldn't hear, so I sat closer to Alice. 'I hope you realise I was serious about what I said to you in the car.'

She had changed into a skirt and blouse and freshened herself with new perfume. 'I only remember the amusing parts.'

'Maybe you already have a boyfriend. Or a girlfriend. I'm not old fashioned. Or maybe you have a husband, though as soon as I saw you I thought you looked too happy for that.'

'I do like my commons, Claud,' I heard Lanthorn boom out. 'I smoke all I want, and eat red meat, and drink what I can hold. I don't put weight on, either. I think it's those vegetarians, non-smokers and mad dieters who are responsible for the country being in a decline. They've got no bloody drive or energy. If you can't consume, what incentive have you got to produce?'

Moggerhanger laughed. 'You should know, Jack.'

Alice smiled. 'I'm divorced. I was married at twenty-two, and split up three years later. My husband was a smooth-talking con-man who wanted me to support him.'

'You walked out?'

'No. He found somebody who would. I was devastated, for a while. His burning ambition was to be idle. He saw idleness as the greatest virtue.'

'You make my blood run cold.'

'I haven't had anything to do with any man since. I even stopped seeing my father. My mother was dead, so it wasn't too difficult. He wanted me to go and live with him, because he'd retired from the bank. But I had my own flat: my husband was so idle he hadn't even signed the lease.'

We sat with plates on our knees. 'I'm really interested in what you're saying. Your fine and subtle face has an expression which shows you're at peace with yourself. To someone like me, who has a passion for work, to the extent that I've not had much to do with women in my life – nor men either, come to that – you're the most attractive and fascinating person I've met. I'd like to get to know you.'

'You may not find as much as you expect.'

I held a piece of meat close to her mouth.

'No thank you.'

'Let me be the judge of that,' I said earnestly.

'I'm up here to work.' She sipped her wine. 'And I'm dead tired.'

'I think you misjudge me.' I clinked her glass, and took a long swallow. 'I've been sexually impotent since I was fifteen. All I do, when I can, and I don't very often, is sleep with women, just for love and comfort. None of them have yet been able to induce me to have proper sexual intercourse.'

I'd used that ruse a couple of times before, yet I regretted trying it with Alice because it should have been possible to get her into bed by normal diplomatic methods. I was inveigled into such a statement because her claim not to have made love with a man for what must have been at least ten years struck me as an even bigger lie. The fact that I fell for it was my second mistake that night. Maybe I was tired as well. Or perhaps I hadn't gone far enough and should cap it with a third lie by telling her I was queer.

'We'll be here for a few days,' she said, 'but I don't think I'll have time to take you on.'

Matthew Coppice gazed as if he envied me being so close to her. Well, I couldn't share her with him and that was a fact. I'd have to call off my campaign and make a real effort the following day. There was a time for everything, and in this case it wasn't now, but she didn't know how right she was when she gave me a lovely goodnight smile and said: 'See you at breakfast!'

Moggerhanger looked from his hugger-mugger game of cards with Lanthorn. 'Being difficult, is she? The thing is, Michael, you don't have the art of courtship. Nobody does, these days. But it'll cost you a pony or two in flowers with her. And why not? It feels all the better when you get there.'

'In my opinion,' I said, 'it always feels good.'

'That's no way for a young swain to talk.' He bellowed with healthy laughter and returned to his double dealing, a man of the world but not completely in it, which made him too cunning by half. I helped myself to Matthew Coppice's trifle of sponge, tinned fruit and custard, into which he must have poured several bottles of strong sherry because at the first spoonful my eyes watered. Lanthorn said it was the best dessert he'd had at Spleen Manor. When Matthew brought in coffee I asked where he'd learned to cook. 'I worked at an old folks' home.' He had only a faint Yorkshire accent. 'I'll tell you about it some time, if you're interested.'

Facing me, and away from present company, I saw him wink, a signal that mystified me, because there was no business I could possibly have with a broken-down old caretaker like him. I swallowed his weak brew and wondered how much he was making on the housekeeping bills. 'Any time. I like stories.'

He looked grateful and relieved, and I almost thanked him for allowing me to make him happy. He shook my hand so furtively that I wondered whether he'd done it.

I heard Alice Whipplegate humming and splashing around in the bathroom, and was tempted to look through a keyhole in passing, or get out my Swiss army knife to widen a crack in the door. Such actions were below even me, but when I came to her room I opened the door and walked in. It was bigger than mine. The wardrobe had a few dresses already hung, and a table was cluttered with various combs and cosmetic pots. I pressed the mattress of the single bed, then noticed that her diary was open, with the ink barely dry:

'I'm quite enjoying my trip,' she'd written, 'though I must say I was dog tired on the way up. I managed to get some reading in, at least, even though it was only a trashy novel by Gilbert Blaskin. The only trouble was that I had this chauffeur practising heavy breathing down my neck. He's a real bore, forcing attentions on me that I definitely do not want. He actually told me he was impotent. The oldest gag in the book. He'll be telling me he's gay next.

'Hell, I suppose I'll have to put him off somehow. It's so tedious. There's always some pest hanging around. I'm sure it won't be easy to get rid of him, though. He's so cocksure. He's not really bad looking, but I just don't fancy him. If I did, he'd be the one to complain after a while.

'Must take a bath. Dead beat after my time with Parkhurst last night. Now, there's a man, though I don't suppose anybody would think so. An ENGINE! He just fucks and fucks as if he's in a ballet on stage at Covent Garden, saying nothing because he's thinking of the money he's going to win at gambling after the show's over. He got THREE jackpots out of me, the brute. Lord Moggerhanger wanted him to come with us, but I'm glad he didn't. I'd never be in a fit state to get anything done.'

I walked out and slammed the door. You can't win 'em all. I got into my flowered dressing gown and waited outside the bathroom for her to finish so that I could go in for my evening ablutions. Clutching my toilet bag, I tapped on the wood. 'Can I share the sink?'

She opened the door, and walked by. 'Good night, Mr Cullen!'

'Good night,' I called cheerily.

I couldn't sleep. A moon lit up the room because there were no curtains. I tried one side, then the other, thinking of my encounter with Ettie in the broom cupboard. I recalled making love in the toilet at 30,000 feet to Polly Moggerhanger on our way back from Geneva. I even longed for Bridgitte. What I wanted most was a drink, preferably a pint of Jack Daniel's. Sounds of shouting from downstairs told me that Moggerhanger and Lanthorn were cheating at cards. I regretted having had only two glasses of wine at supper. I regretted not having scrawled 'Fuck You' across Mrs Whipplegate's diary. In fact I regretted not having torn the page out and posted it to Blaskin for use in one of his novels. Bollocks, I said to myself. Die, I told whoever had got me into this boiling stew.

Insanity was coming on fast. Alice wasn't having an affair with Parkhurst after all. The cunning little vixen had only written that stuff in her diary knowing I would sneak in and read it. She was testing me to see whether or not I would be discouraged. She loved me passionately. Maybe it was the first of a series of many tests that I was expected to pass. She carried the diary with her and filled in a page so as to scare off any bloke she was with, and left her door unlocked so that he could go in and read it. How can I think such things? I thought, falling asleep.

I was chasing her along an avenue of piled woodplanks. There was a tug at my arm and I woke up. A blue Yorkshire dawn spread across the window and showed Matthew Coppice sitting by my head. 'What the fucking hell do you want?' I asked, as humanely as I could.

'Sorry if I woke you, Mr Cullen.'

'I am, as well.'

'It's the only time I can talk to you. In secret, that is. These people here would kill me if they knew.'

'I'm sure they would,' I said, just to comfort him.

'Do you think so?'

'Well, you said so.'

'Did I?'

'You certainly did. But I suppose you're right.' He was dressed as he had been at supper and still reeked of whisky. Ash from his fag fell on my bed. His chin was smooth and he also smelled of aftershave, being the sort who shaved twice a day but had a bath only once a month. Why did I keep meeting people I felt sorry for?

What I needed was Moggerhanger's rock-hard reality – though the thought made me want to puke. Poor old Matthew Coppice, he hadn't even been to sleep. 'Make it short,' I said. 'I'm still hoping for a night's rest.'

'I've fixed you something to drink.' He fetched a tray from the door and set it on my knees: a big pot of coffee, a jug of steaming milk and a plate of hot toast and buttered teacakes. The coffee was ten times better than the slop we'd had after supper, I told him.

'When I meet someone like you, Mr Cullen, my impulse is to be absolutely frank.'

While tucking into the excellent breakfast, I congratulated him on his skill in reading character.

'In my early days,' he said, 'I was a steward on a British Railways restaurant car. The best job I ever had. I don't mind telling you that we made a packet. One of the others was a young woman called Elsie Carnack, and we used to think up ways of making money on the side. Of course, we had to share it with the rest of them at the end of the day, but every week it amounted to quite a bit. We diluted the orange juice, put water in the soup and thickened it with flour, doctored the coffee, took in our own cheeses (some of which fell off the back of a lorry, if you take my meaning,

Mr Cullen), sold our own bread, gave half portions where we thought it wouldn't be noticed, short changed, fawned so that we would get good tips, and dispensed our own wines and liqueurs – oh, I can't remember all that we did.'

He seemed quite excited.

'Elsie and me saved what we could and left our jobs in the restaurant car when we got married. We sold the concession, as a matter of fact, though not long afterwards there was a crackdown and the syndicate got fined, or lost their jobs. The ringleader was sent to jail and Elsie had a good laugh over that. I never liked her laugh, mind you, and should have been warned by it. But love is blind, isn't it, Mr Cullen?'

I could only nod at his wisdom. 'Even National Health specs don't help.'

'Me and Elsie bought a big house in the country very cheap and called it Forget-me-not Farm, which we ran as an old people's home for seven years. As you can imagine, we had quite a rapid turnover. I loved the work. Some of the old folks were wonderful people. I was at it twenty hours a day. I would even read to them if they were blind. And some of the stories they told me! They'd lived long and had been all over the world. Some had been famous in their time, but they were forgotten now. A few were ga-ga, of course, but I did my best for them. Elsie took the business side of it too much to heart. She found a way of keeping the bodies fresh for three or four weeks after they had died, so that we could go on claiming maintenance. The relatives didn't bother to visit them, so there was no risk. And it wasn't doing the old folks any harm if they were already dead, was it, Mr Cullen? Not that I liked the idea, though it made a big difference to our profits by the end of the year. Mind you, we had one or two narrow escapes, though I was working so hard that much of the time I didn't know what was going on. That was my downfall. I should have done. One day Elsie vanished. She took the money, and anything valuable that the residents owned. It was terrible. She'd robbed them blind. She robbed me, as well as leaving me with all the debts. She even took my best Rolex watch which one of the nice old chaps had given me. The result was that the police came and found two bodies in the deep freeze, underneath all the vegetables. I took the blame on my shoulders. Elsie was let off, but I got seven years. Seven years! When I think of what the judge said about me my blood runs cold. "The worst case of vampirism on the elderly that I've ever had to deal with," he said, and it got in all the papers. Did you read it, Mr Cullen?'

'I must have been abroad at the time.'

He seemed disappointed. 'I suppose I deserved it. During the latter part of my time in prison I had Parkhurst Moggerhanger for a cell mate. He was in a very bad way, going off his head in fact, so I looked after him as if he was one of the people in my old folks' home. I saved his remission. He got better, and came to rely on me. I pulled him through his bad patch and when we were discharged we kept in touch. I had nowhere to go, so I went back to live with my old mother in Halifax, bless her. She's dead now, Mr Cullen.'

'I'm sorry about that.'

'Parkhurst told his father about me, and Mr Moggerhanger, as he then was, took me on as a caretaker for whichever property needed me. He wanted to show his appreciation, and I was thankful for it because I was a finished man, done for and never to rise again, when I came out of prison. And yet, having taken this position, which I did with alacrity – I admit it with tears in my eyes – it seems I've only jumped from the frying pan into the fire, because I am an accessory after the fact of things which go on here, so that if there's ever a proper round-up by the forces of justice – if there is such a thing – I'll be over the wall and inside again for even longer than last time. That's why I want you to help me, Mr Cullen.'

I could have choked. Fortunately I'd finished his delicious breakfast. I had helped Bill Straw by bottling him up in Blaskin's roofspace, but Bill Straw was a friend of long standing, whereas Matthew Coppice was one only as of last night – if he was one at all. I was never wary of acquiring new friends, which may have been why I had so few real ones. Besides, an open and unafraid disposition such as mine always made people suspicious. There was something about Matthew Coppice, however, that told me not to trust him entirely. Moggerhanger was no fool, and he was certainly capable of setting this drab minion onto me to find out if I had any resentment at having been put away by him ten years ago.

He set the tray on the floor, and I gave him a cigarette. By my watch it was six o'clock. He spoke so glumly it was hard to imagine he was Moggerhanger's nark. 'What do you think?'

'First of all, my answer is an unequivocal yes.' What had I got to lose by putting him at rest? 'I always help if I can. It almost goes without saying. But having said that, I've got a few comments to make. All right?'

He nodded.

'The first is that you shouldn't do anything hasty.' I laid it on thick, while another level of my mind thought further on the matter. 'You should bide your time. Criminal actions may be going on all over the place, but how can you be sure? When you ran Forget-me-not Farm they were also going on, but you didn't know. You made a mistake last time, and you might make one this time. What I mean is: are you the best judge of anyone else's criminal actions? My second comment concerns Lord Moggerhanger. You tell me that he employed you out of the goodness of his heart. He's famous for it. He never forgets a grudge and he never forgets a favour. Most millionaires are like that. They have to be. It's one of the things which keeps them rich. It also keeps them in touch with human nature – and that also keeps them rich. I mean to say, would you like to repay him by reporting him to the police merely on suspicion?'

He couldn't look at me directly, which suggested that my arguments were getting at him. 'You think I'm mad? One part of me suspected Elsie for months, but I laughed it off to myself in the middle of sleepless nights. I did nothing. Now I've stumbled onto the main drug and gold smuggling racket in Great Britain and I'm expected to turn a blind eye, am I? Just because Moggerhanger gave me a job when I was down and out? The only reason he took on a fellow like me was that he thought he might one day become a lord, and would need someone he could treat like a dog.'

I felt sorry for him, which was the worst thing you could do for anybody. 'You are in a mess.'

There was as much of a smile on his face as the wrinkles around his eyes were able to muster. 'So are you. That's why you've got to help me.'

I thought of Alice Whipplegate's long slim body sheathed in its nightdress next door. 'How can I? You've got no proof for any of these assertions.'

'I know where to find some. But you've got to promise to stand by me when the crunch comes.'

Dawn was my randiest time. My mother told me I'd been born at six in the morning. I had spoiled her breakfast. 'I'll think about it, Matthew, and if I say that, it means I'm halfway there. But can you go to the kitchen and get me a breakfast exactly like the one you brought up for me?'

He realised what I had in mind, not as slow as I'd thought. 'Oh ho! I see. Well, yes, OK Mr Cullen.'

If he was really trying me out he hadn't got much response, and even Moggerhanger would have to laugh, or at best grin, at the way I was using him as a pawn in the seduction of Mrs Whipplegate. A pony or two in flowers, my arse! Since she had scorned me so wickedly last night, at least in her diary, I was more intent than ever on getting my mutton dagger home, and I mulled on the delicious possibility till Matthew came back.

'There it is.'

I looked in the coffee pot. Full and steaming. 'I'll never forget this. You can rely on me from now on. Go down and have your morning whisky.'

'I had it last night.'

'Have tomorrow's, then.'

He threw a definite smile. 'That's an idea! Anyway, I've got to get Lord Moggerhanger's breakfast. He has two kippers, a plate of scrambled eggs and eight pieces of toast.'

'Don't fall into the porridge,' I said, 'or you'll get your nose wet.'

I had gone too far, as if my flippancy threatened him with another downfall. He lit a cigarette and said, with a hint of despair in his otherwise irredeemable glumness: 'All my life I've been the victim of levity. I hate levity. I expected better from someone like you.'

He was genuine, or I was no judge of people. From now on I would believe all he told me. 'You must realise that underneath what you call levity, Matthew, and what to me is only a brash sense of humour, is a seriousness that's almost as solid as rock.'

He seemed to appreciate my effort. 'Thank you, Mr Cullen. I'll see you later. I must work now.'

I picked up the tray before the breakfast got cold, not caring whether I made love to Alice or not. In fact I positively didn't want to and, I was sure, neither would she want me to. On the evidence of her diary, which it had served me right for reading, I was the last person she'd hope to see first thing in the morning, even with a breakfast tray.

My mind was on higher things as I knocked at her door and went in. She slept on her stomach, her face turned away from the wall and towards me. I opened the curtains. The diary was no longer on the dressing table. I edged bottles and tubes aside and set down the tray. My only thought was to go out, but I couldn't leave the coffee to get cold. I had to wake her first, so touched her shoulder. 'What is it? Oh, it's you. What do you want?'

It was hard to say what dreams she had been in, but I could only suppose that she regarded me with the same dislike as I had looked on Matthew Coppice an hour ago. 'I thought you might like breakfast. Hot coffee, orange juice, toast and teacakes.'

She sat up, not knowing where she was and looking as if I'd gone out of my way to injure her during the sleep from which she had been jerked. Her otherwise sensitive face was creased with distrust as she took in the landscape of the tray. I suppose we're all funny people the moment we come out of our dreams. 'What's this?'

It was too much. 'Your bloody breakfast.'

She stared. 'Breakfast?' She held both hands to her small breasts. 'In bed?'

'Why not?'

'Breakfast in bed!' She laughed. 'And served by a man!'

I gave her the juice and she knocked it back. 'What's funny about it?'

'Shall I tell you?' I poured the coffee and handed it to her. She took a sip while I buttered her toast. 'I've never had breakfast in bed.'

'You must be joking.'

'I'm not. No man's ever made my breakfast.'

'You haven't lived.' I had often taken it upstairs to Bridgitte. In fact I'd always made breakfast at home, and felt pain that such a chore was finished. It was the only meal I could cook which didn't cause ulcers. 'It's the least I can do for you. I'm afraid I made a fool of myself yesterday, pestering you and talking all kinds of nonsense. I want us to be friends.' Thinking of the times I had taken breakfast in bed to Bridgitte, after the children had gone to school, and of the occasions when we'd made love among the crumbs, cornflakes and flecks of scrambled egg, got me at the quick for having thought of being disloyal to Bridgitte with an opinionated diary-writing thin-rapped woman like Alice Whipplegate who, when she had finished eating, reached out for me with tears in her eyes which were caused, I thought, more by being too suddenly ripped out of sleep than by sentimental gratitude at my gesture of getting up especially early to go down to the kitchen and prepare her a delectable breakfast with my own hands. 'You're wonderful,' she said.

She kissed me, her lips moistened with a smell of coffee and oranges. I was still in my dressing gown, nothing underneath. She must have slept well, because the sheets of her single bed were hardly disturbed, until I slipped between them and felt her relaxed body folding towards mine.

I was uninterested, yet moved like a snake because I had the biggest early-morning hard-on that I could remember, and I didn't even finger her but rucked up her shimmy-nightgown after a few salivating kisses, and went straight in without a murmur. I'd had enough of tongue-wagging. So had she. We were a duet of moans. Maybe she thought she was still in her sleep. The one-off atmosphere made it seem like a dream. I lifted myself on my hands and rubbed up close. She came once, and soon, and then I let myself go. When the eddies died away we laughed. I wasn't trying to compete with Parkhurst by making her come four times.

'Thank you,' she said.

'What for?'

'A lovely breakfast.'

I liked her sense of humour. 'We do our best at this

hotel.' I gave silent thanks to Matthew Coppice. 'It's all in the price of the Away Weekend.'

'I was certainly away just then.'

My old red lobcock flipped out. 'I must be off. I've got two more breakfasts to deliver.'

She put her arms around me. 'Do you think you'll manage?'

I kissed the lovely shoulder where her nightdress slipped. 'I have to do my best, or I'll lose my job. The management has to live up to its advertisements.'

'Doesn't it wear you out?'

I stood by her bed. 'It tends to. But it keeps my weight down.'

'Did you do any breakfasts before you came to see me?'

'You were the first on my list.'

'That's a relief. It was nice. Doesn't happen often in my life, I don't know why.'

'Not even with Parkhurst?'

She laughed. 'Caught you! No.'

I could have killed her, but smiled. 'What about with your husband?'

'He's dead.'

'How?'

She rested her chin in her hands. 'One evening the police phoned to say he'd wrapped the car, and himself, around a tree. An oak tree, as I remember. Why he added that little detail I don't know. Maybe he took an interest in such things. When he added as a tailpiece that my husband was dead beyond resurrection my first thought was that I would have to get a job. It was more a decision than a notion and it occurred to me in spite of the shock, there being no better time to make one, since it was more than necessary on getting such news not to fall down dead at the sudden emptiness of life.

'He'd gone out that morning and hadn't made his usual enquiry as to how well or badly I'd slept, so I waited all day for disturbing news. Such an unusual omission on his part served, I suppose, as a warning that something was on its way. The clouds were low and grey. I looked at the rain from the living room window, and the extent of my thought was in wondering when it would stop.

'I remember every detail of that day. It was rare for my mind to be so empty, and for me to be so inert. The occasional cigarette tasted foul – though I chain-smoked in the hope that the next would be better. It never was. I cooked an omelette for lunch and even that was tasteless. In the afternoon I went into the bathroom and satisfied myself, something I'd never done at such an hour, and rarely did, in any case. I felt hardly any relief afterwards. My breasts were turgid, as they sometimes are before a period. I even wondered whether I was pregnant. Then the phone call came which explained it all.'

I always kissed a woman when I saw tears under her eyes. What else could you do? 'Sorry about your tragic life.'

'I've never spoken to anyone like this.'

'Because I brought you your breakfast?'

'I suppose so.' She got out of bed. 'I'll use the bathroom first, if you don't mind. Then I must dress and get to work. Lord Moggerhanger is an early riser.'

Matthew Coppice had laid out a breakfast in the English style, which was welcome after my continental snack. Moggerhanger, wearing horn-rimmed glasses, read the *Financial Times* and through the window I saw Chief Inspector Lanthorn striding along the gravel path consuming a cigar. I ate breakfast as if I didn't know where my next meal was coming from – the very opposite, I supposed, of the way an elderly patient at Forget-me-not Farm must have eaten when confronted by the avaricious phizzog of Elsie Carnack.

After reading the *Daily Mirror* I got out a bucket and cloth to swab the car. Moggerhanger had told me to do it and I should have objected since it was not part of my job, but never having been an English workman, demarcation disputes were not in my blood. If they had been I would have said that a skilled driver such as myself should not have to stoop to common cleaning. Neither was it part of my nature to quibble about any kind of work while in the presence of a man who only asked me to do something as a test. Or so I told myself, to save my pride. In any case, at this stage of my rehabilitation with Moggerhanger, I didn't want the sack.

In spite of the drizzle I stuck at the work long enough to wash the number plates, clean dead gnats off the windscreen and polish the headlamps. I was about to go back inside when I heard a car turn into the drive. Lanthorn went down the steps to meet it. He had obviously been waiting, and I was curious, so unfolded the leather and began wiping the side windows.

The Mini-van, recognisable at once by its coat of arms, came to a halt. The wipers stopped, and Eric Alport got out.

'Where the hell have you been?' Lanthorn called. 'You should have got here last night.'

Alport began filing his nails. 'The ship was late.'

'Like hell it was. You got caught up in some pansy boozer by the docks. I'm flaming well fed up with it!'

I'd never seen such contempt on a man's face as came across Alport's. He would have stayed silent all day, rain or not, if Lanthorn hadn't asked: 'Did you get it, then?'

He took his time, while picking a crow out of his nose. 'It's in the back – you pratt.'

Lanthorn's face was only saved from bursting by shouting: 'I'll fucking nail you one day, lad.'

'If you do, it'll be your coffin lid that's going down.'

Lanthorn pulled at the handles as if he'd break them off. 'Where are the keys?'

They flew through the air. He missed. Alport went on at

his filing. It was a wonder he had any nails left. They must have been the pride of whatever club he belonged to. Lanthorn picked up the keys with eyes glittering, and opened the back of the Mini. He put his hands in and touched lovingly whatever was there. 'Matthew!' he shouted. 'Cullen! Come and give a hand.'

I walked around the Rolls a couple of times before getting there. Matthew carried what looked like a five-pound box of tea, a neat wooden package, well battened on all sides. I took one, and so did Lanthorn, but Alport didn't deign to work. He asked if there was any breakfast in that house of iniquity, because he was starving. I said there probably was, at which he put his nail file into its little leather sheath, buttoned his Carnaby Street Mao-style sugarbag jacket that must have cost every bit of fifty pounds, and went inside.

The Mini-van was stacked to the gunwales with boxes which I supposed they had wheeled off the ship on a fork-lift truck. When this lot got loose on the streets of Britain everybody would be flying till the end of the century. They were flying already, but this would take the lid off their heads as well. In my time as a criminal we had smuggled gold, which seemed so harmless it was impossible to feel guilty, but now it seemed the gold was of a different sort and much more valuable, weight for weight. Instead of getting at the government's pocket, it got at the people's minds by rotting them through and through, which would only end by making it easier for the Moggerhangers of the world to gain more and more power.

I didn't fancy making a career in that kind of trade and considered giving notice at the earliest opportunity, though I realised that the best way to do it – so stupidly had I fallen into it up to my neck – would be to send a telegram of resignation from a remote island in the South Pacific. Even then there would be no guarantee that the long arm of Moggerhanger or Lanthorn wouldn't reach me. Strolling out of my palm-thatched hut to smoke an early morning cigar, a giant coconut would fall from a tree and squash me flat. The only way I could get free of such a job was by bringing the whole organisation crumbling down, and in that respect at least I knew that Matthew Coppice was right.

Sixteen

When I got back to Town I called on Blaskin, and found to my amazement that he was playing chess with Bill Straw. Dismal snapped at my collar and tie with affection. 'I'd forgotten you could play chess.'

Blaskin poured us all a glass of wine. 'He's damned good at it. He beat me twice yesterday.'

Bill grinned. 'I learned when I was in jail.'

'He's a boon,' Blaskin said. 'And I'm in despair, so it takes my mind off things.'

'I thought you never got depressed.'

He made a move. 'Don't be insulting. My commitments are numerous and onerous. I have to show Moggerhanger a first draft of his life story in three months. I've also promised to deliver a Sidney Blood story to Pulp Books in a month's time.'

I spluttered into my wine. 'You're Sidney Blood?'

A troubled grin exposed his long yellow teeth. 'What an idiot you are. There must be twenty writers churning out a Pulp Book by Sidney Blood now and again. It pays my club subscriptions for one thing. It's a bit of a challenge, for another. And then, I enjoy rattling off all that violence and obscenity. What's more, to continue my litany of woe, I've also promised my ordinary publisher a new novel in a fortnight that he can bring out in the autumn, and apart from the fact that I want to give it to a publisher who's promised me twice as much money, I tore up the first page this morning because it was no good, so don't have anything to give anybody. I also have to write a lecture on the future of the modern novel before tomorrow. With so much work to do I can't lift a finger.'

Bill gave his usual hee-haw laugh and made another move on the chessboard. 'You're up the creek with a hole in the boat and no paddle, and a three-hundred foot waterfall in the offing.'

Blaskin clutched the kind of head that should never have been without a hat. He was obviously not feeling well. Ever since the revelation that he was my father it had been hard to think of him as such. At twenty-five years of age, when the news broke, I no longer needed a father. Before then, he'd have been a bloody pest. Maybe if he and my mother had managed to live a normal life when they finally got married our connection would have been more convincing, but the last thing we knew she had gone on a bus to join a lesbian commune in Turkey. At least Blaskin said, and if so, who could blame her – the way he had treated her after the first weeks of their reunion had worn off? Not that she had given him much peace, either.

Blaskin resembled a mad uncle more than anything, meaning he was more likable than if he had been my father, because whereas a father might have cast me off when I got into trouble with the police, Blaskin had generously stood by and given some help.

'If you listen to me,' I said, 'your troubles are over, the present ones, anyway. I'll spill what I know about Moggerhanger onto a tape recorder, so that all you've got to do is get it typed. That'll give you a nice wad to show him, and he won't mind as long as you hand something over.'

'He's already had a fat packet of stuff from me,' Bill said.

'That's good, then. And as for the novel by Sidney Blood, you can write that, Billy. Read a couple, and you'll soon spew it out. The typist can correct your bad grammar.'

Bill poured more drinks. 'I've read scores already. They're on every airport bookstall I've been through, as well as in pirated editions all over India. I'm game for having a go at writing one. It'll pay Major Blaskin back for his wonderful hospitality.'

Gilbert threaded his fingers together and smiled. 'Acting Major, please.'

I stood up. 'And so Gilbert can get on with his lecture, which he can finish by tonight.'

'You mean I have to get to work right away?' he wailed.

That was all the thanks and appreciation I got for my ingenuity. 'I read in last week's *Guardian* that the best medicine for a difficult menopause is work. In any case, if you don't want to give your new novel to the present publisher – a novel that you haven't yet written, I might add – why don't you write a shit novel in a week and let them have that one to turn down? Then you're free, and you can write a proper one for your new publisher.'

'Work, work, work!' he cried. 'Will it never end? Now you're asking me to write a trash novel that my present publisher will turn down, and so leave me free to go to another publisher with a real no holds barred genuine 22-carat Blaskin. Do I understand you to mean that I'm to write two novels instead of one?'

'Yes,' I said.

'Pour me another drink.'

Bill obliged. 'You'd better come up with something better than that, Michael. Can't you see Major Blaskin's upset?'

'I'll tell you what we'll do,' I said, 'and this is final. I'll write the shit novel, Bill will do the Sidney Blood and you can get on with the proper novel for your new publisher – as soon as you've written your lecture. All I want is a title.'

Blaskin was very pleased with my arrangements. 'Call it *SPOOF*.'

'Then I want something to eat.' A good heart, plus a sense of humour, were fatal for survival. I had promised too much. You had to be halfway good to cover two hundred pages with trash. I wouldn't know where to start, and was too proud – and stupid – to ask Blaskin for advice, for whom such work was as easy as breathing in and out. I could have done the Sidney Blood tale better, but had palmed that off on Bill, who was already scribbling notes on the back of a cake packet: 'It's nice to have something to do again, Michael. You're a winner. Never at a loss for a solution.'

Inside I groaned, but outside I grinned and said it made me happy to help. I spoke my adventures with Moggerhanger into a tape recorder, and Blaskin put it into a padded envelope for his secretary, Jenny Potash. He already had a wad of material from Bill, but I didn't tell him (and he didn't see Bill look up from his cake packet and wink with his wolf-like Worksop eyelid) that Bill was the biggest liar in the world.

I set the spare typewriter and a box of Croxley Script on the kitchen table, and made a couple of false starts on some crazy tale of adventure. Each time I screwed the paper into a ball and threw it to Dismal he caught it neatly in his jaws and carried it to the trash basket.

Write the first thing that comes into your mind, I told myself. That's how they all do it. It never fails. So I began to type, and knew straightaway that it was the third time lucky – as long as I could keep my fingers pecking at the keys.

> It's true, of course, that you bite the hand that feeds you, but usually there's no other hand close enough. Langham ran away with his best friend's wife, thinking that because he was his best friend he wouldn't hold it against him. In any case his wife had led him a dog's life, made his existence positively dismal, so he thought he was doing him a favour. But when he saw him standing in the doorway with a stubby handgun

> pointing in his direction, Langham knew he must have been wrong.

I didn't even stop to read, otherwise I'd have admired it for so long that I wouldn't have got any further. The secret that came to me naturally was: go on, no matter what trash comes out of the typewriter. Maybe having an old man for an author was at least half the battle.

> John Weems caught them in amorous passion on the rush matting of Tinderbox Cottage.

I described every object in the place, giving its price and history, shape and colour, which took ten pages, before letting the reader (and myself) know whether Weems the husband was going to kill Langham the lover or not. I had fun. They wouldn't know until the end of chapter two – neither would I – maybe not even till halfway through the book.

I thumped away and by midnight thirty pages had shot out of the roller. Dismal followed the carriage back and forth in a very encouraging way so that I even did the first sentence of Chapter Two:

> The sound of his piss rattling into the pan was like the noise of her voice calling him.

Then I stopped. The others were asleep, Blaskin in the bedroom and Bill on the sofa. Dismal was nodding on the rug at my feet as if made of foam rubber. I picked up the first page of Blaskin's lecture:

> Begin by telling them that if the fantasy of truth is fact, the truth of fantasy is fiction. That'll get 'em. Then go on to confess (there's no better word for it) that I treat the novel like a symphony. I mean, in the way of alternating comedy and tragedy, farce and seriousness. I aim for perfect harmony out of widespread chaos. Many individuals inhabit the continent of a novel, but

I'm the Big Chief who marshals their actions and emotions, which lesser folk put down to fate. From wanting to write a novel of serious intent at which there are nevertheless places where you laugh, I will henceforth weave a patchwork of interwoven set pieces, each with its tragic or comic mark, but all related by the desire of the hero to find God among the ruins of his moral but all too human ineptitudes. God help me, isn't that enough? Change course, if you can, without drowning in the Seven Seas of Ambiguity. I wasn't made for this. I'm only a writer.

I persist in writing novels (I'm glad you asked me that one) because I don't yet think that 'the novel' as an art form has reached its apogee. No author should get lost in its twentieth-century cul-de-sac. I try to cure myself of the habit of thinking that the next novel will be my best. If I persist in this belief I will end by assuming, with many critics and reviewers, that the novel is dead – though a more ridiculous statement I've never heard. The best novel is the one you've just written.

England's writers have always been attracted by the demotic. While their limitations in this endeavour have sometimes been obvious, the result has often been fair to middling. Some people like a good sprinkling of the demotic because it opens a window on what they would otherwise never have a hope of understanding. Others like it because, hearing it every day, it reflects their own life. Some may dislike the demotic because they see those who use it as a threat to their way of life. Most writers are unable to use it because if they did they would sound fake or patronising. And another reason is that every time I fart I get a pain near my heart. Say in lecture. Stop this waffle, and make 'em laugh. That's all they want, and who can blame 'em?

It was a poor start, but what could you expect from

someone who was better at telling lies than trying to find out what he thought? Sifting through Bill's pile of paper, I was both appalled and impressed. He'd got the Sidney Blood tone perfectly, but on some pages he'd outblooded Blood in obscenity and violence to an extent that even I had to stop reading. It was bound to be a success. Blaskin didn't know how lucky he was to be running such a dedicated workshop. I took a lamb chop from the fridge and threw it to Dismal as a reward for his cooperation and encouragement.

Restless after being cooped up writing for hours, I put on my Burberry and took a late tube to Piccadilly. I'd cashed money from the bank and it burned a hole in my pocket, so at The Hair of the Dog I flashed the blanket membership card that Moggerhanger issued to his inner circle and went in. One or two drinkers were flush against the walls, and Kenny Dukes sat near the bar. I bought drinks for us both. 'Here's the skin off your lips.'

Such a phrase, straight out of Sidney Blood, brought him back to life with a smile which showed his battered teeth. 'I hear you been to Spleen.'

'That's right,' I said.

'A cushy billet.'

'I've seen worse.'

'Like Peppercorn?'

'That was great,' I said. 'I'm in love with the place. The rats were very friendly.'

He shuddered. 'I hate rats. When I went up there I slept outside. But the fuckers came out and ran all over me. So I walked up and down the lane all night. Don't talk to me about rats.'

'There are worse things.'

'Not to me.'

'If I had to live there I'd take a couple of cats,' I said.

'I hate cats as well. Kick the fucking things. And dogs.'

'Who do you like?'

His face was flushed with sickly spite. 'Women. I can hit 'em and love 'em.'

I shuddered – though didn't let him see it. After a couple of minutes I said: 'Want another drink?'

'Got to keep a head on my shoulders. I'm waiting for a man who owes Claud some money. If he don't pay, I've got to break his arms.'

'Maybe he'll break yours.'

He grinned again. 'He'll pay. He's got lots of money. I'll just frighten him.'

I stood up to go. 'Do I know him?'

'It's Dicky Bush.'

'Jazz pianist?'

He nodded. 'He wouldn't like to lose the use of his arms.'

'I only know him from the magazines. By the way, I've been most of the day with – you'll never guess.'

He tried to look at me threateningly. 'Who?'

I laughed at his half-closed eyes and hunched shoulders. 'Your favourite author.'

He swallowed his bile and fumbled for a cigarette. 'Sidney Blood? Yer don't say!'

I nodded. 'He's in the middle of a yarn called *The Mangled Duck*. It's a real snorter. He read me a couple of pages.' I saw the question in his eyes. 'Well, maybe one day I'll see what I can do. He's a very exclusive person. He lives alone at Virginia Water with a couple of Great Danes. Doesn't like interruptions.'

Kenny understood. 'Them fucking authors are funny people. I saw one once on telly.'

'I'll try and get you over there.'

'I'd give anyfing to meet him.'

I patted him on the shoulder. 'I'm off back to Ealing. I'm dead beat.'

Outside the street door, a tall thin black reeking of eau de cologne almost collided with me. 'Are you Dicky Bush?'

I asked, quick as a flash. 'If you are, you're the greatest jazz musician in the world.'

His expression changed from absolute hatred to the most beautiful smile of goodwill. His hand came out: 'Shake!'

I did. 'By the way, there's a beefy chap with fair curly hair down there wanting to break your arms because he says you owe money to somebody or other.'

A look of caution replaced the shining teeth of his smile. 'Thanks, Whitey.' He took out a knife and licked it. I went on my way, thinking that in the jungle the man with the blade is king, if not god.

I walked along Old Compton Street. There wasn't much trade going on. One or two women plucked my elbow, but I thanked them for the compliment and told them not tonight, darling, wishing I had gone straight home rather than put myself between Kenny Dukes and Dicky Bush. They could take care of each other without my help. I pulled up my collar against the drizzle and walked across Cambridge Circus. Somebody was pushing a pram up St Martin's Lane, and I tapped him on the shoulder. 'Delphick, how's life?'

He glared at me. 'Fuck off.'

London isn't a very friendly place. It even brings out the worst in those who come from the North. 'That's no way to talk to somebody who not only gave you a lift to Stevenage, but bought you breakfast as well.'

He had another look. 'You forgot to pay me for the poem.'

The panda also glanced at me resentfully. The pram was battened down with cord and canvas. Delphick wore a fashionable jacket and cravat under his duffel coat. 'Did you give a reading tonight?'

'Reading?' he said. 'Well, I suppose you'd call it that. The place was full, but when I sent the hat round it came back with six pounds fifty, four Deutschmarks and a

Canadian cent with a hole in it. I sometimes think I'll pack it in and get a job as a tally clerk in a corduroy factory, except that they've all closed down. I'm going back to Doggerel Bank tomorrow, but tonight I've got nowhere to stay, so I have to push this idle panda all over the place till dawn. The person who was going to put me up in Camden Town threw me out because his missis took a shine to me. Where do you live?'

I offered a cigarette, and he tried to take two. 'I sleep above my employer's garage. It wouldn't be any good.'

'I'm losing my faith in people, and that's bad for a poet. I don't know what I'm going to do. Nobody is happy to do me a favour anymore.'

I got annoyed. 'When did you last do anybody a favour?'

A copper looked at us as he walked by. Being young, he didn't know whether to wish me good night, sir, or take me in for questioning. 'Me? Do somebody a favour?'

I heard an ambulance running in circles somewhere beyond the Marylebone Road. 'You could give somebody a poem now and again. It wouldn't hurt you.'

'That's my bread and butter. Poems are priceless and precious.'

'I suppose you only give 'em to girls who sleep with you.'

He squinted. 'How did you guess?'

A bundle of rags tied in the middle with a bit of rope, a bushy grey beard at the top, and a jellyfish of footcloths at the bottom, shifted down the road poking at cardboard boxes in shop doorways. Four bulging plastic bags, like airships at their moorings, hung from whoever it was, man or woman.

'People like that should be shut up for life,' Delphick exclaimed. 'The place is crawling with 'em.'

The bundle of rags, about a hundred yards up on the other side of the road, stopped. He unclipped the plastic bags, rummaged in one, and took out a cigar. 'Did I hear right?' he called in a clear, loud and fairly unaccented voice. 'Or did my hardened ears deceive me? Would my callous fellow man like to try shutting me up for life?'

'You'd better run,' I said to Delphick. 'He sounds like the Son of Almanack Jack.'

'I'll throttle the bastard,' Delphick said. 'He's not going to talk to me like that. He's got to show some respect to a poet.'

'Leave him alone.'

But he was halfway across the road with hands lifted, and the next thing I knew a remarkably agile fist shot out from the Bundle of Rags, and Delphick, after a suitably dramatic cry, was lying on the pavement. I suppose there was some justice left in the world, but when the Bundle of Rags lifted his beribboned footcloths to stamp on Delphick's face I pushed him away so hard he nearly cracked the plate glass window of a car showroom. 'That's enough,' I said. 'Piss off.'

He looked at me while lighting his cigar. 'You must allow that I had a case.'

'I suppose so. But don't kick a man when he's down, even though he would have done the same to you.'

'Allow me to introduce myself,' he said. Then he drew back. 'No, I'd better not. Call me Sir Plastick Bagg, if you like. Suffice it to say that I come out on one night a week to see how the other half lives. I have no sex life, so what else can I do? The Madam sends me out, and I like it. It's like being in the shit pit as a kid, old boy. So nice to have met you.'

'I was going to offer you a fiver,' I said.

'Don't bother. I'll be home for breakfast. Knowing my proclivities, the Ministry of Defence allows me a day off each week, so that I can sleep in. Goodbye. I hear there are rich pickings on the Strand.'

It was a shattering experience. One learns only slowly

what's going on in the world. Delphick was back with his panda-pram. 'Let that be a lesson to you,' I said.

He dabbed his bruised face, and we stood without speaking, an occasional car moving up and down the road. He pulled at the rope covering his pram. 'I'll give you a poem. I've got just the poem. You'll love it.'

'Save it for somebody else.' I was in no mood for verse, but remembered he had nowhere to go, so pulled a twenty-pound note from my wallet. 'Take this, to get a bed somewhere. Or you can borrow it till I'm in trouble and want you to help me.'

He ran to a lighted window and held it up, then came back and pushed his panda-wagon a few yards along the road. I decided that if he walked away without saying thanks I would give him a pasting and kick his panda-wagon to bits.

He was in tears, the bloody actor. 'I'll never forget this. I know you aren't rich, and I appreciate it more than I've ever appreciated anything. And thanks for saving me from that madman in rags. Can I have your address?'

You had to think quick with Delphick. 'I shan't be there much longer. I expect I'll see you around some time. I might call on you at Doggerel Bank.'

'Well, cheers then, mate. And thanks a lot.' He went up the street, while I traipsed down to Trafalgar Square and hailed a taxi that took me to my cosy room above the garage at Ealing.

Seventeen

The business trips Moggerhanger sent me on were mostly short hops by air to the Channel Islands, from which place I returned with hundreds of Krugers stitched into the game pockets of my tailor-made shooting coat. God knows what the customs thought when so many sportsmen and hunters started coming through. It was as if caribou had become the blight of Jersey, and stags were stampeding around on Guernsey. They just loved tomatoes, I could have told them if they'd cared to ask.

I made six trips altogether, for a hundred-pound bonus at the end of each, and soon I had nearly a couple of thousand in the bank. We took a risk, the one condition being that if we were caught we were to say nothing more than that it was our first time and that we were on our own. We had various bits of paper to suggest it, and proof of a bank account in the Channel Islands with ten quid on deposit. It was worked out so that nothing could be traced to the Big Firm itself. One morning Moggerhanger called me in and said he wanted me to go to the New World in a couple of days. 'Where's that?' I asked.

'You'll do,' he said when he had stopped laughing. 'It's a special mission to Toronto, and I want somebody with a head on his shoulders.'

I never anguished over making a decision, in the hope that one day I would make the right one. Be that as it may, what frayed my temper on setting out to get the one o'clock plane for America was the fact that I had such difficulty picking up a taxi, and didn't reach the airport terminal till half past twelve. When I asked Alice Whipplegate why Kenny Dukes couldn't drive me there in the Roller she said he was in hospital swathed in bandages, having told the police he had fallen on a crate of broken bottles in Bateman's Alley.

The plane was delayed and we were still in the airport lounge at three o'clock. I drank a dozen cups of coffee, ferreted my way through the *Daily Telegraph* from back to front and envied a grey-bearded man with glasses reading a fat book called *The Way We Live Now* which, judging by his expression, was telling him something he wanted to know.

At four o'clock I settled myself in a window seat on Shoestring Airways, my briefcase-type travelling bag stowed in the rack above. Our Jumbo 747 was so full that not even a man hoofing up the runway waving a first class single fully paid up ticket could have been taken on board. I thought I would rather spend a week at sea than travel with four hundred people in this sort of random meeting hall where, within two hours, everyone would jump up and start battering their way out through doors and windows. And the trip was scheduled to last for seven. My only consolation was in thinking of the millions of dollars in travellers' cheques pre-packed by Toffeebottle in my holdall and the ease with which I had carried it through the customs. I had been led to understand that the money was payment for goods gratefully received.

'Do you mind if I have your window seat?' She liked looking out, she said, so I moved to the middle and read the tattered safety instructions card. The airline magazine was equally shabby, otherwise all was well in the Sardine Express. Four babies were crying from different parts of the plane, just to make us feel at home. Things had altered since the Glorious Sixties when, loaded with gold for the Jack Leningrad organisation, we had travelled first class.

Getting up to thirty thousand feet, we flew over Birmingham, Peppercorn Cottage, Manchester and the Scottish Highlands. The pilot announced that we would cross the Atlantic along the fifty-eighth parallel, then go over Labrador and Quebec. Every trip I took for Moggerhanger got me thinking that I should make it my last. But a mere hint, and I would have been sent on one in which I was caught and put away for as long as would make no difference to his operations. Once you began working for him, in all stupidity and innocence, you kept on till he in his own pleasure stood you down. I began to wonder whether Bill Straw wasn't his recruiting agent, who spun his likely tales to get candidates standing in line for a job. No doubt Moggerhanger's psychologist told him that those couriers who believed in loyalty to friends were not the types to run off with the gold or money they had to carry. Even racketeers had a use for industrial relations experts, and you could always rely on someone like Dr Anderson to sell his advice.

I saw the cauliflower tops of cloud through the window, when the woman leaned forward to take something from her bag. Maybe the psychologist's mathematical certainties fell to pieces when put to the test by flesh and blood. If every person is different, and they are, he can't be right about all of us, because what if I went missing in Toronto and started out all over again under a new name, using the money in my bag? Would Moggerhanger send someone to cut Anderson's throat? Or did Anderson protect himself with a rider at the end of each report saying that his conclusions were not guaranteed and he would not be held responsible if anything went wrong? A man like that was never without a good lawyer, which was a pity, since my possible desertion could not also be used as a way of settling old scores with him.

An indication of my disturbed state of mind was that I hadn't so far shown an interest in the woman by my side. Perhaps it was because she seemed so ordinary, but a couple of hours on board Air Steerage induced me to take in her short dark hair and pale face, with a skin so translucent I fancied I could see traces of veins underneath. She had a small nose and dimpled chin, and a faint vertical line in the very middle of the lower and slightly protruding lip. I took this in from a few seconds of side view and from what I remembered when she had asked me to change seats, a disturbance which now seemed a waste, because she leaned against the window and was trying to sleep, one arm folded over her head.

Unsatisfied by her position, she woke up, and pouted at the racket of a screaming kid. It began to get dark, settling into a twilight that lasted most of the way over. I offered my hip flask: 'Travelling's not what it was.'

She had a few swigs, and I could see it going down, by the movement of her lovely throat. 'What a wonderful idea, to travel with one of these.'

'I always have.' I felt her body touch mine as she settled back into her seat. 'If I go by train I have a tea-making set. When I'm in the car I have a hamper from Selfridge's as well as a tent and sleeping bag. I like to get my priorities right.'

'You must do a lot of travelling.'

I nodded. 'If I'm not on the move, I'm not living. I can't stand not getting out of England every month or two. When I'm feeling ready to do myself in I go through what I call lifeboat drill – that is to say, escaping from the country at sensing that people are about to go around hanging such as me from lamp posts. Once, I cycled in a panic to the coast and got on a boat for France. Another time I hitch-hiked to Scotland. Sometimes I drive. Or I may go by air. Or I just pick up a rucksack and walk. Are you on holiday?'

'It's a long story.'

'It's a long journey.' I passed the flask again – after I'd drunk some. 'I know how you feel. When I can't write another word of the book I'm doing I go to the Heathcliffe Hotel in Yorkshire for a week. Or to Moonshine Manor in

Cornwall. Either place will unwind me. At the moment I'm off to Toronto for a couple of days. I came on impulse to the airport this morning because I had to get away. I thought I might go to Rome, or Israel. But before I knew what I'd done I'd bought a ticket for Canada. I'll go to Israel later. How about you?'

'That was lovely whisky.'

A single drop stained my trousers when I held the flask upside down. 'Glad you honoured me by enjoying it.'

'I'll get some more when the trolley comes.'

'I didn't mean that,' I said earnestly. 'I do too much drinking alone, and I don't like it. Night after night I sit with a bottle of the best hooch, staring at my typewriter, the blinds drawn, all lights on, and hearing nothing but the odd car go by. I keep the blinds drawn and lights on during the day as well, I get so glued up and depressed. The only thing I've got for company is a dog. I turned him loose this morning, to live on sheep till I get back. Being alone isn't good for me.'

She smiled. 'It's generous of you to share your whisky, all the same.'

'The most natural thing in the world.' I touched her warm wrist, though only for a second. 'I live in Cambridgeshire most of the time. I bought an old railway station ten years ago, and use it as a gentleman's cottage. It's very nice in spring.'

'What do you do?'

I was waiting for that. 'Do?'

'For a living.'

I leaned back in my seat, and let ten seconds go by. 'I'm a writer.' What else could I say? 'In other words, a con-man of the worst type. I tell stories by lying, and make a living out of it.'

'That's a lovely way of putting it. Can I ask you your name?'

'Michael Cullen.' I was unable to lie about that one.

'But I write under several pseudonyms, such as Gilbert Blaskin and Sidney Blood.' I added the names of a couple of novelists from the north, but she said she hadn't heard of them, either.

'It sounds an interesting life. I'm going to Toronto because I've just got a divorce, and I've got to go somewhere. I have a sister there, so at least there's somebody.'

The plane grumbled and bumped, and a notice implored us to *fasten seatbelts*. I stood up to get mine disentangled. 'It's always better to move in a crisis.'

'My crisis is over,' she said, 'and I can never have another as bad as that.'

Oh, can't you? I thought, though I wasn't ill-mannered enough to say so.

'It started the day I was married, fifteen years ago. My husband had qualified as an accountant and we were set for a long and happy life. I admit I was uneasy about it, having just left university. But I don't think I showed it. I was in love, after all. And we know what that means.'

At a particularly big bump, she held my arm. The fact that she was terrified brought out different aspects of my concern. I was happy she was in such a state, yet sad to acknowledge that there was little I could do for her. A baby had been screaming for ten minutes and they could hardly tell the mother to take it outside. Earphones were issued as a last resort and the film began. 'Do you want to look?'

She shook her head. 'The trouble was that almost from the day we were married he wanted to leave me, I don't know why. He didn't tell me, but I felt it, and I knew I had been right when he eventually did tell me. We were driving around in the New Forest and he lost his way so we had our first big quarrel. Then he came out with it. He said he couldn't stand me. He wanted to leave me. By now I wasn't sure I wanted to stay with him, but I hadn't mentioned it. I told him that if he wanted to leave me he could. If he was unhappy (and he was – I'd never seen anyone so unhappy as he sat numbly over the steering wheel), then he ought to go, as long as he knew that he wanted to. He burst into tears and said that he couldn't.

'It was obvious the marriage was a disaster. I didn't even know whether I loved him anymore, and I had to assume I didn't, otherwise I would have left him there and then so that he would at least have been happy at not wanting to leave *me* anymore. You can imagine – you being a writer – what a mess it was. I asked him if he had met anyone else. "No," he said, "but have you met another man?" "Yes," I told him, "I have met another man to the one I married, and he's sitting right by me."

'He called me a whore and said how could I be so disloyal to *him*? I didn't know which one he meant, and neither did he. He was so shaken that I had to drive home. When he was with me he was never less than insane, but I know for a fact that during this time he worked hard in his profession, and got on in the firm. He also made a lot of money freelancing other people's accounts. I supposed for a while it was a pity we didn't have a child, but as things went on without improvement I felt it was for the best. All this time I didn't have a lover, mostly I suppose because he kept me in that state of hypertension and misery that paralysed me, and which put off any man who came near me. It was the same with him, I'm fairly sure, unless he had a quick screw at one of the office parties at Christmas.'

'Why didn't you throw him out?'

'I should have, I know that now. When I thought about it, things hadn't been right from the start. He had a sister who hated me, though I think I know why. I went to his house once to call on him before we were married, and he wasn't in. His sister was upstairs when the bell rang, getting ready to go on holiday to Venice, and because she was neurotic the bell startled her so much that she tripped as she came down the stairs, and broke her ankle. From then on she hated me even more, as you can imagine. I should have taken it as a sign and called the whole thing off but, as I said, I was in love with him.'

'He sounds like a real vampire.' Sidney Blood would have been proud of him, I thought. 'Or maybe he was just waiting for you to throw him out.'

She spoke calmly, as if there was ice in her belly. 'That's what I should have done. But I couldn't. He wanted to go, but couldn't. Perhaps we were in love with one another. It was hopeless. Maybe love is only complete when it becomes your enemy.'

'Excuse me,' I said, 'while I write that down. I may use it for one of my books. You don't mind?'

A faint colour came into her cheeks. 'Why should I?'

I went to the bar and returned with two half bottles of champagne. Rule number one, as stated in Moggerhanger's Handbook of Regulations, said that no heavy drinking was to take place, but I decided to ignore it. We chinked plastic glasses.

'But he did leave,' she said. 'Neither of us could stand it any longer. We talked it over for days. It was as if we were both getting ready to go away together. It was crazy. What had driven him mad I still don't know, but I know that by now I had begun to go the same way. I helped him to pack his suitcases, which he appreciated very much. There was more friendship in the air than I'd ever known. If only we could live like this every day, him always packed and thinking about leaving, maybe life would have been tolerable. We even made love better than for years, on the settee. I couldn't believe it. Neither could he. But he couldn't change his mind. As a silly man who had given his word he couldn't climb out of the ditch he had dug for himself without a nervous breakdown. By now I didn't want him to change his mind, either. I could take only so much. Maybe he really wanted to stay, but wouldn't do so unless I crawled and grovelled. There may have been a chance, but I wasn't strong enough. I was too worn out to take it.

'Everything's got to end some time, I thought. During the few years we were together you can imagine how often I was in a bad mood. That meant that we didn't make love much, because he found it impossible to make love to me when I was in a bad mood. That of course was exactly the time when I wanted him to do it. I would have come out of my bad mood then. But when I was in a bad mood he went into a worse mood, so it was even less possible for him to make love. The only time he could make love was when I was in a good mood, which under the circumstances wasn't very often since I couldn't be in a good mood because he was always in a bad mood. And when I did happen to be in a good mood, in spite of everything, I didn't always want him to make love. Neither did he, as often as not, but when he did I had to let him. Sometimes it worked, but often it didn't. There was endless friction on that front alone.'

I wondered if this long yarn wasn't her technique of putting off men who were about to make a play for her. If so, I would have taken my hat off to her, if I had been wearing one. 'You make me sweat.'

'Do I? Anyway, when the great day came I helped him into a taxi and kissed him goodbye. The only condition was that I wouldn't ask where he was going. That was easy. I didn't want to. When the door closed and he was driven away I was desolate for a couple of hours, but then I began to mend. I was happy. I wanted money to live on, so two days later I got a job as a typist and general office dogsbody. My wages were low, but I managed. It was no real problem. In fact everything was wonderful. No one could understand why I was so happy and calm. I made friends, with a woman or two, and a married couple in the same street. I invited them over for drinks. There was even a man I thought I might fancy.

'Well, you've guessed it. He came back. I found him on the doorstep one day, when I got home from work. My heart sank. I wanted to kill him. Just as I had got back on my own two feet this had to happen. My impulse was to turn round and walk off, never to see him or the house again. If only I had. But I couldn't. I swear it had nothing to do with him. It was just that I lived there. Whatever I thought, he was back. He had become more and more unhappy the longer he was away. It was only three months. We had grown to be so much like Siamese twins, spiritually, that maybe his continuous misery was only at the thought that I was getting happier and happier.

'We had a real quarrel then, such as we'd never had before. It didn't clear the air and end our troubles, either. Things aren't that simple. It made them worse. There was no solution. I went for him with a hammer. No, I didn't murder him. Even that would have been an advance on our situation. I caught him at the temple, and I never knew he had so much blood. Perhaps that was his trouble. Anyway, two weeks later I left *him*, and I didn't go back. He was still at his work, the life and soul of the firm, I suppose. I packed up and got a room. I had arranged a transfer to another office of the same firm, in St Albans. In a couple of years, by which time he'd got himself another woman – thank God, I was quite happy about that – the divorce came through. I'm the manageress of the office now, and they've given me extended leave, because I had to get away. I've been very calm, and maybe the reaction was delayed, but the hard fact of the divorce hit me like a bomb, not because of anything to do with him but due to something in myself. I'm absolutely free now, and at last know who I am. Only I can tell me who and what I am, not any man. I live very well on my own. I've even managed to save money without skimping myself. I have friends, though no man friend who I would let be my lover.'

'If you dislike men so much,' I said, 'why are you telling me all this?'

She held my hand for a moment, and finished her beaker of champagne. 'I'm not one of those who hate men. It's just that nothing good's happened with men, that's all. In any case, you're a writer and I can talk to you. My name's Agnes, by the way.'

'Glad to know you.' I opened the second bottle. 'I'm writing a novel called *The Way We Live Now*, but I'm stuck halfway through. That's why I had to get away for a few days.'

The plane droned on. Now and again I got a glimpse of the film, which seemed to be about an endless car chase, the occasional vehicle erupting into a fireball. 'They gave me a bonus for the trip,' she said, 'and I went to Knightsbridge and spent some of it on underwear.'

The seatbelt lights scintillated, and air pockets scared her. They scared me, too. The stratosphere shook the Boeing as the proverbial terrier is said to shake a rat. Then it went as if on velvet. I didn't mind the plane falling apart, but I would have appreciated having the fuselage lit as we went down. 'Underwear's a good thing to spend money on,' I said. 'Keeps up the old morale.' I put my hand on her thigh, quite unobtrusively I thought, but she tapped it away: 'It's not for you.'

'It's for you, then, is it?' I responded.

'Oh damn,' she said, 'trust me to sit next to a writer.'

'The sort of experience you've told me about takes longer to get over than you think.' I wondered if there would ever be a time when such misery between man and woman would not exist. Even in China, I said to her, a peasant and his wife were not beyond an occasional slash with a billhook in the rice fields when the Red Brigade commissar was looking the other way. No system could cure it, and I suppose in fact it kept us going because otherwise we would be bored to death. At the risk of making an enemy for life I told her this as well, and she said: 'You're wiser than you look!'

Another car exploded on the screen, maybe to get us used to the idea of the plane disintegrating. The fuselage was grumbling so much I wondered if it could stand the strain of the next two thousand miles. She didn't feel me twitch at her remark. The only thing that stopped me slapping her chops was the thought of that sexy underwear clinging to her thighs and arse. I couldn't understand why she had told me such a come-on thing, unless the idea of contempt for men had bitten so deep that she didn't care anymore. 'If I ran an airline, I'd call it Pornair and show blue movies all the way, one that men would enjoy, and one for women.' She took my hand at another lurch of the plane. The film show ended with a convoy of cars and lorries exploding one after the other, and half a dozen babies started crying at the same time, as if we had miraculously taken more on board since the trip began. 'I think the pilot's got a lever on his instrument panel that controls screaming kids.'

The lights came on, and a smell of casseroled meat hinted that food bins weren't far away. 'I'll throw up if I don't eat,' she said.

I was famished, and wolfed the grub as if I hadn't seen any for a week, though didn't omit to pass her tit-bits from my identical dish. 'I'll be at the Grand Park Hotel in Toronto. Smack in the middle. I'll probably only stay two nights, being a restless sort of person. If I'm there longer than that, I usually hang on for a fortnight, or until I'm bored. Is your sister going to be waiting for you?'

'She isn't even expecting me. I'll phone her from the airport. If I had written beforehand to say I was coming she might have told me not to bother. If she isn't pleased to see me, I'll go on to New York. I got a visa before I left, just in case.'

She wasn't to know, but so had I. As soon as Moggerhanger said Canada, I said New York to myself, and though he was certain to put me on such a tight schedule that I wouldn't be able to use it, I got straight down to Grosvenor Square with a photo and the filled-in documentation, and fixed myself up just in case.

'Do you know,' she said, when I ordered wine with the meal and filled her cardboard cup, 'a man's never tried to get me drunk before.'

'It's hard to believe. I often got my wife swined-up when she was tense and couldn't throw off a bad mood. Just to melt the clouds. She even knew what I was doing and, forgive a bit of crude talk, but the fucks we had afterwards were wonderful. I felt the sky wafting my arse as I went on and on. Then she got on top of me, and the wind tickled her lovely arse. Marvellous what a little loosening up with alcohol can do. I would never try to get a woman so pissed that she couldn't enjoy sex, though. I'm not a brute.'

'I know.'

I popped a spoonful of trifle into her mouth. 'That's the nicest thing you said to me since we took off.'

She slopped it immediately back, and luckily it went onto her tray. Her gills were the colour of whitewash. 'Excuse me, but I must go for a pee.'

I pushed the old lady by my side – who had been eavesdropping on our salacious chit-chat – into the gangway. The noise of Agnes's progress up the plane was painful to hear. Perhaps the experience of meeting me had been too exciting for her. I tripped over the old woman's reticule, and led my latest loved one to the toilets.

'It's bloody disgusting,' someone called – a podgy bloke wearing a cricket jersey and a porkpie hat.

A stewardess, swinging a bunch of keys and leaning against what looked like a washing machine, poured a miniature bottle of vodka into a mug of cocoa. 'We get all sorts on planes these days.'

'It isn't her fault,' I snapped. 'Everybody'll have it soon. They must have taken bad food on in London.'

My arm around Agnes's waist went under her plump breast, and I drew it back. Far be it for me to take advantage of a woman in such a state. People were shoving their trays aside, faces bunched up with doubt about the food. Twenty were already queuing at the toilets, but I pushed Agnes in as soon as a startled Indian woman came out, then stood guard, hearing her retch even above the hum of the engines.

I don't know why, but as I listened to her almost rhythmical unloading, I was fixed with the certain realisation that disaster waited for me in Toronto. My life had been filled with occasions on which my most profound feelings, warning me of the wrath to come, had been ignored. Whether or not it was the closeness of Agnes I don't know, but this time I decided to acknowledge the feeling that something nasty was being made ready for me, and take steps to avoid it.

I recalled the expression on Moggerhanger's big-daddy face at the briefing in London. The attaché-case was handed over locked, and when I asked for the key he said I wouldn't need it because they (whoever they were: I was too lowly in the cogwheels of international skulduggery to be told) had it on the other side. The key had gone over by letter. 'But what,' I asked, 'if the customs officers in Canada want me to open it? I don't want to end up in the uranium mines.' I only got a small dose of laughter this time. 'That's a risk you've got to take,' he said. 'It's a high risk business.' Like fuck it is – flashed through my mind. 'Whether you have the key or not, it'll make no difference if they ask you to open it. Tell 'em you lost it. If they axe it open they'll just look foolish, because there's nothing incriminating inside. So no more questions, Michael. Believe me, they won't stop you. It's the neatest little job you've ever been given to do, and as easy as pie.'

I could only suppose that the payment I had to deliver was in counterfeit notes, that I was the fall guy in a plan of deception that would deceive nobody. Those who were waiting for straightforward recompense, believing in honour among thieves, could not credit the fact that, being an out and out criminal, Moggerhanger wasn't as perfidious as many inhabitants of Albion had long since been known to be.

Perhaps I was wrong, and my sanity had taken a turn for the worse, but I was determined, after I had delivered my case, to get out of town as soon as – and as secretly as – possible. With Agnes I would be less suspicious than travelling alone, and so I wondered whether my acting scared wasn't just another plot cooked up by my subconscious to get a woman into bed. I tried not to show my confusion of spirit as I leaned on the bog door, knowing at any rate that I hadn't fallen so desperately in love that I would risk my own throat when I could get there by infinitely safer methods.

Against a sheet just back from the laundry she would have been invisible on coming out of the lavatory. I licked her wrist, I don't know why, and she smiled at me with gratitude as we went towards our seats. 'My husband would have baled out of the plane even without a parachute at this happening,' she said, 'but you didn't abandon me.'

'Is she all right, duck?' A wag with a Nottingham accent (you found them everywhere) called that she should have done her business in the sickbags in the pocket of the seat in front, like others were now having to.

'She'll spew all over yo', mate, if y'aren't careful,' I replied in an even coarser vein.

He turned to his wife. 'Bleddy-'ell, a din't know there wore another Nottingham ragbag on board. Wunders'll never cease!'

I was laughing as we settled back into our seats. 'I'm

very ashamed, though,' she said.

'Don't make me feel sorry for you. After all, you were only sick.' I kissed her cold lips, and she held my hands for having been kind to her. I felt as if we'd been married for ten years, such a homely and horny sensation that the peril I would be in once I got to Toronto came palling back over me. My armpits sweated terror. I didn't think matters through step by step as to how I would avoid the coming trouble, but the picture was played out before me by the time Agnes's lovely head rested on my shoulder, as we drifted over the woods of Canada. When she woke up I suggested we go to New York, via Niagara Falls, and her look found a special place in my photo-archive. I'd never seen a face with nothing in its expression except an unqualified acceptance of my good nature – though it occurred to me also to hope that if things went wrong in Toronto we wouldn't end up under the ice together.

As if we had planned it for months, we rattled on about arrangements for getting to the United States. I told her everything, and explained the dangers I would be in, but she laughed as if I'd concocted a story as a writer to take her mind off her recent sickness. To make life safe for us, but especially for her, I would check in at my hotel and deliver what I had brought over for Moggerhanger. I would, as soon as feasible, go out for a walk, and not show my face there again. I braced myself to carry off the meeting with as much nerve as a British con-man can. Agnes would be waiting for me at the Union Station three hours after we had landed – which would be half past four in the afternoon, Toronto time.

Eighteen

Moggerhanger was right. The Canadian customs didn't open my luggage. I don't know why I was born with such a suspicious mind. Nevertheless, as soon as I was clear of immigration control I bought a map of the city and planned my campaign. I had only to imagine Bill Straw in my place to see how things should be managed, though why I should regard that bastard with such companionable affection when he had been the one to get me into the mess, I'll never know. All the same, I would have given anything for a chinwag and booze-up with him, even if he couldn't stop boasting about how he had nearly wiped out half a battalion of Sherwood Foresters in Normandy before realising they were on his side.

I took a taxi to the Union Station and checked my suitcase into the left luggage, then stood in line and got two tickets to Niagara Falls. I bought a new suitcase into which I flung a few magazines from a trashcan, and after that little bit of survival business went by taxi to the Grand Park Hotel. On arrival I stepped out with a duty free cigar in my mouth and a plastic bag of clinking booze-bottles as if I had come straight from the airport. My Burberry seemed like paper in the sharp wind and I was glad to reach the lobby, where they told me at the desk that my room was waiting. When I got up it was plain that Pole Axe Tours looked after those who did Moggerhanger's donkey work. There were two beds, a desk, wardrobe, bathroom and – I could hardly believe that the future was coming true so quickly – a big colour television which would produce blue movies if I phoned down to the cable clerk. A list of titles in a booklet showed a few choice stills, and I salivated over whether to ask for *The Story of O*, *The Beauties of Coral Island* or *Devil Take the Hind Leg*.

A ringing telephone suggested that other matters were in the offing. I was informed that a Mr Harrow in the coffee shop would like to see my samples, so I picked up the bag and went down, pleased at the speed of events – though there was enough power in the bumping of my heart to run a steam engine.

With his little goatee beard he should have been selling fried rabbit. I met the glare of his teddy-bear glassy eyes, and held out my hand to be shaken. 'Pleased to meet you, Mr Harrow.'

His whitewash brush of a beard twitched. 'I'm his clerk. No need of names. Harrow's that guy over there, wearing the red and white scarf.'

A fair-haired chap of about thirty sat before an empty plate a couple of tables away. 'Five seconds after he moves,' Goatee said, as if his warbling throat contained a miniature tape recorder, 'get up and follow him to his Lincoln Continental parked outside. He'll drive you down University Avenue. You don't need to engage him in conversation. When he stops at a traffic light get out, but leave your bag in the car. Your job's done. Walk north, back towards the hotel. You'll be free to leave. Repeat what I've said.'

I told him to bollocks. 'I'm too old to play such games.'

He stood up. 'I hope not – if you want to be older. But good luck and have a nice day, tomorrow.' He walked into the lobby while I kept an eye on Harrow with the red scarf. I liked travelling, though often felt desolate till I got to such high points of action as this. Harrow stood up and, when the sweep second hand of my watch passed over five divisions, I followed. The commissionaire opened the back door to the Lincoln and I put a dollar into his hand. The afternoon rush hour seemed to be on, unless it was always like that. I only saw the back of Harrow's head, and two eyes when he looked in the mirror to make sure I wasn't poking a gun at his neck and asking him to drive me to Vancouver.

He stopped at a traffic light halfway down University Avenue. I got out, and set off north as ordered. But, as I cannot emphasise too often, I wasn't born yesterday, not even in North America, because at the first intersection I turned right onto Yonge Street, and hopped a taxi to Union Station.

Agnes was waiting at the entrance to the platform and we rushed towards each other like young lovers who hadn't been to bed for a week. I was trembling with passion and fear, wondering how long my clockwork would go on being better than the clockwork of those who would be after me as soon as they opened my bag and saw they had been paid in forged currency. On the other hand, I couldn't be certain there was anything wrong with the transaction, only that I'd got scabies on my heels due to a primitive fear in my stomach.

The train pulled out, shuddering and rattling through a sea of lights, a scintillating air-conditioned rainbow-land all around. Agnes was by my side, and I didn't think about making love, as if we had known each other long enough to have put that kind of thing behind us already. Perhaps the unimaginable had happened, and I was growing up, or getting old, as we went towards the land of freedom and opportunity.

'Shall I tell you something?' she said after we had been on our way for an hour. I nodded. 'I think I've fallen in love. Don't answer. I don't mind what you say, but I think you should know how I feel. I first knew when I was alone in that Boeing toilet throwing my stomach out – the old one. Isn't it funny that it should have begun at that moment?'

I snuggled close. 'It had to start some time.'

'And life's been so interesting with you that I haven't thought once about my boring old problems.'

'I do my best,' I said.

'I'll confess something else. I decided that while I was away I'd try to get pregnant.'

My eyes kept their look of adoration, and at the same time searched out the emergency exit. There wasn't a door in sight. 'Really?'

'Maybe it won't work. Perhaps it was my husband's fault, and not because of me, that I was never able to have a child. But who can say? Anyway, I thought that if I met a halfway decent man during my holiday I'd go to bed with him and hope to get pregnant. I'm thirty-eight, and if I don't try now it'll be too late.'

I may have been nature's gentleman, but I was also flabbergasted. It was usually me who said I was in love, and pressured the woman by a flow of stupid chatter to come to bed. Agnes's gambit of saying she only wanted to make love so as to get pregnant was as perfect as any I could have thought up to get a woman into bed. I again regretted I had no hat to take off to her, because what man could refuse such a sincere and heartfelt request?

'Now that we've come away together,' she went on, 'I thought I'd be fair and let you know what you were in for. If I do get pregnant you needn't bother about the responsibility. I'll look after everything. You just happen to be the one I've chosen.'

'It's a rare honour,' I said. 'I accept your terms unconditionally, but I hope you don't mind if I make one or two comments on the matter. I mean, if you do have a kid – and the way we feel about each other you might well – what are you going to tell him, or her, when he or she gets to a certain age and asks about his or her father? It's bound to be an intelligent little bastard who'll ask awkward questions from very early on. Then again there's the matter of supporting yourself, not to mention a hungry and demanding child.'

She laughed. 'You can leave all that to me.' I felt we would have no bother reaching Niagara now. Maybe she had sensed my worry, and invented this matter of getting pregnant so as to ease my mind, a kind of return for what she considered I'd done for her. The sweat in my groin wasn't exactly the sort to give me an erection, but I must admit that she had pushed Moggerhanger and all his works out of my mind for a few minutes at least. But on realising this, the prospect of being killed in the next hour by the gang I had double-crossed came back to me. I was also sad at having been so callously sacrificed. Not that I'd ever thought there was any friendship between Moggerhanger and me. Outside his family he recognised no such thing. All the same, he could have sent Cottapilly or Pindarry, or some other expendable agent to do his dirty work. But he had to have someone halfway competent to bring off a coup like this and so had chosen yours truly, as if I would appreciate the honour of having a certificate of merit drawing-pinned onto the lid of my expensive coffin before it was let down into the hole and covered with wet soil. He had nothing if not style. He might also have suspected my avowal to get my own back at the first opportunity for the dirty trick he'd played ten years before – and what better way of forestalling me? Fortunately it was something I'd been on the lookout for from the beginning, a state of mind which activated my own warning lights on the aeroplane.

'A penny for your thoughts, my love.'

I drew her close. 'They're worth more than that. In Niagara we can find a hotel and start making that baby. Tomorrow we'll go across Rainbow Bridge and hop on a bus for New York.'

'Or the day after,' she said.

When we got into our room she took her clothes off, lay on the bed with her legs spread as wide as they would go, and closed her eyes. 'Now,' she told me.

Only when I'd kept my promise did she come to life. Such passion was too late, because all I could do was stroke her till she was satisfied, then go to sleep, struck dead by a mixture of jetlag, fear, the unexpected love affair (which I was now thinking I could well have done without), a new country, and the plain passage of time. She lay beside me and we went into oblivion.

Morning was my bad time. As I grew older it got worse, a fact I liked less and less. Whenever I woke up I wondered where I was, even if I'd slept in the same room for years. But because I was in a panic as to my latitude and longitude I invariably wanted to make love if there was a woman in bed with me, just to get my system working.

That morning in Niagara there was Agnes, and as soon as she opened her eyes I knew that she wanted to make love with me as well. Her cunt, cloyed with the sperm of the night before, increased her enthusiasm, and though I tried to hold back it wasn't long before my backbone liquified into her, after which the events of the previous day began to pester me again. I was a hunted man.

Far from this causing me to kick her out and tell her to get back to St Albans, or wherever it was she came from, I embraced her as if never wanting to be separated from her comfortable body. Her suspenders, superfine stockings, frilly knickers, front opening brassiere and lace-edged slip hung over the rail of the bed, things she'd bought for the lucky man chosen to be her consort, but which looked like items for breakfast waiting to be eaten.

I didn't know where the hell I was. For a change, one fuck wasn't enough to get me into gear. If anything was, it was the realisation that I had to run and hide in New York, where I hoped no one would find me. We had to get moving. Her breasts pressed against me, and her night breath was the perfume of her soul. I said such things that came to me. How could a woman of thirty-eight blush? The great waterfall rushed to its doom under clouds of spray. 'I could stay here forever,' she said.

'You're not the only one.'

'The room smells nice after all we've done in it.' She put on a pair of pants but came back, and I held her by the hair and kissed her neck, and ran my hand around that soft material hiding softer skin.

We ate a Canadian breakfast of pork sausages, muffins and coffee. As soon as I saw that waterfall pouring over the precipice I knew she was pregnant. I would have fallen into the boiling spray but for the wire. No wonder honeymoon couples come here, I said. A woman's only got to look at such a mass of water to conceive. Aren't there enough children in the world? Yes, yes, everyone shouts back, but they aren't mine.

We got across the bridge and went southwest through the New England spring. Though I lay back on my bus seat in a cloud of crackpot infatuation and looked at the wonderful scenery, another part of my mind sorted out the permutations as to what form the hunt for me would take. When the boys in Toronto discovered the dud money on opening the bag and phoned the hotel to find out I wasn't there, they would imagine I'd left on the first plane from the airport. By timing, they would guess to within half a dozen different destinations where I'd gone, but at each I could have changed planes for somewhere else, so I had got clean away, unless a couple of planes had left for New York around that time. To be on the safe side, when we got to the bus station I would jump on the next one to Philadelphia, on a hunt for brotherly love. My ultimate nightmare had always been that of falling into a trap, which was why the few I had got caught in had been so deadly. I never liked the idea of people waiting to do me an injury. As the bus drew out I thought I saw Harrow run to get on. My old two fingers went up in the V sign, and the man shook his fist at lunatic me whom he'd never seen before.

Agnes didn't quibble at my plan. 'I feel like a gypsy, going around with a writer who only wants material for his next book.'

Lies came in useful, though I made up my mind to confess as soon as we were back on home territory. 'I'm a very jumpy person.'

'I've got to make sure I'll have my baby. Maybe we need a few more goes.'

I wondered what other plans she'd got for us, and felt morbid and superstitious. 'It may be necessary for me to go back to England sooner than I thought.'

She held my arm, pressing closer. 'If you could manage another night or two, I'd be very happy.'

'I don't want to go. I can't explain fully, but I have to.'

'It's all right,' she said. 'I'll fly back to Toronto and see my sister, then go to England from there.'

Halfway to Philadelphia we stopped off at a motel, and stayed three nights. We were safe, though it was a while before I lost my sense of apprehension. I told the manager and his wife we'd only been married a week, and were travelling around seeing the country. We loved the country. It was a great country. We'd never known such a fabulous country. 'You've seen nothing yet,' the man said. 'America is the greatest country on God's earth.' They were wonderful to us, and made it hilariously obvious that they wanted to leave us alone as much as possible. I couldn't remember such a wonderful time in cuntland and tit-country, the great united states of lips and nipples with its jungle lairs and mountain ranges – oh hymn to outright non-ashamed fuckery. We went at it as if I at any rate was going to be hanged in the morning, and when she said: 'We're certainly making sure of my baby,' I laughed so much she even laughed with me, which showed how much in love we were.

I would take the bus to Philadelphia and she would leave in the opposite direction for New York. Separation was harder than we thought, which was the worst of being casual. She wanted to ask me not to go. I wanted to ask her to come with me. I was brainwashed by my inability to know what was happening. I felt as if I was committing suicide. Parting from her was a bullet in my brain. It would lodge there, but I would go on living.

My jacket was wet with her tears, something which hadn't happened since Nottingham days. Her blouse was wet with mine. I felt as if I had been through the mincer and come out a different person. No such luck. She said nothing about seeing me again. My stiff upper lip had a blister on it. One clause of our contract was that if she became pregnant that would be the end of our affair. In spite of, or perhaps because of her passionate nature, I could see that she meant it.

'Are you sure?' I said.

'Yes,' she said. 'Are you sure?'

'Yes,' I told her. 'Do you want me to stay another night?'

'No,' she said. 'Do you want *me* to stay another night?'

'No,' I said. She was turning me into her husband, but I still loved her. She must have cared for me, in fact, if she was taking the trouble to turn me into her husband – or a facsimile of the man she had turned her husband into. Even though I loved her, I never wanted to see her again. In her suitcase, between the underwear, I left an address card, though I had no expectation of seeing her. I had served my purpose just as she had served her purpose in getting me this far without being killed.

At Philadelphia there was a special Air Nimbus flight to London with one bucket seat left, and with my pack of credit cards I was able to wangle myself on board. I would be safe after taking off, because these days, with so many terrorists wanting to dip their hands in the blood bucket, no one could get on board with a cut-throat razor in their hand luggage.

Flying in a Jumbo at night was like being in a long cellar underneath a laundry doing temporary duty as an air raid shelter, in which you sat until the all-clear went. After four hours I was hungry, but the smart young stern-faced stewardesses were still selling high octane drink, as if wanting us all to be too blindoe to know how foul the food was when it came, or not to care when the plane went into a spin. An occasional tray passed up and down the gangway, but the flight crew were eating first, and then the cabin staff. The smell of food was as fake as the music, which was also out of a can.

People were queuing for drinks near the galley, and when a woman pointed to water all over the floor I said in a loud voice as I squeezed by: 'Never mind, love, as long as it's not petrol.'

After the meal I tried to sleep. There were stars outside, and the movie this time was a long saga of ships bursting into flames. I regretted not having brought a few Sidney Bloods to pass the time. My brooding about Agnes lost its intensity as the journey went on. Misery evaporated, though the hours went by like weeks. Was she only another of my twenty-four-hour passions?

While looking out of the window at the green fields of Southern Ireland the stewardess reached for my breakfast tray which still held half a Danish pastry. As the meal had been one of the most meagre in my experience, and catching sight of her intention out of the corner of my eye, I stopped the tray in mid-air and pulled it back. She snorted and walked off. A gentleman a few seats along, being somewhat frailer than me, had perforce (as Blaskin might say), though after a somewhat spirited struggle, to relinquish the final crumbs of his blueberry muffin to a more determined young woman. They had a schedule to stick to, and no goddamned passenger was going to spoil it.

When we landed I got my luggage from the roundabout and headed for the Nothing to Declare gangway. A hatchet-faced customs officer called me over and thrust his little board in front of my face, as if I had to pass a literacy test before being allowed into God's Little Acre. He made me empty my case, and even felt along the seams and linings. I didn't take the trouble to manufacture a supercilious grin – not having more than my allowance of Philip Morris fags and Jack Daniel's whisky. The search was so thorough I couldn't help thinking that somebody must have tipped him off that I was a notorious hash merchant. Yet no one knew I was coming back, and those who knew I had gone hadn't expected me to return alive. He made me turn out my pockets and when he found nothing asked to see my jacket. My patience and forbearance seemed to encourage him, but he stopped short at a body search. 'Sorry for the inconvenience,' he said.

I was back. Watch out, Moggerhanger. I walked towards the taxi through the beautiful odour of real English rain. They couldn't water that, at least.

Nineteen

Going over Hammersmith Flyover, a maroon Rolls-Royce told me I was back in Mogland. Pindarry wore his funny little Austrian-type hat with a feather up the side, and I recognised Moggerhanger's big head in the back. He leaned against the window and, having much to think about, didn't see me. At the moment only he was in my mind and I thought it a bad omen that I should spot him so soon after my arrival.

The presence of Harrods reassured me and it felt good to be safe home again. Letting myself into Blaskin's flat, there wasn't even Dismal to greet me, nothing except a couple of letters on the lounge table.

Dear Michael, [the first said]
I've decided to cut and run. I couldn't stand it any longer. Not that Gilbert isn't a gentleman. He certainly is that, the way he treats Mrs Drudge. We had some good times together. I had all the food and booze I wanted, but as soon as I finished writing his Sidney Blood story I lost interest in living here, and wanted to get out. Another thing was that that Mrs Drudge was getting on my wick. Every time I laid my hand on her arse she jumped a mile, as if I was going to rape her, or as if I wasn't fit to touch such a person as her. I ask you, what kind of life is that? She wasn't to know, I suppose, that it was only a friendly gesture. She also complained that I didn't make my bed. Me make my bed! Anyway, I knew it was either her or me, and as I didn't want to inconvenience Major Blaskin, Sergeant Straw had to get back into the wilderness and live

under fire. Well, it makes a change.

Another thing is, I got so stir-crazy yesterday I went out for a walk as far as Harrods. You know my weakness for the place, well I went in for a look around. I saw that pillock Cottapilly in the toy department buying a fire engine. He's got the best collection of toy fire engines of anybody I know. He's very queer for fire engines, I can't think why. Anyway, I don't think he saw me, but I can't be sure. If he did it's only a matter of time before they come and get me, or before they tip off the Green Toe Gang so that *they* can come and get me. Life's not easy, Michael. It never was, not for yours truly. Oh, and another thing. I've taken Dismal. I'm sorry about that. I know you're fond of him, but with me it's a matter of life and death. I'll buy a white stick from the Blind Shop, and with dark glasses and my coat collar turned up like on the pictures, I'll be an object of pity and respect to all passers-by. I'll have an impenetrable disguise, what's more, and be able to pull in the odd penny or two if I don't think it's safe to go to my room and help myself to proper financial collateral from under the floor-boards. If I find I can't cope with him I'll put him in a basket and send him back to you by British Rail. That's a risk, I know, because he might well end up in the engine sheds at Swindon running in and out to buy teabags. I'll try and look after him, though. I hope you had a restful trip to Canada. See you some time.

Your old pal, Bill

PS. The probability is that by the time you read this I'll be on some island in the South Pacific being served pineapple brandy by a smiling young girl in a grass skirt and no top.

The other letter, also in Bill's handwriting, was from Lincoln Prison, on official notepaper:

Dear Michael,
I have been arrested but they'll let me go if you send twenty-five pounds for the fine to the above address. I'll explain later.

Bill Straw

I needed a long time to think about that one, but his peril was also mine, so five minutes later I put the money into an envelope, and paper-clipped it to a covering note as from Upper Mayhem. Then I went out and dropped it in the postbox so that it would arrive next morning. I needed all the pals I could get. If I didn't knit myself quickly into some framework of defence I was finished, because whatever had gone wrong in Canada would sooner or later have unpleasant consequences for me. I wanted to throw myself out of the window and smack the ground five floors below. If I had known Moggerhanger was going to be standing underneath I might have done. But to do so otherwise was a luxury I couldn't afford. I would just have to survive. My feet hadn't touched the ground nor my soul the sky for almost a week. I recalled Agnes like the wet dream I always hoped would come true while going to sleep, and had to pinch myself into believing I'd seen her, though without our meeting on the plane I would have walked to my death in Toronto. She saved my life. The phone went and I picked up the receiver: 'New Scotland Yard, can I help you?'

He or she hung up.

I wanted to be with Agnes and hold her close, but she was probably in Hawaii by now, working her emotional way around the world. The phone went again. 'Natural History Museum. Head Keeper speaking, can I help you?'

'Mr Cullen, you're not being serious.' I recognised the melancholy voice of Matthew Coppice. 'I'm phoning from Spleen Manor, just to tell you that my investigations into Lord Moggerhanger's activities are proceeding apace and according to plan.'

'That's very good,' I said. 'Just keep on keeping on.'

'Thank you. I shall. But I do like a bit of encouragement, Mr Cullen.'

A moment after I hung up, the phone bell tolled again. I was beginning to think I was home. 'Michael Cullen here.'

'This is Lord Moggerhanger. Come and make your report. The customs people told me you were in.'

I was so astonished that I didn't know what to say. 'I'm a bit tired.'

He chuckled. 'As well you might be, Michael. I'm not a hard man. Take a seventy-two hour pass. Then I shall want to see you.'

He hung up. I hung up. It was mutual enough to satisfy my honour. He expected me to come running. Let him wait. I wasn't a London pigeon, to eat out of his hand. I'd run when he did. I found a half-bottle of wine in the fridge and wobbled some out for a drink. Air travel not only frazzled me at the edges, it made me thirsty.

Wandering around the flat I saw the first thirty pages of the shit-novel I'd written for Blaskin. A khaki circle showed where Bill had put his tea mug, and the cellophane wrapping of a cheap cigar between the pages told me he'd read it. Under the last line he'd pencilled: 'You can do better than this. Not trashy enough, old son.'

The typewriter would soothe my nerves, so at great expense of spirit I got my erring couple out of Tinderbox Cottage and into a maze like the one at Hampton Court. The husband was looking for the lover, the lover was looking for his girlfriend, the girlfriend was looking for her lover, and they were both looking out for the husband. I carried this on for a few pages to sustain the anguish and suspense, and in the middle of that particular section I typed the first chapters of Genesis word-backwards. I also copied a few paragraphs from a book by somebody called Proust (one of Blaskin's favourites) and ended the chapter in mid-air so that I could start the next one in Peppercorn Cottage.

I was all set to go on, but Gilbert came in with a tall thin woman he introduced as Margery Doldrum.

'I'm happy to see you're working. I think that trash novel's a very good plan.' He told Margery about it while pouring drinks. 'I never thought I would have a son who would stand by me in my afflictions.'

He walked restlessly from kitchen to living-room, from bedroom to study, leaving all doors open in case he got pregnant with another book and started to have labour pains at the same time. I told Margery about my trip to Canada, especially relating to Agnes, and she thought I was mad or lying, or both. She didn't seem all that stable in the eyes herself, but that was because she was acquainted with Blaskin. He came back carrying a chapter of his novel, put it on the table, then got to work trying to open a bottle of ink – so clumsily that Margery looked at me as if to say: 'What can you expect with such a male chauvinist genius?'

'I've been invited to Jack and Prue Hogwash's cottage next weekend, in Wiltshire,' she said. 'Why don't you come, Gilbert? Bring Michael, if you like. There'll be quite a party.'

'I'd rather not, my love.' He went on fiddling with the ink bottle. 'I was invited to Roland Hamstreet's place a month ago, and to my everlasting regret, I went. I've wasted too many hours of my precious life at weekend cottages. It's the hugger-mugger I can't stand, not to mention the fact that if somebody takes a piss in the furthest bathroom from the kitchen, the yolk of your egg shimmers in the frying pan when he pulls the chain. If a tractor goes by in the lane outside, all you see through the window are tyre-treads chucking up mud like water from a mill. Michael, why in tarnation did you screw the lid on this bottle so tightly?'

It must have been Bill Straw after he wrote his letter. 'Let me do it,' I offered. But he wouldn't: 'Walk from one room to another idiotically smiling because you've just survived one of their batty parlour games, and you leave your head stuck to one of the beams like a bit of skin. Try to find the toilet in the middle of the night and you end up in the dog kennel. That's the only room in the house with human dimensions. If the Bomb goes off, though, I expect a cottage will be the safest place to be. Half the population will be saved because the roofs are too low to catch the blast.'

'Oh, stop it,' said Margery. 'You make me sick.'

At which I gathered that she also had a cottage.

'Thank you very much, Margery, but I can't stand cottages.' He got the bottle of ink open, but so suddenly that he splashed half over his latest page. 'Now see what I've done, a whole week's work gone.' He looked at me with a spoiled, malevolent stare. 'Michael, you idiot, how could you have done it?'

'You talk too much.' I spoke without malice, wanting only to take his mind off the accident. 'I told you to let me do it.'

Margery laughed, enjoying herself, and Blaskin's bile got the upper hand. 'Still here, are you? Why didn't you go with Wayland Smith, and see how he gets his material on the great smuggling ring that's threatening our national existence?' Then he turned on me. 'Listen, John Fitzbastard, clear off.' I missed his fist, just. He missed mine, because I didn't really aim. He gets worse as he gets older, I said to myself as I went out, case in one hand and umbrella in the other. I barged into the lift. He ran after me, shouting that I should come back and finish his trash-novel.

Upper Mayhem in late spring was the most wonderful spot on earth, and buying it was the only thing I'd done right in my life. I got there at dusk, clapped out and jet-lagged, unmistakably rejected and utterly dejected, smelling flowers and fresh fields as I walked down the lane, incapable of understanding why I had responded to Bill Straw's letter two months ago and given up such a comfortable den.

Gnats danced in the evening warmth, frogs croaked from a nearby dyke, and birds were like specks of dust between drifting clouds. A whiff of coal smoke blended with the smell of soil. Here was the peace I wanted, and I made up my mind not to leave it again, as I entered my domain via the booking hall, crossed the footbridge over the line to the opposite platform and went up the garden path into the house.

A loving welcome from Bridgitte was a thing of the past, but I thought I had a right to a not unduly cold reception after an absence during which I had been doing my best to earn a living, if not actually to stay alive so that I might do it again – occasionally – in the future. Maria sat by the living room fire knitting a white shawl, and her smile was part of the domestic order which I now craved more than the exciting life I had been pushed into. She had put on weight, which improved her appearance, and she looked happy, as if she also found Upper Mayhem the perfect haven. When she got up and kissed me it was like being welcomed home by a loving daughter.

'Where's Bridgitte?'

'In kitchen.'

Leaving my suitcase by the door, I picked up the jumbo box of chocolates bought at Liverpool Street. Bridgitte sat on the floor wiring up a plug for the electric iron. 'Let me do that,' I said.

'I can manage.'

'The blue wire goes on the right.'

When she got up I gave her the chocolates. She put them on the sideboard. 'What have you come back for?'

I was feeling worse by the second. 'Because I live here. Because I love you.'

She held the iron high, as if to bring it down on my head. I was ready for her, though I hoped without showing it. 'Stop that, you bitch!'

'I didn't believe you'd ever have the cheek.'

'Where else could I come?'

Her face went from a shade of pink to blood red. 'You must be in trouble.'

'Somebody's going to kill me.'

'Oh, when?'

It was the best thing she'd heard in years. 'I'll fix you up with a nice seat in the shade as soon as I know. You seem in a bad mood today.'

She put the iron down and turned away. I knew from the change in the contours of her shoulders that she was crying. An earring fell off as she said: 'How could you do it to me? How could you?'

I'd always thought that what the eye didn't see the heart didn't grieve over, so had she, by some magic message system, heard about my ten-minute grapple with Alice Whipplegate, or my brief encounter with Agnes in the New World? 'How could I what?'

'Do that to Maria, and then bring her here.'

'I took pity on her, the same night I brought her. What the hell do you mean?' I was arrowing into a pit of fatigue. 'I thought I'd come home to my everlasting love. But I'm not staying. I'm off. I've had my bellyful.'

'You've had your bellyful, have you?' She wiped her eyes and took off the other earring. 'You're a treacherous, lecherous beast. You had the cheek to bring Maria here when she was pregnant, and you thought you'd get away with that, did you?'

I staggered back. I really did, hitting my head against the closed door. 'Pregnant?'

'I suppose you didn't know,' she jeered. 'You fuck

women as if babies still come from under bushes. And you pick them when they aren't on the pill. It's the only way you can do it. You walk along the street playing a game called "Is She On The Pill, Or Isn't She?" – and all those who aren't, you fancy. Oh, what a rat you are. Why did I ever meet you? – me, who comes from a good family and had a very religious upbringing?'

'You didn't tell me that when I first met you.'

She was crying again. 'You didn't ask me.'

I laughed. It wasn't hysteria. It really was funny. 'I had no idea Maria was pregnant.'

'Well, she is.'

'Are you sure?'

'She slept with me after you left because she was in terror of the man she'd worked for. She kept thinking he'd come and get her. Then one morning she was sick all over the bed.'

I sat down. 'Maybe it was a tin of salmon.'

'It wasn't.'

'Put the kettle on, and let's have a cup of tea,' I said.

'This isn't the Blitz. Put it on yourself.'

I tried to kiss her. 'Are you sure *you* didn't make her pregnant?'

She was a big woman, and the fist at my shoulder almost spun me off my feet. I put myself in a state of defence: 'If you believe I made her pregnant you'll believe anything. Did she tell you I did?'

'She doesn't say anything. But she's in love with you. Whenever your name's mentioned she looks ecstatic. You think I'm an idiot? It's just one of your tricks.'

I put the kettle on and spread a slice of bread with good Dutch butter. 'It's my fault she's here, that's true. Trust a fool like me to bring somebody home like that. But how was I to know she was up the spout?'

'If you didn't know, who could?'

I spoke with my mouth full. 'We've got to ask her

direct.' I took her by the arm. 'Come on.'

In the living-room Maria was leaning close to her knitting, as if short sighted, black hair covering the side of her face. Her luscious figure was so visible I almost wished I had made her pregnant. If I went to bed with her I'd never want to get up again. The way I looked at her did nothing to convince Bridgitte that I was not responsible for her condition, and the smile Maria gave when she realised I was in the room only doubled the proof of my responsibility. 'Maria, Bridgitte tells me you are going to have a child.'

She stood up, and put her half finished baby shawl on a chair. 'Yes.'

'Whose is it?'

She smiled, and pointed to both of us. '*Your* baby.'

I regretted there wasn't a snowstorm outside that I could turn her into, thick wet flakes piling up beautifully all over the inhospitable soil. 'Maria, you know it's not mine. It can't be, now, can it?'

Bridgitte actually stamped. 'You'll do anything to make her deny it.'

Maria's dark and doll-like face screwed up as if to have a good cry. 'You take baby. A gift.'

I'm sure she was an intelligent young woman, and we weren't too far behind in our powers of perception, but her lack of English, and our turning against each other when in a crisis tended to confuse the issue. 'I'll take her to my father's place.' I didn't know what else to say.

'Not to that monster,' Bridgitte cried.

She was right. It was an unreasonable suggestion, pregnant – oh God! – with disaster. He would make her write a Portuguese novel, then find a translator and pass it off as his own. 'He wouldn't molest a pregnant woman, though.' I wanted to defend him against such outright rottenness though didn't really see how I could. Bridgitte still did not get the drift of what Maria meant, so I decided to be a little more forthright, even if only to clear my good name, and asked as tactfully as I could:

'Maria, who fucked you?'

She stopped crying, and looked at me so intently with her shining brown eyes that I knew she was staring into space. 'Who fucked you, then?' I shouted.

Bridgitte, both hands to her ears, looked at me with contempt and horror.

'Mr Jeffrey,' Maria said.

'Jeffrey who?'

'Har-lacks-stone' – or Horlickstone, something like that.

'The man you worked for?'

She nodded, and fell onto the carpet in a dead faint. We struggled upstairs with her and, on the landing, I edged her towards the spare room. 'She sleeps in my bed,' Bridgitte said.

'Our bed, you mean. What for?'

She switched on the overhead light to tell me. 'Because I don't want to sleep with you. Because I like to sleep with her. Because Maria likes it as well. Isn't that enough?'

'Have it your way.' I was appalled that she didn't trust me even now. She saw me sloping into Maria's room in the middle of the night to have it off with her. I'd never felt so offended. I pushed them into what had been described in the estate agent's information sheet as the master bedroom, and went back to the kitchen to find it filled with steam from the boiling kettle. Enough water was left for a pot of tea. I poured Bridgitte a cup when she came down. 'How is she?'

'All right.'

'Do you believe me now?' I tried to kiss her, but she still wouldn't have it.

'You'll have to go and see this Mr Horlickstone.'

'What good will that do?' I asked. 'He's married. He's got four kids. And nobody would be able to prove anything.'

'Then I'll go and see him. I'll take the shotgun.'

I trembled, knowing she would do it. Man shot dead in the prime of life by Calamity Jane. The newspapers would love it. Any number of photographers would descend on Upper Mayhem. My face would get on the front pages. The lads in Canada would know where I lived. Most of all, I couldn't stand the thought of Bridgitte getting six months for murder.

'I'll do it,' I promised.

'Tomorrow?'

'I'll go now. I'll take the car and be there by dawn. I'll pull him from the new *au pair*'s bed and execute him against the ivy-clad garden wall. He'll love it.'

She thought I was being serious. 'You look tired. Do it tomorrow.'

I had no intention of moving anywhere for a few days. After more bread and butter I went into the damp bed in the spare room and slept till three the next afternoon, a big white whale chasing me eternally through hanging fronds of seaweed. Bridgitte tried to trawl me out about eight, and came up with tea at ten, but even her imagination must have told her I had to sleep myself out.

A gritty floorcloth was being pulled across my face, and I opened my eyes to see Dismal on the bed. Then I heard Bill Straw downstairs shouting that he wouldn't mind a cup of tea and six fried eggs after hitch-hiking all the way from Lincoln.

His demanding voice brought me back to life. I dressed and shaved, and found him sitting by an empty plate in the kitchen, trying to cajole Bridgitte into grilling some beef sausages. 'Thanks, Michael. That's one more life I owe you. You took long enough about it, though.'

'I didn't get back till yesterday, and I posted the money within ten minutes of reading your letter.'

He wiped the fat off his plate with a piece of bread and it was halfway to his mouth when Dismal took it. He looked at Maria: 'Get me some more to eat, duck, will you?'

'Didn't they feed you in prison?' I asked.

'Prison?' Bridgitte looked away with shock. 'I suppose all your friends are jailbirds?'

'I was only in two days,' Bill said, 'so don't get like that, duck. It was a case of mistaken identity and false arrest. A graver miscarriage of justice I've never been involved in. They gave me a good breakfast, though, before I left this morning. It was so big I thought they were going to hang me.'

'Tell me about it later,' I said.

Bridgitte went out, and Bill nodded towards Maria, who put more sausages and bacon under the grill. 'Who's *she*, then?' I introduced them. 'She's lovely,' he said.

Maria smiled as she plied the spatula.

'She's here to help out.' I'd intended to say she was pregnant, but didn't – I can't think why.

He couldn't stop looking at her. 'A gem, a real bloody gem. Is she foreign?'

'She's from Portugal.'

'Do you know, Michael, I never use long words, but if anybody was to ask me, I'd say she was exquisite.'

'I serve you in dining room.' The Gem went before us with a tray. Rain beaded down the windows, and it seemed a good day to be indoors eating breakfast at three in the afternoon. 'Tell me what went wrong in your great venture to the outside world,' I said when we made a start on the big black teapot.

He put two pieces of bread and butter together and began to eat. 'Michael, forgive me if I chide you, but your sarcasm worries me. You didn't used to be like that. Sarcastic people aren't usually successful in life, and I wouldn't like that to happen to you.'

'I'm a bit on edge,' I said, 'what with one thing and another. I'll tell you what happened to me since I last saw you, and then you'll know why.' Maria came in with our full-house English breakfast, and I marvelled at how much Bridgitte had taught her in such a short time. Bill was about to pat her on the arse, but a look warned him off, smitten though he was. While we wolfed our commons I recounted my trip, though managed to leave out my meeting with Agnes and my homecoming at which I'd been informed that Maria was pregnant.

'That puts us in the same mess,' he said. 'If I was you, though, I'd go and see Moggerhanger and find out what the score is. In this kind of business you don't know who was at fault. All you know is that you did your duty, and now that you've survived you're worth twice as much to Moggerhanger than if you had failed.'

'My mind boggles,' I said.

'Don't you see? If he sent you there to make a genuine delivery, you've nothing to worry about. You did deliver it, after all, whatever it was. Didn't you?'

'For God's sake,' I said.

'Granted. What's more, you don't know what arrangements he had for the stuff when it left your hands. That's not your business to speculate about. If he sent you over to get you killed – and I think only your hyper-active imagination could suggest such a thing – now that you've beat 'em he'll have to welcome you back into the fold. Once there, you'll be too big to be knocked off. Or too useful. He's got the others to think about, but if you stay on the run your life won't be worth a light.'

He didn't realise that Moggerhanger already knew I was home again. 'I wonder whose side *you're* on?'

He put his knife and fork down, so I knew things were serious. 'Michael, listen to reason. I realise your instinct is to kill Moggerhanger. It may be understandable, but – bide your time. You may be cunning, but you're not cunning enough. Nobody is. You don't have a tactical brain quick enough, nor the sort of cool thought pattern that stops you just this side of ruthlessness. Cunning without tactical appreciation always leads to unthinking cruelty, which is no good to man nor beast. If you're ruthless without due consideration your opponent may become your victim, but you might also put yourself in the way of becoming his. Savvy?'

'I'll think about it.'

He finished his breakfast in one great swipe across the plate. 'I would, if I was you.'

'How can you be so thin,' I asked, 'when you eat so much?'

He gave me his wide Worksop grin. 'I burn it off. It's thought that does it, Michael. I never stop thinking.'

'You could have fooled me.' I was careful to smile. 'But tell me *your* story.'

'Pass the marmalade, and I'll start.'

'Go on, then.'

'I went to Somers Town, and there was Toffeebottle standing as large as life by the corner of the street. I knew that if I went to my room, even in my disguise, I was a goner, and so was my cash. I backtracked it, hoping he hadn't seen me, and got up to Goole as easy as pie. Taking Dismal was the best idea I had. I just stood by the road, held up my white stick and touched my dark glasses like Maurice Chevalier his hat, and had them bumper to bumper fighting to pick me up. "I'm going up north to see my brother," I said, "I'm almost blind, and if it wasn't for my faithful dog I wouldn't be able to get around at all." While Dismal jumped in the back, the man (or sometimes woman, because a blind man with a guide dog like Dismal couldn't possibly get up to any dirty business) got out and opened the door for me in case I missed my target and walked out into the road and got killed. I must say, though, that with my new rig on, which included one of Major Blaskin's hats – I hope he hasn't missed it yet – I knew I couldn't be recognised when I went snooping around Goole.

'My journey up was a treat – only three lifts, as a matter of fact. One chap who took me straight up the A1 to the Doncaster cut-off even stopped and bought me a meal, and I tell you, when I'd finished I could hardly move. Even Dismal was so full he scraped along on his belly to the door. Everybody seemed to love him all the more for it, though he's a terrible farter, by the way. I can't understand when people talk about a dog's life. And the man paid up without a murmur, though I offered my share. He owned a few shops in Barkdale and drove a nice big Ford Granada, but he was just an ordinary chap like you and me, about fifty-five, I'd say. I told him about my adventures in the Merchant Navy, when I'd had my sight damaged in a fire.'

'I didn't know you'd ever been in the Merchant Navy.'

As Maria cleared the table he looked at her with a mixture of longing and sheer lechery. 'Michael, when somebody out of the goodness of his heart has given you a lift, it behoves you to entertain him if he's half in the mind to hear it. Anyway, he then told me about his three sons, who all won scholarships at eleven and went up through the system till they got to the best universities. The eldest is one of the wonder boys at Marconi, another's in computers in America and the third's just got his master's degree in modern languages at Oxford. I suppose there are thousands of families like that, Michael, and they keep the country running. It gives me faith, honest it does. Merit triumphs. There's hope for us yet.'

He gave his infectious maniac laugh.

'I'm serious. There's a lot of talent in this country, and it's nice to realise Moggerhanger doesn't have it all, although he and the criminal fraternity – the gold smugglers, dope peddlers, pickpockets, money printers, as well as tax dodgers, moonlighters, con-men (and con-women), muggers and cat burglars – cream off reams of intelligence. In the brain power and talent they employ it must be second only to the arms industry. Makes you think, don't it?'

I lit our cigarettes. 'It's the way we live now.'

He rubbed his hands together. 'It certainly is, old cock.'

'So you got to Goole?'

'Ever been there? Of course you have. It's a funny sort of place – ships right in the middle of the town. You only need one of them medieval catapults to swing half a ton of heroin into the square. At night it'd be the easiest thing in the world: just roll your car roof back and the stuff pops in. Then you drive away and nobody's the wiser. All I wanted was to go into a few pubs and see what I could find out. You never know what information you can pick up, or who you can see in pubs, especially when you tap your way in with a white stick, led by a dog. Now, Michael, I don't know where you got that dog, but he has been trained to do some very funny things, because no sooner did we get in a pub than he went sniffing around, and he wasn't just after Woodbines. There were five people in, and when Dismal passed by one and didn't sniff him – a chap with a grey beard, straggly hair, and a Russian-type fur hat – the others who *had* been sniffed turned on him. I didn't know what I was getting into. I'd been hoping for something, but not this. I just stood by. I had to, because I was supposed to be blind. But the others got hold of the chap Dismal had passed over, and held him against the wall. One of them was a big bald-headed specimen with a strawberry mark down one side of his face, a sailor from one of the boats, with the biggest set of fists I'd ever seen. "Who are you?" he asked the chap. "Wayland Smith," he squeaked. That was a made-up name, if ever I heard one. I noticed a pansy-looking chap nearby who seemed to be the ringleader, a nasty bit of work who did nothing but file his nails. "What's your job?" he asked. Wayland Smith shook and trembled, and called to the pub landlord that he should get the police, but the landlord only laughed and said "Get 'em yourself." The sailor asked the same question, and Wayland Smith must have thought it was all up: "I'm a journalist," he sobbed. Well, I ask you – a journalist! That was the worst thing he could have said. "I know him," Nail File said. "He works for the television. BBC, I think." That made it even worse. If it was ITV they might just have thrown him out and that was that. But the BBC! "You'd better put him in the van," Nail File said. The sailor hit Wayland Smith in the stomach, and they dragged him outside. "It's terrible," the landlord said, "the way people can't hold their drink. How was I to know he's had thirty-five whiskies?" He looked at me. "If I was you I'd make myself scarce. And take that dog with you." "I only came in for half a pint of mild," I whined. "Bugger off," he said, "or you'll need a deaf aid as well, if that lot set on to you." His advice was well meant, so I stepped outside. It was too late. Somebody hit me on the back of the head with the town hall.

'I woke up in the cop shop on a charge of being drunk and disorderly. Dismal was put into the cell with me, in case I wanted to go to the lavatory pan in the corner. Whoever struck the blow outside the pub must have dragged me to a street on the outskirts and poured a bottle of brandy over me. Fortunately he wasn't smoking at the time. The beak next morning said I should be ashamed of myself. "A blind man to get into such a state." I was belligerent and nasty, he said, and took advantage of my disability to bamboozle the general public into protecting me. What's more, I didn't deserve the service of that faithful dog "whining so hard because it can't get into the dock with you. However, in view of your condition, I will be lenient. Ten pounds fine, and fifteen costs."

'As you know, Michael, I hadn't got a bean, so they sent me to Lincoln Prison. Why they packed me off there I'll never know: it should have been Leeds, where I know the governor. I'd have been treated much better. They'd have given me a packed lunch as well, when they sent me off. Anyhow, they were glad to get rid of me, though they weren't bad chaps. They let Dismal share my cell and always had a vat of slops for him to eat. When your letter came with the money I was off like a shot and got here an hour ago. I still don't know what it all means, except that those smuggling lads don't fuck about when you cross them. That smack across the skull seems to have damaged my appetite. The only good thing I can say about them is that they were English enough not to push a needle into Dismal and hurl him into the river.'

'What did they do with Wayland Smith?'

'Do you know him?'

'Only what I heard at Blaskin's. Seems he's researching for a TV documentary on smuggling.'

He took a silver toothpick out of his pocket and began to ply it. 'He's probably on his way to Hamburg by now. I expect he'll wake up in the middle of a donkey show, and he won't be playing the donkey.'

'Can they get away with a thing like that?'

He leaned back and laughed. 'Michael, your sarcasm is more than made up for by your sense of humour. Them lads can do whatever they like. That's why I think the sooner you're back in the Moggerhanger compound the better. If you could spend your life never more than twenty feet away from the great chief himself you would live forever.'

I called for Maria to bring another pot of tea. 'That's not my idea of life. I want to finish him off. I want to get him put behind bars.'

He came forward so that I would hear every word. 'Shall I tell you something? Life's too short. And however bad life is, it's very good. Why do you want to get him sent down? Because he's done you a bad turn? If that's the case, your motives are revenge, and that's selfish, Michael. Don't stoop to selfishness. In any case, "vengeance is mine, saith the Lord". And it's right. Why ruin yourself? Let the Lord take care of a lord. He will. And if he don't, somebody else will. And if nobody else does, you and me's got nowt to lose – by and large. But maybe you want to get rid of him because he's ruining the economy? Or because he's drugging the whole country silly? Very good motives, Michael. Far better than revenge. But shall I tell you something? Don't bother. He's drugging the whole country silly? It was drugged before, only the drugs was different. And what do you want to do with the country, anyway? Wake it up? Pardon me while I swim to France.'

'I don't suppose it's much different there.'

'No, but the grub's better. Where's that lovely young wench with the tea?'

I felt as if I was swimming in treacle. I could neither sink nor get out. It was necessary to go back to the centre before I could decide what to do, but where was the centre? 'I'll report to headquarters tomorrow.'

'That's what I'd do in your place. Do you mind if me and Dismal hang on for another day or two?'

'Ask Bridgitte.'

We were sitting around the fire that evening, and she announced that she was missing the children. They'd had enough of a holiday without her. She was going back to Holland. 'Besides, I have a boyfriend, and I'm missing him as well.'

There was silence for five minutes, then I said, packing as much threat into my voice as I could: 'What did you say?'

She flushed her usual high colour when she was inwardly disturbed. 'I've got a boyfriend in Holland.'

I was ready to choke. 'So it's the end?'

'Yes.'

'Really?'

'Really.'

I stroked Dismal's wide head. 'And what about my kids? I'm missing them as well. I haven't seen 'em for weeks, and it's breaking my heart.'

There was a big tear in her left eye. 'You can see them whenever you like.'

'It comes to all of us,' said Bill.

'You keep out of this.' I had been expecting it for a long time, hoping for it, in many ways wanting to be free of her for good, but now that the words had come out, and in front of other people, I felt sick. At the same time I wasn't certain that she meant it, and this made me angry, so in order to make sure, no matter how much more miserable I was going to be, I asked: 'When are you going to take your things from the house?'

'It's my place as much as yours. I'll take them when I like.'

'Make it soon,' I said. 'My girlfriend wants to move in.'

'Do you play this game often?' Bill said.

'Girlfriend?'

It was getting too complicated. 'I'm only kidding. But what about Maria?'

Maria, who sensed things were not as they should be, sat idly with the knitting on her lap. 'She's your responsibility,' Bridgitte said. 'You brought her.'

'That's nice of you. I need a caretaker.'

'I'll stay on for a day or two,' Bill said. 'She'll be all right with me.'

'Yes, and I'll thank you to keep your hands off her if you do.'

'I'll go back to London,' Maria said. 'To get a job.'

'You stay here,' I told her. 'I need you. Look after Dismal and Bill. London's no good for a nice person like you. The police will send you back to Portugal if you haven't got a job. In fact they're probably hunting high and low for you at this minute.'

She began to cry.

'It's all right,' I told her. 'You've got nothing to worry about. I'm going to London tomorrow to kill the man you used to work for. Then I'm going to Holland to kill Bridgitte's boyfriend. Then I'm going to kill myself. Clear the air a bit.'

'A holocaust,' said Bill. 'Take a Bob Martin's and calm down.'

I fetched a bottle of whisky out of the cupboard and poured everyone a glass. 'Here's some medicine, Maria. It'll make you feel better.'

'It's whisky.' Her eyes moistened. 'I like whisky.'

So that's how it happened, I thought. No wonder she didn't know.

'Give me another.' Bill drained his glass before I set the bottle back on the table.

'You won't kill Jan,' said Bridgitte. 'He'll kill you, you coward. You won't frighten me, or him.'

'Of course I won't kill him,' I laughed. 'I'll be too busy with Agnes.'

She swallowed. 'Agnes?'

'The girlfriend I mentioned. I really have got one. She went to America with me. Her name's Agnes. And she's pregnant. This house won't be big enough to hold us soon. It's just as well you're leaving.'

'You're rotten,' she screamed. 'Rotten, rotten, rotten.'

'I don't know about that,' I said.

She stood up.

'You throw that glass,' I told her in no uncertain terms, 'and it'll be the last thing you do.'

She set it on the mantelpiece. 'Maria, let's go to bed.'

Sweating with misery and rage, though I knew I was getting off lightly, I poured more whisky for Bill and myself. Maria had a look which I can only describe as ecstatic when Bridgitte picked up her glass, and the bottle, and they went out of the room holding hands.

'This place has a funny effect on people,' Bill said, 'but I find it restful enough. Jack Daniel's has a lovely taste. I wish you hadn't let them take the bottle.'

'I've got some more,' I said, going to the cupboard.

Twenty

When everything is settled, torment slops away beyond recall. It is arguable, of course, whether anything is ever settled, but I thought it was as I dressed in my two-hundred-guinea bespoke three-piece suit, donned my tailor-made shirt, laced up my handmade boots, put a handkerchief in my lapel pocket and took a brace of duty-free Romeo and Juliet cigars from the box in the spare room. I filled a holdall with shirts, underwear, shaving gear, my hip flask and the air pistol. Last of all, I threaded the gold half-hunter watch across my waistcoat. No one was awake. I said goodbye only to Dismal. Maybe I would be back in the morning. Perhaps I would never be back. The outcasts of Upper Mayhem could look after themselves.

Streaks of pink cloud crossed the sky, blue on the ground and hazy above. It felt good to be alive, the sort of morning that was kind to a hangover as I strode along with my umbrella towards the bus that would take me to the station. I bought a *Times*, and a train came within five minutes. Judging by my state of mind, my middle name was Havoc, no matter how many decisions had been made. To know what to do, and come out of chaos with advantage, seemed impossible. Whatever I did would be wrong, so I was bound to do the worst. My mother would say, not without pride, that it was the Irish in me, but I didn't think so. When your back is to the wall you at least turn round and give it a push in case it magically falls and you are free. All in all, I felt reckless, certainly in no mood for taking the safest option.

Wearing what I was wearing, I could not go into the

maelstrom on anything less than a first class ticket. Bridgitte's announcement that she had a boyfriend and was leaving me for good, made the knives inside turn even more quickly than when I recalled Moggerhanger's dirty trick in sending me to Canada with a load of printed matter which, whatever else was stamped on them, contained my death warrant. Whereas he had wanted to wipe me out physically, Bridgitte, from motives of self-preservation which nobody but me could understand better, was out to destroy me in spirit.

I had always prided myself on never giving in. In leaps of optimism, I was spring-heeled Jack, though today I thought that if I got with alacrity out of the dumps I might land somewhere even worse. People in second class, when I went for a stroll, glanced at me from behind the fortifications of their faces. I looked back from mine. They saw a berk from the first class going through for a walk, and I saw people with expressions put there by too much looking at television, that I had fought to wipe off my own face since birth.

A few miles of walking would get my confidence back. I strode through the City, by the Bank of England and St Paul's tube station, over Holborn Viaduct and down Fetter Lane into Fleet Street, and west via the Strand towards St Martin's Lane. The more I walked the less inclined I was to go into Moggerhanger's den and get chopped into little cubes of meat. London made me cheerful. So much traffic and so many people continually passed that no threat seemed serious anymore. I had accumulated a few thousand pounds since I started working again for Moggerhanger and what a pity, I mused, that I should disappear into the Thames or prison before I could spend it.

I went into one of those new-style eating places with plastic sawdust on the floor and plain wooden tables called The Trough, where the menu was chalked on a board and you could get a wedge of quiche, a lettuce leaf, a slab of damp brown bread and a cup of acorn coffee that wouldn't send a tse-tse fly to sleep, for five pounds. I sat for half an hour while I read *The Times* and watched people coming and going.

A girl came in and, instead of sitting at a table, she went behind the counter and through a door. She came back wearing a grainsack apron, as befitted a waitress in such a dump, and I saw by her reflection in the mirror that she was that same Ettie from the café on the Great North Road with whom I'd had a romantic attachment on my way down from Peppercorn Cottage. That's London, I thought, wondering whether I should do a bunk before she spotted me. There was no time to make a decision. She came up to me, and the flush of recognition disappeared under her blond roots. 'Michael!'

'I wondered if you'd know me. I was going to get in touch with you at The Palm Oiled Cat or whatever it was called, but whenever I went north you were on the other side of the central reservation, and we always came down a different way. Or I had my employer in the car and wasn't allowed to stop.' So much fundamental shifting about had recently happened that no leap of my imagination would take me back to the sort of person I'd pretended to be in order to broach that broom cupboard. 'I would have looked you up sooner,' I went on, 'only I had to go to America for a week. I thought about you all the time I was in New York, though.'

Her little mouth got straighter and straighter. 'I hate rotten liars.'

'So do I. The worst liar I ever knew was my father. The next worst liar was my mother. They made life hell.'

'Oh, fuck off.' She went behind the counter. The trouble with working-class girls, I told myself, is that they always say what they think. I picked up the newspaper and tried to figure out an anagram in the crossword. Ten minutes later she was back. 'Do you want me to chuck this boiling soup over you, or are you going to stop pestering me and get out?'

I wasn't one of her sort, who would respond to such a request by pushing the boiling soup into her lovely, sensual face. I fingered the remaining corner of my mouldy bread and killed a weevil that dropped onto the quiche which I hadn't had the courage to tackle in case I got bilharzia. 'I'll go when I've finished my lunch, or whatever you call it.'

She delivered the soup to the next table and went back to the counter. There was a cashier at one end and – behind the vats of cornmush and gritcakes and wholemeal onion patties and Brussels Sprout paste and melted cheese dips and nut rissoles and codliver oil salad dressing – were two other women, one of whom I fancied very much. She was a mature thirty-five-year-old clandestinely eating a beef sandwich as if she had only taken a job at such a place in order to drive the customers mad, because lengths of meat and fat were hanging from between the bread like living organisms soon to be devoured. She was full-bodied, and had dark ringlety hair, and her high cheekbones were highly flushed as if they'd been too near the fire. Ettie, who was in tears, had presumably complained of my offending presence, as I knew she must if I sat there long enough, so that when the woman had finished her sandwich and poured a cup of strong black coffee out of a hip flask – which being too hot could grow cooler while she was dealing with me – she came swaying beautifully between the tables of satisfied customers, and said: 'You'd better clear off. You've been annoying one of our waitresses.'

I looked up. 'I was waiting to have a word with you, as a matter of fact. I've been here for luncheon on at least five occasions recently, but it's only been due to you, not to that foul-mouthed little chit. You've been under observation.'

'What the hell are you on about?'

'Your name is Phyllis,' I said. 'You are approximately thirty years of age, and one of your parents comes from Ireland. And you're divorced.'

My sharp ears had heard her greeting to Ettie on the way in, and I put the rest together from all sorts of clues. I could also have said she had two kids and lived in Camden Town, but didn't want to overdo it, or spoil the picture.

'How do you know all that?'

'It'd take too long to explain. There's a new restaurant opened not far from here called Raddisher's. Used to be The Shin of Beef. You probably know it. I own it. To be honest, what food I've ordered here wouldn't be enough to energise an ant, so I'm thinking of sloping off for a porterhouse platter at the aforementioned place. I might have a barrel of Burgundy to wash it down. Would you care to join me?'

I saw by her eyes, and the slight turn of her lips, that she'd had quite a bit to put up with in life, but because it had been mostly from blokes like me it was still only blokes like me who could deal with her and hope to get anywhere. The expression around her brown eyes was so subtle and active that her whole life seemed to pass in front of them before her hostility finally went and she said: 'I'm working till three thirty.'

'I'll meet you at seven thirty tonight, for dinner.'

My speedy response pushed her back into the trenches, and her lovely eyes clouded over. 'What did you do to Ettie?'

I yawned. 'I'm afraid it's what I didn't do. That's always my trouble. She worked at a service station, as you know, which wasn't far from my estate in Cambridgeshire, where I breed racehorses. I couldn't take her there because of my wife. I know I'm soft-hearted, I must be, because my mother's Irish, but I don't like making women unhappy, and I stick to that rule so firmly that unfortunately I occasionally end up hurting someone, or making myself even more unhappy because of it. But if I had taken her home with me the chances were that my wife – and it hurts me to say so, but it's the truth, so I don't see why I shouldn't – well, she would have got Ettie into bed before I could. My wife's like that. Even our five kids look askance at her now and again when she's with other women. I'm pretty broad-minded myself, because when she's got tired of some of these women, I have to comfort them, and then I have my innings, you might say. But I didn't want to subject Ettie to her baleful influence. I wouldn't wish that kind of thing on any woman.'

She wanted to go away, but couldn't. She was horrified, which was promising. She was fascinated, which was dangerous – for her. But I was tired of it and wanted to end matters.

Good woman that she was, she wrung her hands together, and looked across at the bar, where Ettie stood as if wanting a news bulletin from the negotiating table. What it was all about I didn't know, and I craved the certainties of an encounter with Moggerhanger.

'When I took my secretary home to do some work, the result was the same,' I went on. 'I hired a male secretary, and took him home, but she had him in bed as well before midnight. I was at my wits' end, but finally decided that I was the only one who'd be safe when I went into that house, simply because she despised me so much.'

'Don't listen to him,' Ettie shouted. 'He'll tell you anything. He's a fucking liar.' Half the happy eaters looked closer at their gritcake and vintage carrot juice, while the rest stared across at her. She rushed over to me, her little bill pad swinging. 'He sent his pal up to The Palm Oiled Cat to tell me he wanted to borrow ten pounds because he was down the road with a puncture. He said he would come tomorrow to pay me back, with love and kisses. But he never did. And now look at him, dressed to the fucking nines and denying everything.'

I pushed the chair over in my haste to stand up. 'What did you say, you lying little tart? What pal? I don't have any pal.'

She turned to Phyllis. 'You see? I suppose he ponces off a lot of women like that. And I said I was in love with him. I can't believe it. He said he was in love with me, as well.'

'Men do,' Phyllis said.

I don't suppose I'd ever been much closer to mental agony than I was while standing there. Or I had, but I'd forgotten the other times. 'What was this chap like? Was he a blind man? Did he have a dog?'

These questions inflamed her even more. She jeered. 'You see? He's trying to get out of it.'

Phyllis had the most honest face I'd ever seen that still had a trace of human feeling in it, and I wanted to make love to her there and then, but knew I had very little chance. 'They all do,' she said. 'Wild horses wouldn't drag the truth out of them. It's enough to break your heart.'

'If any of these knives were sharp enough, I'd cut his'n out.'

Blessing my luck that I hadn't met up with her in some Cellar Carvery, I took a ten pound note from my wallet to pay her back. 'If you can't tell me who it is, it's not fair.'

'Fair?' she said. 'You use that word? That's what that panda bastard said. He kept using the word fair. I said I hadn't got ten pounds, but he said it wasn't fair of me to hold it back while my boyfriend wanted it to get out of a jam. I borrowed it from the cashbox till I got paid that night. I gave it to him. And after I got my wages and went to put the tenner back in the till the boss saw me and threw me out. I had to hitch-hike to London, and nearly got raped twice on the way.'

'You see what you've done?' Phyllis put an arm around her shoulder when she went back to crying.

He must have committed the crime on his way north, the night after I'd given him twenty pounds. I had always thought I was rotten, but it didn't make me feel good to have evidence that some people were worse. 'Here, take this. I always repay my debts, even if somebody else has done the borrowing. But I never was on the A1 with a puncture, and I certainly didn't send Ronald Delphick to you for a loan.'

'You didn't?' Ettie put the note in her pocket.

'No, and I'm sorry, even though it wasn't my fault. I'll be responsible for what I do myself, but not for others taking my name in vain. But as a way to kiss and make up, I invite you both out to dinner at Raddisher's. We'll eat rare beef and drink red wine, and after dessert I'll smoke a Monte Cristo cigar to get myself out of the cellar of depression that the inhumanity of man to woman has put me in. Is it a deal?'

Ettie laughed. So did Phyllis, who said: 'I don't think Banning the Bomb would be any good for somebody like you.'

'There's only one thing: when I next set eyes on Ron Delphick the Panda Poet I'll thump him. No I won't. You can't take the incorrigible to task, a poet least of all. In the meantime I have to get out of this Nutcracker Palace, so I'll meet you at the Covent Garden tube station at seven thirty.'

Before either could object I kissed them on the lips and left, allowing at least half the clientele to get back to demolishing nutburgers which to me looked like objects I'd rather not mention.

A taxi nearly ran me over near Charing Cross, but it wasn't the driver's fault. I can never wait for space between the motors before getting over the road, but dodge the London traffic like a pigeon in a kind of roulette which keeps me fit and alert until one day the big wheels will no doubt trundle over me. But after my encounter with Ettie and Phyllis in The Trough I felt able to tackle Blaskin with my usual filial impiousness. I also wanted to put a couple of finishing chapters to the shit-novel, and he reminded me of it as soon as I opened the door:

'How can I live if you don't get my books in on time?'

'It might help if you wrote one now and again.' I dropped my bag and coat on the floor. 'Is there anything to eat? I've just been thrown out of a vegetarian restaurant.'

'Who threw you in? By the way, your mother got back this morning. After the postcard arrived to say she was arriving, she knocked at the door. I was in bed with Mrs Drudge, so it wasn't a very felicitous homecoming, though I should have known she would come without warning, because the card had no stamp on it. My heart sank so low when I saw it I'll need a bathyscaphe to go down and bring it back. Or a drink. Have another.'

'I'd love one.'

'I at least hoped she'd get back too late for the cocktail party being given this evening to celebrate the publication of my twenty-fifth book. Now I'll have to take her. You're welcome too. Maybe it's not a bad idea to play the family man now and again. I'll know what I'm talking about when I plunge into a loving and horrific family saga.'

He opened the fridge for a jar of rollmops, a packet of Californian radishes, an Italian salami and a melon from Israel. German shepherd bread came out of a drawer. 'Pity Mrs Drudge has gone, otherwise she could slice it for us. I always cut my finger. Be a good chap, Michael.'

I hacked off a few pieces, then got to work on the shit-novel, to bring some relaxation into my hectic life. I pumped out page after page. The lover of Tinderbox Cottage now had the husband and wife prisoner at Peppercorn Cottage, and he proceeded to tell them his life story – in justification for his bizarre behaviour – which included three murders for which he'd not so far been apprehended, though the worst atrocity was when he'd held a red admiral butterfly captive in a cellar and forced it to listen to similar confessions before pulling its wings off and then setting it free. I got three and a half pages out of that. The tension was mounting because, his shotgun being double-barrelled, no one knew whether or not he was going to make it five murders. I was almost sweating myself. Then the police surrounded the place and there was a siege, in which every nettle and blade of grass was an accessory after the fact.

At one stage they heard a scuffle and thought he was coming out to give himself up, but it was only a couple of rats fighting over a piece of bread. To keep the shotgun-lover calm, a policeman began to tell his life story through the door, about how he'd been underprivileged and poor, how he'd studied at home, but mostly at night school, and worked himself up the educational ladder as far as nine O levels and then joined the police force because he wanted that sense of belonging that you only got in the army or with the lads in blue. And he wasn't disappointed. He'd do the same again, because life was worth living, no matter who you were, though a rise in pay would never be unwelcome, because he'd got a wife and two kids. On the other hand, he also had a Vauxhall Viva and a nice flat in a police block and perhaps (fumbling for his wallet), 'you'd like to see a photo of my two kids taken at Morecambe last year . . . ?'

This drivel continued for ten more pages, because the policeman had a lot to say about catching burglars and punching skinheads (with which no reader can disagree) or chasing terrorists when they landed from the Middle East at London Airport.

I could end the book any time because there were two hundred pages on the table, but I went on and on. One policeman, having pissed into the nearby stream, suggested to his superior officer that they withdraw from the vicinity and send a gunboat. He is commended for his sense of humour, then told to go back to the mobile canteen for an extra mug of tea and a Mars Bar.

I went into the mind of the man with the shotgun, who told his prisoners about how he believed in God, otherwise he wouldn't be so ready to kill them, would he? He felt a great loneliness at the middle of himself. He dreamed of falling through it, and woke up screaming. It was a hole he could only fill with a holocaust. God is love, not emptiness.

'Yes, sir, but you ought to put that shotgun down, you know.' The policeman perspired under the searchlights. His wallet was sopping. The argument about God went on. Everyone was waiting. It was on television. The woman hostage began to have a baby. More arc lights were brought up. A chopper hovered overhead. The Japanese television rights were sold. When a camera lens came through the window the husband and lover joined forces and attacked it with hammers because the fees weren't high enough. They tied a message to a rat and sent it to their agent waiting up the hill with a lump of cheese. But, unknown to any of them, a third, fourth and fifth camera took a film of their religious and human objections to having the world pry on them at this fraught time. They decided to brook no encroachment on the universal theme of the birth of a New Man but, dear reader, it availed them not – believe you me. Thomas à Becket was killed when a tip-up juggernaut shed its load of words.

The world looked on at this drama played out in the primitive precincts of Peppercorn Cottage in the Shropshire hills. Taking a lesson from Delphick, I let myself go on the alliteration, and it worked. In poetry it was out of date, but in prose it was up to the minute, for the moment. From the opening vagina of the wife I went into the mind, if you can call it that, of the TV commentator and filled a page of phrases such as ripping the sky, tearing at the stars, clouting cloud out of the way – until Baby was born. Husband, who now had the shotgun, decided to make a run for it.

He climbed out of the top back window and, silhouetted in starlight, fell to the ground and broke his ankle. Copper grabbed him but, before the jump, our Lover had taken his gun and shot at the Copper but missed. Husband zig-zagged between trees and went up the hill. (Film rights sold.) Moonlight also shone. At the top was the frontier of Wales. Once inside, he was saved. (Two pages on Welsh Nationalism.) He ran, a Druid got him with outstretched arms. It was a cloud. He leapt through it, athlete that he was. (A reading on Radio Three.) Back in Peppercorn Cottage, Lover tended Newborn Babe. The harrowing surrender scene had to be read to be believed.

Blaskin was satisfied. It was such an appalling shit-novel – the drivel of a fourteen-year-old – that he laughed. 'Nothing better to get me off the hook. They'll turn it down, and I can send my masterpiece elsewhere.'

'Glad to be of service,' I said. 'I think we're coming up to the climax. I only need a few more pages, so I can finish it in the morning.'

'You'd better,' he said. 'Now get out of the way while I dress for my hour of glory. Where your mother is I don't know, but she'll show herself at the party, woe is me.'

Even though he hadn't been present during a minute of my bringing up, I suppose I got my passion for snazzy dressing from him. In some matters blood tells more than circumstances, and the wish to be seen as smart by the outside world, no matter how ragged I felt within, or how scruffy inside my own abode, was something I'd had for as long as I could remember.

Blaskin donned a black suit and bow-tie, and I could have shaved by the shine of his ankle-length boots. 'Mrs Drudge has a good hand for that.' He looked critically at what I wore, and supposed it was the best I could muster.

When we got out of the taxi and went into the party at Bookman Hall he introduced me to his publisher, Tony Ampersand, as his research assistant. I did not deny it. To be known as his son would have lumbered me with too much I couldn't live down. The brilliantly lit hall was half full, and I made for the table where champagne was poured and food laid out. Blaskin handed me a cigar, which I lit after eating half a dozen sausages, several cauliflower heads and a few smoked salmon titbits.

I stood with my glass at a vantage point to watch whoever came in, though it was soon difficult to see through the crush. Blaskin took me to Margery Doldrum and Mrs Drudge, annoyed at them being together, and hoping I would break up their twosome. Mrs Drudge was tall and icy and I could tell she didn't like me, which made me want to get into bed with her, but knowing it would take too long to engineer, and not caring to run off my own father, I didn't waste any chit-chat. I think she hated anyone connected with Blaskin, though she seemed annoyed when Margery turned sharply and left her alone.

The noise was like waves breaking on the shore at Brighton rather than Blackpool, though it was still hard to hear what was said. Blaskin was at the door, greeting newspaper and magazine people. When Margery asked me how his latest novel was getting on, I told her it would be out next month. She promised to tell Melvin Gomery, who might review it. They had it in for Blaskin, though it didn't seem to reduce his sales. She pointed out the luminaries: Colin Camps of the *Soho Review*, Victoria Plumb of the *Daily Retch*, Peter O'Graffity of *Private Lives*, Christopher Hogwash of the *Bookbag*, Edwin Stowe of the *Hampstead Review*, and Susan Stopwatch of the *Literary Mirror*. They were not the first liners, she said. They had gone to another party, though maybe some would come later, if they hadn't had enough to drink.

Raymond Mangle told me that his latest novel was about Iranian fanatics calling themselves 'The Brothers of Cordoba', a terrorist group working to bring Spain back into the fold of Islam. 'They have thousands of members in training. Secret cells have been set up in Seville and Toledo. The Foreign Office knows about them but doesn't mind really. In fact they are trying to do a deal, promising to give them a free hand in Spain – as far as the Pyrenees – if they won't claim Gibraltar when they come to power.'

'Is it a fantasy novel?'

'Oh no. In twenty years it'll happen. Mark my words.'

'Don't tell Blaskin,' I said, 'or he'll write it.'

'You think so?'

'He's sure to.'

Standing on tiptoe, he looked around the room. 'I like this kind of party. I've had nothing to eat but kippers for over a week, washed down with white wine.' His lipline, not quite lidded by his beard, became rippled with dislike when I answered his question by saying I only read Gilbert Blaskin, Sidney Blood and Ronald Delphick. His eyes turned a more intense grey to signal his disgust.

I told a girl with long auburn hair and a hare-lip who worked in publicity at Lock and Kee that I wrote book reviews for *The Times*, under a pseudonym. She tried to find out what my real name was, so I said that if she followed me into the cloakroom I'd tell her. 'Now I believe you,' she said, and vanished like a fish in water.

'Who's that big pompous-looking chap standing by the door talking to Blaskin?' Mangle asked.

'How the hell should I know?' But it was Lord Moggerhanger, who gave Blaskin a friendly pat on the back, then turned to bury Tony Ampersand's boyfriend in a cloud of cigar smoke. One or two middle-aged publishing women were punked-up to the eyebrows, and Moggerhanger shifted uneasily when they spoke to him. I got close enough to hear one say how privileged she'd be to publish his life story – or even a novel. 'It's taken care of.' He nudged one who got too close, having seen Lady Moggerhanger and Polly observing what was going on. 'Mr Blaskin is doing a book on me, so I expect he'll take care of publication.'

'How did you meet *him*?' Punk-one asked.

Moggerhanger laughed. 'Where does one meet Blaskin? I read a page or two of his books. Or my wife did. All I know is that he's a gentleman.'

'Do they exist?' asked Punk-one.

Punk-two was scornful. 'What *is* a gentleman?' She had made a good job of trying to disguise her impeccable middle-class roots by adopting the fancy dress of the workers.

'A gentleman is someone who never admits to being one – for a start,' he told her. 'Then it's someone who doesn't give a gnat's fart – if you'll excuse the language, though I expect you've heard worse – for anybody or anything, but keeps his eyes open and his trap shut. He knows the world belongs to him, but isn't above a bit of generosity when the mood takes him.'

'You sound as if you'd write the most wonderful book,' said Punk-one, a little fawningly, I thought.

He slapped her on the back. 'And you'd be quite an attraction if you agreed to work at one of my entertainment complexes, my dear. You'd be very good at it. I'll pay you a nice fee. How about it?'

'She already has a complex,' said Punk-two.

'I say, Claud, get me a drink,' said Lady Moggerhanger.

'Nothing's ever any good unless you have two of it,' he said. Then he saw me. 'Michael! Come here, you naughty boy!' He didn't only push the finger with the bloodstone ring on it, but his whole hand, which I shook. Pressures were genuine and hearty. 'I'm glad to see you, let me tell you. You're always close to me, you know that. I was more than glad to know you'd extricated yourself from that Canada business. I knew you would, otherwise I couldn't have sent you. But you're a bit silly not to come straightaway for your debriefing, though I did understand you wanted a rest first. Anybody would have re-entry problems after a trip like that.'

Punk-two indicated me. 'Who is he?'

'My *chief* courier.' He was an emperor awarding promotion on the battlefield.

Punk-one, as quick as a flash, gave me her card. 'Do *you* want to write a book?'

'No,' I said. Moggerhanger looked happy at my correct response. 'In my job I sign the Official Secrets Act, and it's for life.'

'He could do it, though,' he said. 'He's got it in him. I'll bet he'd win a prize if he did.'

'The Moggerhanger Prize,' said Punk-one.

Punk-two spilled her champagne with excitement. 'I say, that's a wonderful idea, Jane. What do you say, Lord Moggerhanger?'

He was in a good mood, because it was his first literary party, as it was mine. 'That depends. If it's a money prize, forget it. But if I can pay in club memberships, or a stolen motor, or forged book tokens, or an ikon one of my lads got from Russia for a pair of tights, we might be able to talk about it.'

He was surrounded by the laughter of fairly young women, but even young men were turning to look. Punk-one came back leading a waitress with a tray of champagne glasses. Polly Moggerhanger took one, and saw me.

'It's been a long time,' I said.

She tried to smile, and succeeded. 'You haven't altered – physically.'

'You haven't changed either, I'm sure.' Her hair was just as black, her face fuller but paler. Her lips were as shapely and her figure had ripened. 'In fact, you're lovely. I was in love with you, and still am. You haven't been out of my mind since all those years ago, but I've been out of my mind at not seeing you.'

She was a real Moggerhanger, as hard as nails. It was she who had connived with her old man in getting me sent to prison, and I thought that if I could get her put inside as well as him at some future date I wouldn't hesitate. Otherwise I would settle for giving her a smack across the chops just hard enough not to loosen any of the perfect teeth which I saw when she smiled. 'You never got in touch with me, though, did you? I often thought of you as well, and was always hoping to see or hear from you.'

'I'd heard you were married.'

Her laugh carried all over the room, in spite of the noise, and Punk-one looked at her so lovingly I thought she would try to talk her into writing a book as well. 'When did you let that stop you?'

'Or you were busy having a kid. I forget which. But I'll be around more from now on. Where do you live?'

'Not far from Daddy. On Pipe Road, number twenty-three.'

'I don't even know your married name.'

'My divorce came through last week. It's the same as it was before.'

'Convenient.'

'We like it better that way.' She touched my hand. 'But I must circulate, and meet Mr Blaskin.'

'Don't,' I said, horrified.

'Don't? Listen, I fuck who I like. And don't you forget it.'

'I'll try not to.'

I turned from the next pointless conversation and bumped into my mother.

'Don't you know me, then?' She kissed me and I hugged her tightly on the understanding that if I did any less I would have her following me around. It was almost seven o'clock and I had a date with Ettie and Phyllis at half past. All the same, my instinct told me to run, though not because I didn't love her. In fact, when I banged into the startling wild-haired creature I thought she was just another appurtenance to the publishing profession, and only her brassy hilarity prevented me from assuming she was Punk-three. In that fatal few-seconds flash between first sight and the death of perception which comes from recognition, I saw this willowy, sallow-faced, attractive, well-worn forty-year-old (she was fifty-five) to whom I was about to say a few flirtatious words before making my way to someone else. 'Gilbert told me you were back.'

Her beads rattled. 'I've just been talking to him, but he told me to fuck off. He's got some hopes. He was chatting up that syphilitic racketeer Lord Moggerhanger. I don't know what he wants out of him. He's the biggest whoremonger in Europe.' Punk-one and Punk-two were standing by, but Moggerhanger was too far off to hear. 'I came all the way back from that lesbian commune in Turkey to be present at my husband's twenty-fifth book party, and the prick-head tries to ignore me.'

She took a glass of champagne from a tray swaying by like a magic carpet, and drank it like sherbet, then grabbed another. Dark hair crinkled down her shoulders, and her kind of beige sack dress was festooned with clinging gew-gaws. She asked how Bridgitte was, and I told her the score. 'You lucky bleeder,' she laughed. 'Bridgitte was always too good to live with you. How are you going to support yourself now?'

'I'm working for Moggerhanger.'

She put the champagne glass into a haversack decorated with CND symbols. 'Well, if you go to prison like you did last time, don't write and tell me. Only don't let him send you to Turkey and get you put in jail there. You may be my son, but I wouldn't like that. I used to belong to the

Society for Cutting Up Men, but now I belong to the Society for Cutting Up Turks, and that means most Englishmen as well.'

Punk-one interposed her presence. 'Can I introduce myself?'

My mother put an arm round her. 'Any time, love. Do you want me to write a book?'

I slid away. My intention had been to cut it fine by leaving at seven twenty-five and taking a taxi to meet Ettie and Phyllis, but at seven fifteen I heard a loud shrill voice: 'And you couldn't fuck half a pomegranate stuck in a lift door!'

What was I to do? Pull her away and take her home? Such a suggestion would earn me a champagne glass thrown in my direction, which is what happened to Blaskin. The scuffle sounded like someone sandpapering the floor. A circle opened. People were shouting, but above all came Blaskin's wounded roar: 'I divorce you, I divorce you, I divorce you!'

He was blind Samson pulling out the props. An unliterary silence cleared the room even of tinkling glass. 'Don't touch me,' she said, 'or I'll kill you.'

'Put that glass down.'

'Show me you love me, then.'

'Did I ever love anyone else?'

'You might be a writer,' she shouted, as if just back from her elocution lesson, 'but you're an upper-class twit to me. You stick pins in people to make 'em jump, so's you can write about 'em. Right now you're writing your twenty-sixth. I know you, prick-head! I can see that little tape-recorder going behind your left eyelash.'

His moan ascended to a scream. 'You push me back into the slime!'

'It's where you belong, you arse fucker. That's all you ever wanted.'

A great Oooooh! went up.

'That was to stop you becoming a lesbian,' he threw back.

'Any woman's a lesbian who lays eyes on you.'

'I don't need you anymore,' he laughed. 'I'm at an age when I can get all the young women I like.'

'So am I!'

I made a track through to her. 'Come away. You're going too far.'

Both had tears on their faces. If this sort of session was in store for me at fifty-five I wanted to run to the nearest bridge and jump in. Or I would accept any dangerous assignment that Moggerhanger could dish out. 'Not half as far as that dirty bastard went. He's English to the core, which means he's worse than any Turk.'

'You're ruining my career.' Blaskin hid behind his hands, though I suspect he was laughing. I didn't wait. They were quite capable of looking after themselves. I envied them, in a way, while never wanting to be so outspoken. It was unfortunate, I thought, as I ran out and put my hand up for a taxi, that a man of thirty-five had to have parents, and just my luck that the quarrelsome pair would live so long that I'd no doubt still be a son at seventy-five.

Twenty-One

As soon as I was away from them the pall lifted. In any case, there's something inspiring about the London crowds seen from the inside of a taxi on a weekday evening when it's still daylight. A girl ran across our track to get to Eros as we rounded the Circus, and lighted advertisements were already flashing, hardly dimmed by the sun. There was a feeling of luxury and well-being, and I would have told the driver to take me up Regent Street and down Gower Street to get to Covent Garden, except that it would have made me late. Some taxi drivers are a rough lot, but I've always had a soft spot for the way they earn their living. 'You just come from that Blaskin party, mate?' he asked, pushing back his window.

'Yes. A good do.'

'Is he drunk yet?'

'Nearly.'

He laughed. 'There are two Mr Blaskins. One is when he's in a taxi, and then he's as good as gold. Another is when he's in his own car. Then he's a devil, and you'd better keep clear. But we like him. You always know where you are with Mr Blaskin. A real sport. I only wish I could say the same for his brother.'

I swallowed twice, and craved a double brandy. 'Brother?'

'The Reverend George Blaskin. Must be older than Mr Gilbert, sixty-five, I should think. He's a mean and cantankerous old so-and-so, believe me. I don't think they get on well. He's always trying to save Mr Gilbert's soul and between you and me I think he's got his work cut out. I heard them arguing once when I was driving them to

Paddington. The Reverend George is a little thin chap with thick white hair, and he was really hammering Mr Gilbert. I could have laughed. Gilbert said he had no soul. Mind you, his sister can be an awkward customer as well.'

I nearly opened the door and jumped out. 'Sister?'

'Gertrude Blaskin. She's the matron of a hospital. I wouldn't like to get on the wrong side of her. She's six foot, give or take an inch. I saw her arguing with Gilbert on the pavement once outside the National Gallery and she hit him with her umbrella, but Mr Blaskin grabbed hold of her and gave her a terrible blow at the back of the neck, then pushed her into my taxi as I drew up. What a family. I thought mine was bad enough.'

'Are you sure he's got a brother and sister?'

'Certain. But they don't see much of each other, and I can understand why. There's no doubt about the relationship – they hate each other enough.'

I was appalled at the thought of such an aunt and uncle, but had no time to ruminate on the fact because at seven twenty-nine we pulled up by Covent Garden station. Being thirty seconds too early, neither Ettie nor Phyllis were there. I paced up and down. Things had been so hectic at Blaskin's party that I'd only had two champagnes, and my mouth was as dry as a tinderbox. A smell of beer wafted up the street, and I was pondering on the delights of a quick quart when I saw Phyllis coming through the crowds. 'Where's Ettie?' I gave her a kiss on her lovely red lips.

'She had a headache, so I sent her home.'

'Where does she live?'

'She's staying in my flat, till she can find a room. Anyway, she'll get Huz and Buz to bed, and meet us at Raddisher's in half an hour.'

The names rang two bells. 'Huz and Buz?'

'Bloody hell-raisers, but she knows how to keep them under. She's a proper little madame, Ettie is, when she sets her mind to it. Which way shall we go?'

'Hungry?'

She nodded.

'Famished?'

'I'm starving.'

We walked to Raddisher's. I didn't know what to say, still jangled by the taxi driver's revelations, and in any case we couldn't stay side by side because of the crowds.

Across Charing Cross Road I took her arm. 'I think I've heard of Huz and Buz before.'

'They're in the Bible,' she said.

'I mean – as living breathing people.'

I had phoned for a table at Raddisher's from Blaskin's, and we sat upstairs by a window. 'I thought you said you owned the place.'

'In a manner of speaking,' I said. 'I come here so often it feels like it.'

'I've only known another liar like you.'

'What was his name?'

'I forget.' The waitress took her tatty-looking coat with its rat-fur collar, and I wondered what I was doing with her when I'd seen such gorgeously turned out women at Blaskin's party. If my mother's Nottingham-style slanging match hadn't driven me away I might have gone home with Polly Moggerhanger.

Yet after a while, sitting opposite Phyllis at our small oblong table, looking at her lively dark eyes and cynically smiling mouth and high flushed cheekbones and little flattened nose, and her attractive bust sheathed in a white satin blouse from Littlewood's with an emerald Woolworth's plastic brooch holding it together, I changed my mind. 'You're lovely. I'm glad you came alone. You know how I feel about you. Ever since I first saw you I've been in a fever of sexual excitement waiting to set eyes on you again. It was a wonder I didn't lay hands on myself.'

'I was looking forward to it as well.' We reached for

each other's hands over the table, stopped from going any further by the waitress asking if we would like to order.

'I'll have the wine first, White Bordeaux. Then Newcastle Pope – or Pope's Newcastle – or Châteauneuf du Pape – a bottle of Jolly Red.'

'What are you on about?' Her annoyance at my rigmarole looked like getting out of hand. Ettie came just in time, flushed and fair, her small face slightly worried in case she had missed something.

Phyllis ordered smoked salmon and tournedos steak, as if I was made of money, and Ettie followed her example, both of them wanting to throw off the demoralisation of the meatless place they worked at. I didn't mind, because Phyllis was worth spending all I had on, the sort of woman whose halfway good looks and exuberant spendthrift spirit would make any man feel cock of the walk. When we chinked glasses and began the meal she said: 'Well then, what do you do for a living?'

'I'm an estate agent, in Nottingham. I'm down here for a week, visiting friends.'

Ettie cut her smoked salmon into little squares, while Phyllis rolled hers up like a carpet and slid it in at one go. 'What do estate agents do?'

'A good question. Me, I'm the cat minder.'

'Cat minder?'

'It's a vital part of our organisation.' My seriousness convinced her. 'Often when we show people around a flat or house they complain that a room isn't big enough to swing a cat in, so we decided to keep a few cats to prove that a room was – or was not, indeed – big enough to swing a cat in. We keep four, as a matter of fact. After that, most other estate agents copied us, and also kept cats.'

'I didn't know.'

'Haven't you noticed, when you go into an estate agent's office, a distinct reek of cats? It's not unpleasant, because they're very well housed. My job is to feed them, clean out their boxes and keep the log up to date.'

Phyllis finished off the buttered brown bread. 'Log?'

I poured more wine. They knew how to knock it back. 'A cat-log, in which is recorded the date, time, place and results of whenever the cat is taken out to be swung in a room to see how big it is.'

Ettie pressed her hands together. 'Isn't it cruel?'

'Well, no, not on a strict rota basis it isn't. And they're used to it. It's their life. They like the outings and look forward to the excitement. They only get used every two or three days. Not all clients argue about the size of a room, in any case. But if one expresses any doubt, or if we anticipate an argument we put the duty cat into the box and take him along. They're very intelligent. If the room's not big enough to swing a cat in, they're wonderful at missing the walls and avoiding bits of fireplace. They set up a meeow like a radar set to indicate that the room's too small, and then it goes back in the box. Once, though, when I was coming through the fishmarket old Whiskers got out. He leapt out of the bag, you might say. As to how I eventually got him back, that's a story for another day. I might tell it when the steak arrives.'

We finished the white, and the red came. 'Enjoying it?'

'Marvellous.'

Ettie's mouth was too full to speak, so she nodded. They half believed my cat nonsense, and if Phyllis didn't I could tell she liked me for taking the trouble to spin it. I half regretted not having worked such an idea into Blaskin's shit-novel, but you can't think of everything. The food and wine put some colour into Phyllis, and I stroked her cheek with my middle left finger. 'You're the most splendid person I've ever met.'

It was obvious she had never been called splendid before, because her eyelashes went like butterfly wings. 'I have a remote and charming little place called Peppercorn

Cottage. One day we'll go there, you, me, Ettie as well as Huz and Buz. It's the most peaceful house you can imagine. How much longer are you both going to work at the Groundnut Café?'

'I've got to earn my living,' Ettie said.

I offered them a brandy.

'Are you married?' Phyllis said, 'or aren't you?'

'Separated.' I saw no reason not to tell.

'Life's hard,' she said. 'I sometimes wonder how I can go on. I can't explain it, really.'

'Don't, then.' I ordered brandy and coffee, and lit a cigar. 'I tried to kill myself last year. I took an overdose of opium, but it didn't work. Then I hanged myself and the rope snapped. Next, I shot myself, and missed. So I decided it wasn't for me to take my own life.' I'd had my bellyful with Bridgitte often wondering how much longer she could go on with her so-called dreadful existence, and I wasn't going to take the same crap from a woman I'd treated to an expensive meal which she had eaten with sufficient gusto to suggest she intended living forever. Ettie just looked, knowing Phyllis had said the wrong thing. It was getting harder to choose the one I would go to bed with. Both, I decided, stroking Ettie's arm so that she wouldn't feel hard done by. 'I love to see you eating all that rich food.'

She'll be telling me she's pregnant next, I said to myself.

'It's because I'm pregnant,' she said.

'Don't say such things, for God's sake.'

She laughed, a wicked little weaselly laugh. 'I can be a better liar than you, if I put my mind to it.'

Phyllis was warbling with laughter again. I told them more about the beauties of Peppercorn Cottage, till the bill came, when I put on a serious face, just to let them know they were having a good time.

Darkness had been switched on outside, a feeble glitter of blue between rooftops. Phyllis held one arm as we walked along, and Ettie took the other. Noises had softened, and on a quiet corner of the network of main drags even the trilling of pigeons could be heard – if you had ears as sharp as mine.

'I can't tell you how much your company means to me.' My words could apply to either of them. 'On an evening like this.' After ten dull years with Bridgitte at Upper Mayhem I was falling in love with every woman I swapped six words with. I was starting to live again, except that getting entangled with Moggerhanger might mean I was going to die.

'I'm having a wonderful time,' Phyllis said. 'But I'm a little bit tiddly.'

'I am, as well,' laughed Ettie.

I kissed her on the cheek. 'What we need is a drink.' We wandered up a darkened street off Long Acre, past Stanford's map shop, turned a few more corners and came to something like a warehouse with a light over the door and a notice that pulled me up short: 'Ronald Delphick, Poet Lariot, Reading Tonite. Admish: One pound.'

Phyllis made a motion of rolling up her sleeves.

'We're going in,' I told them, 'but he's mine.'

Ettie ran up the stairs. 'Don't spoil my fun.'

He was already reading, but we pushed our way in and sat on a wooden form among a few dozen other people. We couldn't help making a clatter, and Phyllis giggled as they moved their legs to let us get by. Delphick stood on a stage, a hand on his panda's head. 'I hate people who come in late, but at least it's another three quid.'

They laughed. He wouldn't be so glad when he saw who it was. ' "Dusk Queen",' he said, 'is the title of the next poem. I hate titles, but my public insists, so here goes. I hate my public, though I've got no option but to love them. I dedicate the poem – I hate dedications also, but what the hell –' more laughs – 'to Prue, a generous little girl I once met, and don't suppose I'll meet again because she's undergoing psychiatric treatment, though to be fair to myself, she would have been, anyway, sooner or later.'

'Get on with it, Ronald,' a bearded man shouted.

'Yes sir, no sir, three bags full, or two rather.' He read each line as if it was a whole poem, sufficient space between the words so that he could get his breath – the same poem he'd let me have just before dropping him off near Stevenage, though it sounded better now.

He stopped long enough for us to know it was the end, so that we could cheer. 'What bullshit,' I said in Ettie's ear.

She stabbed me in the ribs. 'Shut up. It's wonderful.'

Everyone clapped, and so did I.

'I wrote that at Doggerel Bank.' He was breathless with emotion. 'That's the place where I live, or exist, rather, on the pittance I earn as a poet. But when I cut my throat, not having eaten for three days, I'll leave it to the National Trust. They can run it as the Delphick Museum, where my fans can come and mourn. My few belongings will be laid out here and there.' He took a paper from his sugarbag jacket. 'And this is what they'll find. I dedicate this list to the farmer who lets me have the cottage at five pounds a year. It's the least I can do because I haven't paid him since I started living there.' Phyllis was choking with mirth. Everyone clapped, and he hadn't yet read the list. Ettie looked adoringly in his direction, and I wondered what had really gone on between them at The Burnt Fat service station on the Great North Road.

'Of course, it's not a shopping list. That would be too long to read. It's not a laundry list. That would be too short to bother about. It's a list of absolute essentials, which is just about right.'

There was a pause in which he gave us time to think about his eloquence and contemplate the honour still to come. 'Well, the list I'm going to read begins like this. I must explain that it's only the first draft. In fact I'm still making some of it up, which gives an insight into the poetic process of yours truly.

> 'So here's my list,
> And I'm not even pissed.
> In my mess-of-pottage cottage you will find
> French letters on a clothesline
> Greek letters on the wall,
> A pot dog on the shelf
> Hopscotch on the floor
> Girlie-mag pix on the ceiling
> And a hi-fi in the bog.'

'I have a dog called Fido, by the way, and when I call "Hi, Fi!" he comes running in for his daily popsong.' Laughter for at least ten seconds. 'To resume my list:

> 'Eccles cakes in a bag
> Pencils in a row – '

He changed gear, a priestly booming in his voice:

> 'A knife fork and spoon
> To eat up the moon –
> And a tinlid for an ashtray.
> A typing machine,
> With old man ribbon
> Who just keeps rolling along.
> A table of planks
> That I made with these hands,
> And an orange box to sit on.
> A row of books held up by a wire:
> When I choose one for the fire
> I read poems from the smoke.
> An old fag packet
> And a dead beer bottle
> Newcastle Brown, I think it was
> But most of all

The bed I lie on's
Made at birth
And can't be got from
But whose clean sheets I share
With Ettie and Betty and Phyllis and Dylis.
Yet when I'm alone I share a bone
With my randy Panda
(Don't I, pet?)
And watch the snow come down the window
All
Winter
Long.'

The last three words had half a minute between each, and the effect was tremendous. Nobody thought they had been robbed. The interval had come, and before leaping from the stage he reminded us that books of his poems were on sale by the door – and drinks available at a bar downstairs. He would sign any we wanted him to, even Blake's or Shelley's, or T. S. Eliot's, and sink any pints that were offered.

There was a luscious girl at a table by the head of the stairs, with piled blond hair, a broad high forehead, almond-shaped eyes, a small curved nose, full lipsticked lips and a face narrowing to a dimpled chin. She wore rimless glasses and smoked a cigarette from a black holder. There was the faintest sheen of fair hair on her upper lip. She wore a purple high-necked blouse with small white buttons down the middle going between her breasts to a slim waist. A stock of books burdened the table and a tin to one side contained a few pound notes and coins.

I was immediately in love with her because, apart from her obvious qualities, she struck me as being the most intelligent person I had ever seen. She glowed intelligence, as well as mystery and beauty – but above all intelligence. How I could tell, I didn't know, unless it was by looking at other faces around me, especially Ettie's and Phyllis's. I wasn't even interested in seeing what her legs were like, but stood in front of the table as people were going downstairs for their drinks. 'I'll buy three books.'

She didn't look up, but passed them over and took my tenner.

'Will you come down and have a drink?'

She smiled. 'I'm with Mr Delphick.'

'You can both come.'

'You'll have to ask him.'

'Are you his girlfriend?'

'In so far as he can have one.'

'Is he impotent?'

She laughed again. 'He's somewhat promiscuous, as you can imagine.'

'I wouldn't be, with someone like you.'

'You don't have someone like me. At least I don't imagine so.'

'What's your name?'

'Frances Malham. Why?'

'You've bowled me over.'

An even heartier laugh showed her clean and lovely teeth. I'd never been so close to such a person. 'It's nice of you to say so,' she said.

I could feel my elbow plucked from behind. 'Where do you live? Where do you work?'

Thank God my questions amused her. 'I'm at Oxford. Doing a medical degree.'

'You're going to be a doctor?' I was ready to faint.

'I hope so.'

'Are you coming, or aren't you?' Ettie squeaked.

I was ready to turn round and deliver the most vicious but enjoyable smack at her chops, and tell her that if she persisted in pestering me I would rip off her drawers and strangle her with them, but that would undoubtedly have destroyed the good impression I was attempting to create before Frances Malham. I had never known myself to be in such a trap. 'Just a moment, darling,' I said.

'I must see you again,' I told Frances. 'I want to talk to you about Mr Delphick's work. I'm a writer, and I may be able to do something for him.'

Her face became even more intelligent, if that was possible. 'What's *your* name?'

'Michael Cullen. But I have another handle, and I'll tell you about it when I see you.'

She scribbled something on a scrap of paper and slipped it in one of the three books I'd bought. That was enough. I was satisfied.

'Hello, pet.' I heard Delphick's horrible Yorkshire twang behind me, the sort he put on when in London. 'Having trouble?'

I turned, and at the same time he recognised Ettie. The half smile went off his face. She had been entranced by his reading, but the fact that it was over, combined with the callous neglect just evinced by me, wiped out the effect of his performance with surprising speed. 'I've been waiting to meet you, you fucking thief. Where's my ten quid?'

'Ten quid?' he laughed. 'I've yet to meet a person who got even ten pee back from me, never mind ten quid. Anyway, I don't owe it to you. I've never seen you in my life, you filthy little trollop. Piss off.'

The only thing wrong with Ronald Delphick, basically, was that he could speak, and he might just have been all right if he hadn't added that unnecessary dose of invective. I suppose he got carried away, and even I couldn't fault Ettie for the way she reacted, nor could I argue with Phyllis's heavy-handed response. Ettie reached across the table, and put her fingers in the box to take out what she considered her property, even though I had repaid the ten quid at lunchtime, and Phyllis caught Delphick a fairly comprehensive swipe across his complacent mug. Then another smack sounded when Frances Malham, that superb creation of beautiful intelligence, clipped Ettie so hard that she spun several feet backwards and barely stopped herself toppling down the stairs.

Quick as a flash, as they say, I got hold of Delphick's hands and pushed him beyond range. He'd been intent on battering Phyllis with clenched fists, which I couldn't allow, though it was hard to say why. He hit the wall with an impact that caused him to think twice about bracing himself for more. Before Ettie and Phyllis could join forces to go for lovely Frances Malham I grabbed their arms and dragged them kicking and screaming down the stairs.

Perhaps I was saving them from a mauling, because Frances may have more than held her own. Their obscene threats I will not put down on paper, though I suppose Frances must have heard them, which gave me a pain at the heart, until I remembered that she was a medical student, and had heard far worse already, or if she hadn't she would have to get used to hearing it in the future. I also remembered, when I had Ettie and Phyllis pinned against a wall downstairs, and was threatening to knee them both if they moved an inch, that I had left my books upstairs, one of which had Frances Malham's address inside. 'Wait here,' I said, 'or I'll kill you both.'

I went up four at a time, scattering people still coming down. 'I'll never be able to write again. Look what you've done!'

I felt in an ugly mood. 'Belt up, Delphick, or I'll kick fifty poems out of your arse, you troublemaker. You shouldn't rob a young girl who has to work for her money.' I grabbed the books from Frances. 'I apologise for that little outburst. I love you. I'll see you again.'

She smiled, though she was clearly upset.

Slipping the books in my poacher's pocket, I got back to Ettie and Phyllis at the bar. I put a hand on each shoulder. 'You should be ashamed of yourselves, behaving like that.'

'Oh bollocks,' Ettie said. 'I hate you.'

'He ought to be flayed alive,' said Phyllis, 'doing that to poor Ettie.'

'Forget it,' I told them. I longed to see more of Frances, but not with those two slags around my neck. 'Let's go to my flat. I'll give you a better drink than you can find here.'

We got out before Delphick appeared. 'Do we go by tube?' Phyllis asked. 'Or bus?'

'With me, you travel by taxi – and like it.'

Down the Mall and by Buckingham Palace, I sat between them in the back, and kissed them both, and had a good feel of their lovely breasts by the time we reached Hyde Park Corner. I don't suppose Ettie knew I had my hand on Phyllis's breast, nor that Phyllis realised I was getting to know the shape of Ettie's, which was the best of sitting between two women in a half dark taxi. It was the only time in my life I prayed for arms as long as those of Kenny Dukes.

My idea was to lure both women into the same bed, an experience I hadn't had in my so far sheltered life. But the first thing Phyllis did when we got to Blaskin's flat was go into the bathroom and throw up. She said the taxi ride had upset her stomach, but I again remembered Moggerhanger's remark that London was the salmonella capital of the world, and hoped my turn wasn't coming. Perhaps it was only a case of gluttony. She came back with her blouse unbuttoned down the front. I already had my tongue in Ettie's mouth and we weren't far off trying to pack ourselves into each other. I pulled Phyllis to us and kissed her, then I kissed Ettie, and kissed Phyllis again. Phyllis kissed Ettie, and Ettie kissed her, and they smooched each other and me with gusto, and I smooched them, and our threesome went on, until I thought the time had come to carry things a stage further.

For that to happen we had to let go of each other, and

no one wanted to. I sampled over and over the difference between Phyllis's lips and Ettie's. Phyllis's were soft and warm, and she kept them closed so that I got the best out of them. Ettie's were thin, and opened easily, so that my tongue licked around her little white teeth. I wondered what each of them felt towards the other, and towards me. While they kissed each other my hands went up their legs, and I wondered whose hand each of them thought it was, whether they imagined it was mine or suspected it was the other's. The three of us were locked into a love knot so firmly that the perfume and powder which they had on took me back to the days when I fucked Claudine Forks and Gwen Bolsover (separately, however), and wrapped me into a feeling I'd never known before – and was never to know since, because before it could go any further Blaskin and my mother came into the flat.

Gilbert took off his hat, an instinctive politeness on seeing ladies in the room. 'I sincerely hope I haven't disturbed a gang bang. Or have I stumbled on a prime example of Knightsbridge tribadism? Sir Richard Burton would write reams on that.'

'Who's that bleeding geezer?' said Ettie. I didn't know whether she meant Burton or Blaskin, though I imagined it was both. I had hoped that Gilbert and my mother had torn each other so completely to pieces at the party that nothing would put them together again. I thought he would end up blind drunk and despondent at his club, and take a room for the night in which to lick his wounds. And I had assumed that my mother might have gone to Upper Mayhem to cool off, or found a corner for the night in some Hoxton squat. But here they were, and she kissed my father like a schoolgirl. 'Shall I get you some supper, my darling?'

'I'd be delighted to have something to eat, my love. Those poisonous titbits at the party created hollows instead of filling me up.'

'You said your uncle was in Manchester,' Phyllis accused.

Gilbert turned to me. 'Michael, introduce us to your friends, there's a good fellow.'

I didn't like the way he said it, nor the way my mother put her hand over Ettie's shoulder and asked her to come into the kitchen to get some booze and grub on the table. Ever since prick-headed Blaskin had entered the room Phyllis hadn't been able to stop looking at him. She turned away to fasten her blouse, then smiled with simple-minded pleasure when he asked: 'What kind of music do you like?'

She blushed. 'Oh, I love Irish singers.'

'Och, do yer, den, me goil, well we'll see what we can foind for yer!' He sorted among the records, and instead of being insulted by this mock-Irish, she started talking it herself, and actually caressed his fingers as he passed her Beethoven's Kreutzer Sonata and asked if that would do. She laughed, and said no. He suggested she have a drink, and went to the bottles on the sideboard. His hand was at the back of her neck as he poured an Underberg which, he said after much salacious talk about her recent vomiting, would cure her once and for all. He got her to knock it straight back, and she shook from toe to head like a fat adder standing on its tail. Then, as if fainting from the shock to her system, she flopped into his arms and stuck her lips to his.

It was too much, especially now that raucous laughter from my mother, and a high-pitched giggling from Ettie in the kitchen had stopped. I felt I should get out of the flat and drown my sorrows in The Hair of the Dog, but my feet only moved as far as to allow me to lock myself in Blaskin's study and do some more work on his trash-novel.

The saga of Peppercorn Cottage was over, I decided. Two years had gone by. The clatter of the typewriter closed off the sucking and moaning noises from other rooms. I knew exactly what was going on. I sweated mercury. I felt more like writing a Sidney Blood saga than a Blaskin crap-opus.

A shoot-out at Stonehenge was on the cards. Dawn on Midsummer's Day. On coming out of prison, the husband in my tale bought a holiday cottage in Wales, but a year later it was burned down – cause unknown, ha-ha! – so he joined the Longest Day Society and limped on foot from Richmond to Stonehenge. His wife drove after him in her shining Volvo and brought The Child.

I dashed out to make some coffee, and noticed that Ettie was now with Blaskin, and Phyllis was in the spare room with my mother, and a more spaced-out set of fuck-drunk faces I had never seen. But I let that pass, and got back to my novel.

Smoke over Stonehenge. The Druids have it. The Child is carried in, held high. Stoned bikers lying by their machines (mostly 1000 cc BMWs) laugh irreverently as they boil a kettle of opium tea over a fire of burning L-plates. A horsemeat sausage stall does good trade. For two pages I start every word with a capital letter. The next few pages are in italics. That wad of pages are intimately concerned with the pimples on people's faces. Then comes a page with no capital letters at all, concerning a character called Snot, who drifts around crying, and putting people's fires out. The bikers do for him. They have a whip-round, and send him back to Merton on the milk-train – with his head on the wrong way. I'm determined to make this the most trashy novel in existence. Even the trashiest Blaskin novel no longer strikes me as being a very hard job, as I tack-tick-tack away.

The end of the story is near, and so is the end of the world. Every year a new dawn, at Stonehenge. A man with a little moustache and a slick of hair across his forehead, wearing a buttoned and belted mac, makes a fiery speech in favour of CND. After a few minutes he is laughed into silence, and I move elsewhere. The Child begins screaming. Its painted eyeballs portray different hemispheres of the world, and it hates everything about the place. Nothing will quieten its screaming. It is the Noise of the World, I say, and move on from that as well. Babies don't like New Dawns. They are new dawns themselves, and the false dawn of a New Dawn will destroy it. They want to stay snug in the womb of the zillions that have gone before so that none will come after.

All the other children are asleep. They don't care one way or the other. People are singing hymns. A few wonder why they are here. Even midsummer is cold at midnight. It starts to drizzle, the sky's answer, and the wail of tribulation turns into a police siren.

Dogs bark. The coppers are looking for drugs. Little packets are flying into the fires, even aspirin and Beecham's Powders. A weirdo-nark makes incantations over the green and blue flames. A swivel-eyed biker thumps him. Another hits him with a wheel – 1000 cc BMW. One or two people are dragged off. Seven, actually, after I've counted. One person is an elderly novelist who protests that he's only there for the research. They let him go. He bears an 'uncanny resemblance' to Gilbert Blaskin, but I called him Michael Blood. The inspector picks his hat up from the mud and hands it back to him: 'Don't be hard on us, sir, we're only doing our job. Give us a fair write-up.' The novelist brings out his cigar case to offer him a smoke, and half a dozen syringes, plus a few Moggapills, fall from his pocket. The policeman picks those up as well. He puts them in his own pocket, but refuses the cigar, then moves on to put down a disturbance. Some Hell's Angels are overturning the soup kitchen.

The Child is taken back to the car, while its parents stand on the luggage rack to get a better view of the Dawn. Rain stops play, and clouds separate to show a rippled sky, grey rags and TB blood, God's shirt in the morning, or the Devil's, more like it, at this Pagan Festival.

I go on a bit more, and by three o'clock I'm so clapped out I end the novel with terror biting into thousands of hearts as, from the crossbar of a megalith, an enormous beastlike figure is seen stalking across the fields from the east with a terrorist's floorcloth around its head, a machine gun in one hand and a whip in the other, shouting that Allah is Great, and vomiting crude oil over the countryside as people run to escape the tide that catches fire.

I stop the book in the middle of a sentence, as a few stoned bikers are revving up for a counter-attack, unable to take in what I've typed. That should fuck it up. Then I remember that that's what Blaskin wants me to do, but I'm too sleepy to care and, stretching out on the couch, fall dead asleep.

Twenty-Two

My mother woke me at eight o'clock with a cup of coffee. 'Here you are, son.'

She looked smart and fresh in a pair of olive-drab corduroys and one of Blaskin's shirts. I wondered whether I'd also grow tougher as I got older. 'Where's Ettie and Phyllis?'

The place was too quiet for them to be there. She lit a cigarette and gave me a drag, then sat on the end of the couch. 'You mean those dirty young trollops you brought back last night?'

'You did all right out of it.'

'Don't get grumpy. Your father gave them some money, and we told them to go to Upper Mayhem for a few days. They'll like it there.'

I jumped. 'For God's sake, that's my secret retreat.'

'Don't be mean. You allus was a tight-arse. I don't suppose they'll go. Too quiet for 'em.'

'They aren't even battered wives, or unmarried mothers.'

'They're a *bit* battered, anyhow,' she said. 'I had that Phyllis so often she didn't know whether she was coming or going by the end.'

'What a rotten trick.'

'Go on, she had the time of her life.' She came closer. 'You're a good-looking chap, you know.'

'You're not so bad yourself.'

We looked at each other and laughed. She stood up. 'Well, anyway, it wouldn't do. You're more like your dad than you imagine. Don't ever go bald, that's all. You'd better get a wash and come to breakfast. I'm making a big pan of scrambled eggs. And don't say much to Gilbert this morning if you can help it. He's not feeling too good.'

'Neither am I.'

'I know – but he's your dad. And don't fucking argue.'

'I hate swearing,' I said.

She was getting nasty, and dangerous. 'You mean in a woman?'

'In anybody. But don't cook the eggs yet. I want a shower.'

'Make it quick, then.' She kissed me on the lips, and went to minister to Blaskin. I switched on the bathroom tranny and listened to a programme which I thought must be called Mob Rule. Between the whir of the shaver I heard howls and catcalls, jeers and hyena laughter. People in short periods of silence were trying to say something sensible, but others accused them of lying, defaming and vilifying – when anything could be heard at all. As I was fastening my tie the programme came to an end, and I learned that it was called Yesterday in Parliament.

Blaskin forked food into his mouth like a somnambulist. When the doorbell rang he said: 'If it's my publisher tell him I'm dead. I was buried secretly by the light of thieves' candles on Hampstead Heath. He'll read about it in *The Times* tomorrow.' Then he closed his eyes and went on eating breakfast as if he'd live forever.

When the bell rang again a look from my mother told me to get up and answer it. Pindarry stood outside, hat in hand, the feather pointing towards my stomach. 'Lord Moggerhanger expects you at a gathering tonight, seven o'clock sharp, dress informal.' He went back into the lift, having left the door open. Arguing was useless. He was only the invitation card. It was the lack of an RSVP that I didn't like. He was lucky to get back into the lift unscathed.

I laid the morning mail on the table, and sat so quietly that my mother said it was like having two zombies at the trough. Gilbert mumbled that he never became conscious before twelve, unless he had it off immediately on waking up, and then he went back to sleep till one. I'd intended reporting to Moggerhanger that day, whatever the dangers, but his two-fingered summons put my back up, which was never to my advantage, so I made an effort to smile at my mother, and not to dig too obviously at Blaskin's overhung condition.

She fussed over us, buttering toast and refilling cups when the rim line went a fraction below halfway. She'd had the time of her life yesterday, having been to a party, got drunk, lived through a terrible quarrel with Blaskin, made it up, gone out to dinner, then come back to a night of satisfying love; while all I had done was put the finishing touches to a miserable novel, had half a night's sleep, and woken up to have Moggerhanger treat me like one of his lowest minions. To make up for it I decided to play the heavy mob, and frighten the guts out of Jeffrey Horlickstone.

When I had asked Maria what work he did, she indicated that he was very high up in advertising. Not only had he and his family tried to work her to death, but Jeffrey had also managed to get her preggers. If Maria had worked as much as she said, it was difficult to imagine when he could have done the deed, but nobody knew better than me that where a will existed, a way soon opened up.

Blaskin, sorting through the mail, slung a letter at me. He was very particular about the post. While he hunted for cheques and incriminating evidence against my mother, in that order, I opened an epistle from Matthew Coppice:

Dear Mr Cullen,

I hope you have not forgotten your promise to help me to bring Lord Moggerhanger to book. I have been doing my part, and the file of evidence I am getting together is growing bigger and bigger. What I am unearthing would astonish you as much as it pleases me. As soon as I think I have enough I will send it to you, and I trust you will do your best to make it *strike home*. I don't know how you will do it, considering Lord Moggerhanger's friendship with Inspector Lanthorn, but you seemed to be a very clever chap, as well as a good citizen, so I know you will find a way. I must tell you, before I sign off, that Wayland Smith the television man came snooping up here to find out about Lord Moggerhanger's affairs. I wanted to help him, but I knew that that would put me under suspicion. So I shopped him, and that has made them trust me more than ever. I am their golden-haired boy. That was just what I wanted. I think Mr Wayland was taken to Peppercorn Cottage. I don't enquire too closely because I want to stay in their confidence. You will be hearing from me again soon. Please eat this letter, or I shan't be alive to send the next, which is growing apace.

Yours Faithfully,
Matthew Coppice

On my way to the Horlickstones my fist was tingling, as if it had been dipped in a tin of iodine. The tube ticket almost dropped from my fingers as I went through the turnstile. I would teach the bastard to get Maria pregnant. And yet, did she really want me to? – I wondered by the time I got out into the sunshine at the other end. Bridgitte had bullied her into the idea, I was sure. In any case, hadn't I committed far worse actions than Horlickstone? Was I losing my sense of fair play? It was hard to say what drove me on, but, looking back, I'm more than glad that something did.

The trees along the streets smelled fresh, and it felt good to be outside, neither in a car nor in Blaskin's cluttered flat. Horlickstones' house was doublefronted and freshly painted, a garden in front and no doubt a bigger one behind with greenhouse and Wendy hut and a rope hanging from a tree with an old Volvo tyre swinging on the end even when there was no breeze.

It was Saturday, so I hoped he would be home, and not on his way to a football match. I hammered the iron knocker. They were too upmarket to have a glockenspiel or Swiss yodel-alarm. I expected to see a new *au pair* girl, but maybe he had put her up the spout as well, and packed her off home on the Newhaven ferry, because a woman who was obviously the type to be his wife opened up and asked what I wanted. 'I've come to see Mr Horlickstone. They sent me from the office.'

'You mean *Harlaxton*, I assume.'

'That's right. So I do.'

She had a narrow, delicate, fine-featured face, and would have been young-looking for a woman in her late thirties if it hadn't been for the wrinkles around her eyes and at the corners of her mouth. Nevertheless, she had that combination of worry and good looks that attracted me, though it was hard to know what kind of female would not have got me on the hop. My mother was right when she said I should never go bald.

'On Saturday?'

'It's important.'

She was dark-haired and blue-eyed, but didn't have much of a figure. Jeffrey had worn her out by his permanent hard-on, and when he'd got tired of her he had worried her to a frazzle by his hanky-panky with secretaries and home helps. I almost turned and walked off without accomplishing what I had called for, not knowing whether I didn't because I was afraid she would phone the police – suspecting that I'd called to burgle the house but changed my mind on seeing somebody in – or because I really wanted to blat her husband and give her the pleasure of seeing that for once he'd had to pay for one misdemeanour in his life.

'Why didn't they phone, I wonder? They've never sent for him on Saturday before.'

'I know. But it's on fire. Somebody broke in, poured petrol over the art department and set a match to it.'

She went into the house, while I stood with hands in pockets as if prepared to wait all day. But Jeffrey came immediately. He was a stocky man with short fair wavy hair, but rather worn skin, and was dressed in trousers, shirt and carpet slippers. His grey eyes glared at having been disturbed, but I couldn't tell whether it was from looking through his stamp collection or rumpling the skirts of his latest *au pair* while she was picking up Galt toys from the Habitat bedroom floor. 'What's all this I hear?'

'I don't know what your wife told you,' I said, 'but I'm here on behalf of Maria de Sousa, your Portuguese skivvy. Remember? I didn't want to mention it in front of your wife.'

He moved back sharply – to close the door in my face – but I got half inside and held it firm. 'I want to tell you that she's pregnant.'

He laughed, legs apart, head back, as if I'd told him the award-winning joke of the Universal Joke Contest. He seemed such a good sort that for a moment I knew I wouldn't have been there if Bridgitte hadn't made me promise. 'Not another!' His laughter made him so much younger and better looking than when he first came to the door. 'Oh marvellous! Wonderful! I'm populating half the bloody planet. But you see, it couldn't have been me, old boy, and if you think so you'll never prove it. It's impossible, out of the question.' His face turned red, and he pushed me, but with a clenched fist. 'I'll have no truck with blackmailers.'

It's always been my belief that if you're going to do something, then do it when it's unexpected. Surprise furthers. Shock accomplishes. It's not often, though, that the perfect opportunity presents itself. Now it did, because there's often no one more surprised than the bloke who, having taken a poke at you, gets one back. I hit him so that he lost his balance and did a spinning two-step along the hall and knocked an umbrella stand flying. 'Elizabeth,' he called, 'phone the police.'

'Yes,' I said, 'and I'll tell them why you're down on the floor. Anybody can get into that sort of scrape with a woman, but you shouldn't have laughed. Maria's my sister-in-law. My sister's married to Maria's brother. Her whole family are on their way from Portugal to cut you up. I'm in touch with a lawyer, and he'll write to the big chief of your advertising firm telling him about it. Get the coppers by all means, but you've had one fumble too often. When she has the baby it'll be dumped on your doorstep. Make no mistake about that.'

I was wondering whether to hit him again if he got up, when Frances Malham came out of a room further along the hall. 'What's that noise, Uncle Jeffrey?' Not only was she blessed with the most exquisite intelligence, but she had a superior memory to match: 'Oh, it's you!'

Life was too cruel. I'd just hit the favourite uncle of the woman I'd fallen in love with only the night before. I knew she was the girlfriend of the feckless Delphick, but I wasn't averse to a taste of unrequited love as long as I got there in the end. 'What are you doing here?' Her voice was not altogether pleasant, for there was a trace of blood under Jeffrey's left nostril. 'What happened?'

His laughter was almost as real as when I had told him about Maria. 'These damned slippers. I tripped in my hurry to get to the door and banged my snozzle.' His wink was meant only for me as I helped him up. 'What did you say you wanted?'

'I have a message for Miss Malham – for you,' I said to her. 'I was in Town this morning, and Ronald Delphick was beaten up by a gang of skinheads. They smashed his panda-wagon, but I managed to fight them off. I got him into a taxi and took him to my father's flat in Knightsbridge.'

Her lovely cheeks turned pale. 'Oh my God!'

'I've come to take you to him. He's not badly hurt.'

'You are good.'

'It's nothing,' I said. 'But he's asking for you, naturally.'

'I'll get my coat.'

Jeffrey came close. 'Was that true?'

My heart beat faster than when I'd hit him. 'No, but I had to say something. Maria is pregnant, though. My wife and I are looking after her. She's all right at the moment, but you'll have to do something when the kid pops out. As for thinking I'm a blackmailer, you should be ashamed of yourself.'

He came close, his eyes six inches from mine. 'How did you come to be able to lie so well?'

'Quick thinking,' I smiled. 'Sorry I was over-hasty. That's another of my faults.'

He rubbed his nose. 'Faults? It's a quality very much lacking in the world today. What's your job?'

'I'm a writer.'

'Do you get published?'

'Yes, but I write under a pseudonym. My father's Gilbert Blaskin the novelist.'

'You don't say.' He considered for a moment. 'Have you ever thought of working in advertising?'

'Occasionally.' What else could I say?

He reached for a jacket on the coat hook, and took a card out of his wallet. 'Give me a ring on Monday, and we'll talk things over.'

Frances came back with her coat, and a leather shoulder bag. 'Shan't be long, Uncle Jeffrey. Elizabeth's in the garden. Peter's been sick. He's all right, though. Must have eaten too many sausages at breakfast.'

I noticed his touch as she passed by, and wondered whether such a desirable medical student niece had been able to keep him off.

It had never ceased to amaze me how quickly one's prospects could be transformed for the better. Or, now and again, for the worse. But here I was, walking along the tree-lined Saturday morning suburban road with Frances Malham, when on seeing her for the first time the night before I would never have thought it possible, especially with Ettie and Phyllis causing so much trouble over ten paltry quid Delphick had conned out of them.

'You're walking too quickly for me.'

I would do anything to hear the sound of her voice, but slowed down, and she came level so that I could see the bloom of her cheeks. 'I'm glad I found you in.'

'How did you know I was staying with Uncle Jeffrey?'

'You gave me the address last night.'

'That was a friend's place in Golders Green.'

'In the press of the moment you must have written this one.'

She wrinkled her mouth, as if such a mistake was the tragedy of the week. 'Who were those two horrible females at the reading? They certainly took a dislike to Ronald.'

We stood by the main road, hoping to see a taxi. 'I met them in a pub and they told me about how he had tricked one of them out of ten pounds. It sounded too true to be lies. I met Delphick when I gave him a lift down the A1 three months ago. He got money out of me, and does whenever he sees me. He's incorrigible.'

She sighed, as if he'd bled her dry, or would if she let him. 'Is he badly hurt?'

It was as much as I could do to keep my hands off her delectable hips as she went into the taxi. 'Not really. In fact he's hardly hurt at all. To hear him scream you'd have thought they'd killed him. But he was more concerned for his panda. He's very English in his love of animals.'

'Poor Ronald.'

'He's a born survivor.' I thought the joke of her being fond of him had gone far enough. 'I expect he's borrowing money from my father right now, though it won't be easy. He's Gilbert Blaskin, the novelist.'

Her downcurving lips told me she was annoyed. 'Can't you come up with something better than that?'

I realised the folly of taking her to a place inhabited by an old lecher like Blaskin, not to mention by someone like my mother. If they were in the same mood as last night they'd cut her up between them and eat her raw. I hadn't had time to weigh the ramifications of the lie I'd been forced to blurt out, and it was too late to modify it now. Frances had probably seen photographs of Blaskin, and his features were too distinctive for her to have any doubts when she saw him. You could bet that he wouldn't hesitate to pull the great writer stunt when he set eyes on someone as lovely as her. And if she was so impressed with a rotten little half-baked poet like Ronald Delphick how would she react to a fully-fledged author like Blaskin, even though he was sixty, bald, drunk, decrepit and, in all probability, poxed up to the eyebrows? 'I may have my faults,' I said, 'but I don't lie, except in exceptional circumstances, or in a purely professional way, because not only is Gilbert Blaskin my father, but he occasionally throws a bit of writing in my direction.'

'Oh, for God's sake.'

'I suppose you're worried about Ronald? You should be. He's made a lot of enemies. Not that I myself regard him as a bad sort, because he has to live. It might be a good idea, though, if he laid doggo at Doggerel Bank for ten years or so.'

'Doggerel Bank?'

'His house in Yorkshire. Didn't you know?'

She said nothing.

'It's a wonderful place. Quite a mansion. He's got forty acres, though it's mostly moorland, except for a smallish ornamental garden of five acres. I was up there once. It's a solid stone-built house looking across the dales, one of the most beautiful views, I should think, in all England. His wife and two kids love it there. At least he said it was his wife, and who was I to disbelieve him?'

Her shoulders were shaking. Time to stitch your lips – now that she was crying. How could she, or anybody, weep over Ronald Delphick? Little did I know. I told her I was sorry. I really was. I'd have done anything to put back those tears. I'd have spread them on bread and eaten them with relish. We were passing Gloucester Road. 'Shall I tell the taxi to turn round and take you back to Uncle Jeffrey's?'

'No. I'll see Ronald first.' After a pause, near the Science Museum, she said: 'Is Gilbert Blaskin your father, or isn't he?'

'He is.'

My determination never to lie again was as strong as ever, because I was quickly coming to realise that telling lies never did me any good. On the other hand they rarely caused those I told them to much harm. It seemed hardly worthwhile acquiring the moral taint of being known as a liar. On the other hand, I didn't know why – if my lying was so ineffectual – I was made to feel so tainted. As I got older my guilt in this respect became worse, especially sitting beside Frances Malham in the back of a taxi, as I took her hand to try and comfort her. If the intention of my recent bout of lying was to put her off a sponging fraud like Ronald Delphick, then they were told in a good cause, but if they were told to draw her in some way closer to me, then the sooner I acted on my determination never to lie again the better. On the other hand (how many hands have I got?) I was so in love with her that any amount of lying seemed justified. These thoughts having gone through my mind, I felt much improved. After helping her out of the taxi, I left the driver a good tip.

Going up in the lift I sensed a new curiosity coming from her regarding my good self. I smiled, and she couldn't have been too despondent because the beginning of a return smile settled on her lips. 'I hope he hasn't done anything silly like doing a bunk,' I said. 'He was certainly making himself comfortable when I left.'

I stood aside to let her out first. She may have been a supporter of Women's Lib, but I was taking no chances. If my politeness struck the wrong note she could have the pleasure of being scornfully indulgent, but if I was impolite when she expected me not to be her contempt might be fundamental. I was canny enough to know, however, that no female who attached herself to Ronald Delphick could have believed in Women's Lib.

The flat was uninhabited.

'Ronald!' I looked in all the rooms, and came back rubbing my hands – almost. 'Let me take your coat, then we can sit down and have a drink, while we think the situation over.'

'Perhaps that's the most sensible idea.'

Could there have been a more wonderfully intelligent-looking young woman with such a Venus de Milo figure? If only she had no arms to match, though I supposed in that case she would have been very dextrous with her feet when it came to defending herself. 'What would you like?'

'Vermouth.'

'Splash?'

'Please.'

'Ice and lemon?'

She nodded. 'I wonder what's happened to Ronald?'

'I expect he's gone off to Hamley's for another panda, and to Mothercare for a pram.'

She put on a show of concern. 'You don't like him, do you?'

'Well,' I said, 'put it this way: no.'

She looked around. 'I still can't believe this is Gilbert Blaskin's flat.'

'Do you like his books?' I said nonchalantly.

She thought for a while. 'Well, yes – though I think his attitude to women is putrid.'

I held up my glass. 'You can say that again. Cheers.'

'Cheers.'

I was unable to bite off my tongue. 'This place isn't a patch on Delphick's Yorkshire manor, I admit.'

'I didn't mean that.'

I looked into her eyes made smoky by the rimless specs. 'What *do* you mean? Do you mind telling me?'

She made a little tremor with her mouth. It was impossible that such a sensitive mechanism as her face couldn't detect even the most feeble lie. I held out my hand. 'Come on, I'll show you the flat.'

I drew her into Gilbert's study. 'Look around. Feel free. His first editions are in that bookcase. In the drawers underneath are his press cuttings. On that filing cabinet is a photograph of him as an army officer with two of his mates. You can easily pick him out. He's already bald, and you can see by his features that he's hopelessly corrupt.'

She walked from wall to wall, sipping her drink. 'You don't seem to resemble him very much.'

'You've made my week.' I passed a couple of pages from his latest novel. 'Read this. Apart from Blaskin, you'll be the first one to do so – and I doubt if even he has, he was so busy writing it.'

Flushing, she sat on the couch. 'Really?'

'You're the first one.'

'Shall I read it aloud?'

'If you must. I mean, if you like.'

'I can't read as well as Ronald.'

'Nobody can.' I sat by her side. 'But I'd love to hear *you*, all the same.'

' "As soon as he saw her," ' she read, ' "he knew it was The Road to Cheren all over again. The paper flowers on the table were pretty, and when he lit his cigar at the candle he tried not to blow smoke into her face. She didn't trust him, and didn't like him, but when did that have anything to do with love?

' "The coppery glow of spring spread over the flat fields. Nothing comes of waiting. He told her that he loved her. She said he never had. He never would. Nor much of hoping, either. Only out of doing does a light show through. And that, all too often, incinerates. There was but one thing he wanted, and he hoped she too was in the mind for it. Moral regeneration was his only hope, and therefore hers.

' "She looked at him, and realised that for all his thirty years, he wasn't grown up. He never would be, so what was she doing at the Fenland Hotel? But if he was to grow up, she could see all too clearly what he would grow up to be, and she didn't like it. The fact that she could see into the future, however, made all the difference between a live and a dead relationship. 'If a rolling stone gathers no moss,' he said, 'whose loss is that?'

' "(If I don't get her knickers off, I'll burst. Never say it cannot happen here. It always might, whether it does or not. That doesn't make sense. Or does it? Everything's too turgid. Write it fourteen times. You need a drink, you lazy swine. No, get her as far as that four-poster bed at least. Lead up to it slowly. Make 'em wait. Make yourself wait, you awful old prick. Why don't you admit it?)

' "She sipped her brandy, and the pursing of her lips boded well for when she lay naked on the bed and he lowered his head to suck an orgasm out of her lovely full-lipped cunt. He loved women, but loved those women more who loved women. Oh, Lady Samphire of the Ouse! What do we have to lose except the reek of virtue?" '

It was time for me to cough. He always spoiled it, and things would get worse. Such vile words coming out of Frances Malham's lovely mouth in the purest of accents seemed, to say the least, incongruous. I put my arm around her shoulder. 'Maybe you should stop. It's only the first draft.'

She laughed, flushed though she was. 'It's funny.'

'It's foul.'

'I'm getting an insight into the way he works. It's wonderful.'

'It gets worse. It must be the specimen sheet that he lets lady thesis-writers read when they come to interview him. Then he lays them down where you're sitting now – if they get the message. It's almost as bad as Sidney Blood without the violence. There's no trick he doesn't stoop to.'

She put the papers on the table. 'I suppose all writers are the same.'

If Blaskin walked in she was lost. I dreaded the click of the door. 'It's the creative process. They're in a permanent state of randiness. I've written a couple of books for Blaskin, so I know.'

'You?'

I kissed her hair. 'He has so many ideas he has to farm them out. He gives me the gist, I knock it off, he polishes it up, his secretary types it, the doorman posts it, some daft publisher prints it. One day I'll branch out on my own. You learn a lot working for Blaskin.'

She took off her glasses, and our faces touched. We were fully clothed, but I noticed the heat of her body. I could only assume she felt mine, for she moved a few inches. Being scientifically minded, she realised that such narrow space would make the heat increase, till the flashpoint came.

I had such an elegant hard-on that, if need be, I could have balanced a plate of black puddings on it as I made my way towards her up a flight of stairs. I put my hand on her leg and gently touched the thigh under her skirt. My hand went as far as it could go. She was in flood. I wasn't far off. Being in love, I came too quickly when we lay back on the couch. I wanted her to take her clothes off, but she said it was too late. Such easy success was bad for me. I had expected to pursue her for days, maybe weeks, but she had arranged for events to rip along at her own special pace, something which women did more and more these days. It was the way we fucked now – sometimes. Back from the bathroom, she said: 'I'd like another drink. I made myself come, otherwise I feel lousy.'

'Sorry it didn't work together.'

She smiled, and kissed me on the cheek. 'I'd like a cigarette as well.'

We sat in the living room. 'I don't know who you think I am or what I'm like,' she said, 'but I'm sure your ideas are wrong. My father was a doctor who died ten years ago, when I was twelve. He went to the surgery one day and the receptionist phoned my mother two hours later to say he'd had a heart attack. He was sixty and they'd been married fifteen years. He smoked and drank very heavily and that was what killed him. As well as overwork. I was the only child. My mother was over twenty years younger. She had practically no money, and got a job as a doctor's receptionist to pay for my education. If it hadn't been for Uncle Jeffrey I think she would have gone under. He's my mother's brother. He's been wonderful, and still helps out, though he has a family of his own. But he won't have any more children because he had a vasectomy three years ago.'

Was there never going to be a dull moment, an uneventful minute without one single surprise? Working for Moggerhanger was employment for senior citizens by comparison. I had given Jeffrey a punch in the face for having put Maria in the family way – just a few months ago – and here was Frances telling me that such a thing couldn't have been possible. I was too numb to pray that the earth would devour me. No wonder he'd laughed. Was it at the thought that his vasectomy hadn't worked again? Or did he know it was foolproof, and he was justifiably amused at my crackpot accusation? Yet if it wasn't him, then who had got Maria pregnant? She'd lied to me, though if she hadn't I would never have gone to the Harlaxtons and met Frances so as to bring her back to Blaskin's abode (by an equally outrageous lie) and confirm our friendship by a more delectable fuck than the hugger-mugger in the broom cupboard at The Palm Oiled Cat with Ettie. There seemed little hope of stopping that old roundabout as long as I breathed. A start in life goes on to the end.

'Are you sure he had a vasectomy?'

'I know the doctor who did it. He was one of my father's old friends. I also know the doctor who talked Jeffrey into having it done. His name was Dr Anderson. Jeffrey was going to him for analysis at the time, because he'd had a bit of a crack-up, and his advertising firm paid for the treatment. Jeffrey was in absolute terror of the world ending. He said he couldn't bear the thought of his children going up in smoke and flame at the same time as himself. And the idea of having one or two more children so that they would also be incinerated was even more terrifying. He called such anguish paying the Moloch Tax. He had apocalyptic visions of slaughtering Elizabeth, then the children and himself. He thought he might wake up in the middle of the night and soak the house in blood and paraffin – he said. So at least he was determined to have no more children and add to the casualty list.'

'He's such a cheerful-looking, extrovert bloke,' I said.

'I know. But the issue paralysed him, and even the fact that Aunt Elizabeth was on the pill didn't convince him that he wouldn't have more children. After the vasectomy he was normal, positively exuberant in fact, and went back to work. If I had to give anyone my idea of a good person, I'd tell them about Jeffrey.'

There was something wrong here, which was not surprising considering her opinion of a shit like Delphick. Still, I owed Uncle Jeffrey an apology, just as I owed Maria a smack across the chops. Another item which scratched me on the raw side was the way Dr Anderson, the evil genius of the psychology underworld, kept turning up. He seemed to be as big a pest on the body politic as was Moggerhanger on the social fabric, and if I had any say in the matter I would pull the plug on both. The only question was how. 'Do you know anything about Dr Anderson?'

I fully expected she would bring out a list of his good deeds, telling me of how he was the benevolent supporter of five thousand orphans in the Third World, that he personally washed mugs in a soup kitchen by Waterloo Bridge on Saturday night, and that he ran a home for battered wives in Glasgow.

'I think I would like another drink.'

'Willingly. Cigarette?'

She smoothed her skirt and stretched out her legs. 'All I know is that for some time after Jeffrey had his vasectomy, Dr Anderson was having an affair with Elizabeth.'

'He was screwing Jeffrey's wife? You're joking.'

I caught in the openness of her mirth a similarity to that of Jeffrey. 'I never joke about things like that. I often think that if I could bring myself to tell lies my life would be easier. Anyway, the upshot of Anderson's affair with Elizabeth was that she got pregnant. Would you believe it? It seemed that Anderson recommended vasectomies to his married patients as often as it seemed convincing to do so, and then, if their wives were halfway attractive, he had an affair with them to get them pregnant.'

'But you said Elizabeth was on the pill.'

'She came off it after Jeffrey's vasectomy, and Anderson

provided pills which weren't effective. Isn't that diabolical?'

'I'm appalled.'

'So was I.'

'And Elizabeth got a bun in the oven?'

'What a horrid way of putting it. You see, Anderson is investigating a breakdown theory, pushing people as far as they will go, to see at what point in their decline they begin to pull out of the dive naturally. Some do, some don't. After a certain point he's not interested in those who go down to the depths never to come up, but only in those who get out of it. It's this point of rebound that fascinates him.'

'He wants to remove it?'

'He wants to control it,' she said.

'So that's his game.'

She nodded. 'But he didn't have the chance to break Jeffrey. Elizabeth got rid of the foetus without him knowing. I helped her. It was a bloody awful experience for her. Not too pleasant for me, either.'

'You poor kid!' I drew her to me, and received a warm kiss which I matched with my own.

'That's all I know about Dr Anderson.'

And I knew that during or after his rave-up with Jeffrey's wife he had got hold of poor innocent Maria, who was now inflating with another of his monster-kids.

'I expect he's writing a book on it,' she said, 'full of graphs, statistics and obscene mathematical formulae that in reality mean extremes of emotion and misery. He wants to chart and document the point of return – or no return.'

'He probably sends his findings to the Ministry of Defence.'

'Or the Russians.'

'Or both. How does one stop him?'

'He'll end by running himself into the ground,' she said.

'I wouldn't bank on it.'

She looked at the window, as if Delphick was going to come flying in triumphantly on his Winged Panda. 'I wonder where he's got to?'

I could think of no one except Frances and myself. The world stopped, and I'd have a hard job to kick it spinning again. 'Drowning his chagrin in The Jolly Scribblers because Hamley's wouldn't take his cheque.'

She looked at me, and even with my ever-burning optimism I could hardly call it a loving expression. 'Maybe you really are Blaskin's son. Anyway, where is The Jolly Scribblers?'

'Near Mornington Crescent. But I expect he's gone somewhere else by now – our peripatetic Panda Poet. It's catching.'

'What is?'

'You start to imitate those who sponge off you.'

'I don't, but maybe that's because I'm a woman. Anyway, I must be going.'

I was in a state of terror, thinking that if she went I would never see her again, a feeling I would normally have despised. 'It's time for lunch. Why don't you have something to eat?'

'I'm not hungry.' She picked over the records by the Bang and Olufson hi-fi that was as thin as an After Eight.

'I am.' I went to her. 'For you. For your spirit, for all the thoughts you've had since you were born, and all the thoughts you'll have till you die. To say that I love you doesn't express what I feel.'

'I'll put this Schubert on, if I may.' She looked at me. 'In a way it's a pity we made love. I don't have to get to know you now.'

A stone hurled from the wall of a castle had hit me on the heart. 'I feel the same about you. I hated making love just then, not that I didn't enjoy it, but because I knew you were the sort that would use it as an excuse for calling it the end. I thought you expected me to make love, and so

I was forced to choose between disappointing you, or damning myself. The fact that I proved myself right doesn't make me feel any better. I can always use it for one of my stories.'

'Maybe I'm wrong,' she said.

I didn't give a damn whether she was or not (I certainly did) and told her so. 'I like Schubert, though not better than Bach.' Bridgitte used to play them. 'I'm going away tonight, and won't be back for a few weeks.'

She was lost in the music, so I had to become lost as well. I would follow her anywhere, through snake-pits and dog-tunnels, though I would resist the idea for as long as I could.

'I don't really know you,' she said. 'Perhaps I was wrong.'

I sat by her and kissed her. 'I don't know myself, so how can you? I'm not so sure I want to. Know yourself, and die. I have a stab at it now and again.' I came out with any nonsense because to mystify her was my only chance of getting anywhere. She was so knowing that to compete with her quality of mind and brain was useless, whereas gibberish might have some effect. I spoke into her warm ear. 'You're the last person I expected to meet in my life, because I've been searching for you from the beginning. That's why it won't kill me if you vanish forever. To live with an ideal woman would be like being born again, and I don't think I could stand it. Self-destruction was never in my line.'

Such rubbish was a pointer as to how I really felt. I was half laughing as I spoke, but hoped she would mistake it for a state of emotion near to tears. I stopped, as if overpowered by the beauty of the music (maybe I was) and to see whether my words would fetch a response.

'Have you ever written any poetry?'

I let a minute go by, as if I'd been waiting for such a question. 'I'm sorry you asked that.'

'Why?'

I watched another fifty seconds slide by on the clock. 'They're locked in a drawer at my house in Cambridgeshire.'

After a while (she was good at the game as well) she said: 'Can I see them?'

The speed of our conversation was sending me dizzy. I was beginning to crave a ding-dong battle with Bridgitte, or a bit of argy-bargy on the state of the nation with Bill Straw. 'They're not finished. There are only six. I burned fifty last week. They were too much like Delphick's twaddle.'

She twitched.

'I'll sort some out when I come back. If I come back.'

'Where are you going?'

'I won't know till tonight.'

She turned and kissed me. My hand went up and down her blouse, but I felt no response in me. 'What poets do you like?' she asked.

'Peter Lewis and John Jones. They're new young poets. They're sensational. They write so that people won't get any reaction at all when they read them. They're all the rage – or will be.'

'Who publishes them?'

'The Silence is Golden Press. No other poets can get a look in while they're on the scene.' I went on with my stroking and stoking. Her legs opened and I reached the crotch of her drawers. She was ready, but I was stone-cold. These young girls were shameless and wonderful. Five years older and I could have been her father. Even that thought didn't give me a hard-on. Schubert came to an end and left the field free.

She gripped my arm. 'I don't want you to go away.'

'I've got to.'

She undid her blouse and opened her bra in front so that I could knead the warm flesh. 'I love you,' I said. 'I think you know that. But my life's not my own.'

'Nobody's is,' I thought she said, as my lips went to her nipples. There was nothing I could do but go back to kissing her lips, and gaze at her pale brown eyes through the gold-rimmed glasses. My lips kept sliding off her nipple, which was so small there was hardly anything for a purchase. I sent a single finger under her hair and around the back of her neck, then drew it forward to her ear, and felt the curving slim wire of her glasses. I prised it up, and put a hand also to the other ear, and lifted them off to see her naked eyes beneath, and the effect of such misty and undressed eyes, and the feel of her light glasses hanging from one of my fingers, and their release as I let them drop gently on the table, gave me a surge of blood that put me in the mode of action – and no mistake.

Twenty-Three

I made my way along Kensington Gore and the High Street, then turned into Holland Park, heading for the Bush. Young mums pushed their prams down leafy paths and across lawns, proud at having done the most ordinary thing in the world, while peacocks with spreading feathers observed them haughtily. After our day of love Frances had gone back to Oxford, saying she wasn't sure about seeing me again. We'd quarrelled and shouted, and reduced ourselves to silence, and my zombie-half could only hope that she would reappear sometime, somewhere.

A con-man whose ambition was to bask in idleness, whose only ability (if he had any) was in telling lies, comes sooner or later to a point when the lying and the laziness have to stop. I decided this was it. In answer to Moggerhanger's summons via his pillock-in-chief Pindarry, I walked seven miles to Ealing to let the fact sink in.

I made westerly at a steady pace so as not to arrive in a sweat, a warm wind flicking at my face as I stepped out on my stint through all the Actons. My shoulder bag was heavy, but that was part of the game. At Upper Mayhem I often did twenty miles a day around the Fens with Smog, packing a weightier rucksack with gear and grub, and a big tea flask, and setting out in early morning to spot butterflies at Wicken Fen and birds at Dugdale Wood, and not getting home till dusk.

Kenny Dukes was at the gate of the Big Chief's house. 'You're the last one in. It's a real gathering. There's going to be something big on.'

The cuts from his meeting with Dicky Bush had healed,

except for a nasty-looking ridge under his left eye. I aborted a witty remark about having fallen over a Sidney Blood book. 'I'm glad you're on the mend.'

He growled. 'I'll disembollock him the next time I bump into him. I fuckin' will.'

We walked along the covered hall and into the main part of the house. Nobody frisked me to see whether or not I had a Sabatier carving knife strapped to my leg. I was one of the family, it seemed, which is what I wanted to be. Or maybe if he intended killing me after the Canadian fiasco (if it had been a fiasco – I had begun to doubt it) he would do it with a couple of well-sighted Kalashnikovs.

'If I see him crossing Frith Street, I'll run him down with the Roller. What did Claud say?'

He hit me on the back, then lowered his voice. 'He'll give me one more chance. If I get cut up again he'll put me on the dole. Said he couldn't have people who couldn't look after themselves. Well, I fucking ask you, that fucking Dicky Bush came through that door like a human cannon ball. I didn't stand a chance. Next time, though, it'll be him who's for the mincer.'

I gave him a crash on the back that sent him three yards forward. 'Even Sidney Blood won't recognise him, eh?'

He righted himself. 'I don't know how he knew I was there, though.'

'He saw you through that crack in the door. Then he went back up the stairs and wound himself up like a spring. A bloke like that don't go into any place without finding who's inside first. We haven't got to be too proud to learn, Kenny.'

He followed me into the house, where the party was as normal as you'd find anywhere on Saturday night in Richmond – or Ealing. I sauntered into the main drawing room, which was furnished in the best Harrods style. A wall had been knocked down, and an Alhambra-type archway connected the two halves. Crystal chandeliers scintillated from the ceiling, and mock old masters in heavy gilt frames decorated the walls. Persian carpets that looked genuine covered the floor. It was lucky I'd togged up in my best, having stumbled into an obviously grand occasion.

About a dozen people were present, and I didn't know who to talk to first, a problem solved by Moggerhanger coming across and putting an arm around my shoulder. I wanted to shake it off because it felt like the tail of an anaconda which was looking out for a secure purchase to an oak tree. He led me to the table where Mrs Blemish and Matthew Coppice were serving glasses of Moët et Chandon. 'I'm more than glad you could come, Michael. It's a real pleasure to have you with us again.' He handed me a filled glass from the table and steered me into a corner. 'We're going to need your services as we've never needed them before. Thank God you've honoured me with your presence.' He wasn't drinking.

It sounded like a knifing at least, but my wonderful day with Frances Malham had ensured that I was beyond caring. 'I intended coming tonight, whatever happened. I don't see how anybody could have done better than me in Canada, even though it didn't work out.' I stopped myself. Pride wouldn't let me grovel to that bastard.

'I'm the one to say whether it worked or not.' He laughed, until he saw Parkhurst, who was standing alone, let his cigar-end fall on the carpet and tread it in. 'Can't you pick 'em up and put 'em in the ashtrays provided?' He could play the heavy dad when he liked. 'I'll blind you if I see you do that again.'

Parkhurst looked red-hot pokers at him, then turned and said something to Cottapilly who had a glass of champagne in each hand.

'It seemed to me you sent me to Canada as a decoy,' I said. 'Or because you thought it was the easiest way to get me killed.'

His arm came over me again, this time as if the anaconda had got a real grip on the south-east leg of the heavy walnut table, and squeezed my shoulders. 'You've got guts, Michael. And you're clever. You're also lucky. Not only that, but you've got a sense of humour. If ever I want someone for a hard job, I don't ask whether they're intelligent, or lucky, or experienced (though they've got to be all of that), but if they can take a joke.'

'One of these days I'll die laughing, though I wouldn't mind knowing exactly what did happen when I got to Toronto.'

He took out a couple of Partagas and we lit up. 'Let me say this: in the bag you carried was a lot of paper work which couldn't be trusted to the post. It was worth a lot of money, so we had to send somebody like you, otherwise the Green Toe Gang wouldn't think it was genuine. Now they do, and they're acting on information that's ruining their operations in North America. Certainly, it was a dangerous job, but what do you think I'm handing you this thousand-pound bonus for?' He slipped the cheque into my lapel pocket, behind the tip of white handkerchief. 'I expected you to get back. I can't afford to have a valuable and trusted friend like you get hurt.'

'I feel reassured.'

'Imagine, Michael, if I'd sent someone of lesser calibre than your good self.' He took a good long puff at his cigar. So did I. 'Take Kenny Dukes. He'd have bought the biggest teddy bear at London Airport as a present for a tart he knows in Toronto. Cottapilly would have gone for a giant fire-engine to keep him company on the long flight. They'd have been spotted straightaway because those hot-heads over there would have thought they didn't intend to deliver the goods. No, it had to be someone like you, who's got no foibles and would deliver the stuff without a hitch.'

'I feel better all the time.'

' "If the earthenware pot floats downstream with the

brass ones we all know what must happen to them." '

'It's kind of you to say so,' I said in the right tone of voice.

'You're so cool and clear-thinking it's as if you're not as working-class as you say you are. Still, life is a bit of a mystery at times. I would have had you to dinner after the Blaskin party, but that's not my way of doing things. When you invite only one person to dinner he's always unnerved because he doesn't know whether he's come to eat or be eaten.'

We laughed, as if we had been nothing but friends for years, and that even in death we would not be divided. 'When the ladies have retired,' he said, 'there's going to be a meeting. I've a job in the offing that I've been contemplating for years. We're going to deal the Green Toe Gang a blow which will settle their hash in this country. In the meantime, go and enjoy yourself, while I talk to my dear wife.'

I could never decide whether life was too short or life was too long. Mrs Blemish was dishing out champagne at the drinks table and either she didn't know me, or she was playing the part of waitress which included not knowing anyone at all. She wore a white cap across her grey hair and a short black apron, and looked far more self-possessed than the forlorn woman I had given a lift to near Goole. I reminded her of the occasion, but she smiled, and said while filling my glass: 'I'm on duty, sir.'

I drank to her. 'Congratulations on getting away from Percy. That's all that matters.'

She had the most beautiful bow-like lips, suggesting that her teeth were still perfect. But those lovely lips trembled, and I felt like kicking myself for having reminded her of less fortunate days.

'A month after I got this job, he found me. I don't know how. He pleaded with me to go back to Tinderbox Cottage. I said I wouldn't. I was polishing the silver at the time. He threw a bundle of it across the floor, and Lord Moggerhanger heard the dreadful clash and came in to ask what was going on. He swore at being disturbed. Percy said he was my husband and wanted me at home, but Lord Moggerhanger told him that I had agreed to work for him, and that he and Lady Moggerhanger were so satisfied with me that they wouldn't let me go, and that if Percy didn't clear out he would have him thrown out. Then Percy pleaded to be given a job as well, and Lord Moggerhanger, after thinking about, it agreed to take him on as a handyman. He could catalogue the books in his library. Percy did this in a couple of days, and I'd never seen him so happy. But when he finished he attacked me with a knife. Lord Moggerhanger came in and knocked him down. He wouldn't let him go, even then. In fact he was even less inclined to do so but sent him to be the caretaker of a place called Peppercorn Cottage. I've never been there, and don't want to, but Percy can stay forever for all I care, as long as he's out of the way. I told Lady Moggerhanger that I would only remain providing I didn't see Percy. She said she would talk to Lord Moggerhanger, and see if he wouldn't keep Percy away from me. I haven't seen him for a fortnight, and that's longer than at any time since before we were married. I feel a new woman.'

'You look it.'

She filled my glass without gauging the amount, though none was spilled. 'I'll never forget your help. When you gave me a lift to the Great North Road, you brought me luck.'

'The luck of the Irish.' I wished her more for the future.

'There's something about my husband that Lord Moggerhanger likes,' she said. 'He seemed to regard Percy even more highly when he became violent and dangerous.'

'That's how some people are,' I said, reluctant to go further into the matter. A couple of waiters wheeled in the food, so I went to get my share. Toffeebottle was a small, bald but very compact man with big hands, and eyes of pig-cunning. God knows where Moggerhanger had picked him up. He wore a black suit and bow-tie at the throat of his ruffled white shirt, which made him hardly distinguishable from the waiters. He reached for the boneyard of chicken legs in aspic jelly and put three on his plate. Then he helped himself to chips, boiled potatoes, rice, corn salad and bread and butter. 'You can come back for your cheese and dessert,' I said.

He turned, from an acquiring world absolutely his own, and I put his accent a few miles north-north-east of Manchester: 'There'll be bugger-all left then, Mr Cullen.'

'That's probably true.' I heaped things onto my own plate. 'Are you in on the big job as well?'

'We all are.'

'I'll feel safe.'

'It's very nice of you to say so.'

Oh no it wasn't. The Boss could hardly get all of us wiped out. 'Is Lord Moggerhanger coming?'

'He'll be staying in the control tower,' he whispered.

I bumped into Pindarry, who avoided a flop of mayonnaise onto his electric blue suit. It went onto the carpet. Moggerhanger, talking to Polly, saw it. He saw everything. Pindarry saw him seeing it, so took a napkin from the snap-table and mopped up the mess. It was more than his bonus was worth not to. It was part of Moggerhanger's nature to see everything, but it was also a talent he cultivated. He had read, or he had been told by Dr Anderson (for a fee or a crate of whisky), that great men notice everything. They had an omnivorous grasp of detail. True, yet not true. Child of the Bedfordshire parish, Moggerhanger had been born with keen eye and windmill touch. He'd abandoned school at fourteen, Blaskin told me (who had jollied Drudge-Perkins into doing some detective work), though he had not been attracted to it from birth, considering that as long as he learned the three 'R's' any other knowledge he needed was accessible to someone of his intelligence, curiosity and greed. But just as it is true that great men owe their success to a grasp of detail, so it is equally true that their downfall is caused by an inability to delegate tasks whose success is vital to their continuing prosperity. Those who fall into this trap are not great men at all, Blaskin remarked, adding that Moggerhanger was just a nosy old bastard who couldn't keep his hands to himself at a time when there were more blind eyes in the country than missing arms. I walked over to Matthew Coppice by the door. 'How are things at Spleen Manor?'

He spoke so that no one but me would hear. 'Alport's gone east.'

'I nearly went west,' I laughed, 'in Canada.'

'The finest dope comes from the poppy lands of Turkestan,' he said. 'Farmers grow it in secret on collective farms. Some say the Russian government knows, but doesn't mind. They'll do anything to get foreign currency. The stuff's delivered to Alport in East Berlin by a Russian general. I heard you-know-who saying that next time we'll pay them with a few sacks of grain, which they seem to need more than money. You'd be surprised how much white stuff comes from Russia. Somebody sells a lot to them, and they sell most of it to us. Then (and I don't know how this is done, but it is) we sell it back to them for furs, diamonds and ikons. Breezeblock Villa at Back Enderby is bursting at the seams. So are one or two police stations. We send it to Russia on ships to Odessa and Rostov. It goes on barges up the Dnieper and the Don – then on to the Volga-Don Canal and up to the Moscow-Vladivostok railway. Russian Sailors can't get enough of it.'

I didn't want to know so much, verbally, but couldn't resist asking: 'Why don't they bring it from Moscow by plane, and save all this hole-and-corner trouble?'

'Aeroflop's too unreliable. You never know when the Russians are going to invade another country, like Afghanistan. They needed half their civilian air fleet to ferry in troops and guns. Lord M had a man carrying a valuable suitcase by Aeroflop to Australia. In Moscow there were no more planes, so they sent everybody back to Warsaw. The Poles didn't know what to do with them, so they sent them back to London. Lord M's courier had to book another route, and got there too late. The Green Toe Gang operating out of Amoy via Hong Kong made it first. Money was lost on that deal.'

'Anything else?' I was sweating because Cottapilly and Pindarry weren't far away.

'As long as it don't snow,' Matthew said loudly, in his simpleton fashion.

I laughed, as if at the end of a long joke.

'I'm writing it down,' he said. 'A packet of papers will be waiting at Upper Mayhem, like you told me. It's dynamite. We can't lose.'

Only our ears, I thought, and a few fingers. The Arabs aren't the only ones who chop your hands off for stealing. I slapped him on the back, then rejoined the crowd. 'There are lots of new gangs coming up these days,' Jericho Jim was saying.

'Kid's stuff,' Kenny Dukes said. 'Think of their names. Looting Tigers. Molotov's Angels. The Window Smashers. Flames of God. Fucking riff-raff.'

'Footpads and pickpockets.' Cottapilly was also scornful. 'Gaol meat.'

'What's wrong with pickpockets?' Jericho Jim tapped me on the shoulder, and held my wallet in his hand. 'You should watch this.'

I grabbed him by the jacket, my fist lifted. 'You fuckpig.'

Moggerhanger smacked himself at the waistcoat with laughter. 'It was only a joke among the lads, Michael. I bet him a pony he couldn't get it off you.'

He turned white, so I let him go. 'Next time, I'll beat the living shit out of you.'

'No harm done,' the boss said. 'You aren't a proper Londoner if you haven't had your pocket picked. Good job it wasn't on the street. You'd never have seen it again.'

Jericho Jim straightened his tie. I shouldn't have lost my temper. 'Sorry about that.'

He grinned. 'Sorlright. I learned it in Borstal, but I never had to earn my living at it, thank God.'

Lanthorn lit another of Moggerhanger's cigars. 'Those rioters and burners can expect little sympathy from me, Claud. What are they looting? Televisions, washing machines, videos, fags and booze. They should bring the army in and shoot the buggers like dogs. If they were taking bread and groceries I could understand it. My lads 'ud still go for 'em, though.'

Scottish George hated such talk. 'The social fabric's coming to pieces. Only communism can put things right.'

Moggerhanger liked a party. He was having a good time. 'I don't think so, Jack. Communism's nothing but a middle-class plot to cure wild-cat strikes. Your free-born Englishman wouldn't stand for it, God bless him!'

'Well, I'm a Scot, sir.' I liked George because he wouldn't be intimidated. 'It's the only hope for the poor.'

'Maybe so,' Mog said. 'But look at how my only begotten son is pushing that delicious food around his plate as if it was yak shit.'

'Bollocks,' Parkhurst drawled.

'I wish you wouldn't swear.' Lady Moggerhanger and Polly came over from the drinks table.

'You don't know you're born,' Moggerhanger said to his no-good son. Then he addressed us all. 'You're stinking rich, that's why. You should have been alive before the war, and put up with what we had to put up with. I expect some of you remember. My mother and father were turned out of their cottage one autumn, and the five of us lived through the winter in a tent. And winters were winters in those days! When we got a house the following year my younger brother died. I made up my mind I'd never put up with that again. And I didn't, eh, Jack?'

Lanthorn nodded, and pulled on his cigar. 'You were right. Some things are more than flesh and blood can stand.'

'My mother's eighty-five,' Claud said, 'and has a beautiful home in Golders Green. Somebody's there all the time to wait on her hand and foot. She has enough money settled on her never to want, even if she lives to be a hundred.'

'She'll live longer than that if I know her,' said his wife.

'Maybe she will.' I'd never seen him closer to tears – though he still had a fair way to go. I'd tell Blaskin that he had the human touch after all. He rubbed his hands together: 'It's no use wanting the impossible. Duty calls. It's time we got down to work. And that means YOU,' he roared at Parkhurst, who opened the door to slive out.

'I'm going for a slash,' he said. 'And besides, I've heard your stories fifty times already. And for another thing, don't expect me to work. I tried it once, and I didn't like it.'

Moggerhanger joined in our laughter, which said a lot for him. 'I know when to concede defeat. That's another reason why I am where I am. Flexibility furthers, Confucius, he say.'

Mrs Blemish brought in a huge tea urn and a tray of mugs, and cake for everyone. Lady Moggerhanger and Polly went out, which left – apart from me and Lord Moggerhanger – Cottapilly, Pindarry, Kenny Dukes, Jericho Jim, Toffeebottle, Inspector Lanthorn, Matthew Coppice and Scottish George, and Mrs Whipplegate who stood by the telephone with her notebook.

Moggerhanger had learned from Lanthorn that the Green Toe Gang stored their loot in a farmhouse near Great Creaton in Northamptonshire. It was their number-one depot containing counterfeit money, airline tickets, national insurance stamps, traveller's cheques and real money, amounting in value to more than two million pounds. There was also, as it was quaintly put, a quantity of poppy seed. 'The value of which,' Moggerhanger said, 'doesn't bear thinking about – or it won't till we have it safely under lock and key.'

'I could have the lads move in,' Lanthorn said, 'but if you promise me a quarter, which is not asking too much, I'll give you three days to get the stuff out first. All I want is you to leave a bag of poppy seed for me to charge the Green Toe Gang with when I make my raid on Day Four.'

Cottapilly said they could pull off the raid with no trouble, providing they had plenty of back-up, plus a couple of decoy cars. Buckshot Farm was a mile from the main road, and close to junctions of the M1, the M45 and the M6. In a couple of hours we could be anywhere in the country. With four getaway cars no one would know which one to chase, even supposing they were in a condition to do so, Cottapilly said, accentuating his hatchet face. If it happened that the laden car was pursued, the other three could close in on the pursuers and, as it was put, see to them.

It was a neat idea because nobody would be breaking the law. To rob robbers seemed a reasonable thing. And if we did stray onto the wrong side of legality I could justify it with the argument that I was taking part in the raid only as a means of trying to find some way of getting Moggerhanger and Lanthorn put behind bars.

Cottapilly showed us a map of the area. Polaroid photos went around the table, of a plain, slate-roofed farmhouse, six windows at the back and six at the front, an isolated building without sheds or barns, suggesting that it was no longer a working concern, if ever it had been. 'It's a good name,' Moggerhanger said.

'Buckshot it could be,' George laughed.

Toffeebottle straightened his bow-tie. 'There's often no other way with the naughty boys of the Green Toe Gang.'

Parkhurst sat to the right of the door, mindlessly striking matches and letting them drop into an ashtray placed there by Alice Whipplegate – who was also shorthanding the notes of the meeting. I wondered if Blaskin would ever get access to the obviously extensive archives.

'It's a third of a mile off the main road,' Moggerhanger said, 'but as a car turns up the lane, the warning flags'll go up from the house. Don't imagine they'll be sleeping on the job. But you can see from the map that Snowdrop Wood comes to within two hundred yards, and another lane passes the far end of the trees. So use the cover. Car A will set Kenny and Jericho down at the back end of the wood at eight-thirty. After the car's dropped them it will be driven around the area, but make sure to be on station at the lane junction with the main road by nine o'clock – when all hell will be let loose. Parkhurst will drive that car. Oh yes, he'll do it, don't worry.'

'If I must,' he said.

'You're not my son if you don't want to be in on a bit of fun like this. Cottapilly will drive car B, with Pindarry and Toffeebottle. At one minute to nine they'll shoot up the lane to Buckshot Farm, to make the full frontal assault. Do it quick. You'll be supported by Kenny and Jericho, who by this time will have got through the wood. At four minutes to nine they'll race the two hundred yards to the back of the house and force an entry. So it's A at the back, and B at the front.

'Car C, with George driving, will wait on the main road two hundred yards north of the lane-opening while the argy-bargy's going on. He'll be facing south, and will stay on station to ram any pursuit car coming from Buckshot

Farm after the aforementioned argy-bargy's finished and car B with the loot has shot out of the lane, though I hope the occupants of that car won't neglect to immobilise any motor transport at the farm that could possibly be used against them. When the Green Toe lads have got their quietus, load the stuff up as quick as you can. Don't start checking to see what you've got. It ain't a clipboard operation. Just work like navvies and get it inside the transport. Car D, Mr Cullen driving, will wait one mile north of the village. Car B will transfer the load to him. Michael will have the yellow Roller, and be in position by five minutes past nine, and facing north. As soon as he's loaded, he'll set off for Peppercorn Cottage, which only he knows how to find in the dark.'

'What do I do when I get there?' I was thankful not to be in on the actual assault. I wasn't afraid of rough stuff, but firearms might well be involved, and I neither wanted to kill nor be killed. They were only there for a threat, said Jericho Jim – but if the other side had similar threateners, anything could happen.

'Mr Blemish will help you to unload. All you have to do then is wait, rats notwithstanding.'

Kenny Dukes shivered. 'Better you than me.'

'As for the rest of the cars' – Moggerhanger spoke as slowly as his excitement would allow – 'after car B has transferred its load to Michael it'll follow car D for a while. Car C (the Range Rover) will deal with any pursuers by running them off the road, if need be. Car B will be the Jaguar, and will go south if any pursuers from Buckshot Farm decide to follow. If you're not pursued, keep after A and D to make sure D is not molested. When D is finally safe, A goes north to Spleen Manor, C comes back here, and B goes to Breezeblock Villa at Back Enderby. And no quiet booze-ups in a village pub, neither coming nor going. Any questions?'

I think our heads were spinning. Mine was.

'I'll go through it six times more, just to make sure you can recite it backwards before midnight.'

I put my hand up. It was like being at college. 'What about air cover?' I was going to ask, but didn't, because Moggerhanger had no use for levity, unless it was his. 'Air cover?' he'd say at best. 'I'll lay on a fleet of choppers from Luton, if you like.'

'When do we set off?'

'I'm glad you asked that.' He was sarcastic. 'You've got three days, and all leave's cancelled from this point in time. I'd prefer dry weather. No thunderstorms, fog, freak hail, or lengthy periods of rain which will turn the countryside into either a skating rink or a quagmire. I've seen too many things go wrong in bad weather. So I'll keep tabs on the met office and wait till they can give me a halfway decent forecast, though I can't leave it too long because I want nights of maximum darkness. We don't want even a sliver of moon in the offing. On the day, though, you'll set out from twelve hundred hours. As there are four cars, you'll leave at half hour intervals – as long as you're on station at the appointed time. All vehicles will be in perfect condition, and topped up with petrol, by which I mean it'll be at least a month since they were serviced. I say that advisedly, because in my experience cars in this country are more likely to break down immediately after they come back from the garage – if they're going to do so at all. It's disgraceful the way long-haired overweight ignorant bloody lads are allowed to crawl over a car with a Taiwan tranny belting out monkey-yammer while they tinker about with a spanner and grease-gun. No wonder they leave half the things undone, and do everything they shouldn't. They can't even write their own names. Now, where was I?'

It was hard to say.

'Mrs Whipplegate will give you a hundred pounds each, so that you can cope with every eventuality. But I warn you: no drinking. I want ice-cold brains, or none at all. Remember that this is a big job. The Green Toe Gang are sitting pretty at their secret warehouse. Make it so they don't know what hit 'em. Our information says there's no more than two guarding the place. They'll be easy meat for five of you. It's vital that we get everything, except some of the poppy seed for Jack's lads to find next day, as well as a few tenners with the ink still wet. If the job fails, you're done for – every one of you. But there's no reason why it should. Some of us have been working on the details for a long time. I need hardly say that there'll be healthy bonuses thrown around afterwards. Now, let's do a bit more studying. We'll carry on till midnight, and go through it again between ten and eleven tomorrow morning. This is an all or nothing operation.'

I thought he was going to add that the fate of European civilisation depended on it. I wouldn't have been surprised. The only reason he didn't was because he didn't think of it. My guts were bubbling. I was in it up to the top of my head, and there was no way I could back out.

Twenty-Four

At half past twelve on The Day I checked the car out of a garage in Kentish Town and made my way to the North Circular through a maelstrom of traffic. I intended joining the M1, which would take me into Northamptonshire, so why did I go right, and hook up with the A10 for Cambridge? The fact that I couldn't say gave me hope for the future, in that at least there would never be a dull moment in my life, or in anybody else's I happened to be close to.

But I was truly mystified at the time because, having been programmed to do one thing, a force to which I could give no name pressured me gently but decisively into doing another. As in every case when I do a crazy thing, I began to see reason in the move. If I went straight to the area of Buckshot Farm I would be so tempted to reconnoitre the place that my description would be taken fifty times before the others arrived and we moved in. Moggerhanger had cautioned us against going to within twenty miles of the locality before Zero Hour, but I would park by Snowdrop Wood and, with map case and field glasses, wellingtons, combat cap, and air pistol cocked, sneak through to have a look at the nut we were to crack. I would be spotted of course by someone shaking carpets out of a back window. I would then return to the lane to find a couple of youths joy-riding away in the Roller. Those in the house would in the meantime clear everything out, and leave before we could get our hands on the dope and cash. So it was safer for all concerned if I did a very wide approach ride to get there, and what better place to call at on the way than Upper Mayhem?

Everything, on paper, was mapped out, yet I felt as if I was taking a step into the unknown. My brain encompassed Moggerhanger's arrangements with no trouble, but my own private scheme had to dovetail into them, and for the moment I didn't see how it could. I didn't take easily to such fine-point organisation, because no room was left for ingenuity, flair, improvisation – those qualities (if such they are) of British genius that put them for five hundred years under the heel of the Roman gestapo. All the same, the programme seemed tight – and unnecessarily complicated – and I sniffed weaknesses everywhere, though knew I had to abide by the plan for safety's sake. Only if something went wrong would I come into my own.

It was hot, and the sky was clear, but I resisted the temptation to stop for a few pints of lager, or even to listen to Moggerhanger's Favourites as I rolled along. On paper everything looked fine, but what if one of the cars got banged into by a juggernaut on the motorway and burst into flames? Or had a puncture and found the spare tyre flat? I supposed we could afford to lose one car, as long as it didn't contain either of the assault parties. Again, what if it was the annual general meeting of the Green Toe Gang, and a score of the worst villains were present that evening? Everything had been taken care of, Moggerhanger said. Even Jack Lanthorn was on our side, the biggest bent copper in the business. What more do you want? I asked, as I pulled up outside Upper Mayhem railway station.

Bill Straw was asleep on a swinging seat in the garden, the *Daily Mirror* spread over his face to preserve his complexion. Dismal lay by his side, head between paws, and neither looked up as I opened the squeaky gate. Maria, her belly certainly higher than last time, came out with a tray, ice chinking in a tall glass, and a dogbowl full of water. The tinkling ice woke Bill, and a smile came onto his face before he let the newspaper slip off. 'Oh my darling! Another lovely drink. Oh – hello, Michael, what brings you here?'

Maria kissed him, and he held her close. They snogged awhile, the most tender-loving couple in the world. 'Ain't she wonderful? She's perfect, Michael, perfect. Aren't you, my pregnant beauty? You're perfect, aren't you? Aren't you, my duck?'

'You wonderful too.' She set the waterbowl before Dismal.

I kicked him, but not too hard. 'Don't *you* know me, at least?'

He yawned, rolled a lolling tongue back into his mouth, then stood on two legs and rubbed his cold nose against my cheek. Formality satisfied, he gobbled up the water in two licks.

'Your mother came last night, and went this morning. Said she was going to Holland to see Bridgitte. You can never tell, though, with a woman like that. She took a bit of a shine to Maria, but I put my foot down. I had to, Michael. I looked her in the eye and said: "She's mine. Leave her alone." And she backed off. I just had to be firm.'

'Get me a drink, Maria,' I said, 'for God's sake. Only, no alcohol.'

Bill stood up. 'She's a treasure, Michael. We're as much in love as two school kids. I never believed it could happen. I can't tell you. I'm glad you've come, though. We're out of money. Can you spare a bob or two? The local shops are complaining, so I'd like to fob 'em off with a bit.'

I gave him fifty quid out of my hundred. 'Let that last a few days.'

He put on his all-knowing bottom-dog Nottingham look. 'You're out on a job, are you?'

I nodded. 'It's D Day. Twenty-one hundred hours. Tonight.'

He drained his glass. Maria came out with mine. 'Bring some more, sweetheart, will you?'

'You're a bone-idle bastard,' I said. 'Why don't you lift a finger and do it yourself?'

He laughed. 'Do you know, Michael, I'd be glad to, but she wouldn't let me. She'd be offended. Wouldn't you, duck? I tried taking my carpet slippers off once, and she sulked half a day. It broke my heart to see that disappointed look on her face. Well, she does love me, and I love her. Besides, you don't know how long it will last.'

Part of the fence had been painted. 'Who did that?'

'Well, I mean, she insisted. Said she didn't have enough to do. You know me, Michael. I'm not a cruel man. I didn't want to stop her.'

I envied him. 'You've fallen on your feet.'

'I know. But think of all the times I've split my head open.'

'I don't see many scars.'

'That's because I've got a good head of hair. Nine o'clock tonight, is it? The Green Toe Gang get their come-uppance?'

I had no secrets from Bill, nor him any from me. 'We're after their warehouse.'

He whistled. 'Two million?'

'Knocking three, with the dope. Maybe four.'

'Better you than me. But if you want any help, put me in the boot of the Roller. I'd do anything for a ride in Claud's best motor. He must be pretty sure of pulling it off if he's let you have that. It's the best kept car in England.'

'I can manage. There'll be eight of us altogether.'

'Nine would be better.'

'I'll take Dismal.' I tapped the brute with my boot. A party of bird watchers walked along the bridge, each with binoculars and a recognition manual. 'Let's go inside where we can talk.'

'It's scorching today,' he said. 'I do nothing but drink.

Maybe Maria will make us a pot of her strong tea. I've trained her to mash a pot of jollop in true Nottinghamshire style. I'm very proud of that, Michael. I've not been completely idle since coming here.'

We sat in the cool living room. Even Bridgitte had never made the place gleam like this. 'How does she find the time to do so much?'

'She's at it from morning till night.'

'She's pregnant. She should be taking care of herself.'

He lay back on the settee. 'I know. I try to tell her. But she won't listen. And do you know, Michael' – he got up and leaned forward – 'she's a little bogger. She's at me all night. Bloody marvellous. I feel like the Caliph of Baghdad. It's as if there was three of her. I keep telling her she ought to stop because she's having a young 'un, but it don't mek a blind bit o' difference. It's just one more thing I've got to thank *you* for.'

'I'll regret it to my dying day.'

He got up and chucked me under the chin. 'I'm going to marry her, though. We're all set for it. I don't do owt by halves. I'll just ask her to bring us some tea, and cheese sandwiches.' Dismal must have heard, for he came in and lay by the empty firegrate. I stroked his head. He would keep me company while I was driving through the night to Peppercorn Cottage. He might earn his keep by devouring a few rats, and maybe holding Percy Blemish at bay if he got sufficiently deranged to come at me with a knife.

'The fact is,' Bill said, 'that eight of you might very well be enough. On the other hand, if there's Tu-tu to reckon with, it might very well not be.'

'Who?'

'Tu-tu.'

'Who the hell's she?'

'It's he. He used to be known as Bantam, because he's under five foot and very thin, but he took against the name all of a sudden and said he didn't want to be called

Bantam anymore. Well, because he was a crack shot with a two-two rifle, we called him Two-two. He didn't mind that. I never knew his real name. I'll tell you one thing, though, there might be eight of you, but if Two-two spotted you he'd pick you all off if you tried to rush him from a hundred yards.'

'Not the way we're doing it.'

'Oh, it's two at the back and two at the front, is it? But you'll need to send two down the chimney as well if Two-two's anywhere near.'

'Are you sure he's in their gang?'

'Was, last time I heard. Where the hell's Maria got to with that grub?'

'Take your sweat.' I had a couple of shotguns and a two-two rifle hidden in the house, with plenty of ammunition, from the days when I went shooting for the pot. 'I can't take you with me.'

He shook his head, a glint of envy, his teeth clenched. 'With your rifle I could cover you. Anybody showed his snout at an upstairs window and I'd have him in half a second, right between the eyes. I got a rabbit and two pigeons with it the other day.'

'I thought I'd hidden it.'

'Michael, from me? Hidden anything from me? Don't grumble. We should both get in that car. None of Claud's lot will see me if you throw a couple of blankets over me in the back. We'll take the rifle and the shotguns. Just tell me your plan of attack, and I'll explain how we do it. I was in the Sherwood Foresters all through the war. With a few chaps from the Old Stubborns I'd clean half London up.'

Maria came in with a laden tray, and he couldn't resist stroking her arse as she set it down, but she kissed him, so he had his reward twice over. I was tempted to take him to Buckshot Farm, because he was capable of doing all he said, but his presence would alter the balance of the plan. I explained the scheme in case he could offer any constructive criticism.

Three sandwiches and a pint of tea went into his trapdoor. 'Four cars is too much.' He drew a hand across his mouth. 'Two's plenty. Then you've got six blokes for the assault. Claud always was extravagant with motors. You want precision, not saturation. If you've got three at the back and three at the front, you've got one man at each side to cover the two who go in. Right?'

'I suppose so.'

'Right. Of the two who go in, one bloke runs straight upstairs and works his way down. The other bloke stays as a door-block with a cosh to catch 'em. Same from both sides. Can't miss. Depends on the size of the house, but it definitely sounds as if you need six, not four. If it was one of a row of houses we could approach it on a parallel track by blowing holes through the walls with grenades till we got to the house we wanted. I was a bloody dab hand at street fighting. Loved it. It'd be a picnic for me, Michael. I'll cover you from the front, and make four Molotov cocktails before we go, to lob through the windows if things get sticky.'

'Fuck you,' I exclaimed. 'We want to capture the place, not have a holocaust.'

'I was getting carried away, I admit. You can scrub the Molotov cocktail bit. But you see my point, Michael? Just drop me off in the vicinity half an hour beforehand. I'll saw the end off one of your shotguns and stick it under my coat, and take one of your kitchen knives. I'll put a hood over my face and blacken my hands. When you hear me whistle from the front upstairs window you'll be able to walk in. I'll have 'em trussed up neatly for you.'

'I thought you were in love,' I said. 'You sound bored out of your mind.'

'A bit o' both never comes amiss.'

'We don't want a conflagration,' I said, 'and we don't want a massacre. We only want the goods.'

'That's as maybe, Michael, but if Two-two's anywhere near, watch out. I wouldn't like to see you come back on crutches. You wouldn't live very well on a pension from Moggerhanger.'

'The plan's not only been fixed, but it's already in operation. They'd die if they knew I was talking to you about it. I must be out of my mind.'

'I've got your best interests at heart. I owe you too much not to have. I suppose I'm getting sentimental in my old age.'

I finished my first sandwich, the last on the plate. 'I'm taking Dismal for company. I'd also like a few flasks, tins of food, and parcels of sandwiches. You never know. I like to be well supplied with grub when I'm on a car trip. There's less chance of having an accident. I also want the two-two rifle with fifty cartridges, and one of the shotguns.'

'You're very wise,' he said. 'Maria will go to the village shop and get some more bread. I tried teaching her to drive the other day in your old banger, but she didn't seem to get the hang of the steering wheel, so she'll have to go on the bike.'

I always kept the keys on me, but starting the engine with a bit of wire would have been no problem for him. 'As long as she doesn't take too much time. I can't be late for my appointment.'

'What's the hurry? It's only four o'clock. You don't have to be there till nine, which means you can lounge around here till seven, and still make it if you crawl along at thirty miles an hour.'

'Maybe I'll have a bit of a kip beforehand, then, if I can rely on you to wake me by six.'

'I'm as much interested in this as if I was going myself. I'll see you get woken up, and have a royal send-off. I still wish you would let me come with you and give the lads a hand. I'd enjoy it, what's more.'

Dismal finally realised I was home, because he followed me upstairs and spread himself across the bed. It wasn't easy to get to sleep for either of us. What troubled Dismal I had no way of knowing. He'd make an effort to get his head down, then stand up and walk across my legs for no reason, finally flopping back with a sigh across my ankles. From the woolly caves and tunnels of my half-snooze I would push such leg weight off in case he bent them permanently and turned me into a modern-day victim of rickets. Every few minutes I would wake up from the nightmare of Bill having forgotten to call me. It was nine o'clock, getting dark, and the raid had started. Searchlights criss-crossed the sky to the sound of cannonfire, and Moggerhanger's paratroops were descending sedately through the shrapnel.

He tapped me on the shoulder at five minutes to six, and I would have felt better if I had gone for a five-mile walk instead of taking a nap, though a few doses of Maria's Nottingham tea – on a mug of which a bricklayer could walk forty storeys up and not feel nervous – followed by a long cold shower, soon steadied my shaking hands. I insisted on Dismal's bowl being filled, and he lapped it clean with such gusto that we gave him another, after which he stood on a leg and his tail, and flipped the bowl bottom-side-up with his tongue.

'I'll miss that dog,' Bill said. 'For God's sake, don't let him get killed. I'd never get over it. He runs a mile every morning to the village for my newspaper and sixty whiffs. I don't know where you got him, but he's a godsend.'

Dismal farted in appreciation of this eulogy, and slid under the settee. His inability to converse as a human, as hurtful to his soul as it would have been to ours if he ever succeeded, occasionally lured him into disagreeable alternatives. 'Don't let him get near the Roller,' Bill said, 'or the paint'll fall off. It's a distressing habit he's got into lately. That strong cheddar plays hell with my guts as well.'

At half past six we packed the grub into the spare front seat, plus a couple of blankets to cover Dismal during the time at action stations, and to conceal the two-two rifle and shotgun. Dismal clambered in like an old age pensioner, though he couldn't be more than three years old, and I fastened myself in the driver's seat.

'Contact!'

'Give 'em hell,' Bill said. 'I wish I was coming with you. I'd be in that house like a three-bellied snake.'

'I'll be safer on my own than with a bloke like you. You're barmy, and that's a fact.'

He turned on that immortal berserker grin from Nottingham. 'I know I am. It feels marvellous, though – at times.' He thrust an umbrella through the open window. 'You might need this. Only don't prod Dismal. It's the one you picked up in the tube station, remember?'

He patted my cheek, and then I drifted down the lane on a day when the pollen count was high. My anxieties vanished. Where they went I did not know, and cared less. In spite of my waving him back, Dismal flopped over onto the front seat and took silent snaps at the smoke rings from my cigar as we bowled along towards the Huntingdon road.

The cloudless day began to scare me. I wanted to turn north or south, or even to spin back east, rather than continue west for the job I had to do. I would have felt better if dusk and rain threatened and all heaters were burning to keep us warm, because then my one impulse would have been to stick to my task and get it done, just to escape the winter and jump back into the snuggery of home.

There was something festive as I glided through the lanes. My feelings were out of control. I wanted to put on my party hat – I actually looked in the glove box in case one was stashed there – and pull into the next layby for a suck at my brandy flask. I waved at a red-headed young woman by the roadside on going through a village, and she gestured with a smile that made me scared at the notion of doing something indisputably daft during the period of the raid.

The green and yellow belly of England pulled me along. My eyes fed on dark woods, on waving corn and meadows. I drove by wealthy houses. I threaded steadfast villages, no face starving or anybody in a hurry. I was glad to be travelling on a perfect evening, and happy at feeling different to everyone I passed. It was like going into battle as a soldier, because I didn't place myself one second in front of my life. Otherwise I might stop and cut my throat.

Crows disputed for the shade of a tree when I stopped at a give-way sign. Dismal yawned, but when I pushed his snout aside I'm sure he laughed inwardly. Even a dog could sense our luck at being inside a moving car. The familiar traffic island on the Great North Road gave me a peculiar feeling to be cutting it at right angles instead of going north or south. I let half a dozen juggernauts go by before getting onto it, and a car behind hooted, expecting me to shoot into the stream with such a fast car. But I was careful, for if in my life I was to have a traffic accident, the time was now. In one way I wouldn't have minded a collision just deadly enough to get me into hospital yet not kill me – a Blighty one, as Bill might say – but failing that I was cautious in getting across the island which actually smelt dangerous, though soon I was waving my hat at the Duke's big shadow over the village of Ellington. On a straight but narrow bit of road a Cortina full of laughing kids drifted by at eighty, a pink rubber pig bobbing at the back window.

The tape deck treated us to popular marches by the Band of the Royal Artillery, which seemed just right for the job in hand. Even Dismal liked it, his fat tail flopping around the seat. Then came Exhortation 974 from

Moggerhanger, saying I shouldn't turn the car into a kitchen by leaving potato peelings and onion skins, pea pods and cornflake packets all over the upholstery. He must have chuckled while fiddling about with tapes in his spare moments. Dismal barked the hectoring voice down, so I buzzed the window and threw the tape over a hedge.

I mapped my way through Burton Latimer to dodge Kettering, and from then on a network of lanes took me over uplands and across the middle of Pitsford reservoir. Every two or three junctions I stopped to look at the map, because on this jaunt I couldn't joyride and hope for signposts to put me on track. The sheet of water made Dismal scratch at the window, and before clambering back in he was thirsty again, so I emptied the plastic container into his mobile dog bowl.

I lit another of the chief's cigars and off we went. Close to the raid area I drifted onto the main road facing north after an inconspicuous run through the village in which I saw a woman walking a dog by the post office shop, and a Volvo estate with green wellingtons in the back parked outside a thatched cottage.

By nine o'clock a peaceful dusk was seeping in. I don't know why, but it struck me that a yellow Rolls-Royce was an unusual car to use on such a stunt, a vehicle you would never steal if you wanted to get far without being caught. A cop-chopper would spot it from two thousand feet. We should have had Escorts or Cortinas, or a Morris that you couldn't pick out from twenty miles away.

While waiting in position I fed Dismal a Mars Bar. He loved them, the only disadvantage being that he licked my hand afterwards to show his thanks and appreciation. Someone flashed me from behind. It was George in car C, going to take up his station half a mile south. I assumed that cars A and B were already preparing to do their stuff. I flashed George before he could turn the bend.

Another fact which came to me – and all the more

sharply for being too late to be of use – was that I had committed my life into the hands of as big a set of numbskulls as it would be possible to find on God's earth. They must have done a hundred years of bird between them, and if that didn't prove their incompetence I don't know what did. Yet who else could Moggerhanger have chosen? Even I had done my share. Those who had never been inside would be even less competent. Nor would they be so daft.

If Bill Straw, who I regarded as the most sensible bloke I knew, had volunteered to give a helping hand, it hadn't been for gain, or a desire to practise his profession, but merely to have a bit of fun at the shoot-out, and then vanish into the countryside in order to test his ability at getting back to base undetected. Once a Sherwood Forester, always a Sherwood Forester. To Bill Straw, crime was the logical extension of an orienteering exercise, and in that sense I looked on him as being the typical Englishman – one also to whom the notion of class had no meaning.

Such reflections were too late. I was in it up to my neck. Even if I abandoned the Roller and made off with Dismal I'd be a marked man. The clock said it was a minute to nine, and I was on the left hand side of the road facing north, as instructed. A cloud of gnats danced above an elderberry bush. A sparrow flew over a patch of fully flowered nettles.

I was drowsy, so Dismal yawned. The western sky was pink high up and red below. Half a minute went by. I was roused by a car coming towards me with all lights on, swaying on its way south. Cottapilly with bulging eyes was at the wheel of car B, Toffeebottle and Pindarry in the back, poised to make the frontal assault. They were late, hence the hurry. Where the hell had they been? Kenny Dukes and Jericho Jim should already be out of Snowdrop Wood and approaching the farm, to take it from the rear – unsupported, unless they too were late. 'It doesn't bode well,' I said to Dismal, who was asleep.

It would be futile to go back step by step and find out how I got into such a situation. Far better, I decided, to prepare the Roller to expect the load shortly to be thrown into it. I got out and opened the boot, and stood smoking another cigar. Since Moggerhanger would be lucky to see the car again, I saw no point in stinting myself. Dismal thrashed about the hedge after rabbits and partridges, maybe hoping for a fox. The time was five minutes past nine. The assault on Buckshot Farm should have been finished, in theory.

The light was dim enough to warrant the hazard blinkers on. They made the car more conspicuous than I would have liked, but in case the lads had difficulty locating me in the gloaming they would serve as navigation beacons. I fancied I heard a series of light cracks from the south, and my guts iced up at the notion of deadly Two-two going into action. The flatter echo of shotguns may have been from a party of farmer's men after rabbits for the pot. I'd heard such sounds frequently on a summer's evening from the open windows of Upper Mayhem.

At nine fifteen I began to worry, though not unduly. If Bill Straw had been in my place he would probably have had the stove out, calmly brewing a can of tea, as befitted an ex-Sherwood Forester, and be lying on his groundsheet scanning chapter one of a Sidney Blood novel. Ten minutes later he would blow out his stub of candle and turn in till midnight, when he would wake up, mash tea again, fold his bivvy, and steal off into the night to do twenty miles across country by dawn, before hot-wiring a car at a service station and melting into London by daylight.

I got Dismal back in the car and shut the door, settling him down with a blanket underneath and one on top. A possible future development would have been to have the stuff loaded, but with Dismal playing hard to get, me giving chase over six fields and becoming more and more exhausted as every horizon scintillated with the flashing blue lights of cop cars.

I was reading the clock by the minute. Either there was so much loot that they needed more time to load than had been anticipated (though with four such beefy bastards I didn't see how this could be) or the attack had failed and, with one dead, two wounded, one prisoner and one missing (but being hunted for) they had conceded defeat and the venture was off as they beat a retreat to a late supper at Watford Gap cafeteria. If so, how would I know? And if I couldn't know, how long should I wait?

By twenty past nine I considered going south to reconnoitre, yet such a move would be foolhardy, because no doubt as soon as I set off, car B would pass me, and wouldn't find me in position to transfer the goods. Confucius might say that flexibility furthered, but in that case it would only confuse us. The cigar began to taste like shit. To take my mind off matters, I mulled on my encounter with Frances Malham, less than a week ago, but it seemed ten years. If I came out of this lunatic expedition in one piece, or even two, I would find her, and renew our acquaintance. Her face haunted the darkening air and lifted me so much out of anxiety that I hardly noticed a pick-up truck coming towards me, a rainbow light flashing from above the cab. It stopped a yard behind the Roller.

Kenny Dukes, hair matted with blood, jumped out shouting: 'You've had it easy, haven't you, mate?' He wanted to kill me for it.

Parkhurst slid off the back. He had bruises on his face and a sleeve of his jacket torn away. Toffeebottle came out of the other side and banged into the cab door, unable to see with his closed left eye.

Twenty-Five

'What happened?'

Parkhurst threw the first parcel across. 'Complete success.'

'They broke me fingers,' Toffeebottle moaned, who nevertheless was able to play pass-the-parcel with the rest of us, during which five minutes I gathered that Kenny Dukes and Jericho Jim had come out of Snowdrop Wood on time, but hearing no roar from car B shooting along the lane to the front of Buckshot Farm, lay concealed in dead ground, spitting tacks with impatience. Parkhurst, who had debussed them half an hour before, instead of stationing himself at the junction as he'd been told, watched for car B driving up to the farm, and then followed it along in case they needed him as a reinforcement. It was as well that he did. That bit of flexible thinking proved him a true son of Moggerhanger. Both cars were spotted as they came up the lane. A shotgun appeared at an upstairs window, but Moggerhanger's stalwarts zig-zagged in lizard fashion up to the house and reached the door unhurt.

At such a racket Kenny Dukes and Jericho Jim threw down their fags and slid in by a back door to do their stuff. They disarmed two men who had shotguns, but there were more members of the Green Toe Gang than had been expected, and a struggle took place. The first thing Parkhurst did when he came in was clip the telephone cable, then knee one of the blokes who reached for a walkie-talkie. He hurled the radio out of the window, atmospherics crackling in the evening air. There was fighting all over the house, and a Green Toe bloke who got outside threw a match in the petrol tank of the Jaguar, which blew up. The second car was also damaged, but not so seriously that they couldn't use it. 'I've known worse cock-ups, let me tell you,' said Parkhurst.

A cold breeze wafted over the hedge. The drivers of the few passing cars must have chuckled at the thought of a broken-down Rolls-Royce. The flashing light of the pick-up truck was a godsend, though we were lucky that the local cop car didn't stop on its nightly trundle and ask if we were all right, though maybe Lanthorn had told them to stay longer at their tea and darts that night.

Parkhurst slammed the boot and gave a loud laugh suggesting that, in his element, he had come back to life. 'Take it away, Michael, all three million. Or is it four? Don't hit a petrol tanker head on, or fall asleep at the wheel, or get it on a boat for Spain, either. God wouldn't like it.'

'He'd get his wrist slapped for a thing like that,' Toffeebottle laughed, still hugging his fingers.

My blood dropped forty degrees. 'I've got to get some fun out of my dull life.'

Jericho hee-hawed. We were having a wonderful time. We laughed all over the road, a birthday of back-slapping. Kenny was pissing himself with the giggles, his matted head, old razor scars, missing teeth and octopus arms showing plainly in the headlights of the pick-up. Toffeebottle jumped into the cab and sounded the horn. I got into the Roller and sounded mine, two lighthouses talking through fog. Dismal lifted his head, and I pushed him down. He howled, and they fell about with more laughter, thinking I was imitating a dog. Probably the whole village was listening, and wondering if they would be on telly next day.

I shot off, with no preliminary revving-up. I poked Dismal again. 'Don't show your napper, or you might get a bullet through it.'

I was on my way, no pursuit cars behind, not even an escort vehicle to bid me farewell. They didn't give a fuck now that things were more or less all right. After a mile I took the first turning left and set a compass course west-north-west towards Peppercorn Cottage, about a hundred miles away. I felt so relieved I almost hit a hedge, but the left front wheel bumped the verge – and shot me into the clear. It woke Dismal. 'Nothing wrong,' I said. 'Go back to sleep.'

On my own I might get careless and let my eyes close, hit a wall, shoot a cliff, scrape a tanker and burst into flames, but I couldn't let anything happen to Dismal, an animal who hadn't done anyone a ha'porth of harm – well, not knowingly. He licked my hand and lay down again.

The Green Toe Gang would break free from their boxroom. One of them must have run to the nearest phone booth to report. But who to? What tight-lipped, blue-eyed, fair haired eminence with dark glasses would lift the phone and hear those urgent pips before whoever called got the ten-pence in? I'd have given a lot to know who he was, then I could have formulated his response to the raid, and done something to avoid whatever might be put in my way. We had come out of the raid well, and me best of all, with little worry and not even a scratch, and here I was in my motorised palace, central heating on and a cigar in my mouth, and a dog curled up on the mat, trying to read *The Times*, driving into the peace of a dark pink sunset with goods to the value of millions in the boot.

Things had gone too well. It was time to think, and take evasive action. If the head of the Green Toe Gang had a halfway decent intelligence section he would know about Moggerhanger's various hideouts. His know-how hadn't been good enough to warn him of the raid, but that was another matter. Defeat sharpened the faculties. Whoever he was he would be stung into a bout of clear thinking. He would know about Back Enderby, Spleen Manor and

Peppercorn Cottage. He would look at his RAC motoring map and make a big black mark at each location. Then he would put his finger on Buckshot Farm, and he would see that Peppercorn Cottage was farthest away, and he might be inspired into believing that the loot-laden car was heading there. He would alert any motorised henchmen who happened to be in the Midlands and tell them to block my progress along the A5.

Our tactics had been sound enough to have the yellow Roller parked well away from the scene of operations, so they wouldn't know what make of car to look for. In any case it was dark. My respect for Moggerhanger increased by the minute. Even so, I was taking no chances. What if one of our own lads knew who to phone so as to get the Green Toe Gang on my trail? The outlook was unlikely but, being totally untrustworthy myself, I knew that in this kind of racket you couldn't trust anyone.

Then again, even though there was little chance of intercepting me en route, whoever was head of the Green Toe Gang had only to send a car to wait at Peppercorn Cottage. The fact that you had to think of everything didn't faze me. I would deal with such a calamity when I came to it. At the moment I was only interested in convincing George's car, or Parkhurst's car – either of which might be following (and the occasional vehicle did come up and overtake) – that I was a good lad who was doing what he was told by taking, as anyone could see, the road to Peppercorn Cottage.

Half an hour later, I swung off the main road and made my way into Nuneaton. I played around the place for ten minutes to make sure nobody was on my trail, then went south along a straight bit of dual carriageway at seventy miles an hour, crossed the M6, and got into Coventry. Easy as pie, as Bill might say. I wasn't followed, nor would I be ambushed. I was off everybody's radar screen except my own, and that was how I liked it, for as long as

I could believe it was true.

My plan was to trundle via Warwick, Bromsgrove, Kidderminster, Ludlow and Knighton, passing the Black Country to the south instead of the north. Then I would strike northerly to reach the vicinity of Peppercorn Cottage, a tricky route to follow at night, but they didn't call me Tactical Jack for nothing. The hands of the clock glowed half past ten.

'Dismal,' I said, 'you're a clever dog, but why can't you read a map? One bark for left, two for right, and a howl for stop? With me driving, we'd get on like a car on fire.'

He staggered up, and snuffled around. Before leaving Upper Mayhem I'd thrown in six tins of Bogie left over from a pup that got run down by a van five years ago. Dismal couldn't talk, but I could sense he wanted food, even if only because he was bored, so I would have to stop and victual him soon. I wasn't hurrying, but my progress was good. At the rate I was going I would hit Peppercorn Cottage at two in the morning. My orders were to wait there, but like hell I would. The fact that I didn't like the place had nothing to do with the rats.

I didn't intend to let Moggerhanger get his maulers on those bags and boxes jammed in the boot, yet what use was such a load of hot goods to me? There was no doubt enough hash speed dope or maryjane to keep me and half the country stunned till the twenty-first century and beyond. The counterfeit or stolen money would set me up in Papeete forever likewise, in which place I could light my cigars with the reams of national insurance stamps and think of all those working in Blighty (when they could) who had to shell out for them towards the pittance of an old age pension.

Maybe I would find a dumping ground and set fire to the car with the loot still in the boot. Or I could leave it outside some rural cop shop with a note pinned under the wipers and the boot key in a little plastic bag of the sort they fix parking fines in.

Perhaps I should, after all, leave it at Peppercorn Cottage, without waiting for further instructions, and walk off never to contact Moggerhanger again. Whatever I did beyond the call of duty I was a dead man. I wasn't in Canada now, where I had a whole continent to get lost in. I was in Albion fair and square, and never you forget it, I said to myself, ceasing to think of the problem for the time being.

Beyond Warwick, and heading for Henley, the road was narrower. A souped-up Mini was honking to overtake. They must be local lads who knew the route. Their horn played a truncated version of 'Colonel Bogey' so loudly that my backbone shook. On a straight bit I slowed down and they shot by. It was pub closing time, so I would have to be careful. I'd never had a serious accident, but didn't want my turn to come now.

I waited for the next stretch of dual carriageway so that I could slow down and look for a layby. On England's arterial lanes you often see a sign for one just ahead, but when it comes it's two hundred yards long. Twenty cars try to overtake a hundred-ton lorry, and the scene develops into a madder version of the whacky races.

The stiff breeze had a bit of rain in it, showers approaching from the west, as it said on the news. The layby just before Bromsgrove was slippery with spilt diesel oil and plastic bags, and after doing his stuff Dismal wanted to get straight back in the car. I told him it was the best I could do and opened a tin of Bogie. He sniffed it, took a lick, then began to gobble as if a TV camera had started whirring away. I sat on the step with a packet of cheese sandwiches and the giant flask of coffee, coming back to life after not realising I had been so hungry, and blessing Bill and Maria who had stocked me up so well. Bill's old-sweat touch had also thrown in a small gas stove, and everything necessary to make me self-contained for a fortnight.

When Dismal had finished and I was having a smoke, we heard footsteps between the lion-roar of a lorry and the gazelle-purr of a car. Someone trod wearily into the layby as if about to fall after a very long walk. Dismal growled and I told him to hold back in language he was coming more and more to understand. The man was out of breath. 'Is the dog safe?'

'He wouldn't hurt a fly.'

'I don't expect he would, but a chap like me can't afford to tek chances.' He leaned against the car, and in the dim light I saw the unshaven face of someone about sixty. He had a rucksack on his back, but there didn't seem to be much in it. The open neck of a white shirt came over his sports-jacket collar. He wore a pullover, flannels, black boots and a cap, more like a traveller than a hiker.

'What are you doing out at this time of night?'

'You might well ask.'

I took his response to mean he had no option, so got the flask and gave him a cup of coffee. He drank it straight down. 'Good Lord, I don't think I've had one like that in years. It's nectar!'

I passed him a couple of cheese sandwiches. 'Where are you going.'

'The next town.'

'You're hungry.'

He glared. 'It's the human condition, for somebody like me. Or it has been for ten years. Before that it was another matter.' He stopped talking so as to eat.

'I'll give you a lift, if you like.'

Humour just outweighed the bitterness. 'I had a damned good car once. I had a house, a wife, a job – the lot, and I loved it. When you're sitting pretty you don't know what's going to strike in the next year or two, or even the next ten.'

His look made me uncomfortable. 'Whoever did?'

'Thanks for being kind to a bloke on tramp, anyway. They were excellent sandwiches. Don't think I can't appreciate it. It gets harder for a bloke in my position to explain himself properly. I've had more tribulations in the last ten years than Israel ever did in Egypt. Or so it felt, though I don't like to complain.'

'Another coffee?'

He nodded. 'Yes, please.'

I gave him more sandwiches and a bar of chocolate. 'I have to be going now.' I opened the door. 'So if you'd like to get in.'

'What time is it?'

I went to the headlight and looked at my half-hunter pocket watch. 'Five to eleven.'

He leaned close. 'I had a watch like that once, but I lost it. Or it got stolen, probably by the removal men. Such things happened to me in those days, when I still had a watch to lose. I was far too careless.'

We settled ourselves in, and I offered him one of Moggerhanger's prime cigars on the assumption that all fugitives were born equal.

'I'd better not, but thanks all the same. That supper was a treat. I hadn't eaten since breakfast.'

I waited for a car to pass, then drifted onto the road. 'Haven't you got any money?'

'Oh yes, I've allus got a bit. Don't want to get pulled in for a vagrant. It happened once, so I never have less than five pounds in my pocket, though that ain't worth a sight these days. But I'm always economising. I set myself to spend so much a day, and I even try to save a copper or two out of that. It's a rigorous regime, but I never go really hungry. I think a Spartan existence does a man good, don't you?'

'No,' I said.

He pulled out a tattered map. 'I intended getting some fish and chips at the next town. Bromsgrove, ain't it?'

'I hope so.' I saw the glow of lights in the distance. He asked if I owned the car. 'I'm taking some stuff to a place in Shropshire. I'm the chauffeur.'

He settled back. 'I'll have that cigar now, if you don't mind.' He stroked Dismal's head, and if there was one thing Dismal liked more than having one person to fuss over him, it was having two. 'Lovely dog, this one.'

'He's my best friend.'

'Looks like a cross between a Newfoundland and a St Bernard.'

'Could be,' I said. 'Where are you going after Bromsgrove?'

'It's anybody's guess. I keep on the move. I come from Nottinghamshire originally, and funnily enough I never seem to get more than a hundred miles away from the place. I go in ever increasing circles for a while, then in ever decreasing circles till I hit Slab Square, when I start my ever increasing circles once more. I suppose it comes from having been an engineer. I was a mining engineer, but I retired early because I came into some money. It wasn't much, so I don't know why I did retire. Stupid, it was. I let it go to my head. But my wife had left me the year before, though the time had come for us to go our separate ways in any case. We'd been together so long we were like two maiden ladies living together. When she'd gone I sold my house and moved to Leicester. I was fifty then. It was just over ten years ago. Seems like the ice age has come and gone. But I was happy enough to sell my house at the time. I got £4,600 for it, which was fair enough in those days.'

He settled himself more comfortably. 'In Leicester I bought a small flat, took it on a kind of cooperative basis, organised by a man who said he had been a socialist all his life and wanted to put his principles into practice. I don't know who you are, but never have anything to do with anything like that, no matter what the principles are. If ever you get close to anybody who starts talking about the future, run for your life. But I fell for it, in reply to an advertisement. Never fall for an advertisement, because they are just a mirror to what's in the rest of the newspaper. Anyway, this smiling damned villain with his blond locks, fisherman's sweater, army boots and pigskin briefcase vanished one day, and the next morning the council moved in to demolish the house. I just managed to get out before the ball and chain came through my window. As it was I lost my books and records.'

A tearfulness came into his voice, but he checked it firmly, which endeared me to him. 'I went mad. What money I had left I spent trying to sue them. In the end I was penniless. I had some family in Leicester, but from then on they wouldn't even speak when they passed me in the street in case I asked 'em for the price of a pack of fags. Even their children snubbed me. I got ulcers, and then I was in an asylum for a few months because – so they said, but I didn't remember – I threw a ten-inch nut and bolt through the windscreen of a councillor's car. Doughty props were giving way all round me.

'The only thing I could do was take to the road. That was the saving of me. Every few weeks I pick up a bit of money from national this and national that. They all know me in the offices at Nottingham and Leicester, and it's not much money but it keeps me going. I'm lucky it's this world and not in Russia where a bloke like me would be put in jail as a parasite. But I've never felt so healthy since taking to the road. Summer or winter, I'm out in all weathers. Sometimes I get a bed, but often I sleep rough, inside a sewage pipe, or a barn, or under a hedge, or in an old car, or a derelict building – of which there's usually one round about. I never get colds, nor any aches and pains. My feet hardened after the first fortnight. I get a bit forgetful, that's the only thing. Ever since I set out, though, I've kept a Level Book to record my ups and downs.'

He laughed. 'That's a joke, really, but I do fill in a log.' He held up a red, stiff-covered notebook which he kept in his pocket. 'I record the date, distance and place names travelled to every day. Very brief, mind you, no description or stuff like that, otherwise I'd get to need more than one book. It's my only companion. Every mining engineer has his Level Book. If ever you meet another, just ask him. When there's black ice in winter, or bitter pouring rain, I go into a public library and read Shakespeare or the Bible. I never look at newspapers. I don't care what's going on in the world. They don't have any news to effect me. They write for themselves, not for us, so I just sit in the library on bad days, reading and keeping warm. They're my holidays. I never touch booze and I allus manage to stay clean. I don't know whether you've noticed, but I don't smell.'

He didn't.

'When I've walked a long way you might get a whiff of sweat, but that's natural. In my rucksack I've got soap, toothpaste, shaving tackle, deodorant, boot brush and a tie. Not much else, except a pair of opera glasses, a bit of string, a small flashlight and a couple of pencils, a change of underwear and a clean shirt. The only luxury is a slide rule and a book of tables. Usually a bite of grub. When I want a new coat I get one for next to nothing from one of those Oxfam ragshops.'

He sounded more cheerful. 'So you see, it's a healthy life. Plenty of exercise, fresh air, always something interesting in the view, or in people I meet. I never pass anyone without a good-day, and I don't care whether or not they answer. If they don't, that's their problem. I don't often accept rides like this, but when I got into that layby back there I was feeling a bit weary after walking from Leamington. It's not unusual for me to hike thirty miles a day when I'm in the mood, which isn't bad for a bloke turned sixty. Perhaps you chaps who work for your living think I'm sponging on the social system, but I did my share of work up to the age of fifty, and in all conscience it's not very much of the world's resources I consume.'

I was icy at the back of the neck. We were beyond Bromsgrove, but neither of us had mentioned any need to stop there. His story put such a decision out of my mind because the fact was, I knew him well. He was the man who had sold his house at Farnsfield through me when I was working as an estate agent's runabout in Nottingham. I had done a bit of fiddling because several buyers were after it, out of which he got an extra few hundred pounds. He generously gave me a hundred and fifty, but I was given the push from the estate agents, Pitch and Blenders, because they found out about it. However, I used the money to buy an old banger and finance my coming to London, so this tramp in my car was responsible for me being where I was and doing what I was doing – which was giving him a lift while ferrying Moggerhanger's loot to Peppercorn Cottage. Even Blaskin wouldn't believe me if I told him, and he's a novelist.

His name was Arthur Clegg, and I'd spent a couple of days helping him clear up his house after the contracts had been exchanged. We'd had fry-ups when we got hungry, and played draughts while a Handel oratorio blasted out of the gramophone. The valuable half-hunter gold watch in my pocket was none other than one I had pilfered from a chest of drawers. I later gave it to that elderly dropout Almanack Jack who came to live at Upper Mayhem, so that with a little red flag and a gold braided cap, which Bridgitte put together for him, he could play at being station master. When he kicked the bucket from a heart attack I got it back, and had carried it in my waistcoat ever since.

Such a long tale had exhausted him. 'I don't know why

I went on so long.'

We were intersecting the M5 and heading for Kidderminster at ten minutes past eleven. 'I'm glad you did. You may find this hard to believe, but we've been acquainted before.'

His hand twitched on the back of the seat. 'It seems unlikely, if you don't mind me saying so.'

'It's true, all the same.'

A liveliness came into his voice. 'Well, I do detect a trace of the old Nottingham in your accent. It's barely noticeable, but I would say you hail from Beeston – or somewhere near.'

'You're spot on. The fact is, Mr Clegg, I was the estate agent's assistant who sold your house at Farnsfield. We practically ran an auction on the matter. Remember?'

During the two-minute silence I could almost hear the wheels of his rusty mind working at top speed. 'Michael Cullen?'

'The same.'

'If ever I lost my memory, I'd do myself in.' Another minute went by. 'I don't particularly know why, but I have occasionally thought of you during the last twelve years and wondered how you'd got on.' He came out of his sombre mood and chuckled. 'You lit off to London, then?'

'On the money I made out of you.'

'I can't believe it.'

'A hundred and fifty pounds was a lot more then than it is now. I had a bit besides, so I bought a car.'

'What are you doing in this Rolls-Royce?'

'I'm a chauffeur.'

He tut-tutted. 'You haven't come very far.'

I wanted to stop and throw the old sod out. Who was he to condemn me for the balls-up I'd made of my life? Instead, I unhooked my watch – his watch – and swung it back to him. 'That's yours. I stole it when I was helping you to pack up your household belongings.'

I was left holding it. His face in the mirror was lantern-jawed, moustached and grey-eyed. He had wrinkled skin and a mardy mouth.

'Take the thing, then.'

'I don't want to,' he said.

'Must be worth a hundred quid.'

'I'm flabbergasted.'

'So am I.'

'It's not surprising.'

The road was narrow and full of curves.

'My arm's aching. I don't like driving with one hand.'

He switched on a light before clicking the back of the watch open. 'You're right. My initials are on it. I suppose I ought to thank you for keeping it safe. The other watch I had was stolen in hospital, so I'll never see that again. I'm glad to see this one, though. It belonged to my father.'

I'd have to buy a new one. 'I'm sorry I nicked it.'

'So am I.' I didn't expect him to be grateful. 'I suspected you at the time,' he said, 'but we'd been so friendly I couldn't believe it. You'd better stop this car, and set me down.'

I shouldn't have been, but I was annoyed at him not saying what a good chap I was for giving his watch back, and the idea of him leaving me in this frame of mind didn't suit me at all. I hadn't thought about the Green Toe Gang for half an hour, or worried about the priceless goods I was hijacking in the boot. I patted Dismal on the head. At least he loved me. 'I can't let you go like this.'

I heard his friendly and open laugh. 'Are you trying to Shanghai me?'

'I'm offering you a job,' I said, without thinking.

'That sounds like Michael Cullen of the old days. If I remember, you worked a bit for me, didn't you? I always thought you had flair, and would go a long way.'

'I'm a bit more than a chauffeur,' I said. 'I'm a courier, really, and in the boot there's a cargo worth a lot of money. I'm moving it from one place to another and I need somebody to be with me for a few days, as a sort of driver's mate. It's a temporary and non-pensionable post, but I'll pay you ten quid a day starting from this morning.'

'You're joking.'

'Oh bollocks.' I was fed up with his sanctimonious presence. To our right, beyond Kidderminster, stretched the gloom of Wyre Forest.

'I suppose swearing is the only way you know of being serious,' he said. 'But I'll tell you one thing, Michael. There's a lot to be said for the stiff upper lip, by which I mean not saying anything, and especially not swearing the minute it comes into your mind. You're a man of too much substance to let yourself be carried away so easily.'

I acknowledged that he was right, and that the first thing I should have prevented myself saying was to make that stupid offer of a job. But I took his advice to the extent that I resisted hurting his feelings, though I was strongly tempted to do so. 'Of course your job with me will mean working at night. There are no set hours. It might also involve a certain amount of danger.'

He laughed. 'What have I got to lose?'

'Can you handle firearms?' I thought that on saying this he would run away from the car as fast as a March hare up a chimney.

'I was in the Home Guard during the war,' he said calmly. 'There aren't many types of small arms I didn't learn how to handle. I also taught others how to use them.'

'Somebody might try to rob the car.'

'I don't want to hurt anyone.'

'Just to frighten 'em off. I don't expect it'll come to it, though.' I could smell the ups and downs of Shropshire. Clegg fell asleep and Dismal went on snoozing. I drove up into Ludlow, and the sight of its cosy old-fashioned hotels made me sorry their dining rooms were closed and that it wasn't possible for me to rumble into a courtyard and put up for the night. I trawled along the few lighted streets and circled the one-way system twice. Even the gloomy castle seemed comforting. At midnight I drifted downhill and coasted west, the familiar technicolour dashboard glowing below clear shapes along the road lit by my headlights. I'd been at the wheel forever, or so it felt, and might have gone to sleep over it if I'd been on my own.

Not knowing what to do about my cargo, I was all cold fronts and depressions. I thought of driving as deep into the nearest forest as I could get and staying undetected till I made up my mind on the next best thing to do. In a clearing, with shovel and pickaxe, Clegg and I would bury the loot, a hurricane lamp hanging from a tree branch, while Dismal looked on like a disapproving gaffer at our clumsiness. But I didn't have tin trunks to put it in, so the stuff would go rotten in a week. Still, with a rifle, a shotgun, a Great Newfoundland dog (or whatever he was) and a mining engineer, we might survive till the Moggasearch was called off.

The 'Treasure Island' picture vanished, and I looked to the ever-winding road, drawn towards Peppercorn Cottage – which maybe I wouldn't have been if I hadn't known that Wayland Smith was held prisoner by Percy Blemish. My mind was in knots, but I kept going, determined at least to set him free.

Half an hour later, turning north over bare high hills, I heard Clegg yawn and stretch. Dismal leaned over and nudged my hand with his snout. Time to stop. To the left and right were huge patches of wood. The road descended into a valley towards Bishops Castle, whose lights winked as if somebody had forgotten to turn them off at midnight and would be called to account in the morning for such extravagance.

'A nap makes a new man of you,' Clegg said.

Dismal romped and farted up and down the hedges while I opened a tin of Bogie and put water in his bowl. Clegg made a start on the ham sandwiches and I got out the oval tank of coffee. 'You look after your employees well.'

'I do my best.' We leaned against the car and I saw his face in the light, a man of anguish whom fate hadn't kicked until quite late in life. My last ten years had been peaceful, but his had been full of trouble. I had another fifteen years to go before getting to the point he had started from. Things had to change, if I wasn't to go the same way. Black clouds were drifting up in a line from the west. 'Looks like we're in for it,' Clegg said.

A tree at the edge of the field creaked in the wind like a wooden battleship being pushed up the rocks. 'I don't suppose we'll be the only ones to get it.'

When Clegg poured more coffee Dismal looked up mournfully, so I set the remains in his empty bowl, and even above the wind heard him lapping it with pleasure. A passing car mistook the shape of ours and nearly ran off the road. 'We'd better be off. I have an appointment at Peppercorn Cottage and there's still thirty miles to go. I want to get there in an hour and be away before dawn.'

He settled himself in the back. 'What's the hurry?'

'If I don't do things in a hurry I don't do them at all.'

'It's like that, is it?'

'It is.'

Rain beaded the windows, so I put the wipers-and-driers on. We went northwards, over hills and across valleys. Clegg and the dog dozed again, while I thought of Frances Malham. When too much was tormenting my mind I cut off from it by thinking of sex, and when there was nothing on my mind I thought of sex so as to put something into it. Certainly, a mind ought not to be either tormented or empty. So while driving the dark roads I mulled on beautiful Frances Malham the medical student who, I could be sure, wasn't thinking of me. At the same time, I could be reasonably certain that if there was any woman at the moment mulling on me in similar terms, I wasn't thinking of her. Telepathic wires almost always crossed. But in spite of my recent randy philandering, and the equally randy philandering of those women who had chosen me (and at the end of it all, who was to say who had chosen whom – if it had not been mutual?) my only yearning was for Frances, not only because she had been the most recent of my encounters, but because I was in love with her, and I hoped I would be till the end of my life, though I didn't see how we could get together again, because even though she didn't hate me, she would probably avoid me as if I had got scabies.

Midsummer clouds, filled up by the Atlantic and the Gulf of Mexico, let water drop over the hills that streamed into the valleys. Even on the ridges I was driving along a river. Dismal woke at the noise and tried to stop the windscreen wipers with his left paw, his head moving like the victim of a tennis season. I plunged on, Captain Cullen of the Yellow Roller clipping around Cape Horn. As a kid I'd wanted to be a sailor, as well as a pilot and a train driver, little knowing I would end up at the wheel of a car like everybody else.

Dismal howled at a flash of lightning. When thunder broke he got on the floor and buried his head in his paws. I laughed, and he looked up resentfully, then hid his great juff again at the next sizzling flash across the windscreen. I slowed down in case a fallen tree blocked my way around the bend.

I swayed on, both hands at the wheel, drenched in my oilskins and thrown against the scuppers but getting back to the poop deck on all fours, gallantly assisted by Able Seaman Dismal, before another wave struck us. I snarled at the rest of the crew, and braced myself for the next great sea-change as we made westerly.

'Quite a blow.'

'I've had worse, Mr Clegg.'

'We should beat back a bit, sir.'

'No!' I roared. 'Make westerly. Make westerly.'

And we did. North as well, till we were through, and rain subsided to a drizzle. Water ran down the sides of the road, and sometimes along the middle, and there was obviously more to come. Only two other cars had passed in half an hour. 'Anyone out tonight, and they're up to no good.'

'You can say that again, Mr Cullen.' I turned off the A road, and went along one which ran up the steep side of a wooded spur. Branches met overhead. 'It's like going along a gallery underground. I hope the props hold.'

After a mile the road levelled, a wood to the left. Rain stopped, but water still dripped. Over the dip was Coldstone Hill, four hundred feet higher. I read the map at a crossroads, then forked right and, after a mile along a descending lane, recognised the village of Mainstoke. We were getting close. Wind was thumping the car, but it stayed solid. Flurries of rain came back and front. I cruised up the track towards Peppercorn Cottage and Clegg opened the gate, shutting it after I'd driven through. 'This is about the most remote place I've ever been in, except underground.'

Stars between clouds were like confetti thrown up into the sky that had stuck, each with a bulb inside. We went gently upwards on dimmed lights. Water that ran between the concrete strips of the paved lane was an inch or two deep in places. I stopped a mile short of the cottage and parked under a chestnut tree after turning the car round. I changed into wellingtons. 'You stay here, Mr Clegg.'

'You can rely on me.'

'Have this two-two rifle. It isn't loaded, but at the sight of it nobody'll take a chance. Stand ten yards from the car so that they don't catch you inside. But I don't suppose you'll see anybody.'

'I hope not. I'll do the humanly possible, though.'

I didn't altogether like that. 'Can you drive?'

'I had a car for thirty years.'

I slid two shells into the shotgun. 'Can you get the car back down the lane if I don't show up in an hour?'

'I expect so.'

I buttoned my green overcoat to the neck and put the heavy duty air pistol in my pocket. 'If you can do that, you can get it to Upper Mayhem in Cambridgeshire.'

I wrote the address, and he looked at the paper. 'I should be able to.'

I played it like a bloke on the cinema. 'Come on, Dismal. Don't make a sound, or I'll cut your tail off.'

We trod carefully so as not to splash in hidden pools, and I got used to the dark by keeping the two hedge-tops in view. Dismal was so quiet I thought he had disappeared, but every few seconds I saw his shadow moving against my wellingtons. The track around the house was a quagmire. Rain was endemic in these parts. If I'd brought the car down it would have sunk without trace.

I looked in through the window. The main room was lit by a gas lamp hanging from the middle beam. A large wood fire burned in the grate, a black kettle on top spouting steam. Percy Blemish sat in an armchair reading. Crockery was on the table, with a few tins and packets of food. It seemed a shame to disturb such domestic orderliness. Percy as a caretaker, and his wife as a housekeeper, had found their places in life, and I wondered why it had taken so long.

I banged at the door, but he must have thought it was another bout of wind. He only responded when I tapped on the window. 'Who is it?'

I told him, and at the same time tried the door. 'Lord Moggerhanger sent me to deliver some stuff.'

He opened up, pointing a revolver at my face, which I

did not like. 'Put that thing down.' Had I escaped the skill of quick-firing Two-two, only to fall at a sluggish bullet from Percy Blemish? The thought didn't bear thinking about. I stepped aside. Dismal launched himself at Blemish's chest. In pushing past, I swung and kneed him in the groin. He went flying towards the fire, but was quick enough to get off a shot which hit the wall just under the ceiling and sent plaster all over the room.

It wasn't the nearest I'd been to death, but it was close. I turned to make sure Dismal was safe. He guarded the door, tail flicking with nervous anger as he looked at Blemish lying in a heap. A sharp piece of ricochetting dust had hit me at the temple, and the liquid trickling onto my best overcoat was blood. I thumped Blemish for good measure, regretting that I had changed into wellingtons. My overcoat had cost nearly two hundred quid. 'You stupid prick. Get up.'

Another such bullet and I'd be on the floor bleeding to death. At the best I'd have an agonised journey up the lane, pulled on a blanket through the mud. Then again, a stint in hospital might get me a few weeks rest. I remembered Blaskin telling me about his spell after he had lifted a suitcase and busted a gut. The nurses often laughed as they remembered his stentorian scream up and down the corridors of the private clinic where he went to have his hernia pushed back: 'You know I'm not going to last till morning: wank me off!'

Stop woolgathering, I told myself just in time, as Blemish made a move towards a carving knife on the table. I banged down on his wrist and it fell to the floor. Dismal leapt across the room, his canine spikes grazing my wrist. I pointed to the door. 'Stay outside.' He walked away, pleased with himself.

I turned to deal with Blemish, and lifted the shotgun. 'Next time, you'll get this across your chops.' I pushed him into the armchair. 'You might even stop both barrels.'

But I wasn't getting through to him with such threats. He wore a collar and tie, a Fair Isle pullover, a tweed jacket and flannel trousers – the Master of Peppercorn Cottage. His grey eyes and downturned lips made an expression of murder. 'Lord Moggerhanger said I wasn't to let anybody in.'

I told him who I was. He'd obviously been notified.

'Cullen?'

'Yes, you old fool.' I picked up the book he had been reading, offended at seeing it on the floor. I read the title: *A Knife in Your Guts*. So that was it. There was a shelf of them across the room. The silly bastard had driven himself even crazier on a surfeit of Sidney Blood, that swine of an author who had a lot to answer for. I threw it back on the floor.

'Why didn't you say so, Smiler?'

He tried to grin, in genuine Blood fashion.

'The Boss said you'd give me a rough time.'

His face lit up like Eddystone lighthouse in a gale. 'He did?'

'Told me you was a hard case. Said I might have to kick the door down and go in shooting. If I could get close enough. There's a Dormobile up the lane, full of the boys. He was taking no chances, after you cut up two of his best men last week.'

He got up to smooth his clothes. 'If I do my job well I might be able to go back to my wife in Ealing.'

'The rats blew town.' I hadn't noticed any, unless our rowdy entrance had scared them off. 'How come?'

He looked at me with unblinking eyes. 'I declared war. Traps and poison. They became discouraged. I played a flute and caught one alive. I stunned it, and hung it upside down till it died. Rats are very sociable and intelligent. They could do nothing about their colleague's awful fate because I stayed close. We made a pact that they only come back when I've gone.'

I swabbed blood from my face. If he scared me it was only because I thought that in taking care of myself I might end up killing him. 'You nicked me. What makes you so hasty with the rod?'

'Can't be too careful.' He took a medicine bottle from the shelf, poured some into a glass, and drank it straight off. 'Shoot first and ask later. I'm a hasty man, Mr Cullen.'

Someone was walking upstairs. 'I've come for him.'

'Mr Smith won't go. He's a very sociable and intelligent person. We've had some long talks. He told me about socialism. He's a progressive chap.'

'He's going to make progress now. The Boss told me to take him for a walk.'

His face was pasty and his smile was no smile, though he did his best. 'A walk?'

'He wants insurance. He knows too much. I'm to take him for a stroll up the primrose path and show him his face in the water. You know what that means?'

He laughed. 'Concrete shoes?'

I held out my hand. 'Gi' me the key, and I'll bring him down. But don't say anything. Get me?'

He nodded. The stairfoot door was locked. I turned to see Blemish reaching for the gun again, and butted him so hard he scooted against the table. Half a dozen tin pans fell on the floor. His features scrunched up like those of a little boy hit by his teacher. 'I don't like you.'

'Nobody does. I don't even like myself.'

'I never will.'

'You think this is Kung-fu Castle?'

He didn't like my humour, either. 'I'll kill you, first chance.'

'Try it, yeller-belly.' I spoke from the corner of my mouth, and put the gun in my pocket, hoping he didn't have another stashed away. The loony swine might shoot to kill. 'Give me the key.'

He threw it in the hottest part of the fire. Time was moving, ten minutes gone. A crowbar leaned against the wall, but I needn't have bothered. The door was rotten. I went up the lighthouse-type stairs and into the first room. A small bearded man wearing a black Russian-style fur hat sat writing by a calor gas lamp. There was a mug of something by his side and half a dozen beer cans at his feet.

'Wayland Smith?'

He looked up. 'What do you want?'

'I'm taking you out of this.'

He smiled, but didn't stand. 'What was the fighting about?'

'Move,' I shouted.

'No.'

I was genuinely interested in his stupidity. 'Why not?'

'Who are you, anyway?'

'I'm springing you, Sunshine.'

'You're jolly well not. I could have escaped any time, but I didn't want to. This is the most peaceful time I've had. I've no worries, and I can write and think. So clear off and leave me alone. I'm getting on very well with Mr Blemish, and don't want to be rescued. I'm also closing in on Moggerhanger. I'm onto something big.'

He was. You could see it in his eyes. 'You'll be into something small if you don't do as I tell you.'

He picked up a bundle of papers. 'This is only half. I'll have the rest if I stay. I've got more information on Moggerhanger's drug empire than anybody ever had before. It'll be a great documentary.'

I admired his courage in risking his life for a television company, but gave him a head-on close-up view of the revolver. 'Move, or you won't live to tell the tale.'

He took an anorak from a nail on the wall. 'If it's like that.'

'Have you got any luggage?'

He had a sense of humour. 'They didn't let me pack before jumping on me.'

I followed him down. We stood in the living room. 'Say goodbye to Mr Blemish.'

Percy ignored him.

'I don't think that's necessary,' Smith said.

It was a diversion. I snatched his bundle of papers and threw them to the back of the fire. He burst into tears. 'Why did you do that?'

An arm went towards the flames, but I got him with the full butt of my shoulder, so that he flew one way and his cat-hat another. If anyone was going to get Moggerhanger it would be me. I pushed him towards the door. 'I'm saving your life. You'll be kicking up daisies if they find that bumf on you.'

'I can remember every word.'

'Keep 'em in your head.'

Blemish sat in his armchair, interested only in a Sidney Blood yarn. I didn't see how Moggerhanger could get anything like duty out of him. 'Write and tell me how it ends.'

Dismal followed us up the hill, zig-zagging from side to side as if not knowing that our job was done. We stumbled through potholes and soaking ferns. Fat-arsed clouds slid across the sky. Wayland was in difficulty because he couldn't get used to the dark, but Dismal nudged him on when he slackened. I whistled as we got near the car.

'I thought it was you,' Clegg said. 'Who's that?'

'A bloke I rescued. He doesn't seem to appreciate it.'

'They never do.'

Maybe he was right, and it was the shock of freedom. 'Wayland, this is Mr Clegg, my first mate.'

I sat on the step and changed back into my boots. Wayland had gone. Not even Dismal had seen him skive off. That was all I needed, a midnight chase for the Shropshire lad. I couldn't go back to Festung Peppercorn because Blemish, realising what I'd done, would be walking in circles with the manic energy of a hornet's nest. To go near him again might mean death for both of us. I got Dismal by the nose. 'Find him,' I said angrily, 'or I'll stop your Bogie.'

He whined, and ran off with his nozzle to the ground. I walked as if I was blind, here, there and everywhere. The gateway from one field to another was pitted by the hoofmarks of cows. Each foot had gone into the mud and, when withdrawn, had left a circular hole of water. There were scores of them in the beam of my flashlight. I tried to step onto dry spaces between the holes as I went along with my loaded shotgun, but the grass broke down under pressure, and mud that welled over my boot tops came in through the lace-holes.

Something moved, a rabbit running away. Why it strayed from a snug burrow on such a night I couldn't imagine. I cursed Wayland Smith, and got to the top of the hill. Peppercorn Cottage was in deep shadow to my right. Lights twinkled on a hill in the distance. A loud cracking of twigs sounded near the path, and I heard a bark from Dismal.

'Get him off! He'll bite me. The brute!'

He hadn't had any Bogie for an hour, and might well be squaring up for a nibble, so I put on a spurt. A low branch tripped me and I half stunned myself when I did a header. The shotgun, luckily on safety, flew in front. I landed on grass, which turned my overcoat greener.

Wayland was in a snivelling mess but, my boots and trousers being splashed with mud, I gave him such a shove he nearly went flying off the hillside back to Birmingham. 'What the hell do you think you're up to?'

'You gave me no alternative,' he gasped.

I prodded him as we made tracks to the car. 'It'll be all the more to put in your article.'

'Documentary,' he said, in a normally offended voice. I

blindfolded him with a piece of rag in case he thought to find his way back after I threw him out of the car. He'd obviously been brought in the same way, because he didn't grumble when I pulled it tight. We trundled down the track in the Roller, and after Clegg let us through the gate we were soon back on signposted lanes.

I began to wonder what I would do. I didn't even know where I was. I drove in circles, having lost my sense of direction. Looking at the map made no difference. The twists and undulations of the sunken lanes, the unfamiliar names of hamlets and villages, and above all the darkness, plus the presence of three conflicting spirits in the car, made my hands shake in a punchdrunk fashion. I stopped at a fork – hoping the middle-of-the-night milkman wouldn't come smashing into me – and got out the map again.

'You're exhausted,' said Clegg.

'Thanks for nothing.' What I wanted was a dose of alcohol, but it was more than I dared do. I never drank when driving, and even less when I was knackered. I looked at the dashboard. It had just gone two. Apart from the nap at Upper Mayhem I'd been on the go for fourteen hours. I'd taken part in the robbery of the year, met an old acquaintance and given him a job, and liberated a kidnapped member of the media. I had also hijacked the loot from the aforesaid robbery, which was an indescribably stupid act and meant I was as good as dead. All I craved to bring me back to life was a sight of the super-intelligent face and beautifully creamy bosom of Frances Malham. But it was no good. She didn't love me. No sooner had I discovered the love of my life than I had done something to lose life itself.

'Give me the map.'

Clegg walked to the signpost, turned the map round a few times, then came back. I lifted my head from my hands. 'Well?'

'We're only five miles from where we came from. Where do you want to go?'

'Shrewsbury,' I whispered, so that Wayland Smith wouldn't hear.

'Turn left at the next fork. In half a mile you'll hit a B road. Go right, then left almost immediately. After another couple of miles it should be signposted. It'll be just over twenty miles from that point.'

I set off.

'I'll get you to wherever you want to go, as long as you know where you want to get to,' he said. 'I can't say fairer than that, can I?'

For a start he could shut up, but I maintained a stiff upper lip, as befitted the captain of the Flying Dutchman. 'When we hit the main road I'll want a layby to stop at, so that we can eat. There's a jumbo flask of tea and fifty more sandwiches in the snapbag.'

By the lights of a village junction, not far from the main road, a car came towards us with all beams on. They showed him the way, whoever he was, but they burned the macadam, and sizzled the eyeballs of oncoming vehicles. It was like God on wheels. You didn't stand a chance. The big light was coming, and you had to get out. I held the steering column gently and bumped the verge, but stayed on the road.

'He was in a hurry,' Clegg said calmly.

'What sort was it?'

'One of these, I think.'

'Then so are we.' If it wasn't Moggerhanger himself it was part of the gang, going to Peppercorn Cottage to make sure I had turned up with the swag. On the other hand it might have been Chief Inspector Lanthorn, who had borrowed a Roller from the local car pound and was going to Peppercorn before any of Moggerhanger's lot so as to take the loot for himself. It wouldn't be above his line of thinking. He'd anticipate no aggravation, getting the swag off me. But he would discover that I had been and gone. 'Calling all cars . . .' Let him find me. If that was the case, and I made it back to Gog-Magogdom, I'd be Claud's golden boy forever.

It was a fantasy to get me through the worst of the shakes. Whoever was in that car, they had seen me for sure, especially in such light as they had generated. My guts were turning to Mazawattee, as my mother used to say, but my fatigue was forgotten for a while.

On the main road, I was flat out for Shrewsbury, with no thought of stopping. They could turn round and come after me, though I guessed it was more likely they would go first to the cottage to check on what I had deposited there. It didn't leave much time in which to lose myself. I explained the situation to Clegg, though he had guessed quite a bit already. 'What would you do if you were in my shoes?'

'We all are,' he replied, 'including Dismal. But give me a minute or two.'

'Be my guest.'

He let that pass. 'From the point he saw you at, you could have been heading for London.' He spread the maps out like a general, or an examining engineer. 'On the other hand, you could have been going north. They've only got one car, so they'll have to make a choice. They could make the wrong one. On the other hand, they could make the right one.'

'Thanks.'

'I'm doing my best. I said I needed a minute or two. On the other hand, we could turn back and go into Wales. But there's less road density, and you'd be spotted from afar, and then trapped. Steady as you go, and veer left at the next lane. After two miles you'll be on the main route to Shrewsbury. Then you can let rip. At Shrewsbury, or on the outskirts' – he lowered his voice – 'put your passenger off, then head for the Manchester-Leeds-Sheffield triangle.

Nobody will find you there. I'll navigate you via Stafford, Uttoxeter, Ashbourne and Matlock.'

The road climbed, higher hills to our left. 'I'll never forget you.'

'I haven't enjoyed myself so much for a long time,' he said. 'Not for more than ten years, and that's a fact.'

'What's happening to Wayland?'

'The lucky chap's asleep. Turn left at this major road, and set your compass north.'

I felt better. 'There's a box near your right foot. Open it and pass us a sandwich. And dish out the tea. We can feed on the trot. Take Wayland's blindfold off when he wakes up.' I wanted daylight to come, because though night conceals I felt that, at the moment, we would be less conspicuous in daytime. Headlights could betray you for miles, whereas in the confusion of extra traffic we'd be comparatively hidden. I explained this to Clegg.

'You're learning.'

'I'd have known it at five years of age, if I'd had a car.'

'I mean you're sharing your thoughts.'

I decided to shut up. Yet it wasn't in me to stick to such a whim. I had always spoken what was on my mind. In any case, it was too often on my face. 'We've come a long way in a few hours.'

He got out the map, and was even sarkier. 'As the crow flies, it's forty miles.' He passed a bundle of sandwiches like a postman handing letters. The one I held for Dismal went in a single snap. I threw him another before managing to wolf one myself. Wayland woke up: 'Do I sense food?'

Clegg undid the blindfold and gave him something.

'I'm dropping you off in half an hour,' I said.

'Thank you very much for the favour.'

I wasn't very good at taking sarcasm from someone I didn't like. Dismal nudged me for another bite. 'No favour.'

'And where will that dropping-off point be, in this benighted country, if you please, chauffeur?'

'In the nearest fucking ditch if you don't shut up,' I said.

Clegg passed a plastic cup of scalding tea, otherwise I'd have carried out my intention, especially as it had just started to thrash down with rain. A post office van nearly hit us as it came round a bend. Then a Telecom wagon overtook me and almost skidded into a tree. They didn't dip lights in this part of the country. 'You'll be set down in Cheltenham,' I said. Unfortunately the signposts would tell him where he was.

He made an attempt to laugh, and almost succeeded, then took another sandwich from the box. 'I know exactly where Peppercorn Cottage is. Blemish is such a fool. His heart's full of steel wool. I'd have worked it out, anyway.'

'Go back,' I said. 'It'll be your funeral.'

'I'll stay with you, after all.'

'Think you'll get a new lead?' My laugh wasn't exactly hollow, but it was certainly concave. 'It'll still be your funeral.'

'Don't I have any choice?'

I avoided a hedgehog crossing the road. 'How long is it since you walked five miles?'

'I've forgotten.'

'Well, watch those Shrewsbury signposts, because when it says five, you're out. If your legs give way you can walk on your arse.'

Clegg asked if he had any money for the train.

'Some.'

'Drop him at the station, Michael.'

Since I'd had the foresight to load up with grub and feed everyone so well, I supposed I was captain of the ship. I also happened to be driving. Even Dismal had no cause to get broody, though the only disadvantage of topping him up as much as it pleased me to was that the car became filled with odours suggesting that we were passing an endless gasworks on one side of the road, and an extensive rotten egg plant on the other. No air-conditioning system could deal with the clouds of his guileless effusions. To open a window would set the rain against us. The only solution was to stop and let him out, otherwise we'd choke. 'Three men in a car found dead in mysterious circumstances,' people would read in *Offa's Mirror*.

I pulled in at the first possible place. A pause in our flight was necessary so that we could rest. While the others drank more tea I stayed in the front seat and wondered what to do. At half past three we were near a place called Pox Green. Nobody was following us at the moment, but the thought of daylight showing us plainly from every hill seemed like a promise of death – an adventure all the same, but how long could it go on?

Clegg was happy, Dismal carefree, Wayland Smith apparently content, while no word would tell me what I was. What was I? Don't ask. I knew who I was, and that was a fact, but as to what I was, no answer suggested itself until I was behind the car taking what seemed an endless piss. I was as rotten as ever. Would I piss myself to death and end up clean, but dead? I was as much of a bastard as ever, in spite of (or even because of) the fact that my father had eventually married my mother. Once a bastard, always a bastard. Moggerhanger was as straight as a thief could be, and generous after his fashion, but I was out to cause him trouble from which he would be lucky to recover. There was no one left except this bacillus-colony of a car moving at random over the dripping bosom of green England.

Bridgitte had left me, and with good cause. The only injustice was to herself – in that she hadn't done it sooner. I wanted to change, but it was impossible to reverse the flow of the stars, or my star at least. I got back into the car, beginning to think, not without a shaft of fear through my liver, that I was the sort who never changed from within. That being so, I could only invite the world outside to do its worst.

A sudden revelation suggested that, in such a situation, recklessness pays. From this point on, I thought, anything deviously plotted will only land me in a bag of chips over which someone is pouring blood sauce. Planning would deny me the benefits of my deepest and most life-saving feelings – which are epitomised by recklessness. Every full breath was a landmark, no more than that. I got out my hip flask and celebrated my surrender to a new-found life-saving recklessness by a long swallow of delicious whisky. I passed it to Clegg.

He took some. 'I haven't had more than half a pint of beer in years.'

Wayland drained it, which was just as well. 'Next time I hope they hold me hostage in a pub. Cheers!'

I went to the back of the car with a torch and a knife, opened the boot and slit packet after packet of paper till I came to a bundle of five-pound notes. When we got back inside, out of the rain, I gave a wad to Clegg.

'Do you mean it?'

'All yours.'

He counted. 'Must be a hundred.'

'I've paid you back that hundred and fifty pounds from long ago. I always pay my debts.'

'I didn't lend it to you. I gave it.'

'Please don't argue. I'm too tired.'

Wayland pocketed his wad after a short hysterical laugh.

'Fuck it,' I said. 'We're rich.'

Dismal sat on the driver's seat, paws at the steering wheel. He caught a bundle of fivers in his mouth on turning round, then got down on the floor to play Monopoly with himself. I stuffed mine, the biggest part, into my briefcase with the air pistol. 'Are you happy now?'

The miracle was, they were. So was I. We laughed like kids just landed on Treasure Island. I couldn't understand why I had been so careful. Somewhere along the way, with all the planning and calculation, I had stopped being myself, and that was bad. Look where it had got me. I'd even starved myself of adequate running expenses. You couldn't fund the operation I had in mind on a shoe-string. Interpol would see my point absolutely. All we needed was to stock up on food, petrol, booze and a trio of hitch-hiking girls. The rain drummed so heavily that, without knowing how or why, I dropped into sleep. So did my highway companions, including Dismal, who bedded down with Wayland's Russian-style fur hat between his paws as if it was a dying orphan which had crept in from the rainstorm and needed bringing back to life. The rhythm of falling rain on the roof rocked us to sleep.

Twenty-Six

Clegg woke me. 'I don't know how aware you are of the fact, Michael, but it's nine o'clock.'

'What?'

'The sun's up – a bit of it, anyway.'

It was so late I got the horrors, until I remembered that the password was recklessness. 'Is that all?'

'I didn't know you wanted a lie-in, or I'd have left you till this afternoon.'

We formed a row and pissed into the hedge. Dismal endeavoured to stand up but didn't quite manage, though if he persisted I might have sold him to a circus. 'We'd better find a place for breakfast. I need a bucket of tea to swill the sleep out of my gorge.'

Dismal got back on four legs and barked into the mist. 'Are we going to drop you at a railway station, Wayland, or are you coming with us.'

He looked too scruffy to be seen in a Rolls-Royce – bleary-eyed, beard untrimmed, face pale and lined, and hair hanging raggedly around his bald head. He wore a billowing jersey and stained trousers and stank as if he hadn't had a bath for weeks. Luckily he couldn't get the fur hat away from Dismal, because he looked even worse in that. 'I'll stay, if you don't mind.'

'In that case, maybe you wouldn't mind having a wash-and-brush-up at the next place we stop at.'

He turned sulky. 'Who the hell are you to tell me to get a wash?'

I hadn't meant to scorch his pride to the roots, but at least he was no longer pale. 'We'll be crossing the Severn soon. Maybe you'd like a dip in that?'

'You're just a driver.' He was fit to burst. 'And you're telling me to get a wash, boyo? What's the idea?'

It was hard not to laugh, which was lucky for him. 'We all need a wash, I suppose. But if you'd like to walk' – I opened the door – 'feel free.'

'I'd enjoy one,' said Clegg, 'but I don't like the idea of having to dress for dinner.'

Wayland sat like a graven image. As I got back into the driver's seat I noticed that someone had picked up Dismal's fivers. 'I put 'em in the glove box,' said Clegg. 'The saliva will dry off in no time.' To give more visibility for his navigation I invited him onto the flight deck, and Dismal could hardly believe it when I ordered him to the back, but a thump on his great flank helped his understanding. God knows why he had to feel so humiliated. To offset it he kept trying to sit on the armrest between the two seats, an impossible task, you might have thought, especially in the swaying car, but he managed it after a while, balancing with a forlorn and suffering face. When he had made his point (whatever it was) he got down and sat on the seat, to look over my shoulder at the instrument panel.

A toytown fairytale valley rolled to our left as we went downhill. 'We'll give Shrewsbury a wide berth,' Clegg said. 'The ring road's too close in. It'll mean about fifteen miles of winding lanes, but if you listen to my directions we'll be across the Severn at Atcham in half an hour.'

I took three Monte Cristos from the glove box and handed them around, but there were no takers except myself. Clegg pulled it out of the tube for me, and I lit up. 'Which direction, Navigator?'

'East-north-east, then northerly. Fork right after the next village. I'll tell you when.' A bread van slowed us down for a mile or two. I played it cool. The driver and his mate were pissing themselves at delaying a Rolls-Royce. It was a highpoint of their lives which they would talk about for months, if not years – heroes of the public bar.

'This country'll never get back on the rails,' Clegg said, 'while this sort of thing goes on.'

'What can you expect?' Wayland piped up. 'They've been crushed and exploited since the day they were born.'

I don't know why, but I was more mad on hearing that than at the lads in front. After all, they were only having a bit of fun. I might have done the same in their place fifteen years ago – though I was tempted to get the shotgun out and blast their tyres. 'Crushed and exploited, my arse.' We were going about fifteen miles an hour, so I couldn't lose my temper without matters becoming dangerous. 'They've had the time of their lives, the idle bastards. They've been pampered from the word go. If ever they feel crushed and exploited it's only because pratts like you tell 'em they are – because you *really* want to crush and exploit them.'

'I don't think it's any use talking to you,' Wayland said, as if I was no better than the sods in front. The van stopped on some spare ground at a row of cottages, and I went by without even giving them the satisfaction of a blast on my horn. 'That'll teach 'em,' I said, 'if anything will.'

There wasn't much traffic, and we made good time, though every car that floated up behind had me nervously expecting to be topped and tailed or have the windscreen flaked to pieces from the blast of a shotgun as they overtook. I was glad when Clegg gave the right fork which took us onto the lanes, where we met nothing but tractors and the occasional Volvo Estate.

'It's glorious country.' Clegg was in raptures. 'I'm glad we came this way. What a coincidence, Michael, to meet you again after all these years!' I thought it was fate, and fate was often worse than death, I told him. 'Not with me,' he said, 'or so I hope.'

Nobody could have tailed us through such a zig-zag of

lanes. Every half mile at a fork or crossroads Clegg gave out his cool instructions of left, right or straight on. Dismal didn't like staying in the back seat with offended Wayland, and every so often, usually when Clegg spoke and we made a turn, he bit me – just about playfully – in the neck, but almost immediately his long fat tongue came out and the big soft thing licked the hurt better. Then he smiled, as much as a dog can smile.

We got something to eat at a café on the main road, of sufficiently good quality to keep us alert and fit. We were reluctant to feed the white bread to Dismal, however, in case it sent him mad, so apart from the odd bacon rind and end of sausage, it was back to tins of Bogie in the parking lot. I didn't envy anyone trying to do an emergency stop after he'd used the place. While waiting for the others to terminate their ablutions I sorted out a 50p piece to telephone Blaskin.

'This is Gilbert Blaskin speaking,' his automatic answering device said. 'Point One: if you are a publisher, send the money. If you don't pay within three days I shall come around with a bomb and blast you out of your office. If you report this threat to the police, don't forget that all characters in this novel are fictitious and bear no likeness to anyone dead or alive. Point Two: if you edit a magazine and want me to write something, treble the price you have in mind and meet me in The Hair of the Dog. Point Three: if you are my publisher's editor and want me to alter my novel because it is too obscene, incoherent or inflammatory, get psychoanalysed somewhere else. Point Four: if you are a female student who wishes to talk about my work, take off your knickers as you get out of the lift. Point Five: if you are under the delusion that I owe you money, I suggest that you masturbate on the steps of the Wedlock Advisory Association, for it will do you just as much good as trying to get a bent stiver out of me. Point Six: if you are a member of my family, put your head under the cold tap and think again, unless the caller happens to be my only acknowledged offspring Michael Cullen, to whom I say, phone back later, because I have news for you, you eternal bastard.' He gave a five-second donkey laugh, and the machine clicked off.

Dismal had run back into the front seat, while Clegg was taking in the view, and we didn't have the heart or the strength to pull him out. Because we were going onto fast roads I put him into the safety belt, not wanting him to fly through the windscreen if I pulled up dead. But, like Houdini, he got out of it before we'd done a mile. Clegg continued his navigation, though from then on it was easy going. We crossed the M6 and went through Stafford to Uttoxeter. Beyond Ashbourne we got into the Derbyshire hills, by which time we were famished. There was nothing like being on the run to make you hungry as if, should our pursuers suddenly strike, death would be more agreeable on full bellies. Wayland hummed a pop tune and tapped out its rhythm on the window. 'You can say that again,' he exclaimed, when I spread my thoughts around like Marmite.

We walked into a hotel near Matlock, and sat by the dining room window looking onto the hills. I ordered four meals. Dismal was chained to the fender in case some light-fingered bastard should think to open the boot and make off with a few million pounds' worth of goods.

'Four, sir?' Seeing three of us, the waiter wasn't able to put two and two together. What worried me was that I had seen his face before, and couldn't fathom where.

'I've got my chauffeur in the car. Just deliver four of each course as they come up, and I'll take his out to him.' The waiter was about forty, with thick black hair and large hands, and I was certain I had seen him in prison. He seemed offended that we hadn't let our chauffeur dine with us. Were we communists, or something? Or big trade union nobs?

We ordered a pint of ale, then salami salad, followed by roast lamb, peas, cauliflower and potatoes. This was backed up by a grisly trifle made out of sugar, lard and turpentine. Dismal even gobbled the vegetables, and then licked the ale from his dog bowl. He sat dizzily belching while we had our coffee, brandy and cigars at a table in the sun. The meal cost twenty-five quid, and none of us complained as we stumbled back to the car.

Five miles up the road, and well over the hills out of Matlock, I realised that the hotel waiter had been Bill Ramage, who I had worked with smuggling gold for the Jack Leningrad organisation in the late sixties. He'd given no sign of recognising me, but gold smugglers were always too cunning to share their thoughts, and it was hard to think I'd altered so much. If Ramage was going straight we were safe, and if he wasn't and suspected me to be on a job he might easily phone Moggerhanger and report my presence.

Clegg worked his slide rule and played with the maps like a kid with toys at Christmas. 'I know Derbyshire so well I don't need to look at the scenery. I was brought up only a few miles from here, over at Tibshelf. It was a close-knit mining community in those days. God knows what it is now. Like the ruins of Pompeii, I expect.'

'I suppose the Tories have broken their spirit,' Wayland said. I drove in my own dreamworld, unable to chip in on their talk.

'The spirit of Tibshelf would take some breaking,' Clegg said. 'My father was a collier, but he died at forty in an accident. Then my mother married a clerk at the pit who made me stay at school after I was fourteen. He only earned seventy shillings a week, but you could manage on that in those days. He'd had a bullet through his face in the Great War, and if he spoke too quickly a whistle came into his voice. At first I thought it was funny, but I learned different, though he was never cruel or unjust. I didn't much like him, but I respected him. If he'd had a sense of humour I'd have been a bit happier, but you didn't think much about happiness in those days. Now, you hear it mentioned so often on the wireless and the telly that it's got no meaning. One winter's evening I asked him a question about Napoleon that he couldn't answer, so he gave me a pencil and a notebook and sent me to the reference section at the public library to find out. Libraries stayed open late in those days, but the only thing was that it was two miles away, and it was snowing a blizzard. I got back all right, but only just! Talk about gaining a respect for knowledge! He sent for me when he was dying, during the war. It was only then that I realised he actually loved me. Life's a hell of a funny country. The strange thing was – or is it? – my mother loved him, and only survived him by two weeks. She was fifty, but she was worn out.'

In the Town of the Crooked Spire there were roadworks all over the place. 'We'll soon be safe,' Clegg said, 'in the Leeds-Manchester-Sheffield triangle. A real jungle. We'll have six hundred and forty-eight square miles of towns, dales and villages to get lost in.'

'How do you make that out?'

'Well, it's an equilateral triangle, each side measuring thirty-six miles. Half the base multiplied by the height, or the length of one side multiplied by another, and the total divided by two, gives you six hundred and forty-eight.' He held up his slide rule. 'Simple. Or if you don't feel safe enough in that, you can make it the Leeds-Blackpool-Liverpool-Sheffield Equilateral. That gives you sixty miles from east to west and thirty miles from north to south, making an area of eighteen hundred square miles. And believe me, Michael, with that kind of space to play about in, and the money you seem able to get your hands on, you can drive around in safety forever. All you have to do from time to time is stop for petrol, food, some new maps, and to answer the calls of nature. You can get in the *Guinness*

Book of Records as the first man to grow old on the run. It wouldn't be a bad life, when you think of some.'

'Count me out,' said Wayland.

For a joke, I stopped the car. 'You're counted out.'

'I'm not quite ready,' he said, in a reasonable tone I'd not heard up to then.

I started off. 'Cheer up, Wayland. If you don't have a sense of humour, cultivate self-control. It's only sensible, in the circumstances.'

On the dual carriageway which spaced itself out towards Sheffield Clegg said: 'We'd better have our passports ready for going into Yorkshire. We should have got visas at their legation in Stafford, but maybe they'll let us in. Dismal will be turned back as an undesirable immigrant, though.'

I blessed the fact again that I had given him a lift. 'It's all right. He's on my passport.'

Traffic was thick, coming and going. Dismal was having bad dreams after his hotel dinner. He reeked of beer more than any of us. Hot sun came through the windscreen, at which I thought we'd soon look as if we'd just got back from Benidorm. In spite of my recent onsurge of recklessness I was dead set on staying alive, however serious the misdemeanour I'd tangled with. In front of my eyes was the sky, a clump of bushes, the brick side of an inn advertising Real Food in big white letters half a mile away, and a broken white line down the middle of the road. But inside me, in no uncertain manner, was the vision of lovely Frances Malham. Her features haunted me as if they belonged to some maternal (or even paternal) aunt or grandmother from generations ago, though whether from the Cullen or Blaskin side I had no way of knowing. It was almost as if she was a long-lost sister, and because of this notion I had the feeling that falling in love is the nearest to incest that most of us get. Why, otherwise, her face affected me more positively than anyone else's (I almost got a hard-on thinking about her) I didn't know, especially having met her when she was fawning around that crackpot poet Ronald Delphick – one of his groupies, no less. Or was she? Now that I was in the north, heading into that vast equilateral, as Clegg designated our intended guerilla base, I decided to spy out Doggerel Bank, which was quite near, and see what sort of a place it was that Delphick inhabited, but also on the off-chance that Frances had lied about going to Oxford and was up there visiting him for a bit of hearthrug pie.

'I want to go through Barnsley and Wakefield.'

Clegg looked at his map. 'You'll be skirting the rim of the safety area.'

'I know. But I have to call at a house near Kirkby Malzeard called Doggerel Bank. It's not far from Ripon.'

'It's a risk. Still, we won't be much beyond half-an-hour from safety. We'll run up on the M1 for a while, and then go through Leeds.'

I belted along, but kept my ears as wide apart as they'd go in anticipation of a Wailing Winnie with a flashing blue light. We skirted Sheffield and got onto the motorway, and since there was only one more service station before Leeds, I drove onto it. Why I wanted to phone Blaskin I don't know, but in my reckless state perhaps some voice from the past might persuade me to believe that a future was in the offing.

I parked as near to the entrance as I could get, and Wayland ran in to get coffee. Clegg put Dismal on a lead and was last seen being pulled towards the dustbin area behind the kitchens. The phone was answered after five rings. 'Mr Blaskin's residence,' a woman said.

'This is his son. I want to speak to the shabby old wanker.'

'Please moderate your language, Mr Cullen, while I see whether the eminent novelist is at home. He's in rather a temper today.'

I didn't have time to say a mantra before he came on.

'Michael, is that really you? Last night I dreamed that you'd fallen into the mincer and was dead. I woke up laughing, it was so horrible. Where are you? Are you really alive? If you are, don't come to within five miles of me, or I'll blast you asunder. How could I have given birth to a monster who knows how to strike vitals which even I don't know how to find and didn't even know I'd got? How could you have done such a wicked unfilial thing? I can't believe it.'

He would have gone on for three volumes, but I shouted him down. 'What have I done now, fuck-face? You know I would do anything to hurt you, I love you so much, but I never thought I would succeed, you're such a selfish, hard-bitten old bastard.'

'Don't swear,' he said calmly. 'It's only an excuse for rotten English. Shows deplorable lack of style, and I don't like that in a son of mine. Give me a moment, and I'll tell you what you've done.'

I thought he'd hung up, and found myself getting worried, in spite of everything. He was robbing me of my recklessness, and I didn't like that.

'Do you remember,' he said, 'that you wrote me a trash novel?'

'Of course I do. It was very trashy indeed. It was the best rubbish I could write.'

'Maybe it was. I don't know what's what anymore. I thought it was putrid too. I couldn't have done worse myself.'

'I did it to get you out of a jam, if I remember. You wanted to leave your publishers, but were contracted to hand over one more novel. So I suggested you give them a rotten one that they would have to turn down. Out of the goodness of my heart I wrote it for you.'

I thought he was crying. 'Do you know what happened?'

'How the hell should I?'

'He accepted it!'

I laughed. 'You must be joking.'

'You won't laugh if you get a javelin through your throat. He says it's the best thing I've done. It was "hats off"! He wants to put it in for the Windrush Prize. Michael, why did you do this to me? Where are you, so that I can kill you? Why did you write a prizewinning best seller, you awful abortion you?'

It was getting harder and harder to do the right thing in life. 'I'll never help you again,' I said coldly. 'But why don't you calm down and look at the situation rationally? It won't do you any harm, for a change. Ask your publisher for a twenty-thousand quid advance. He won't pay it. You're free. If he does cough up, give me half. It'll only be fair.'

'Never!' he croaked, and I heard no more.

I was getting sleepy, and looking forward to a night's kip on Delphick's flagstoned floor, or at least an icy wash from his cold-water butt. After a quick swill of coffee I went out to see Clegg and Dismal coming back from their promenade around the dustbins. Dismal must have emptied at least three, because a fragment of plastic cup still adhered to his jowl. 'You disgusting beast, don't we feed you enough?'

He licked my hand lovingly, and left a streak of stale ketchup over the back. Wayland shuffled out of the cafeteria and got back on board. We soon put Leeds behind us (thank God) and headed for Harrogate. It was a very up and down highway, with nice views of the dales left and right, between the built-up ribbon of road. The scenery soothed me, and I soon forgot Blaskin's insane maledictions. With a father like that, who needed friends? I pushed in a cassette for some music. Wayland said it was Brahms, so I turned it a bit louder for him. In Harrogate I dropped Clegg outside a supermarket, telling him to go in and buy everything, then get maps of the Ripon area from a bookshop. Because there was no parking I played Red Indians till he reappeared on the pavement with a trolley spilling over with food and booze. 'There's hardly room to sit,' Wayland complained when he loaded it into the back. 'Why do we need so many stores?'

I marked Doggerel Bank on the map for Clegg. 'I don't feel secure unless the car's loaded with victuals. It's one of my weaknesses.'

'You must have had a deprived childhood.'

I let that one go, and we glided up the hill with a puff pastry in our mouths. Dismal was so full already that he played with his like a cat with a mouse, but when I cursed him for making a mess he licked it up, then got back on the seat to be patted.

Clegg, the rally navigator, didn't take us directly through Ripon. A few miles beyond Harrogate he gave the fork left by a park, and after half a mile told me to split right up a steep hill onto the moors. my nervometer settled down to zero at such a straight and narrow road which went closer to the sky than the main drag to the east. There was little traffic, and we made so many turns, forks, bends, dips and steep ascents that I couldn't imagine anyone staying on our tail.

Clegg guided me to Doggerel Bank without going through a village. A piece of slate stuck on a crumbling wall of boulders pointed towards a track paved with stones, in some places rubble, in others only grass-grown ruts. On either side walls made the lane so narrow I was afraid we would scrape against them.

A bend took us through a belt of tall trees, and after a while I spotted a yard, a broken gate thrown to one side and almost covered in nettles, and across the cobbles was a simple stone-built slate-roofed cottage. Clegg, Dismal and Wayland got out, while I turned the car in case an urgent getaway was necessary, though I had no reason to think it would be. I bumped a drainpipe, tapped a wall and hit Delphick's reconstituted panda-pram, but with Clegg's expert guidance I managed to set the gleaming snout of the Rolls-Royce pointing towards freedom.

A wireless was playing. 'I love Haydn,' said Wayland, who hoped he was coming to a civilised place. I thumped the door but there was no answer. When I banged the knocker it fell off, so I laid it on the lid of the water butt and pushed the door open. Dismal sniffed his way up the corridor like Inspector Javert back on duty. The music got louder, and I walked into a room furnished like Ali Baba's cave.

It was a smallish parlour, but dressed up like an interior as far from Yorkshire as it was possible to get. The floor was covered with mock oriental carpets, and a kind of green blanketing had been tacked around the walls, going a third of the way up, above which was plain whitewash turning yellow. On a round low table was an Indian-style vase with several sticks of smoking joss stuck in it. The bed by the wall was more of a platform, about eighteen inches off the ground, but covered with blankets, pillows and cushions, rugs and sheepskins, in all kinds of piebald or gaudy colours. It made my eyes ache to look at it. On the turntable lid of the hi-fi system was a box of Turkish Delight. Cigarettes, half a bag of sliced bread, a roll-up tin, a bunch of keys and a biker's helmet lay on the floor.

Naked Ronald Delphick leaned against the wall, his arms around the shoulders of a woman who would have been altogether bare but for a pair of flimsy pants. Both were apparently far gone in listening to the music, but on our party entering, and especially at the advent of the Hound of the Baskervilles leaping on the bed and pushing his nose at the woman's breasts (God knows what he had in mind) she screamed: 'Oh God, a fucking nightmare! Get that dog off!'

Delphick looked up, shouting: 'Not you and that mongrel again. I can't believe it.'

It was encouraging, and indeed touching, that even in his panic he remembered us. I kicked Dismal off the bed, and apologised. 'I'm sorry about that, Miss. I've usually got him on a hawserchain, but he slipped out of it.'

Delphick put his trousers on. 'I know who you are, but fuck off. I'm not at home today. Unless you have a block or two of cannabis resin. Otherwise, get up that hill and never come back. I'm tired of intruders and fans who come down here just to see me. An East German tourist bus came looking for me the other day because they'd heard there was a working-class poet living here. I saw it coming down the lane so I took to the woods. I'm not a National Landmark. All I want is peace to go on writing my immortal poems. I'm writing one now, as a matter of fact, which only has words ending in the letter T and it's a very hard job. You're not taking all this down?'

'Oh, you're such a fucking bore.' The woman turned her back to us, and reached for a yellow cotton blouse hanging on a nail. I noticed a large tattoo on her back which said 'I love Janet'. Then the blouse covered it and she turned to us, still fastening the buttons. 'The only time I can put up with you is when you're silent, or when you're fucking me. Otherwise, you're full of shit.'

Delphick belched. 'Don't take on, love.'

Clegg had gone out with Dismal, while Wayland stood in the doorway, and I stayed in the room. I recognised the woman, and told her so. She was in her mid-thirties, slender and with a fine pair of legs. She had shoulder-length but straggly dark hair, an oval thinning face and, as I had seen, small rounded breasts. She was one of those outspoken bi-sexual specimens with one illegitimate kid who comes from a working-class home north of the Trent. I knew her, all right.

'I've seen you before, as well.' Her smile was friendly. 'In London, wasn't it?'

'And on the Great North Road. I gave you a lift once,

when I was going down to the Smoke for the first time.'

She pondered for a while, then laughed. 'In that old banger, with Bill Straw? I remember. That bastard had just got out of the nick. You're Michael?'

'You're June.'

'And if you've forgotten me, I'm Ronald Delphick.'

'Piss off and sulk.' She turned her back to him, and asked me: 'What the hell are you doing in this place?'

The information I had on her was coming back. She'd known Delphick since they were teenage lovers, and he'd put her in the family way, then deserted her. She had taken off to London, had the baby, and got a job as a stripper in one of Moggerhanger's clubs. She'd even been Mog's girlfriend for a while. I'd seen her occasionally in London during my gold-smuggling days, and once made an unsuccessful attempt to get into bed with her. What the hell she was doing with Delphick again, I couldn't begin to say.

'I'm a friend of Ronald's,' I confessed, 'though you might not think so, in view of the welcome he's giving me.'

'I didn't realise he had any friends.' She lit a cigarette. 'He's got sponsors, and people he ponces off, and a few little gang-banging groupies, and one or two idiots who grovel down the lane on their bellies so's they can touch his little finger, but friends – he wouldn't know one if you burst into flames and died for him.'

The smile on Delphick's face got wider the longer she went on. 'If a mark of friendship is to know your enemy,' she said, 'then I suppose I'm about the only real friend he's got, and I hate his guts. The only reason I can stand him is that I know him, and he's only harmless if you've got no illusions. But watch out, all the same, because his inventive mind with regard to treachery is always one notch ahead of yours. Otherwise I love him, and within his very narrow limits I believe he feels a pale shade of regard for me now and again. We occasionally meet for a fuck, for old times' sake. I write and say that Beryl – that's the little girl I had of his, she's twelve now – is asking about him. But he'll never see her in case she looks at him with her big give-me-a-quid-eyes. So I see him just to torment him with the fact that she's still alive. But he's as dead as ever. I don't suppose he'll ever grow up because if he did he'd be even less genuine than he is now, and then he wouldn't know me at all.'

'I love you, Petal, you know that,' he said. 'Such bad opinions almost give me a hard-on.' He grabbed her, but she got free and pushed him onto the bed which, if it hadn't been built on boxes, would have collapsed.

'Let's go into the kitchen,' she said, 'and make your visitors some tea. I'm sure they've paid for it a hundred times over or they wouldn't be here.'

'We've got no tea,' he said.

'No tea?'

'Nor sugar.'

'We'll have coffee,' I told him.

'We're out of that, as well.'

'What about cocoa?'

'I don't buy it.'

'What about a glass of ale?'

'If there was ale in the house there wouldn't be any. I'd have drunk it all.'

'Do you think you could spare us a cup of water?'

'That's different. Why didn't you say so? Just go on down the lane to the farm. There's plenty there. Tell him I sent you. He'll give you all the water you want. He's very generous, old Jack. A real good sort. Man of the people. Salt of the earth. He'll give you a cup of water.'

'I'll settle for a double whisky, on second thoughts.'

'Are you joking? People bring whisky here. They take a sip, and leave most of it.' He laughed. 'There's nothing in the place. We've got to go shopping sometime, Pet.'

June went ahead, leading us to the kitchen. 'Take no

notice of him. He wouldn't give you a hair from his nose. I'll make you some tea.'

She lifted the lid of the Rayburn and set a kettle on. The place was rough, but adequate. There was even a stool to sit on. Dismal sniffed at the bread bin, more out of curiosity, I hoped, than hunger. Clegg stood by the door, waiting for the word to sit down, while Wayland took a stool as far from the stove as he could get because of the heat. I was near the window with Delphick who, following my gaze, saw the back of the Rolls-Royce. He stopped smiling when he saw me looking at him. 'Nice car,' he said.

'You had a ride in it, remember?'

'And how.'

'It's not mine.'

June came to look. 'So you're still working for Claud? How is the savage old bastard?'

'Prospering.'

She took the cigarette out of her mouth. A tooth to one side was darker than the rest. 'Why did you come here?'

'I was in the area. Claud's got a place called Spleen Manor not far away. I always wanted to see Delphick's house. He told me it was a cowshed.'

Delphick laughed. 'You know why? If all my patrons in London saw how nice it was when they came up they'd never leave.'

'It's bloody opulent,' I said. 'I don't begrudge you, but how did you do it?'

June poured the tea. 'I'll tell you. First, an aunt died and left him a few thousand pounds. That was eight years ago. Our canny Delphick doesn't tell anybody, least of all me, in case I ask him for a bob or two to buy Beryl some socks. He picks this place up for a song. Then every little scrubber he inveigled here did something to the place. And every little groupie spent what money she had, and brought something to beautify it. When he'd fucked 'em silly and bled 'em dry he booted 'em out. A gushing middle-aged admirer put in a damp course. Another had a carpet laid – then got laid on it. A third improved the bathroom. Then he severs diplomatic relations with them all.'

He sugared his tea, and put the bowl back in the cupboard. June took it out and passed it round. 'Can you blame me, though?' he said. 'It's a reflection on how society treats its poets. If I got proper payment for my work I'd earn as much as a barrister. If only I was a novelist! I'd shamble around all day in my dressing gown, sit on the lawn in the sun, do a sentence now and again, and call for my housekeeper to bring me a drink, or serve tea which would include delicious little paper-thin cucumber sandwiches. I'd ask her to dish up some lunch of chips and venison whenever I felt like it. A novelist has it easy compared to a poet. I wish I could be a successful novelist.'

'Is there any cake with the tea?' I wasn't hungry, but wanted to do him a favour by giving him a chance to be hospitable.

He turned sharply, as if worms were eating his guts. 'Gritcake? Linseed cake? A cake of salt? I think we ate the last for breakfast, didn't we, Pet?'

She brought a tin of biscuits from the cupboard.

'Have you ever written a novel?' I asked.

He wiped a tear from his eye when Wayland took two biscuits. I threw one to Dismal. 'I'm trying,' he said, 'but not under my own name. A firm called Pulp Books wants me to write one.'

I trembled for the good name of English literature. 'Not Sidney Blood?'

Sheep bleated from the hillside. 'They're paying me two hundred pounds. I'm halfway through. It's only sex and violence, but that's all the people want, whether they live in Gateshead or Hampstead. June's helping me, aren't you, Pet?'

She sat down, and stroked his greasy oil-cloth hair. 'I always was good copy.'

'I never knew it was so easy to write novels. I'll do another if they want me to. Gets cold in winter.'

I'd noticed plenty of dead wood between the trees on my way down the lane. 'Why don't you get some in during the summer?'

'Me? You must be joking. If you want to come up from your soft life in London and do it, you're welcome. I'll give you sessions on oriental religion and the craft of poetry in the evening – if you aren't too tired after spending all day in muddy boots pushing a wheelbarrow. But I don't suppose anybody like you, with your short-back-and-sides, would be interested in that kind of profound edification, would you?' He sneered. 'No, Philistines like you would leave me to do my own rough work, and ruin my hands so's I couldn't write poetry anymore. I'm not going out in the wind to cut logs. It's bad for my hands. Not long ago I had to lift some bricks to fix the wall – didn't I, Pet? – because the sheep had been getting into my garden. When I'd put the last brick on I thought of a poem, but I could hardly write it down because my hands shook so much. I couldn't hold the pencil.'

His lips trembled as if he was about to cry. He put his empty cup on the saucer.

'Just shut up,' June said to me. 'You're upsetting him.'

Delphick put his face against her shoulder. 'Are they going soon?'

'In a bit, Pet.'

I didn't think I'd even arrived. Doggerel Bank seemed the ideal hideout. Neither Moggerhanger, nor Chief Inspector Lanthorn's police force, nor even the Green Toe Gang would ever find us. 'I don't care how much you blubber, you inhospitable bastard, but we're staying. It's important that we hole up for a day or two, but before you have a fit, let me inform you that the car's full of provisions. We spent sixty quid on booze and grub in a supermarket on the way. I'm not so unrealistic as to imagine that a greedy bastard like you would put us up for fuck-all.'

He smiled. 'Why didn't you say so? We can have a party. How much booze have you got?'

'Bottles and bottles.'

'And meat?'

'A couple of legs of mutton, sausages, pork, ham, bacon, and veal pies. We'd better start bringing it in,' I said to Clegg and Wayland.

'I'll help you,' Delphick said. 'Is it in the boot?'

I pushed him back. 'We'll do a human chain between car and kitchen. There are five of us, so that'll mean me at the car and June in the kitchen.'

'I'd be a much better person if people trusted me. Anyway, I've got to go and work on a poem. I'll be in my study when it's time for drinks.'

He was so much himself I couldn't help but admire him. I almost liked him for the fact that you certainly knew where you were when you were with Delphick, something you couldn't say for everyone.

The notion of going to Doggerel Bank certainly seemed a good one when I looked at the land round about. The track to it descended in one or two curves through fields and then woods, to the house which was invisible from the minor road above, which seemed to go nowhere and had hardly any traffic along it. Below Doggerel Bank the track led to a clear stream which was fordable by my sturdy vehicle, and which had a kind of plank-and-girder footbridge over it. I explored the area with Dismal, while June and Clegg got a meal together out of the provisions we'd disembarked.

Beyond the stream the motorable track curved westerly up the hillside, though after a few hundred yards it was lost sight of in more trees. I reconnoitred far enough to see that there was an outlet to another road running parallel to the eastern side of the valley.

Doggerel Bank was a world of its own and miles from anywhere. It was as much of a hideout as Peppercorn Cottage and it was a wonder Moggerhanger never got his hands on it. Dismal splashed and leapt, telling me that he thought so as well. We went back up the hill, sun dropping behind the ridgeline like a yellow Smartie. I dragged in a couple of dead branches and jumped on them in the yard so that they would fit the fireplace, because even in August it was cold in Yorkshire.

Wayland was asleep in the car. Clegg had gone for a stroll. June informed me, as she laid the table in the large kitchen, that Delphick, as befitted the Lord of the Manor, was in his workroom until supper was ready. Dismal flopped lengthwise in front of the stove. 'Anything I can do?'

'Reach in that high cupboard,' she said, 'and get some plates and glasses off the top shelf.'

I set them on the table. 'What else?'

'Talk to me.'

'Glad to. Doesn't Ronald ever talk?' I sat at the table and poured two whiskies. 'Water?'

'A drop.' She put bread and knife down. 'He only says "I want", and complains about his hard life. But I'm with him for such a short time that it doesn't matter.'

'What are you doing these days to earn a living?'

'I'm a hostess in a gaming club.'

'What does that mean?'

'We rob people – mostly Arabs.'

'Do you mind it?'

'I don't like robbing anybody. It bothers me more and more. So much robbing goes on I often think I'll choke if I put up with it a minute longer. But I have to. I've got my daughter at boarding school and that costs three thousand a year, apart from the uniform and all the extras. She has dancing classes and goes riding. She goes on a foreign holiday. I couldn't provide that on a saleswoman's wage. And then I have to live in London, though I only run a small flat in Kentish Town, where I live with my girlfriend.'

'Janet?'

'That's right. I have to keep her, as well. She's unemployable, and totally unable to look after herself, so what can I do? I got her a job last year serving dinners at a school for backward girls. She should have been at the school herself. She couldn't cope. Another woman worked there who was happily married with five children. I came home one night and found them in bed together – my bed. She'd seduced the woman, and the woman had fallen for her. It had been going on for weeks, and I didn't know. What a fuss and bother that was. I threw them out, never having fancied a threesome, not with women, anyway. They're enough bother one at a time. Some weeks later she came back, sweet as pie. I could never make out what happened to the woman with the five kids. I expect she went back to her husband. Sometimes I feel like giving the whole thing up, but how can I? Ronald's hopeless. All men are, but who isn't? Most women are, as well, but I can cope better with a woman. I lived on my own for a while, early on, between affairs, but it was impossible. I lost my job, and all but went to pieces. But I came out of it somehow, and got my present work four years ago. It's hard, but it pays marvellously.'

I poured more drinks. She took the leg of mutton out of the oven and stabbed it with the knife. 'Is it one of Moggerhanger's places, where you work?'

She pushed the pan back in. 'Yes. When I was down in the dumps I went to see him, and he set me on. Gave me two hundred quid and told me to buy some clothes. He's very loyal, Claud. We'd finished our affair years before, but he remembered me. He always sticks by you, if you've been connected in any way with him. There's not much old-fashioned loyalty these days, but Claud's got it. I'm not saying he's the best of people, but he's been good to me, so what more can I say? Anyway, I don't know why I'm telling you all this.' She tried the potatoes, but they weren't done either. She got to work making five plates of hors d'oeuvres, putting a hard-boiled egg, half a lettuce leaf, a tomato, black and green olives, a pickle, a blade of chicory, a sardine and a sheet of ham on each plate. The sight made me hungry. 'You'd make somebody a good wife.'

She laughed. 'Maybe. But get down five wineglasses, love, and open those two bottles of red.'

I was glad to help. She wasn't a bad sort. If I ruined Moggerhanger with my plan of handing the contents of the boot over to Scotland Yard or Interpol I would ruin her as well, and God knew how many others. I would certainly put the kaibosh on myself, because even if Moggerhanger got sent down there would be a skeleton organisation left to keep his firm going, and get even with people like me. If June knew what was in the car and why it was there, I thought, she would do all she could to stop me getting away, and see to it that the news went through to Moggerhanger that I was at Doggerel Bank.

I supposed she wondered in any case what I was doing there with his Rolls-Royce, and coming with sufficient provisions to last a week. Moggerhanger never gave his hirelings such leave to hang around. She must have become suspicious the moment Dismal sprang at her tits. I'd been very dim, otherwise I'd have woven a story to explain my presence more convincingly.

Fortunately there was no telephone at the house, or she might well have been on the blower while I was out for a walk, trying to do Moggerhanger a favour in return for those which he had done for her. The only way to get in touch with the outside world was to walk up the hill and use the phone box at the crossroads about a mile away.

My heart nearly stopped beating, but she was too busy to notice. 'Where's the bathroom, love?'

'Outside the door, and up to your right.'

Such directions had always given me access to every room in the house. On cat's feet I went upstairs, opened all doors, and saw no one. Downstairs, I entered Delphick's study, and that was empty as well. So was every other room, except the kitchen. I even looked in the broom cupboards. It became plain that Delphick had gone. For once in his life he was doing something for June, the mother of his child, and I supposed she had talked him into it by suggesting that if it turned out to be important that Moggerhanger knew of our presence the reward would be so great he'd be able to put in central heating.

Her plan was a pretty one, and the five plates were arranged with the precision of an executioner over the last breakfast of the condemned. She would feed us a banquet, get us drowsy if not blind drunk – all at our expense – and put us to bed so that, on waking up, Moggerhanger's squad cars would be coming down the lane and blocking it. They could get from London in under three hours, a fact which set my tripes shivering. Spleen Manor was only thirty miles away, so if any of the mob was there they could be here in an hour. If Delphick had phoned London half an hour ago, they might appear any minute.

I went into the kitchen. 'It's a lovely house.'

She smiled, tense and flushed. 'Ron's lucky.'

'He isn't in his study.'

She folded paper napkins and set one by each plate. 'He must be somewhere.'

'Give one to Dismal. He likes to sit at table with the rest of us.'

She took me seriously. 'All right.'

'All this house needs,' I said, 'is a telephone. Then you

wouldn't need to go to the crossroads every time.'

Her hand trembled. 'We never phone. We don't need to.'

I knocked a bottle of wine onto the floor, as if by accident. My guts were hot with murder. Dismal leapt up at the smash. 'Sorry about that.'

'I'll clear it up.'

I pushed her aside. 'You must need to, sometime.'

She was beginning to catch on. 'What's got into you?'

'Delphick's gone to phone, hasn't he?'

'You're off your rocker.'

'Do you want to be a basket case?'

She stood, cloth in one hand, pan and brush ready. She was frightened. 'No.'

'He's telephoning Moggerhanger, isn't he? If they catch me here, I'll be a basket case.' There was nothing else I could say, and nothing she would tell me. I ordered Dismal out of the door. She backed away, hands protecting her face. As if we had been married twenty years, I could no longer stand the sight of her. I got hold of the table, and sent plates, bottles, food and cutlery flying to the four points of the room. She and Delphick could feed off that.

Twenty-Seven

Clegg and Wayland walked in from the trees. 'Get in the car,' I said. 'We're leaving.'

Dismal snugged down immediately in the back as if it was more home to him than any of us. I told them in a few words what had happened. 'They'll be here any minute, and if they catch us they'll cut us into little pieces and feed us to the pigs.'

I heard June crying, as I stood by the kitchen wondering whether to go in and apologise, or set fire to the house. I had a vision of Delphick puzzled as to where the smoke was coming from as he walked back from the phone booth. Life was too short, dangers too pressing. I felt the chill wind of the gasworks around me, that same old grandad breeze that at dread moments pushes me back into reality.

My natural fuck-you-jack-I'm-all-right ebullience immediately shot me out of it but, just the same, the fix I was in was tightening. Pull off a stunt like robbing Claud Moggerhanger of his ill-gotten gains, and you find you have no friend to shield you. I'd expected this, of course, which was why I had gone to Doggerel Bank, but it was just my luck to find June there. She was the sentimental sort that made the world go round a bit faster because she couldn't forget a good turn. And she was right, in spite of the fact that it might be the death of me.

Clegg accepted that we must leave, and got into the car. Ten years of adversity had made him easy-going, but Wayland was cantankerous: 'How do you know he's gone to phone Moggerhanger?'

'June will tell you.'

He stood there sourly. 'I thought we were set for a party? Is this place too dull for your excitable temperament?'

I was at the wheel, and switched on. 'I don't particularly like you, but I wouldn't like to see you kicked around so much that your girlfriend wouldn't recognise you. You won't be in a very good shape to write your article –'

'Documentary.'

' – if you stay here. On the other hand, you'll have some first class material. Take your choice.'

I was glad when he got in. The more we were, the safer I felt. I drove towards the stream, and as I turned a bend saw out of my mirror the glint of a car coming down the lane behind. I had slid so quickly under cover that he hadn't seen me. Or so I thought. I couldn't understand how they had got here so quickly, though there was no mystery when I worked it out. Delphick had gone up the hill two hours ago. Moggerhanger phoned Spleen Manor on hearing from him, then phoned Delphick back at the box and told him to wait so that he could guide the car from Spleen Manor down to Doggerel Bank. Otherwise they would never have found it. Moggerhanger was nothing if not quick of thought. The fact that he could put me to shame in the matter was one reason why he was where he was and why I was where I was.

The car went so fast over the stream at the bottom of the hill that a bow-wave hit trees and bushes on either side. I slurped up that half-paved track like a rally driver, bumping against roots and jerking into potholes. The way curved between trees which cut out the light, so I gave it the big beams. After a straight bit across a field, a solid five-barred gate blocked us from the road. Clegg jumped out with the agility of a much younger man, unravelled the chain, and dragged it open. 'Get back in,' I shouted. He closed it, and looped the chain into place.

'For God's sake, we're in a hurry. Let's go.'

'What holds us up will hold them up,' he said as I drove off, 'and I left that chain in a far more complicated knot than when I found it.'

The wind wasn't faster than me around those lanes. If I'd been in any seat but the driver's I'd have heaved my guts up. Twilight was coming on, an illuminated sheet of blue to the east, and a band of threatening vermilion to the west. I turned so much at the cool commands of Clegg's navigation that pale blue and bloody rays seemed in every direction at once. If the car had followed us up the hill we had already lost it. If it had chased us any distance I hoped the manoeuvres had curdled Ronald Delphick's innards. Not that I thought either he or his stomach were tender. In my view he was as tough as old iron, though he would need to be even harder if I caught up with him.

The direction was southerly. Clegg turned round. 'They're still after us.'

'Are you certain?'

Being in the lead, we had the harder job. All the other car had to do was look for the scintillating roses of our brake lights and stay locked on. All we had to do was pick out the twisting wink of their dazzlers to know they were still with us. Even Dismal was tense. If I'd been alone in the car I'd have used all my shoe leather on the pedal, but such bad driving would have been hard on the others. In meeting so few cars we could not confuse our pursuers and throw them off the trail. The way the car was sticking to us, even though some distance off, suggested that it was driven by Pindarry.

'We can't edge so far west,' Clegg said, 'or we'll be on the moors. But if we can hold them off for twenty miles we'll have a better chance.'

My brain was melting through lack of sleep. We went a mile without turning. Clegg's cool instructions to go left and then right brought the adrenalin back. 'Do you feel like giving it the gun?'

'If you two don't mind.'

'I'm prepared for anything,' Wayland said eagerly.

'In that case,' Clegg said, 'I'm going to take you onto the main road for ten miles or so. Slow down a bit. You're going through a village.'

A pretty picture it was, fit for a tin of biscuits going to India. 'If anyone gets pulled up for speeding,' Clegg said, 'let it be them.'

I turned onto the main road and went southerly. The sweeping-brush of the pursuer's light swept the sky behind. 'We'll never shift 'em.'

Clegg was so maddeningly calm I had an impulse – luckily fought off – to stop the car and fight it out with whoever was after us. 'Don't despair, Michael. I can see from the map a manoeuvre which will drop them into limbo for good. We're coming to a railway bridge. That's it, we've just gone over it. Hard to feel the bump in a vehicle like this. Anyway, after a quarter of a mile – any minute now – there'll be a sharp turn to the right. It's only fifty yards or so after it. Then you angle ninety degrees onto a minor road to your left. We know it's there, but for the others it'll be concealed. Luckily, we're still on the large scale map. I wonder how many other lives the Ordnance Survey has saved? All right! NOW! Here's the right turn coming up.'

Headlights full on, dead keen and sweating, I swung, and barely missed a van, which hooted fit to burst. Then I turned left along a lane, and dipped every light I dared.

'Very good. They didn't see us come down here. They'll go tootling on and a quarter of a mile beyond they'll find that the road forks, and whichever of those forks they take will be the wrong one, so they'll lose precious time. They've already lost us. Our troubles are over.'

Could I believe him? Funnily enough, I did. The straight lane went up and down, and into a village. I slowed, in appreciation of Clegg's tactical victory. Lanes branched left and right. The more the better. We were going east, wending and winding towards the Great North Road. The idea, Clegg said, being to avoid the conurbation of Harrogate. 'You can go up to eighty on the main road without attracting attention, because it's a dual carriageway, besides which there's plenty of traffic. We can get into Leeds from the northeast.'

'You're a talking map,' I said.

'I think it's one of the least difficult problems I've ever had to solve.'

We had ditched our pursuers because he regarded our flight as a challenging kind of game. He'd also be a crack shot with a crossbow in an amusement arcade. 'The only thing is,' I said, 'we've got to have food and rest.'

'To think we left all that food and drink with Delphick,' Wayland said.

'After twenty miles,' Clegg said, 'we'll find a place to eat.'

Though there was no frightening flashlight in the sky behind, I was still worried by the fact that, heading down the Great North Road, we would be spotted by another of Moggerhanger's cars that had been sent up a couple of hours ago to reinforce the one already despatched to Doggerel Bank. Any such car would have come up the M1 at a greater speed than could be made on the Great North Road. In two hours they would be passing Nottingham. In less than three they could certainly be where we then were. Whoever was not driving in the car would, as became the best of Moggerhanger's lads, be observing the traffic, even in the darkness, coming down the lane in the opposite direction. When I put these cogitations to Clegg, he thought them worth acting on, unless it was too late, although he added – and I saw him smile in my mirror – it almost never is. 'It's only ever too late once in your life, and by then there's nothing you can do about it.'

'One of these days I'll be laughing with my throat at one of your witticisms.'

To which he replied: 'I sincerely hope not.'

Dismal began to howl. 'We've got to stop, or it'll be all up with us. We can survive hunger, lack of sleep, even a shoot-out, but not Dismal being taken short.'

'It's like having a baby in the car,' Wayland said.

'Well,' I told him, 'he's one of us.'

Dismal's snout gave an approving nudge. His distress wasn't immediate, but we'd had our warning, so at the next transport café I parked as far in the dark and behind other cars as I could get. 'Shall we risk going inside?'

Clegg twitched his glasses and switched off the map-reading flashlight. 'I think we can.'

We waited for Dismal to finish, and went into the usual place of scorching fat and soggy chips, which seemed like paradise. I bought forty fags, and pints of tea for us all – including Dismal. I ordered four plates of everything and a pile of bread and butter, as well as a dozen sweet cakes and more tea. Who knew where the next meal was coming from?

'I believe we've done it,' Clegg said.

I was superstitious, every moment expecting Kenny Dukes to burst through the flimsy door, having learned so much from Dicky Bush that he'd end up drowning in hot fat and Mars Bars. 'There's a long way to go yet.'

'But where?' said Wayland.

'How the fuck should I know?'

'You must have some idea.'

I had never been a master of planning and forethought. I lived and acted by the minute, and had survived well enough up to now – I told myself – but I knew that if I was to go on living I must begin to see at least one move ahead in Moggerhanger's Great Game. But again, my innate nature, or whatever it was, took over. 'We keep south on this fast road and go to my house at Upper

Mayhem.'

'Given up the Equilateral?'

'For the time being.'

The owner came with our plates and mugs, covering the small table. Wayland ate a cake at one gulp. 'Moggerhanger might be waiting for you.'

'They've been and gone already.' My mouth was also full. 'Maybe they never went. I flatter myself that they don't think I'm so daft as to go there. In any case, you'll be in no danger because I'm putting you out in Cambridge. You can make your own way to London.'

'Suits me.' He sounded relieved.

'When you get there, hide for a while.'

'I'll be too busy.'

At Upper Mayhem I would collect the documentation on Moggerhanger's drug empire which Matthew Coppice had promised to send. Then I would get the boat to Holland via Harwich so that, being safe, I could nail Mog and Jack Lanthorn at my leisure.

'Thanks for the excellent meal,' Clegg said. 'It's good to stuff the old belly now and again.' He went out for the flask and got it filled at the counter.

'Tell me, Cleggy,' I said when he sat down, 'I don't know whether this is a stupid question, but do you think your life has been worthwhile?'

He took a long drink from his pint mug. 'It's only a stupid question insofar as my life's far from ended. But if you mean to say *is* my life worthwhile, I can only answer that while a few days ago I wasn't convinced, at the moment I'm damned sure it is. Funny thing is, Michael, I've never asked myself that question, so I assume I've always thought my life was worthwhile. Right now I'm positively enjoying myself. What more do I want? I'm turned sixty, but I'm strong, healthy and free. What about you?'

'If I didn't think my life was worthwhile I'd kill myself.'

I dug Wayland in the ribs. 'What do you think?'

He brushed a hand over his bald head, down to his short grey beard. 'That question's too meaningful to play around with at this point in time. If I have a lucid moment before I kick the bucket I'll try to ask myself then, in the hope, I suppose, that there won't be time for an answer.'

Clegg smacked his hands together. 'It's nice to have a man in the car who's really thought about it.'

He was serious, so I nodded. 'You can say that again – but don't.'

At half past nine I drove south like a zombie, just on the right side of safety. My idea had been to cruise at fifty-five, but as soon as I saw a car or lorry in front my foot went down and I swung out to overtake at seventy or eighty. It was impossible to go slow to wherever I was going.

My mood oscillated from wanting to burst out singing, to an urge to throw the car at full speed against the concrete supports of a bridge or embankment. But I did neither, and we travelled in silence. Perhaps I was intoxicated, and kept alert by the amount of rage which I knew my zig-zag actions were generating in Moggerhanger and Lanthorn. I imagined them going up the wall with anxiety, indecision, fury and maybe even fear, a picture which brought a smile to my face – till I myself was no longer cramped by fear, fury, indecision and anxiety.

What positively cheered me was the pleasure of getting back to Upper Mayhem, even if it would only be safe to stay a few hours. I would warn Bill and Maria, and give them a comfortable lodging allowance from a packet of Moggerhanger's fivers so that they could play mummies and daddies somewhere else. I'd get there about one in the morning, pull Bill from his uxurious embrace, and have a talk about the way things had turned out at Buckshot Farm, until I fell asleep though my lips went on moving, and they had to carry me up to bed.

My head nodded at the wheel, and I saw four rear

lights in front instead of two. Often there was only one, on English roads. I began to weave without realising, and passed so close to the car which I overtook – though my focusing faculties seemed more or less normal – that I must have scared the shit out of the driver. Dismal nudged my leg as if warning me to take care. 'Go back to sleep. I can look after myself.'

'What did you say?'

I nearly hit the verge, but it was Clegg who had spoken.

'I thought you were asleep.'

'Maybe I was, but I heard you say something.'

'I was talking to Dismal.'

'Pull in for ten minutes.'

'I don't need to, Arthur.'

'You remembered my first name?'

It pleased him. I imagined his smile. 'It just came back to me.'

'After all this time.' Another half mile went by. 'Do as I say. Pull in at the next layby.'

'Don't worry.' I overtook a double dose of juggernaut. 'I shan't kill you.'

'I don't expect you will. Pull in, all the same.'

'Getting nervous?'

'Just pull in.'

'We'll be all right.'

'Pull in.'

I had to. No sooner had I switched off than I was asleep.

I felt a hand on my shoulder. 'Come on, Michael. Time to be going.' Clegg held a cup of tea under my nose. 'Get this down you first.' There was nothing like that comforting Nottingham tone to stop me losing my temper.

'How long have I been out?'

'An hour. But it's enough. You'll be all right now.'

'We won't get there till two.'

'What's the hurry? Better than not getting there at

all.'

I had another beaker of tea, then lit a smoke. It was eleven o'clock. Wayland also lit up, and seemed more cheerful. 'I think the car ride was worth it, to have such good cigars.'

He would never appreciate my favour of getting him out of Peppercorn Cottage. Maybe Moggerhanger had already sent someone to cut his throat – after last night's fiasco. I told him, but he said with a touch of bravado, 'You think I can't look after myself? I've been in some tight spots in my life, let me tell you.'

'I hope you get out of this one.'

I lapped our way along, to make up for lost time. I felt wide awake, having gone so deep under in that hour of sleep that it seemed like eight. I tore past everyone, never at less than eighty. What was the hurry? The highway was endless. You never got there. But I couldn't relax the chase. My blood was up, I didn't care what for. There was only me on the road. Others were toy rabbits in their tins, my sport to overtake. I shall overtake. He shall pursue, it didn't matter why. If God existed, He liked it that way.

I came back to life, my sight sharp and clear. At the yellow crossbars before an island when fellow motorists slowed down I pelted along in the outer lane and pulled up only when the white line was in sight. Sometimes I hardly braked but, keeping my eyes to the right and seeing no traffic on the island, shot almost straight across. The top speed of my faculties had come back, and driving to me was like water to a fish.

We made fair time down that wonderful Great North Road. I put Wayland out in the middle of Cambridge, asking him to deliver heartfelt greetings to my old college.

'Which one is that?'

He tried to gibbet me with biting scorn, but I disdained to answer. Couldn't he take a joke? Not Wayland. But now that the time had come he didn't like having to leave our covered wagon, especially in the middle of the night, though it was only half past one. He knew the town from his student days, and could kip at the station till the milk train left for London. At least he wouldn't be hungry because, apart from money, I gave him more cigars and the rest of the sandwiches, this latter being an action which Dismal took a very poor view of, for he tried to bite them out of Wayland's hand before he walked off with never a thank you for our hospitality.

At two o'clock I went slowly along the lane towards the old railway station of Upper Mayhem, country residence belonging to Michael Cullen Esquire. The house was in darkness, as I had expected. I thought of sounding the hooter to give Bill and Maria fair warning, but couldn't resist seeing their shock when pulling them out of bed. Clegg and Dismal came through the gate behind while I fumbled for the key. The smell of soil and vegetation from the garden, and the sweet night air, was a real tonic. It was the first house I had owned and I loved the place. I would bring Frances Malham here and she would love it, too. She would come and see me whenever it was possible to get time off from her studies, and even after she qualified as a doctor. By then my divorce would be through from Bridgitte. I decided to get one as from that moment. Frances and I would get married. I might even think well of Uncle Jeffrey and forgive him for what he had done to Maria. Or hadn't done. I still couldn't be sure. It wasn't his fault that his vasectomy hadn't worked. I would ask him and his family to stay the weekend. I'd even hang a car tyre from the footbridge for his kids to swing on. Frances would bloom in a place like this, lying back in a deckchair in the sunny garden, the two top buttons of her blouse undone. Maybe she'd even be pregnant. How could someone of my age think like that? I was twelve years older, so she probably looked on me as a dirty old man.

A radio was playing, but it was between about three

stations. The noise came from the living room. Just like those irresponsible lovebirds to leave it on. At least it was a sign of life, and I felt quite affectionate towards them, as if carelessness made people human and mistakes made them – almost – divine. I switched on the light.

All I know is that I didn't say anything. A catalogue of woes and curses would be needed to describe what I saw. The radio was going because it had been smashed open with an iron bar. The indestructibility of technology was a delight to see, but that was about all I could say for it at that moment. Half the time I had never been able to get that gimcrack Russian radio going, but Kenny Dukes seemed to have had no difficulty. He had simply laid the back open with the poker. Cupboard doors were hanging off. The dresser had been pulled over and Bridgitte's heirloom Dutch pots smashed. Chairs were ripped and the table lay on its side. I shut the door and ran upstairs.

Perhaps they had given up by this time, or taken Bill at his word. Unless he and Maria had got out, before reaping the whirlwind on my behalf. The beds had merely been tipped up. As if domesticated to my fingertips, I went from room to room and put them right before going back downstairs.

'Looks like the worst's already happened,' Clegg said.

There was no sign of the large buff envelope I was expecting from Matthew Coppice. Perhaps they had found that as well. I checked the letterbox and it was empty. I pulled the batteries out of the radio to stop it squawking, while Clegg righted the table, shut the cupboards and set the chairs upright. It didn't look much worse than the shambles after one of my quarrels with Bridgitte in the early days. Dismal lay in front of the fireplace, in which the ashes were still warm from when Bill had kept a blaze permanently going to brew tea in case they cut off the gas and electricity. I put my hands in them. 'They were here this evening.'

We went into the kitchen. There was a half-eaten sandwich on a plate, and a pot of cold tea. It must have broken his heart to leave that. I gave the sandwich to Dismal. In the middle of the table was a typed letter, and after circling three times, I read:

> You're giving us a lot of trouble, Michael, and I don't like it. What's got into you? I trusted you. I never thought you would be so stupid. I thought at first you were running around the country because you thought the Green Toe Gang was on your trail. I thought you thought you were doing me a favour by your evasion tactics. I stretched a point. You disappoint me. It seems as if you're the victim of a nervous breakdown. It can't be anything less. Whatever it is, I'm angry. Things are serious. So as to get the situation straightened out as soon as possible my lads are taking Bill Straw and his girlfriend. If you don't get in touch, or deliver our possessions, or both, they will meet with a very prolonged accident. You know the sort I mean. If they do, you will have only yourself to blame. And when we get our hands on you, you will have an even worse accident. If you turn over the stuff, however, without undue delay, I still won't forgive you, though I might be induced to forget you.
>
> Believe me, yours very sincerely,
> C. Moggerhanger

Clegg filled the kettle for tea. 'Some news?'

'Yes. From Moggerhanger. Special Delivery.'

'Will they be back?'

'If we're lucky we've got twenty-four hours.' There was even fresh milk in the fridge.

'Will that be enough?'

'It'll have to be.' There was little to be said, though much to be thought. We drank. I poured some for Dismal, who hadn't even clamoured, as if he realised that our plight was grave.

'All we can do is go to sleep till morning.'

'I can't enter into competition with a decision like that,' he grinned.

'I wish you wouldn't take every possible advantage of my misfortunes to polish your style. It's getting on my wick.'

I brought the car in from the side of the road, then stood looking at those clear and numberless East Anglian stars, and wondered when I would be able to do so again.

I lay in bed puzzling over what had happened to Matthew Coppice's promised papers. I'd thought up to now that if all went wrong with the disposal of the goods in the boot of the car I would at least have his depositions to fall back on, and that even if I got the chop they would already be on their way to Interpol. From a sky of bright prospects I was in the non-visibility gloom of nothing. Yet it didn't seem an unpromising condition in which to try getting some sleep.

Dismal lay across the bottom headboard, which meant I couldn't stretch full length. I didn't mind, because sleeping curled up as if I was back in the womb seemed to work, for the next thing I knew I waded through thick and perilous activities called dreams, trapped in clotted caverns like the murkiest insides of a whale, my feet invisible, and head drawn onwards by some gleam I never reached, the tip of a needle which, if I did get close enough, would jab forward and put out an eye. I heard the wafting slow swing of an enormous bird and turned my head in terror to watch it coming, waiting for it to get close and be seen. I never did see it, yet the two feet that gripped my shoulder made me shout and wake up.

Twenty-Eight

I thought they had come to get me. A sheet of Fen light was fastened at the window. I kicked Dismal off the bed, but it was Clegg who gripped my shoulder. 'It's seven o'clock.'

I felt worse than when I had gone to sleep, but then, I always did. If I had woken up feeling wonderful I'd have felt awful, especially on the Day of Days. I knew that if I was alive this time tomorrow my chances of living to the extent of my biblical stretch would be fair to middling. Dismal went down to reconnoitre for food, while I lay an extra few minutes and sipped Clegg's tea.

Why was I so dead set on ruining Moggerhanger? If he vanished into the dungeons, there would be a hundred others in the fresh air above, jostling to take his place. They were the people who would benefit, not the clapped-out druggies perishing on wastelands and parking lots all over Britain. But Moggerhanger, the tin-pot god, had got me sent down for eighteen months to save his own skin, and now I was in a position to get my own back. I was feeling more optimistic by the minute that I would escape his wrath. Even without help from Coppice I could put enough information together, provided I was able to get the boat for Holland.

Clegg put eggs and bacon in the pan, while I gobbled a dish of cornflakes. The only hole in my scheme, and my heart fell through it like a lump of lead, was that by going to Holland I would be separated from Frances. There was no saying how long I'd be away, yet I had no option but to skedaddle. I hoped she'd remember me, and respond to my love letters homing in from different places.

I shaved, showered, put on clean underwear, changed my suit and polished my best zip-up boots, all in double-quick time. The gold cufflinks were awkward to get into the shirt-holes, and Dismal shook his head as I swore. I threatened that if he didn't show a bit more sympathy I'd send him back to Peppercorn Cottage so that the rats would get him. At which he sloped off to look for leftovers in the kitchen.

'There's some post for you,' Clegg shouted.

I found a large envelope, which nobody else could have sent but Matthew Coppice. I put it aside, though, to open a letter with an Oxford postmark, which I knew was from Frances Malham. I skimmed it to see whether she hated me and, when it seemed she did not, sat down to read:

> Dear Michael,
> I'm back in Oxford and can't stop thinking about you. I'd like to thank you for spending your time with me, when I know how busy you are. The whole episode was a lovely surprise! I didn't mean it when I said I didn't need to get to know you because we had made love. I'd like to see you again, and hope you'll be able to visit me in Oxford. I share a house with another girl. I hope you're not toiling too hard.

She signed off with love. A short letter, but with its scented paper packing my wallet Moggerhanger's threats would fall on stone ears, while I had any ears at all.

Clegg sat by the range with shirtsleeves rolled up, while I looked through the papers from Matthew. Spots of rain flopped at the window, a summer shower brewing. Coppice had done his job. The future programme of world drug transport was set out in detail. Albert Croy would be coming from Brussels with five hundred and nineteen grammes of cocaine and two kilos of cannabis. A gang, whose names were given, was coming from Bogota, each member carrying cocaine in bottles of Scotch whisky.

Another group would leave Bogota, three going to Paris and two to Frankfurt, each coming separately into London with a large cargo of cannabis. Pindarry would bring a car from the Continent, half the petrol tank for petrol and the other for cocaine paste from Peru. Jack Mullion from Barbados would bring in (date given) four kilos of cocaine in the false bottom of a suitcase. Cocaine would also come in from Montreal concealed in a false-sided Samsonite-brand case. Luis Gonzales and his daughter Rosanna (daughter, for God's sake!) would travel the Mexico City, Rio de Janeiro and Los Angeles route with cocaine. From the Hook (Amsterdam) a lorry would bring cannabis resin in thirty-five boxes of fruit juice, which load was to be met by Alport and conveyed to Breezeblock Villa at Back Enderby. Twelve kilos of cannabis would come from Beirut, and forty kilos of heroin from Damascus. And so it went on, page after page, the complete plan of Operation Hop Garden. Zero hour was in ten days.

I whistled, and whooped, and smacked my thigh. And that was not the end of it. On another couple of sheets were details of false investment companies to lure money from the Continent, and from Middle East nationals who had so much liquidity that they hardly knew what to do with it. There were schemes to launch false insurance companies, and plans to defraud genuine insurance companies by making false claims, especially in Germany and Austria. I laughed at the ingenuity and admired the enterprise, though I was determined to put the kaibosh on all their schemes.

'Good news?'

'Put it this way,' I told him. 'I think I'm on my way to a breakthrough.'

He looked at the window covered with colourless beads of rain. 'I'll get back on the road then. It was certainly an unexpected pleasure, bumping into you again.'

'What do you mean?'

'I must resume the circuit. I don't want to get used to the good life. In any case, my feet have a distinct itch – at both heels.'

'You can't leave me so soon, Cleggy. We're not finished yet.' I told him what was in the papers from Coppice. I had a weapon to bring Moggerhanger's hopheaded operations to a standstill. The only flaw was that there was nothing to incriminate Lanthorn, though if Moggerhanger and Company Limited collapsed he would be forced to lie low at least, and wouldn't be able to use his police resources to get even with me – for a while. He might also be afraid of Moggerhanger turning Queen's evidence, or of me getting my hands on other material to bring him down. Nor was it by any means certain that they would connect me with Moggerhanger's crash, though I wouldn't be so daft as to rely on that to save my neck.

'I suppose you're worried that things might not turn out as you expect?' he said.

It was eight o'clock, and a move must be made. 'There's a gulf before me.'

He squirted washing-up liquid over dirty crockery. 'Right's on your side. This time, anyway,' which was a sly dig at me for having pilfered his watch. I let it pass. 'When God is with us,' he said, 'who can stand against us?'

I got up. 'If only it was that easy.'

He drew a hand back from the scalding water. 'If you want it to be easy, there's nothing more to say.'

'The first thing I must do is phone Moggerhanger. I've got to turn the car over to him with all that stuff in the boot so that he'll let my friends go.'

I went to the station so as to talk from a public call box rather than phone from home. I wanted the pips to keep sounding between me and Moggerhanger. They would put a feeling of urgency into the conversation and stop it going on too long. I could pretend to run out of ready coins, though I had been careful to bring plenty.

I left the engine going, and the wipers wiping in the rain, and lit a cigarette before dialling. Alice Whipplegate answered, but I wasted no small talk. 'I'd like to speak to Lord Moggerhanger.'

'I'll see if he's out of his bath, Michael.'

'Alice, I'm in a public call box, and can't wait.'

But I did.

'Michael, where are you – in latitude and longitude, I mean?' Moggerhanger's voice was as smooth as silk. I hardly recognised it.

'In a phone booth.'

I sensed his chuckle. 'That's a mistake, unless you have five hundred ten-pee pieces burning under your arse.' He laughed at his own witticism.

I waited.

'Michael?'

'Yes?'

'I asked where you were.'

'I told you.'

'You didn't.'

'I thought I had.'

'I don't think you did.'

'You mean what part of the country am I in?'

He simulated a very expressive sigh of relief. 'Yes.'

'I'm in Kettering.'

There was a costly pause, then:

'Michael?'

'What?'

'I can wait. As long as you have money to put in the box, I can wait. All day, in fact. I'm a very patient man. You should know that by now.'

'Wait for what?'

'For you to tell me where you really are. But I don't like waiting, all the same. The idea of wasting money on the phone doesn't appeal to me, even though it's your money.'

I laughed. 'As a matter of fact, it's yours.'

I detected a slight gear-change in his voice. 'I shall want an itemised expense account.'

'I'll send you one. From Norway.'

'Michael?'

'What?'

'I know exactly how you feel. The world is nobody's oyster, nor is the lemonjuice. Money has to be earned. You've got several million pounds' worth of goods of mine. You haven't earned it. I'm just a little bit more entitled to it than you are. I've at least done something to assemble it in one place.'

'I may not have earned it.' I couldn't help gloating. 'But I've got it.'

'That's very true. But shall I tell you something, Michael? I'm an extraordinarily patient man when I'm dealing with someone I like who has indulged in the luxury of a misdemeanour against me. I really am. Now, the situation as I see it is that you've been working too hard lately. I should have grounded you for a while after your recent tour of operations. That's what I think now. Perhaps I was foolish to give you such a key part in the Buckshot Farm job. But what's past is past. I did, and it's no use crying over spilt milk. I did it because you're one of my best men, and your sort don't grow on trees, though occasionally they do end up hanging from them. Forgive that little joke, Michael. I had a good breakfast this morning, and I haven't got rid of it yet. Have you anything to say for yourself?'

'Not till you say a bit more to me.'

Ten-pence worth of silence went by.

'As I was saying, I used you because I needed you, and I didn't expect you to carry on like this. I won't call it lack of moral fibre, but there's certainly a stress element involved. Only the best are afflicted by it, but after a few sessions with Dr Anderson, the eminent psychiatrist, and a three week vacation on the beach at St Tropez looking at all those topless dollies playing volleyball, they're usually as right as rain. Atomic rain, that is. See my point?'

I had imagined something shorter than this, a rancorous bit of argy-bargy ending in verbal fireworks and a mutual slamming down of telephones. 'I do. The fact is, though, I don't like you taking my friends and holding them as hostages. That may happen in other countries, but I didn't think anybody in England would stoop to it.'

'Michael, I hope you are not accusing me of provocative, unconventional, unpatriotic behaviour?'

I had to be careful. 'Well, Lord Moggerhanger, I'm not accusing you of anything. I'm merely describing the situation as it seems to be.'

'That's better. I knew we could have a discussion without entering into a competition regarding what was actually happening. I've always known you to be a man of the world, Michael. I like you. I've been proud to employ you. You've done work that others might have quailed at. I suppose in the normal world, which people like us healthily despise, you would have got put inside for three hundred years for doing work like that. Fortunately, we don't belong to that world. It's not for the likes of us. We're freeborn Englishmen, who not only began at the bottom of the ladder, but from the bottom of the hole in which the ladder was placed to keep it from toppling backwards. I won't say it's all we have in common, but it's sufficiently similar to allow us to understand each other without so much hanky-panky – and without this shameful waste of ten-pee pieces.'

'I've got a big canvas bag of them standing on the floor.'

I rattled a few.

'I believe you. You always were resourceful. But, Michael?'

'Yes.'

'I don't know whether it was the same with you, because you're not old enough to remember the worst of times. But when I was a lad I used to walk to Bedford from our village, eight miles there and eight miles back, in rain or frost quite often, to try and earn a copper or two to take home to my family. Don't laugh. There's only one way by which my hand could come down this telephone cord and strangle you, and that would be if you laughed when I told you that my family went through times when they were half starved.'

'I'm not laughing.'

'I didn't really think you were. Forgive that little outburst. But in the days I'm telling you about, one of those ten-pee pieces – that you are slotting into the box like three-o-three rifle cartridges as if the fuzzy-wuzzies were coming up the hill to slit your throat – would have bought me a cup of tea. Another would have purchased a cream bun. There was many a time when a cream bun and a cup of tea would have given me much satisfaction. Do I make myself clear?'

'Abundantly.'

'So where are you?'

'Near Newmarket.'

'I thought as much.'

There was another long pause.

'Why did you wreck my house?' I asked.

'You know that I regard private property as sacrosanct. I would never do such a thing.'

'But Kenny Dukes did.'

'I have to delegate, Michael. My life would otherwise be impossible. I'd have no time for my family. My boys didn't like being sent up on their day off.'

It was useless to argue. 'Where are Maria and Bill Straw?'

'All in good time. First of all I want to know when you are going to arrive at my house with the Roller and all the goods therein.'

'I've got news for you, Lord Moggerhanger.'

'And what might that be, Mr Cullen?'

He was having fun. So was I. 'I'm not coming to London.'

The next pause was so long that even I found it uncomfortable.

'Michael?'

'What the fuck now?'

'I think we shall have to meet soon. And don't swear.'

'You'd better get in touch with my agent.'

'Don't you think we ought to come to some conclusion?'

We were speeding up. 'Not until I see Bill and Maria safely back.'

'Granted, Michael. I don't want to go on feeding them, not while the National Assistance could be doing it. What do I pay taxes for?'

I laughed. 'Taxes?'

'Oh, if only you knew what I have to dish out. It's my greatest headache. There are some things even I can't get out of. But when can I get my hands on my goods? I won't disguise my anxiety on that score.'

'I'll drive the car to London.'

After a pause he said: 'On second thoughts, I'd rather you didn't.'

'When can I see Bill and Maria?'

He sounded amiable. 'Anytime.'

'I'll tell you what. I don't want what's in the Roller. I hope you never thought that. I don't know how this misunderstanding could have arisen. When I got to Peppercorn Cottage I just didn't like the look of the situation, so I didn't unload. I was dubious about leaving it in the care of that idiot Percy Blemish.'

'He wouldn't have had it long.'

'I didn't feel sure of that. And I'd had a few brushes with mysterious cars on my way there. The situation didn't feel good. So I thought I would give the Green Toe Gang a run for their money and stay on the road for a few days.'

'How do you explain going off with that television crime reporter, Wayland Smith?' he said dryly.

'I fed him reams of false information that will throw him off the trail for good. Even when I seem to be working against you I'm working for you. I can't help myself.'

'I wish I could believe you. But you're wandering away from the issue. You begin to annoy me, if only because while the goods are out of my hands I am losing money. Every twenty-four hours that they are prevented from being turned into money I lose approximately six hundred pounds sterling in interest alone. Six hundred pounds! Only in interest! How many cream buns and cups of tea would that buy? You see, even in the midst of tribulation I don't lose my sense of proportion. Or humour. Do I?'

'No, sir.'

I wasted more cream buns on another pause. Then the voice came back, as if after a long weekend in Miami. 'Just tell me where you're going to leave the Roller, and the key, and I'll send the lads up with your friend Bill Straw, and Maria – as you call her. She's a delicious little woman, except that she just about bit Kenny Dukes's balls off.'

I nearly choked laughing. 'I hope he does better in his next life.'

'I think he sincerely hopes so as well, though if I have anything to do with it I don't think I'll allow him to have one, in case I have one too. Your friends will be let out of the car as soon as the Roller has been checked, and everything is seen to be safe inside. You don't even have to be present. In fact I gather you'd rather not. Am I right, Michael?'

'Right.'

'That will make the transfer so much simpler.'

'I'll keep my part of the bargain,' I said. 'But can I rely on Maria and Bill being delivered safely?'

'The first point, Michael, is that you are in no position to distrust me. The second point is: what do I want them for? I don't hurt people unnecessarily. That would be un-English. I must admit I feel like giving you a clap around the ear-hole with my brass knuckles for having given me such anxiety, but that's neither here nor there – since you're not here. Maybe you did zig-zag around the country because you thought someone else was after the loot, but there was nothing to stop you phoning through to base and letting me know. That's the third point, by the way.'

'I apologise for the mistake.'

'It's just not like you, Michael.'

'I'm afraid I forgot myself.'

'I think you did. There isn't anything else, is there?'

I was freezing. Then I was boiling, in that confined space. If it wasn't one thing, it was another. Maybe I was getting pneumonia. That would be a relief. 'What do you mean?'

He cleared his throat. 'Well, you're not contemplating anything else, are you?'

'Like what?'

'Against me.'

'That would be stupid.'

'It most certainly would.'

'Do you think I'd bite the hand that feeds me?'

'People sometimes do,' he said. 'It's usually the only one that's close by. But it's very short-sighted.'

'I'm not so daft,' I said, in the northern accent that he liked to hear so that he could feel superior to it.

'I didn't think you were. Where will you leave the car, and the goods?'

I fed in my last ten pees. 'As from twelve o'clock it'll be outside my place at Upper Mayhem. You can drop Bill and Maria there. The car keys will be sellotaped under the front left bonnet.'

'You're doing a very wise thing. In the meantime, take a quiet holiday.'

'I intend to go to Holland, via Harwich. Today, if I can make it.'

'I may be a little hard of hearing, and correct me if I'm wrong, but I thought I heard you mention Norway.'

I was losing my grip. 'Since then, I changed my mind.'

'All right, but don't send me a postcard. Maybe sometime in the future I'll have a little job for you, but not yet. I want to give you time to recover.'

'By the way,' I said, 'I had to use a few of those old fivers from one of the packets. For expenses. Not many, but I ran short of cash.'

'That's all right,' he said. 'I owe you a few hundred anyway. As long as you didn't get greedy and take too many. Money like that costs fingers.'

He hung up. So did I. The steam and chill went on mixing. I was glad to get out into summer drizzle. The bargain was made, in a fifteen-minute phone call which felt like a week. I drove to Upper Mayhem in a state of profound contemplation, as Blaskin (on a good day) might have said in one of his novels. What is treachery except a desire for revenge? Explain it if you can, yet mine in this case was more than that, though it was the last thing I preferred to admit. If Moggerhanger hadn't got me put in prison I would have followed a different kind of life than the ten year stint at Upper Mayhem. It took that long to get over the shock, and my present troubles stemmed from it, though I suppose I had deserved to go to jail for gold smuggling. So did plenty of others, but I was the chosen one.

Gold smuggling was one thing, however, and to flood the country with drugs, as Moggerhanger was doing, was another, and the desire to get my own back fused well with putting a stop to such dirty work as the reason for what I intended doing. It was a close-run thing within me, all the same. In some films I saw as a kid the hero decided that crime did not pay and he was going to go straight, a sign that there would be no more excitement from then on. My interest died. I much preferred him to be unrepentant to the end and, after yo-yoing between the pits of vileness and the peaks of generosity, get shot dead on the steps of a bank he was trying to get out of. I now knew, though, that repentance had just as much excitement, especially when it was coming out of yourself and not being seen on a film.

Fun-life was over. Moggerhanger was going into action, already ordering Cottapilly, Toffeebottle and Jericho Jim, and maybe Kenny Dukes as well, to close in on the Upper Mayhem area at twelve o'clock. My wrist watch said half past nine, so I had half an hour to pack if I was to catch the boat for Holland.

Clegg put on his optimistic smile as I went through the gate. 'How did you get on?'

'Pretty good.' I pushed Dismal away, who asked the same question with muddy paws and his give-me-a-Mars-Bar eyes. 'You see that old Ford banger over there?'

'What about it?'

'Start it up for me. I'm off to Holland in a bit.'

'Holland?'

'Just for a week or two. Then I'll be back. But while I'm away I want you to look after the place. Keep an eye on Dismal as well. Can you do that for me?'

He seemed dubious.

'You won't be alone. Bill and Maria will be back at twelve. You can live together as long as you like. With Dismal, you'll be four. There'll soon be five, because Maria's pregnant. When I get back it'll make six. If a certain Miss Malham comes to stay there'll be lucky seven. My mother will make it eight, if she drops in. She might have a girlfriend, so make it nine. Or a boyfriend, or Gilbert Blaskin. If it's a tight squeeze I can open the ticket office and renovate the signal box. This place has extensive possibilities. There's even an old carriage on a siding up the line that's mine. It's a residence after my own heart, so I know you'll look after it.'

'It'll be safe with me. Are you all right, though?'

'Never felt better.'

He made a pot of coffee, and we ate scones he had bought in the village while I was at the phone box. I handed him another bundle of notes from Moggerhanger's pile. 'Here's money for food. I wouldn't like to see you go short.'

The Ford started a treat. Dismal got an eyeful of exhaust that made him drunk, though happy, for the next few minutes, so that he found our parting less tragic than it might have been. My guns and belongings in the Rolls-Royce went to their usual hiding place in the house. Then I plastered the key where Moggerhanger's lads would find it. I packed my briefcase with money, passport, car logbook and driving licence, as well as Matthew Coppice's bulging envelope and Frances Malham's letter. Clegg laid two suitcases of my best clothes in the back seat of the Ford. Dismal sloped around, lost at such activity, and I was sorry I couldn't take him with me. I ran to the Rolls-Royce for the umbrella without which it seemed impossible to go abroad, even to Holland. Having walked away with it so easily, it was now part of my travelling equipment. In any case, an umbrella made me look half-way eccentric, and therefore respectable.

Whatever I was, while being so busy I did not feel like my old self to such an extent that I began to feel myself again, proving, perhaps, that things had changed, I said to Clegg.

'Changed? I'll believe that when I see it. In my view, you're unchangeable – or should I say incorrigible?'

Maybe he was right. A sense of freedom and adventure was coming back. I was going away, and didn't know where, which was the only satisfactory condition in which to set out for a foreign place. Without a return date, I'd get a single ticket to the Hook, but wouldn't visit Bridgitte because I didn't want to disturb her new-found idyll, no more than I would want her to crock up mine if she came back to Upper Mayhem to see whether or not it had burned down. 'Look after yourself.'

We embraced. 'Have a good holiday.'

'Just give me a fortnight,' I told him. 'After a week, read the papers. Things will start to happen. At half past eleven, take Dismal for a walk, and stay away for a couple of hours. Then you'll be all right.'

'I'll do that. And as for you – don't get into trouble.'

'I'll try not to,' I said. 'But life goes on.'

'It generally does.'

At a minute to ten I kissed Dismal on the nose, and backed the car onto the road.

Twenty-Nine

I joined the A45 for Bury St Edmunds. At one point I felt an urge to return to Upper Mayhem, come what may, without hemming or whoring. I was no longer attracted by adventures that might lie ahead. My mind was more up and down than the road, and I was even bored with driving. Did I want to live at all? I was either no longer among the numbered, or I had a dose of shellshock. I let the car crawl at thirty.

A Toyota van had a sticker in the window saying 'Darwin Was Right'. Maybe he was but, unconsciously speeding up, I overtook a Mini with four golden oldies inside. I watched my hands shaking at the wheel. Perhaps I'd gone to bits because it seemed I'd settled Moggerhanger's hash. The opposition had fizzled out, and there was nothing left to fight. Take away the wall and the shoe pinches, my grandmother said.

Stop this wishful thinking. Pull yourself together. I was playing a con trick on myself, always the first sign of a con-man's downfall. To avoid the trap, I told myself that the unknown in front was more unknown than any unknown had ever been before, even more unknown than prison which, given my character, should have struck me as being less of an unknown than many places in the wide world.

I pressed my foot on the accelerator, otherwise my timetable would shake to bits. If I missed the morning boat from Harwich I would have to hang about, and that might be dangerous. I had told Moggerhanger I would leave from Harwich, knowing he wouldn't believe me, and would not in that case send the lads up on a right hook from London to stop me getting on the boat. His jampot manner on the phone had not deceived me. He would get me if he could. Maybe a car was reconnoitring the environs of Dover in the hope of spotting me.

I arranged it so that I would get to Harwich with minutes to spare. A traffic holdup in Ipswich would do for me, but I had to take the chance. Buying my ticket, going through passport control and customs, would delay me, though I hoped not for long. If there was no car space on the boat, I would leave it parked and run on as a foot passenger. The car wasn't worth a hundred quid, and if it got me to Harwich I'd be lucky. I almost wished it wouldn't, but was surprised at its performance as I picked up speed out of Bury.

The old mechanical bullet of a Black Bess began to make fabulous headway. The pump bottle was empty, but one rainstorm after another came heaven-sent to wash the windscreen. The heating worked to clear the steam. Below Stowmarket a lorry was on its side and a car upended with doors open, the windscreen a patch of white glass in the middle of a field. There was a gap in the hedge where the madcap had gone through. Two youths were helping the police with their enquiries. An ambulance stood by for someone on a stretcher who had been unlucky. A couple of jam sandwiches with flashing lights, and a few friendly coppers, guided us between bollards.

Whenever you're in a hurry there's either floods, roadworks or a pile-up. It's the law of the road, but past experience suggested that you hardly ever got more than one such stoppage in a hundred miles, and I hoped this was the last between me and Harwich. Ages passed while queuing to get by the accident, though it was only six minutes.

I cut off the town of Ipswich and shot down onto the London road. On the dual carriageway I thrashed my ancient banger to the limit, which even in its dilapidated condition put to shame many a better-off car that I overtook. I'd have jumped it over a turnpike gate if one had appeared. The unnerving feeling came to me that when the left fork for Harwich came up in a dozen or so miles I would shoot by and continue my way to London by force of habit, because wonderful London was a giant vacuum cleaner sucking up any bloke like me who got within smelling distance. I'd never felt less like escaping from the country, as if every bone in my body warned me off such an uncharacteristic course.

The Rolls stationed itself parallel to my car, so that our relative velocity was nil. I wondered what the hell he was up to, but then glanced to my right and saw Pindarry at the wheel. The nasty spasm quietened down after I realised I had nothing to fear except death. Kenny Dukes was in the spare seat, so close I could have reached through my open window and touched him. In the rear section were Eric Alport and Jericho Jim. It was four against one in the game of the century.

They had shadowed Upper Mayhem and followed me, and in my stupidity I hadn't spotted them. I was losing my grip to such an extent that it really was time to get out of the country. My position seemed hopeless. I dreaded to think how long the hunt would go on. They had even been in the vicinity of Upper Mayhem all night, which explained Moggerhanger's smarmy tone on the blower. He must have been tempted to call them in while we were talking and hear me being strangled.

If they stopped me now, and found the envelope with details of their gaffer's plans, nothing less than a massacre would take place, beginning with me and Matthew Coppice. I was filled with regret because I had not posted the envelope in Newmarket and taken a chance on it reaching Interpol in Paris. Now that my scheme was on the point of failure there seemed no doubt that it would have got to the right place.

Going along at fifty, I slowed down slightly to consider

how I could, with my hands at the wheel, reach for my briefcase, take out the wad of papers, and eat it page by page. Such action no longer seemed feasible when Kenny Dukes lifted a gun and pointed it at my head. Sidney Blood had nothing on this. Nor would the clapped-out author (or authors) have imagined what subsequently took place, and I hesitate to tell it because I'm sure everyone will think I'm lying. But I believe it, since I was there, and I can't say fairer than that – as one of Sidney Blood's characters might have put it, in a trash book almost as pernicious as the drugs that the Master Dope Peddler scattered about like Dolly Mixtures.

The Rolls-Royce kept its pace so neatly that I felt part of a catamaran-vehicle two cars wide. Pindarry the demon driver was tops in the business. My window was half open, and Kenny Dukes's hand holding the Luger came out of his own window and right into my car. His arm was so long that I almost felt the cold touch of steel at my right cheek. I expect they thought to give me a fright before swinging into my track and forcing me to stop. Anything for a lark, with lads like that.

I don't remember the mechanism of my actions, but what I did was – rapidly, and before Kenny could either fire or withdraw – wind up the window sharp and tight. It was as simple as that, lateral thinking in the absolute sense. Such a thing is hard to believe and I didn't credit it, either, even at the time, till I realised that poor old Kenny's hand was trapped.

His expression changed from a leer of triumph to a look of pig-lip panic. He shouted something to Pindarry who, in the pursuit of his driving art, lived in a world of his own. That was his undoing.

Kenny's wrist was held fast between the top line of the Plexi-glass window plate and the roof of the car. He couldn't move, nor could he any longer control the gun, at least not sufficiently to take proper aim. Being Kenny

Dukes, who saw courage as the last refuge of the Dummkopf, he tried. The grip seemed to paralyse his fingers and the gun wriggled about, so that all I had to do was reach over and take it, before a bullet could smash my temple to mincemeat.

The sides of both cars breathed against each other. They occasionally touched, but as light as a kiss, then glanced away. On that score my worries were nil. It was fortunate for Kenny Dukes that Pindarry was the sort of careful driver who would be welcome in any south-coast old age pensioner town. But he could also be very fast, though he knew it was not advisable to speed up at the moment. In the back Jericho Jim was telling him to stop, while Eric Alport shouted for him to 'get a move on'. Our world was small in those few minutes, and I had immediate plans for making it bigger.

As good a driver as Pindarry, I still needed all my skill to maintain the same velocity as his car. We had to keep the same distance as well, for fear of mangling Kenny's arm. He'd been much in the wars lately, and I hoped the fact would encourage him to put in an application for danger money from Moggerhanger's exchequer.

The situation, then, was that two cars were travelling side by side down the dual carriageway at the same speed, and the same distance apart – such as it was – and almost joined in matrimony by the fact that Kenny Dukes's wrist was trapped in the window of my vehicle. It was a predicament that called for quick thinking, because for the first and last time in our lives we were united by a common desire – that his arm should not be pulled out of its socket.

I had often noticed prior to this incident that whenever quick thinking was necessary, my reactions managed to speed up and make a perfect adjustment. As long as the window stayed closed the car could not overtake and bring me to a standstill. On the other hand, if I kept Kenny's hand a prisoner we would go like this the whole way to

London, which I no longer wanted to do. The turning for Harwich would come in a mile or so, but I wouldn't be able to take it with Kenny's helpless arm pegged in my window, the fingers faintheartedly wriggling as if the blood had been drained out.

When I dared, I glanced at Kenny's face in the other car. His distress would have been terrible to see if he hadn't been a member of a lynching party whose first target was me. It was a quick course in lip reading, and I learned more of the subject in that minute than in all my previous life. I read every threat, every plea, every curse. If after the fight which would ensue on getting to London I lost the hearing from both ears, I would at least have learned something useful, which wasn't much of a bonus, though it was more than I had any right to hope for.

Pindarry was also pleading with me to do something. Alport and Jericho Jim threatened and despaired in turn. Even lip reading became unnecessary in the end. 'Let me go, bastard, let me go!' Kenny roared.

'You shouldn't have wrecked my house, you ape.'

'It wasn't me. It was Parkhurst. And Toffeebottle.'

I wasn't listening. I planned the severance some seconds in advance. Speed and timing was vital. Cars hooted to get by. Another few minutes and the rozzers would be onto us. I saw the turn-off. Whether Pindarry had been briefed as to my possible Harwich intention I didn't know, but he was too preoccupied with his companion's peril to remember if he had. Almost at the junction, I wound the window quickly down. At the same time I veered sharply.

Kenny's hand was free, though his bones must have taken a drubbing as the arm grated out. Their car went straight on, while I swerved left and, in good old Black Bess, got onto the slip road without turning over.

As I went away I heard the car that had been behind me crash into the back of the Rolls, because no sooner had Pindarry realised my escape than he panicked, tried to cut in front of me, and slammed on the brakes to stop me when I was no longer there. Too late, he caused the biggest pile-up on that stretch of road since the black fogs of yesteryear.

I won't say I was laughing. Almost certainly, I had lost the boat to Holland – though my resurfaced optimism told me there might still be a chance. If I missed it, I would drop my incriminating evidence in the nearest Royal Red pillar-box so as not to have it in my possession if Moggerhanger's lads finally ran me to ground.

There was no advantage in speeding the last few miles. I would leave things to fate. When a tractor swung in front from a field beyond Manningtree I was as patient as a superannuated brigadier out on a pleasant country drive using a map from the 1930s. The young tractor driver had an earphone system clamped over his cloth cap, and was listening to the Jungle Blues from Radio Zombie as his vehicle moved sleepily along. Both of us waved in friendly fashion when I shot by.

I could smell the North Sea, and sensed a rough crossing, which would be appropriate enough on such a day. Then the sea was in sight, as well as cranes and great sheds, fences and the car parks. The boat was still there. I ran into the ticket office, wondering whether Chief Inspector Lanthorn and his lads would be at the passport control waiting for me.

'Hello, Cullen! Where is it this time, then? Continental holiday, eh? I hope you aren't getting a bit above yourself. We wouldn't like that down at the station. We're getting to love you more and more. Without you our lives wouldn't be worth writing home about. Our careers would be in jeopardy. Stand still, you bastard. There's nothing you can do. It's a fair cop, I think you'd call it. I'd like to say, though, that that little incident on the A12 just now had us absolutely brimming over with admiration. We had a chopper overhead filming the whole thing. No, I know you didn't notice it. You were somewhat preoccupied. We'll run the film for you one day – when you come out. Trouble is, film doesn't keep very well. After twenty-five

years it'll be pitted and smudgy. You'd better come with me. And I don't want any fucking nonsense. All I have to do is warn you that anything you say will be used to your detriment at the trial, and thrown back at you by the beak to get you the maximum possible sentence.'

'You're too late, mate. The boat's leaving.'

'I didn't ask you that.' I bit my tongue rather than snap at him. 'Just sell me a ticket. I'd like a cabin, if you've got one.'

'Oh well, maybe it's not too late, sir.' He loved playing with late arrivals, but lifted the phone. I stood so calmly I didn't even light a cigar, though my innermost tripes shook like jellies.

'Room for one more?'

I looked idly around the room as seconds went by. My troubles weren't over. They never would be. Moggerhanger might have someone waiting for me, even supposing I got on the boat, when I drove off at the Hook. There was no saying how far his vindictiveness would reach. The only reason for pursuing me was if he had proof that I had got the envelope. I didn't see how that could be, though I was blind enough to believe anything. He wouldn't stop me entering Holland, even if I had to leave the car on board and walk off. Such were the whirlings in my brain as I waited by the window.

'You're in luck. But you'll have to get a move on.'

I took the ticket without a word, then drove to the passport window with that vital laundrybook in my hand. I got it straight back, and the customs didn't bother me. An old salt took half my ticket and pasted a chit on the windscreen. 'That's a vintage car, sir, ain't it?'

I thanked him for the compliment, and trundled ever onward into the car deck, hearing the steel wall fall to behind. A matelot offered to wash my car, and such was my relief at being on board that I gave him a fiver in advance. I felt the vibration of the engines while struggling upstairs with my briefcase, overnight bag and umbrella.

Bursting sticks of chalk drew the ship out of harbour. I stood on the top deck, cold spray hitting my face. Lights winked from the flat countryside of Essex, and we were soon on the watery big dipper. There was a slight rust about the ironwork of the lifeboat derricks.

I sat by the wreckage of my lunch, staring at paper flowers on the cafeteria table. Loudspeakers put out audio-masochistic music which I had even been too old to appreciate as a kid. One song had the word 'Revolution' wailed over and over by a group drugged either on Moggerhanger's wares or their own souls.

I couldn't stay in that plastic maritime palace for processing tourists into foreign parts, so got up to walk. The rhythmic tinkling of pinball machines dominated every gangway and recreation place, though I was glad to be out of Moggerhanger's reach. A man wearing a newspaper-hat led four kids in a conga-dance along the deck.

Safe at last, I felt weak and purposeless though what else could I expect? Only my worst enemy would know that to make me powerless all he had to do was stop threatening me. Maybe Moggerhanger wasn't that subtle, but I stayed on the alert, all the same.

I left my case in the saloon, though I wouldn't let go of the briefcase, and went on deck to watch a ship go by. Tinkling morse came from the wireless office. Was Moggerhanger sending a telegram to his agent on board, telling him to throw me over the side? Not on your big fat Bertie. All said and done, he was only a racketeer, one of many, and not even my wildest imagination suggested that his influence went beyond the land. Trying to reach a higher deck, the gate wouldn't give, and I was about to get it open when I noticed the words GREEN TOE GANG painted there.

The sea was heaving, with an invisible menagerie in the

rigging, snarling and roaring. White cock-heads went to the walltop of the horizon, spumed up and never far away. I wanted to throw myself at it like the laughing man, but went on laughing after reading the words GREEN TOE GANG over and over. There was no mistake. I got under cover from driving rain, to the popsong noises I had despised a few minutes ago, but wherever I walked I sooner or later came upon the same GREEN TOE GANG label pinned over a door that I tried to open but couldn't.

I had stumbled on the flagship of the Green Toe Line, the gang's *Titanic*, no less, gone from one frying pan into another. I staggered like a blind man, but found the first class bar and sat with coffee and brandy, a little internal bandaging for the nerves.

Smoking the last of Moggerhanger's cigars, I was filled with admiration at how the Green Toe Gang had affixed their name to so many doors and barriers. After all, they could have owned the ship without advertising the matter. To take over such a vessel was even beyond the power of Moggerhanger. He may have had the money, but hardly the panache. After a while I began to laugh on the other side of my sandpaper face at the thought that, having with such expertise escaped one racketeer's minions, I had imprisoned myself on the good ship GREEN TOE GANG from which the only escape was to swim through a Force Nine Gale. The sensible course was to meet the Big Chief face to face. A jaunty crew member was walking between the tables, and I called him over. 'Where does the boss of the Green Toe Gang have his cabin?'

He looked at me as if I was crackers. 'What gang?'

'Green Toe Gang.' He thought I'd walked on the ship straight out of an Essex loony bin.

'Was it on telly?'

'It could have been, I suppose.'

'Well, I wouldn't know, then, would I? I work shifts.'

'The Green Toe Gang,' I said. 'It's written all over the

place. You can't fool me. I can read. Where's the boss of it?'

Something occurred to him, and he laughed. 'Oh! Ah! Green Toe Gang! That's a good 'un, mate. And to think – I never thought of it! There ain't no boss, though, except the skipper, and Green Toe Gang don't bother him.'

'Doesn't it? Why not?'

'Well, you see, Green Toe Gang's Dutch for NO ENTRY. See? It's in English underneath.'

He walked off, laughing, while I stood white-faced at the bar, thanking God for my narrow escape. Maybe the situation wasn't as bad as I thought. I'd have another brandy, then go to my cabin and sleep so as to arrive in the Netherlands as fresh as a tulip. On landing I would drive to a lovely small town in the south, and put up at a hotel for a couple of days, where I could feed myself silly. But I had reckoned without fate, a mistake I had made too often in my life.

'Get me one, will you, Michael, my owd duck? A double, if you don't mind. And a nice black coffee for Maria. She's feeling a bit queasy with the rocking of this superannuated troopship.'

I tried to stop myself sliding into a dead faint. 'You must be joking.'

'I'm not,' he said blandly.

'How did you get on board?'

'Well,' he said, 'we didn't come on hidden in a crate of oranges. Bill Straw travels like a gentleman – you ought to know that by now.'

Maria wore a fur coat and a hat. She looked at me with her large, beautifully liquid eyes. Bill was impeccably got up, a Burberry on his arm and a large holdall by his feet. 'Aren't you glad to see us?'

'I'm stunned out of my mind with the shock' – which must have been true, because I ordered the brandies and coffee, and we took them to a table.

'Perfectly understandable,' he said. 'You've been through hell in the last three days.'

'It was my impression that you had, as well.'

He leaned across Maria, who stroked the back of his neck. 'The only thing wrong with these boats is that they don't sell them little custard pies I like so much. And the tea-bag tea's rotten.'

'If you'd told 'em you was coming, they'd have mashed a real Worksop pot.'

He lifted his brandy. 'You're as sarky as ever, aren't you, Michael? Here's to a lovely trip abroad for all of us.'

'I didn't know you fancied a threesome.'

Maria slapped my hand, spilling some of the brandy.

'What I'd like to know,' I said, 'is how you came to be on this boat. I thought Moggerhanger had you in Durrance Vile up to a couple of hours ago.'

He took such a while over lighting his cigar that I knew he was about to tell me a pack of lies. 'You'll never believe me – but what do I care? He let us go last night.'

'Why?'

'He saw no point in holding us. It was you he wanted to frighten. He knew the three of us were like one happy family, and that the mere idea that he had got us at his mercy would make you cough up the doings. Claud's a reasonable man, though he did make it a condition of our release that I wouldn't phone Upper Mayhem and tell you about it. You can understand that, can't you, Michael?'

'Go on.'

'There's nothing to go on about. We had a talk with Lord Moggerhanger before he let us go. He and Lady Moggerhanger had us in for tea. They're not a bad couple, Michael. And the cakes were delicious.'

'I'll bet they were. On your grave they can write: "He sold his best pal for a Nelson Square".'

'Hey, steady on – a cream bun, at least!'

'It'll be in the Guinness Book of Epitaphs. You fucked up my plan.'

'Michael, be realistic. You would never have got on this boat with Claud's three million quids' worth of kay-li. It wasn't on, and you know it. Or you ought to.'

'It's a bitter pill to swallow,' I said.

'Most pills are, Michael.'

'Fuck off,' I told him.

'That's more like the old Mike Cullen.'

'So how did you get here?'

'I'll tell you. When Lord Moggerhanger let us go, we went to my room in Somers Town. I wasn't followed, and the Green Toe Gang – I say, have you seen them notices all over the place? In't it a bloody scream? Green Toe Gang everywhere! So that's where they got their name? Makes you wonder, don't it?'

'Get on with your yarn.'

'Let's have another brandy first. And a pot of camomile tea for Maria. She's getting worse, aren't you, darling?'

She only stopped kneading her hands together when they went over her bosom, or against her mouth, or were drawn across her glistening forehead. She nodded, but wouldn't say anything in case the effort made her sick. She was obviously on the verge.

'Make 'em doubles, Michael: there'll be a queue soon.' His sponging was a tidal wave, a wall of water stretching from the horizon that you couldn't avoid. I got the drinks. 'You see,' he went on, 'I pulled the money out of the mattress, fifty thousand pounds of it, and this morning we took the boat train from Liverpool Street. The money's in this holdall at my feet, so go easy with your cigar ash.'

'You mean to say you've cadged two rounds of drinks off me, and you got fifty thousand shekels in that bag?'

He was offended. 'I didn't want to arouse your cupidity, or your suspicion. But now I've told you. I never had any secrets from you, did I, Michael?'

'If you don't stop calling me Michael every few seconds I'll clock you one.'

'That's the ticket, duck. But don't worry. I'll buy the next round.'

'What else did you talk about with Claud?'

'Oh, it was just a general, wide-ranging sort of conversation.'

'What, though?'

'Travel. Things like that. We jabbered about holidays abroad, and I said I preferred the Dover-Calais run because it was the shortest and because there was a lovely little cake and coffee shop I could stoke up at. It had to be admitted, though, that some people liked longer crossings, for all sorts of reasons. I knew what he was getting at, mind you, and he fell right into my trap. "Michael allus goes to Holland to see his everloving wife on the Harwich to Hook run," I said, as if you'd told it me only a few days ago, and I'd believed it hook line and sinker. I told him because I knew that in the next few days you would take any other crossing but this.'

He was living proof, if proof was needed, that one Nottingham man can think for another, and more or less get it right. In that sense his treachery had little meaning. He understood my look.

'I can see I was wrong, but Michael, what bloody crazy thought led you to take this crossing today?'

'I'm safe on board, aren't I? Though I only just made it.'

'I suppose that's all right, then. Eh, Maria?'

She tried to laugh, but looked awful, her eyes opening wider at each wilful flip of the boat. I felt as if I could drink fifty more brandies and not get drunk. My brain was iced up, and I had hardly any contact with it.

'What I'm certain of is this: that when I get to Holland and disclose all I know to Interpol, Moggerhanger will never be the same again. They'll lock him up in the Tower of London till the end of his days.'

Maria fell half fainting across the table.

'Michael, give us a hand.' I was surprised he was so concerned. He was stricken with anguish. 'She's going to spew by the look of her. Let's get her on deck.' He held her between us. 'She told me she got seasick, but I hoped it would be calm. You can't rely on anything, can you?'

'Not even with fifty thousand pounds,' I said. 'You left it by the table.'

'Oh my God!' He ran back, and hung it over his shoulder. 'I thought these posh boats were supposed to have stabilisers,' he said, staggering a few feet.

I held the door open with the hook of my umbrella. 'Don't make much difference in the storm.' We went to the leeward side, where only a few sprinkles reached us.

'Let's make her walk up and down a bit,' he said. 'Might bring her round. It's funny she gets so seasick, a member of a great seafaring nation and all that.'

'England's oldest ally,' I said.

He cracked me so playfully in the ribs I had to tighten the grip on my briefcase. 'Your general knowledge is nearly as good as mine.'

The wind blew in circles, first clockwise and then anticlockwise. Fortunately, when Maria let herself go, the contents of her stomach went clear away from us. 'You'll never get Moggerhanger put inside,' he said. 'There can't be any evidence to do it.'

'Oh yes there is. And I've got it. The T's are crossed and the I's are dotted. I've got so much on Moggerhanger and his world import drug business they'll have to build new prisons for the crowds that get pulled in.'

'Michael,' he said, 'what's the use? You can't do it.'

He was spineless. He was inert. Or he was amoral and anti-social. He didn't care. The trouble was, he was easygoing, and that was the reason we had stayed pals for so many years. Finally, we trusted each other. We'd always done what was best for each other. He didn't want me to shop Moggerhanger because such an action would disturb the *status quo*. It would rob people like him of employment, and there were enough on the dole already. As for my own living, I was prepared to sacrifice that for the common good. 'I'm turning him in. That's all I've wanted to do for the last ten years.'

'Michael, I won't say it's not right.' He held my arm as if to prove his affection. 'Why should I worry? I won't go to jail. And I hope you don't. We both could, though, but let's not consider that for the moment. All I say is that however much evidence you've got, there won't be enough.' He chuckled. 'If there was, you'd bring the country down.'

The sea was heaving so much I wasn't feeling too good myself. 'I have more than enough evidence.'

'You haven't,' he said, beaming with simple good nature – or so I thought.

How dense and disbelieving could he get? However good a friend he was, the holes in his understanding were big enough to drive a lorry through. 'Haven't I?' I raged. 'Haven't I? Don't I?'

'I bloody well know you haven't,' he shouted against a sudden change of the wind, veins standing out on his face and throat.

I fiddled with my briefcase and pulled out Matthew Coppice's envelope. 'What's this, then? What is it? You want to know what it is? I'll tell you. It's everything. All I've got on Moggerhanger is in here, documentary evidence that's going to shake the criminal world to its foundations.'

'Don't be so bleddy daft.' He thought his Nottingham accent would make me back down. My beloved, fatal, powerful packet of damning evidence against Moggerhanger and all his works flapped in the air only a foot from Bill Straw's nose. 'This,' I shouted, 'will hang the drug-peddling villain!'

His bottle-blue eyes, like a pair of kid's marbles about to hit each other in the game of the century, couldn't believe their luck – I realise now. He snatched the envelope. 'What do you want that for?' – and threw it into the sea.

Maria vomited again and again, but Bill was too busy to console her. My gorge solidified. I was safe from seasickness, though not, for a while, safe from doing the bastard in.

'Your envelope may look like a lifeboat.' He held me from jumping after it. 'But it's too small, Michael. It'll sink without trace, and so would you. I like you too much to let you kill yourself in such a cause. An old Sherwood Forester doesn't let that happen to a mate. And I like myself too much to let you kill me. So stop it. We didn't come all this way for it to end like that. There are better things in life than death, as your good father once said to me. It's no use struggling. I know what you want better than you do yourself, at the moment, and I'm only doing it knowing you would do it for me in similar circumstances. Life's all we've got, Michael, and it behoves us to keep it. God wouldn't like it to be otherwise. And when a Sherwood Forester brings God into the issue you know he's serious. He's on the firing step. So keep still, will you? We're both on the firing step. Stop struggling and spluttering, because you're not going over the top. I'm not going to let you. The only way you'll get over that rail is if you take me with you, and you may be strong but you're not strong enough for that. I'm staying where I am, and so are you. Those bits of paper aren't worth it. The only way to dispose of Moggerhanger is to kill him, but don't try that either, because you'll get killed first. And if you're not, you'll be killed afterwards. You can't fight him and Lanthorn as well, and the whole of the British nation, because Moggerhanger is so powerful that he's one of *them*, and if they insist on clutching him to their bosoms that's their affair, because believe me they clutch worse things to their bosoms than Moggerhanger, and for you to kill yourself to get rid of him, and to do them in the eye as well, which is what it would mean, is just not worth you losing your life. Nor is it worth me losing mine, which is what would happen if you lost yours. Moggerhanger is as rotten as the whole country, Michael. They're one and the same thing, and for you to think you can do anything about it not only astounds me but saddens me. Let them rot, because though the country deserves a better fate – and I love England just as much as you do, if not more – you're not the one to cure it. It'll have to do without you. One person can't alter the course of history without the whole country being on his side, and if the whole country is on his side anyone can alter the course of history. I suppose Blaskin said that as well. Or I don't know what I'm saying. You're upsetting me, I'll tell you that. I'll go out of my mind if you don't stop struggling. Look on the bright side. The three of us can take a holiday in Holland on my money, or part of it anyway, and drive down the Rhine to Switzerland in your jalopy. Then we'll come back to Blighty and go to Upper Mayhem, where Maria will have her baby.'

'You fucking won't,' I said.

'Oh, don't get like that. Let's go inside to that cosy bar, and you can buy me another drink. We'll take Maria with us. She'll be lighter going down than she was coming up, and that's a fact, won't you, my lovely little duck?'

I hated his guts, but no more intensely than I hated my own. I knew what he had talked about with Moggerhanger, and why Moggerhanger had let him and Maria go. I knew indeed that he had been working for Moggerhanger all along, that the despicable bastard was nothing less than his recruiting sergeant who from the beginning was set on to get me for a few hard jobs, and to keep an eye on me while I was doing them. Even Eric Alport being on the train when I came into London at Bill's summons had been no accident.

At that moment by the boat rail, my life cracked in two, and I saw the halves, visible at last with my own clean insight. People like Straw and Moggerhanger had known them all along and put each one to good use. While I had been philandering, the world had fucked me rotten. True, I had sensed treachery at odd moments, but lunatic vanity had prevented me following the hints and realising that, far from being a man of the world, I was the most gullible person in it.

The shock of this revelation, that only friends could betray you, flared my murderous rage up again. I remembered my umbrella, with which Bill had prodded the dog in Charing Cross Road and, recalling the results of that inadvertent jab, I lifted it to deliver a similar thrust at him, which I hoped would prove fatal.

I don't suppose my attack was serious, but I had to make the effort, otherwise I wouldn't have been able to get a proper night's sleep to the end of my days. Old Sherwood Forester that he was, he anticipated the move, easily took the umbrella from me, and slung it after the packet of papers into the water. 'It's unethical to use a thing like that.'

I looked failure staunchly in the face.

'You can't win 'em all, Michael.'

'Tell me something new.'

He laughed. 'There's no such thing, old son.'

I stood by the rail, hypnotised by the lift and fall of the ship, a repetitious movement which emphasised the scale of my downfall. What the connection was, I did not know, but for the first time in my life I realised that I was not going to live forever. I had never thought so, but for the first time I was afraid, and gripped the wood to steady myself. I felt death happening like a dress rehearsal that could turn at any time into the real thing, and I would have no say in the matter when it did. The certainty that life no longer went on was absent. I would exist from minute to minute, and I'd have to be grateful for every fresh second that ticked by.

I stood till I couldn't see the waves for darkness. Bill had no doubt put Maria to bed, then gone to phone or wireless Moggerhanger to inform him that Operation Get Cullen had been successfully concluded. By playing his cards right – which he had certainly done – he had saved me from worse trouble than I was already in. Because it would sooner or later have happened, he might have done me a favour by making it come sooner, but I could see no way of thanking him.

The storm became worse, and the temptation to turn the dress rehearsal into the first and last performance became harder to resist. One flash, and I would be over. I was too inert. A calm sea might have drawn me, but not this spume-ridden upchucking wilderness. It was a killer I wanted no part of, a spider's web of violent water which would not get hold of me if I had anything to do with it. And I still had. I wouldn't even give it my vomit. If I spat to leeward I would get it back in the eye. The sea had to be treated with respect, and would get me if it could – though I would never fraternise.

I had tried to nail Moggerhanger, and had failed because I had neither the gut, the guile nor the patience. I hadn't tried hard enough. I was too few. Let go. The sound of music came through a lull in the wind noise. The animals were out, in the ship and on the sea, in the air and in me. There was no telling who they were after but, if I was going to die, I might as well live. Knowing I had come to such a realisation late in life glued my eyes open. Chagrin and misery made perfect matchsticks. It would be the way I lived now. All I could think of when I got to my cabin was Frances Malham. A start in life goes on to the end.

Thirty

Reader, I married her.

Or she married me. I no longer dodge the traffic like a London pigeon in its prime. Moggerhanger lost interest in me as soon as Bill Straw reported that the evidence against him had gone into the sea. How had they found out? Matthew Coppice was the weak link in the none too strong chain. Chief Inspector Lanthorn, in his ferreting and always busy way, had suspected him. He was all ears and eyes, and nailed him one day at Spleen Manor, where he tricked, shamed, then bullied him into confessing by the obvious and simple expedient of making me out to be a more evil villain than either Moggerhanger or himself. Coppice's moral sense was riddled with idiosyncrasies, which made him as vulnerable as a colander in a millpond.

Lanthorn didn't enjoy his triumph for long, because a fortnight later, while walking across Whitehall, he cracked up from a heart attack as powerful as if he'd been hit by a lorry load of Katyusha rockets. Moggerhanger continues to prosper, however, though things for him aren't as easy as they were.

I also prosper, and I'll tell you what happened. As soon as the boat docked at the Hook of Holland I drove to where Bridgitte was living with her boyfriend. He was a straight and decent bloke, and I knew she would be happier with him than she'd ever been with me. I returned to Upper Mayhem with the children, which was what I went to see her for. She let them go, knowing she could visit them at any time. They were glad to be in their old rooms, and back with their pals in the village. They loved

Dismal who, since Polly Moggerhanger had lost interest in the selfish beast, became the Hound of Upper Mayhem.

My next move was to find out whether Jeffrey Harlaxton's offer of a job at his advertising agency had been serious. It had, and still was, he said. My creative lying and quick thinking had made a firm impression, talent which would be put to proper use at last. I was given a contract with rates of pay and conditions which no person could refuse. If I had realised that such cushy jobs were available from the beginning, I might always have been honest and industrious.

I gave Clegg the signal box to live in, and made him caretaker, head gardener and child minder of Upper Mayhem – and also dog handler, because Dismal lodges under the table that runs the length of the signal box. 'My ambition in life is to be as happy as you are,' I said to him during the first supper after I got back from Holland.

He gave a wise smile. 'You're not old enough for that – yet.'

Bill Straw, the second arch-villain in my life after Lord Moggerhanger, wrote to say that he and Maria were married and living in Portugal, where he had bought what he called an 'estate'. His subtle entrapment of me on the boat had been his last professional job, for which he must have been paid according to its importance.

Maria had her kid, and also another – 'so I don't expect either the underworld or the inland revenue will be hearing much more from yours truly,' he informed me. He sounded as besotted about his wife as when he first set eyes on her hips, which maybe was the only good thing to be said for him. They invited me to Portugal for the summer, but I'd had more than enough of Bill Straw to last one lifetime.

Bridgitte remarried after our divorce, and stayed in Holland. Smog went to work on a kibbutz for six months, and in his last letter wrote about marrying his girlfriend, who was born in Israel. Frances and I are going out to see him in a couple of months.

What about Blaskin? Life goes on for him as well. He motored up to Upper Mayhem with Mabel Drudge-Perkins and they stayed a few days. It made me sick to see her shining his boots before he got up in the morning, though when he ill-used her, a bit more spit went on them than polish. It took him a week or two to forgive me for writing the trash-novel which won him the Windrush Prize, but he generously gave me half the swag of ten thousand pounds, and used the rest to pay off debts before setting out on his travels.

Moggerhanger had taken umbrage at the fact that nobody would touch the book that Blaskin had ghosted. After getting the Windrush Prize, even though he despised it, Blaskin considered it would be unbecoming of him as a recipient of the award, and as an officer and a gentleman, to send out Moggerhanger's life story under his own name. So he re-wrote it as if Moggerhanger had done it himself, then told him to take it or leave it.

Not unnaturally, and having paid out so much money, Moggerhanger did not like the portrait of the elderly Dorian Gray which it turned out to be. No publisher would take it, in any case, perhaps because the Tories were back, and times had changed. If the seventies were less spaced out than the swinging sixties, the eighties promised to be as tight as a drum. Blaskin thought it necessary to absent himself for a while both from Moggerhanger's wrath and an era which would look less tolerantly on the antics of someone like him. He went to live with Mabel Drudge on the island of Vanua Leva, a place so far away I didn't even know where it was. Neither, I think, does he.

Not long ago a letter reached me from some Australian backpacker going the rounds of the Pacific, saying he had heard a report that Mabel had killed Blaskin. The incident hadn't even taken place after a quarrel. A further epistle, this time from Blaskin himself, said that she hadn't in fact killed him, but had only half killed him – which fell in nicely with her plans for their future because she hated him so much. She was now nursing him back to half-spate.

My mother has gone to America, and I last heard from her in California where she was living with a women's group at a camp in the mountains. She asks for money from time to time, and I send it.

Where else could I have told this tale other than in Blaskin's flat? I spend my nights here during the week, and do him the favour of forwarding mail. Frances is with me as I write. She listens to music, and occasionally comes over to tell me to hold nothing back in the account of my final adventures with Moggerhanger, and to let myself rip in my own true voice – something harder to do the longer I work at the advertising agency, though I've come to the end of my story just in time.

Jeffrey Harlaxton looked a bit shocked when he heard Frances would marry me but, as I said to him, you can't win 'em all. I sometimes think I'm only holding my job in advertising until something better comes along. Whatever I do, I have great hopes for the future. Perhaps a start in life really will go on to the end, unless another adventure proves once and for all that it decisively does not. But that is in the hands of fate, more than it is in mine, though I'm keeping my options open.